A No

Bo
Elizabeth of England Chronicles

By G. Lawrence

This book is dedicated to my friend Anne
who helped me to face my own battle,
offering friendship, humour and strength
when I needed it most

"Help me now, O God, for I have none other friends but Thee alone.
And suffer me not, I beseech Thee, to build my foundation on the sands but on the rock whereby all blasts of blustering weather may have no power over me."
Elizabeth I
A prayer written whilst Elizabeth was imprisoned by her sister Queen Mary I

"A thousand years after the Virgin birth, and after another five hundred more allowed the globe, the wonderful eighty-eighth year begins and brings with it woe enough. If, this year, total catastrophe does not befall, if land and sea do not collapse in total ruin, yet will the whole world suffer upheavals, empires will dwindle, and from everywhere will be great lamentation."
The Prophecy of Regiomontanus

"To me the waves that ceaseless broke
Upon the dangerous coast
Hoarsely and ominously spoke
Of all my treasure lost.

Your sea of trouble you have passed
And found the distant shore.
I tempest-tossed and wrecked at last
Come home to port no more."
William Cowper

"O, train me not, sweet mermaid, with thy note,
To drown me in thy sister's flood of tears:
Sing, siren, for thyself and I will dote:
Spread o'er the silver waves thy golden hairs,
And as a bed I'll take them and there lie,
And in that glorious supposition think
He gains by death that hath such means to die:
Let Love, being light, be drowned if she sink!"
William Shakespeare, Comedy of Errors

Prologue

Richmond Palace
February 1603

"Once they named her mermaid, to disgrace her," I say to Death. "My cousin, who hides behind you now."

I stare from the dark window. Mary hides her eyes from me, I hide mine from her. There were always games between us in life. Death follows and the games go on. There is an element of the children we once were in all of us.

I see the waters of the Thames. Lapping waves alight with the fire of torches on the banks. Little waves rising, curling, crashing. England is not an island complete, having Scotland as its head, Wales as its belly, yet always we thought ourselves an island race. We tell stories of ourselves and believe in them, that is the way of life. Those who come of islands are special people. Removed from others not only by lines on a map, a separation man invokes upon his own kind, but by natural borders, by water. Water dictates we stand apart, alone. Something I have ever understood.

"They called you mermaid to disgrace you when Darnley died," I say to Mary, not looking away from the window. "Mermaids are a symbol now of lust and depravity. Your people thought to shame you, make you to blame for what Bothwell did to you, but perhaps they did not know the older stories, tales with more power. People say once the mermaid was a goddess, a form of Aphrodite, goddess of love. Clans of Scotland and Ireland claim descent from women of the sea, as did my ancestors. In ancient times it was claimed the line of the Counts of Anjou sprang from a spirit of water, a woman who was part demon."

My hand rests on the pane. In the subtle surface of glass, my face is become a silhouette; light crests the edges of my cheeks, my chin, making a mask of slim radiance, but my eyes and skin are black as night. At times, we all become ghosts of ourselves. "And as goddesses of old, if the mermaid offers love and life to drowning men, also she offers death. She is the light and dark of water, of life, of love. Like all creatures of the distant mystery of life and death, she is both elements in one form."

My hand curls on the pane, fingers of a wraith touching deepest night. "And perhaps that was where your soul went. Something of water, that restless, changeable essence was always within you, cousin. Phillip and his men claimed that you were with them, your soul joined to their cause, your wishes to their wishes. But I wonder."

I turn to her. Death and she stand side by side. I smile gently at her coy face. Even in death she is beautiful. Even in death my cousin keeps secrets close. "I wonder if your soul went into the waters we sailed upon. I wonder which side truly you thought to support. It might have pleased you if Spain and her Armada had won, for I would be disgraced and deposed, but I wonder..."

Mary's smile is wide, but surrender secrets she will not.

"Did your soul enter water, mermaid?" I ask. "Did your vengeance wish to rise from the heart of the ocean upon which sailed the might of Spain, or did your soul wend another way? Would you have welcomed Phillip on my throne?"

I shake my head. "I think not. For all his faults, for all your disillusionment in me, you always wanted the same man to take the throne as I did. For all the revenge you desired to take of me, James you always wanted triumphant. It would be a better revenge, a more lasting one, if the son of Scots came to rule, supplanting the line of English Tudors, would it not?"

Glittering eyes tell me my cousin will not answer. She would prefer my questions remain questions. I do not blame her. She has no reason to satisfy me. From her I stole much.

"That was where your soul went," I say. "Into water. I know which side you chose. For you knew the fate of England rested upon the oceans. And our fate was entwined, mingled with waves, with water, with that of your son. There was something of the future working for us in water, something of you."

She does not answer.

"Water is God's element," I say, staring at the Thames, grey water lit up by the lanterns of ferries and wheals passing on the murky river. Light, red and golden, flickers on a surface of dark glass. "And perhaps He, in His wisdom and mercy, grants His element to the dead He thinks worthy, to wield in His name."

I look to Mary again. "You will not answer. Perhaps you cannot. The dead do not speak to the living. It would invite too many questions. Questions that should not be answered to mortal minds. Once we had great knowledge, but it is said with each generation since Adam we have lost a little more and a little more. All we discover now is not enough to fill the void of all we have lost. But someone must speak, someone must answer. This part of my tale is not mine alone. It belongs to others. I was not there to see what unfolded upon the sea. Once, Robin told me he would make me a pirate Queen, but never did that promise come true. Never did I stand on a ship, bare boards and strips of cloth between me and death. I was a creature bound to land; my element was earth, not water. Part of this tale I cannot tell."

I stare into Death's hood. "If my cousin will not speak, You must. If not to me, to the memory of the world. Speak, so the deeds done upon the sea do not die. Tell the tale that people might remember. In mind and memory will You speak."

A glimmer of interest in the hood tells me much.

I will not be alone in telling this tale.

Chapter One

Richmond Palace
February 1603

Death

She stares with those dark eyes, presenting something.

A challenge…

It is not the first. Men love to challenge me, to test death, to see how far their power pervades. She wishes to test me.

It will be done. I am all time and none. I linger where I please.

This Queen was right to say I speak only in mind and memory. That is where Death lives; images preserved in thought of the last moment. Pictures of when the essence of life leaves, when the hollow shell, always so much smaller in death, becomes all that remains. Death cannot speak. Words are for the living.

Other sounds accompany me; noises of my existence; heralds that bear witness to my presence. I am the soft step outside the door. I am the sound of hair rising on nape and neck. In the gentle whisper of hands reaching through air to clasp a throat, am I. I am the swish of silver blade in morning light, and the dull thud upon the scaffold. In the twist and hiss of the hangman's rope I am. Inside the shrill cry of battle I am heard. I am the gurgle, the cry, the scream, the choke and the rattle.

Noises come when I am close, yet I make them not. These are the noises of man, and of his dread of me. My own sounds are softer. I am the supple fall of night, the crackle of grass in the first light of day. I am the soft groan of the endless sea, echoing deep. I am the silence before birds sing, and the still, waiting hush of expectation before storms of summer crash across rolling, churning skies. I am the burble of water, the thin crack of ice, the call of the fox in the night. Where life is heard, so Death is too. Where life is born, Death comes to stand.

Man does not hear me. My step is too soft, my hands too gentle. Man hears the heralds who call that I am near, but not the true sounds of my presence. Those, man attributes to life, to living, not understanding that we are joined too deep and long to separate. Poor fools, for they fear me, not life, and yet life brings more pain than me.

Sometimes they see me, standing at the end of a bed, rushing past them, a shadow on the stairs. Sometimes they reach out, take my hand as friends, sometimes they cringe from me for fear of the unknown, the unknowable agony of leaving life, to enter death.

She stares at me. She cannot hear me. I make sure of that. She thinks I do so for sport, and perhaps there is an element of that. Eternity can be tiresome. Men think it would be well to live forever, and they are wrong. The value of a life is measured by it ending. When time is spare, time is valued.

We who live forever must find ways to amuse ourselves, or run to madness. For the sake of those living and those yet to come, it would be a bad thing if I, Death, lost my wits and descended to insanity.

So I play. With some mortals the game is long. We dance, and they escape my hands. The old woman before me now many times dodged me when she was young. People think I come only at a certain time, a fated moment. It is not always true. For some, there is a time and a place, for others there are many. Mortals make choices which affect the moment I claim them. Fates change, destiny alters. If life were predictable, and death too, existence would be a tiresome realm. There were many moments in which I might have taken her, but she side-stepped, feinted, tripped away from my waiting hands.

She thinks this is why I came so often to her. It is not.

I wanted to come close, for something in her called to something in me.

There is, in all aware beings, loneliness. Some, who even though they possess minds that can become aware, never do. These are the fortunate; never once do they consider how alone they are. And yet they are alone.

Some know loneliness. It is the one constant in lives of change and unrest; the sense of separation, the void, dark and long, between them and others. Most people are so very lonely. They seek to fill the void, hoping to make it smaller, less threatening. Music, art, books, love… humans reach out, they grasp them. They do not let go. They believe these things define their lives, and they do, but not in the way they think. The more they cling, the lonelier they are. The more they surround themselves with fine cloth, books, song, dance, noise, the more they become aware of the gaping hole inside them.

And they are all one thing; a cry in the darkness, a hand reaching out, desperate to make contact even for a moment, so they will know they are not alone. People fall in love with people, with music, with books, with art, with friends, so for one bare moment it will feel that something inside them is understood by another. That for a second in the rushing waters of time they will know someone else is there, they are not alone.

But the woman I gaze upon now is not like that. She did as others did, reached out, screamed in the deep blackness of night, yet all the time she knew the futility of it. Since she was a child, she knew herself to be alone. That is how I found her. Because I heard her.

Even Death feels the agony of what it is to be alone.

Sometimes they learn the truth. Humans learn they are least lonely when alone, when able to face themselves. But we all feel it. The restless urge to connect, to be with others, to stand as a pack not as the solitary wolf.

That is why I came to her, why I stayed. That is why I listen now, and why I will do as she asks. She thinks she, a queen, may command me. She cannot. But as a friend, one who has always been with her, I will acquiesce.

The burden of loneliness is great. I, most alone of all creatures, know this better than any. Her sense of solitude cannot match mine. For eons I have walked alone, and I will for eons more. And yet there is an echo of my pain in hers, this frail figure who pretended so much might; this mortal in whom I see a glimmer of recognition.

We, she and me, know what it is to be alone; the void over which you stand, staring down into eternal darkness, where only the sound of your breath and the pounding of your heart is heard.

And so she asks and I will answer. For that is what we do for friends, for those in whom we see a connection. I will help her to find herself in the darkness of the void. For once you find yourself you are not alone. You are always in company, with the only person you have ever really needed.

For that is what I am, in the end; a guide. I am the darkness in which there is no more hiding. I am the place where mortals come to finally understand they were not alone. Not because I am with them, but because they were. I am the guide who teaches this. I am the last thing to fear, not because of pain, if anything I am the antidote to agony, but because when I come there is no more pretending. No more covering loneliness with cloth and clothing, with things and trinkets, or even with other people. I am the truth of the darkness, where souls stand alone and find they have never been alone. They always were in company, with themselves. And that was all they needed.

I spread my hands and bow to her, this lonely soul. I will help her tell this tale.

Chapter Two

Plymouth
July 19th 1588

Death

Let me take you far from the Palace of Richmond, to a time long since passed. We will watch the past unfold.

Plymouth was busy that July day. It was only seven dawns since the English fleet had returned to port after sailing out to seek the dreaded Armada in the open seas. They had not found their foes, and rough wind and rain had sent them home. There, preparations had gone on, for war.

Rigging and sails were being mended; men sitting on the decks of ships, or upon the harbour stitching, the soft swish of thick thread ripping through cloth, binding it together. Carpenters were hammering, making last repairs to the hulls of ships. Others were trying to gather supplies, which were few. Barrels of fresh ale were not easy to fill in Plymouth, and food was not plentiful. The fleet had used up a great deal of resources whilst in port. Captains were hoping more provisions would come from Cornwall and Devon, shipped along the winding estuary which led to villages like Millbrook and Cawsands, where yeomen had farms which had been called upon to send food, but they were running out of time, and they knew it.

The Spanish Armada, which many called invincible, had left Lisbon. The enemy were coming, their plan to invade England underway.

On the Hoe, a natural vantage point where the direction of the wind could be gauged, two men stood, watching. The waters of the Plymouth Sound moved, little white waves cresting and falling. Trees shifted on St Nicholas's Island, leaves whispering in the muggy air. The estate of Mount Edgcumbe was not far away, the sea lapping on the round, grey and brown pebbles of its little beach, so fine beds and good food might have been found, but the two men standing on the Hoe were not lusting for food and a safe place to sleep. They were watching the sea. It was low water, the flood tide starting to run into the port, and they knew any day they would see the sails of the Armada.

Fishermen were coming home, hopefully with supplies that could be salted, if time was granted for that task, and taken aboard their ships. These small bobbing boats of working men would head for the harbour, then for their homes, squat, thatched cottages milling in confused lines along the shore, grey smoke from their cooking fires filling the air. To the men who stood on the Hoe it seemed these small dwellings were, too, watching the sea, waiting for a sign of the enemy.

Lord Charles Howard of Effingham, the Queen's noble cousin, stood beside Sir Francis Drake. Howard's clothing might be considered modest, indeed if he had been due to appear at court it might have seemed inappropriate, but beside Drake, even more simply dressed, Howard was clearly a lord. He may even have been named a fop, by men out of range of hearing. A ruff about his throat, and jewels on his fingers and chest denoted his rank. Howard's tunic was black, but it was fine, costly material. Drake's clothing was made for hard use; a woollen shirt with a leather jerkin and a long coat.

The wind was blowing from the south-west, and an hour ago as church bells pealed for three o'clock, the tide had started to rush into the Sound. Despite the breeze, the air was close. Gulls winged overhead, curling cries arching into the heavens, their screams bouncing from the walls of the port as they followed the fishing boats home. Even though Drake knew their feathers to be white, they seemed as black arcs in the sky, the pale sun and wispy clouds brilliant against their curved darkness. Their cries rang out as they spied fishermen below, and down they sped, hoping sharp bills and keen eyes would find many a meal to filch from the catch being brought home.

Screams of birds were not alone in breaking the hushed whisper of the waves. People were upon the harbour, washing out from close-cobbled and grit-lined streets, from the labyrinth of shady houses packed tight along the harbour. Eyes glimmered from behind diamond-shaped windowpanes in wealthier houses, watching men work and people gathering, standing about mounds of horse shit and rotting refuse of vegetables steaming in the pale sunlight. Children were scavenging in the rubbish, trailing the harbour and its tiny beaches, looking for anything of value, like bone-white bleached wood to burn, or rope. The inns, usually crowded, were not. Most men had been called to the ships. They had not the time to drink ale and visit their favourite whores.

Crowds watched men as they grunted, rolling barrels into holds, mending sails, lowering beams and pulleys to waiting carts, hoisting rigging, running rough hands over rope. The people of Plymouth always came to watch the ships, many contained kin and friends after all, but this day there was no talk of plunder their pirates would bring home. All talk was of the awesome forces to be faced. Everyone had heard the tales, and although the people of Plymouth were better informed than many in the country, since their men had sallied out into the roaming waters to seek the Armada, the tales told were wild. Five hundred ships were coming, carrying fifty thousand men, devils of Spain come to rape the women of England and burn the children. Drake knew the number of ships and men was not so many. Walsingham, his spies all over Spain, had sent word of one hundred and fifty at most, carrying eight thousand sailors and eighteen thousand soldiers, but even that number was daunting. Some bragged that one English ship was more than a match for three Spanish, and Drake had fought them often since the days of his youth so knew where their vessels were weak, but all the same, great danger was coming. He was not alone in feeling its approach.

From the crowds, fingers pointed to the Hoe, towards Drake and Howard. Plymouth knew Drake, its most famous son. The people could always spot him, and he was glad.

When he wandered the streets, which often he did, strangers called out to him as friends. Men offered to buy him beer. Women would touch his sleeve for luck, children would catch the tails of his coat and run away screaming and giggling when he turned, a fierce grin on his weather-burned face. They loved him as he loved them. Drake was kin to all people of Devon and Cornwall. He was their chosen son.

They knew all his tales; the bold escapades that had brought him to the attention of the Queen and had kept him at her court. They knew he had been knighted by her, a reward for plundering from the enemies of England. That a man of no blood could rise for the skill of his sword and sharpness of his eyes was a thing of hope to them. To many, Drake was a good luck charm. They all needed a little luck, that day.

Drake's eyes trailed over the English navy. In Plymouth they had a good number, one hundred and five vessels. Sir Henry Seymour, guarding the Straits of Dover, had another thirty-seven. Seymour, and his *Rainbow*, were in company with the more experienced, and cooler tempered William Wynter, in his ship the *Vanguard*. Wynter was the Surveyor of the Navy, an experienced sea dog, there to control and counsel Seymour, who, like Drake, was known for fire and rash zeal. With them were the heavier vessels of the royal navy, as well as a squadron of ships paid for by the City of London. At the Downs, between the North Sea and the Channel, they waited, guarding Kent from the troops of the Duque of Parma, the Spanish King's General in the Netherlands. Rumour had it Parma would invade along with the Armada, two fearsome forces combined, sailing upon England to wreak devastation.

Drake would rather Seymour's fleet were at Plymouth with them, but the Queen and her Council had demanded some ships to guard London, and perhaps there was sense in that. If Parma decided to ferry his men, thirty thousand highly-trained and experienced soldiers, over from Flanders, it would be good idea to have someone in position to sink their ships.

That was the plan. But Drake knew the reality of ships sinking was low. Even with great guns it was a hard task. Ships carried carpenters and divers to mend holes. Seymour and his fleet might not be able to stop Parma, just as Drake and Howard might not be able to hold back the Armada.

Drake's eyes rested on the ships. Twenty were royal, warships crafted for attack, their sleek lines pleasing to the eye. They sat low in the water, offering greater stability, and many were fully-rigged, boasting three masts all with square rigging. The rest were ships of merchants, some better than others, hastily requisitioned for the fleet. His own ship, the *Revenge*, was the finest, of that he had no doubt. It was not the largest, but speed and manoeuvrability mattered more to Drake than size. Some said she was too high-maintenance to be considered the best ship. Drake disagreed. He was well aware the best ships, like the best women, demand and are due the most attention. She was worth it.

The *Revenge* was more than one hundred feet long. A merry seabird, her deck, rails and forecastle were painted green and white, the Queen's colours. Some of the paint was faded, but the hull burned black, freshly painted with tar, the scent of pitch rising upon her, thick and rich. Sand was upon her deck, to stop men slipping. When night came, the planks of her body would let loose the scent of warm wood, a perfume familiar and reassuring to Drake's nose.

The other ships, some larger, some smaller, were about the harbour. Men swarmed over them like ants. He could see some making use of the hogsheads chained to the rails on either side of the ships; piss-buckets, to be used if fire broke out. Urine, as all sailors knew, put out fire better than sea water. Black Africans and *Cimarrons*, former slaves, many personally released from Spanish slave camps by Drake or brought to England by Hawkins, where they attained freedom, raced up rigging and dived into the water, checking the underbelly of the ships. The sight of them made him sad for a moment, thinking of Diego, a former slave who had become his right-hand man. Diego had died as they sailed about the world. Drake missed his friend. This was a time he would have liked him at his side, for no man had faced danger with better spirits than the man who had escaped slavery and charged aboard Drake's ship, all but demanding he be granted a post.

It was a good fleet, and it was a new fleet in many ways. There had been no permanent royal navy in England until the days of Her Majesty's father. From money he took back from Rome and stole from the monasteries of England, Henry VIII had built his boyish dream; a fleet of active ships crafted for war. His feat had been more a boast than anything. His ships had gone to war, but not a war of distinction. Few sea battles had been fought with his grand navy.

The truth was that most kings used ships merely to ferry men to land, where they would fight. Bluff King Hal had liked to boast, and his ships were a brag; a sign of power, but he, like most kings, had not really understood how they might be used.

But Drake saw something in ships that kings did not. How a ship might become not just a horse to carry a man into war. Drake saw more potential.

When the Queen had come to her throne, the once great navy had been long dwindling, ships falling to rot, in need of repair, others only good for sinking into the dark belly of the sea. But the Queen understood the power of ships, how they might protect, deter enemies and gain spoils for her coffers. From twenty-seven, she had built the fleet up to thirty-four. Six ships present that day dated from her father's time, but the rest had been designed by William Wynter, John Hawkins and others, and they were not ships as had been seen before.

The ships bobbing in the harbour were sleek, built to use the wind, race upon it and against it. Their sails were flatter than those of Spain and although no one had fathomed the reason, it made them easier to handle, more efficient and faster. Their keels were long, and they dipped lower in the water than those of other lands. The high forecastles of their counterparts in other kingdoms were reduced on these English ships to a single deck, the aft-castle now just a poop where officers slumbered. Their hulls were lined with four-inch planks, fine English oak, the gap between filled with tar and animal hair. The pinnaces of the navy were faster than those of Spain, deadly in shallow water and a match for smaller ships.

Only seasoned oak had been used in the warships, no green stick, liable to warp and rot. Unlike Spanish ships, the English had no towers to spy the seas, or to house archers. All this meant the English ships were lighter, quicker, and not as top-heavy. These ships were nimble and quick, built for the waters which lapped upon England's shores.

"… And if Admiral Sidonia fails to meet with General Parma," Howard said, one finger rubbing his nose as his words drew Drake from contemplating the fleet. "They will look to land upon England, in a deep water port, using it to bring men here."

Drake inclined his red head, fire shimmering in the afternoon light. "I would guess at the Isle of Wight, my lord."

"That would be my guess too, but I am glad to hear the same from your lips."

Drake smiled. Howard was not an unwise man, but his experience at sea was smaller than Drake's. Howard was not, however, a man afraid to face his failings, or to accept advice. He knew his experience was limited, so had asked that Drake be his Vice-Admiral. The Admiral was in charge, yet ready to listen. And Drake liked him.

In May, when their forces had first met, it was thought there would be trouble. The chances that Drake would be selected as Admiral were spare at best. The highest posts in army or navy went to nobility. It had always been that way. And yet Her Majesty had, at times, done much that was unexpected, such as knighting Drake. A small part of his ambitious heart had wondered if it was possible she would choose him.

She had not.

Howard had been selected as Admiral for his noble blood, his relationship to the Queen, and for the fact that the title ran in his family; his father and his great-uncle had both been Lord Admiral before him. But Howard was no son of the sea. He admitted a love for the water, had taken passengers and troops to Ireland, sailed along the shore of France, so he had seen more of the ocean than other nobles, but he was untested in battle. Howard was fifty-two years old, and even when he had been a youth, he had been better known for distinguishing himself in the lists rather than on water. His experience was a marsh light to the glaring sun of Francis Drake, the scourge of Spain, plunderer of the New World; the man who had circumnavigated the globe. Many men had thought Drake would resent Howard.

So Howard had made sure Drake did not.

On that May afternoon, Howard had sailed into Plymouth on his ship, the *Ark Royal*, to meet Drake, with the flag of the Admiral and Vice-Admiral flying from his sail. Sixteen more ships came in procession behind him. Drake and his men knew that when Howard got to them Drake's sole command of the fleet at Plymouth, his home ground, would be lost, and the Queen's personal pirate had reservations about Howard quite aside from his lack of experience. Howard had been at court and spoken against the naval offensive, preferring talks of peace. Drake had no doubts that naval action was required. Spain was coming and it needed to be faced. He had urged not only that the navy form, but that they attack the Armada before it could set out. At the same time Howard spoke about court of settlements of peace.

It was therefore not without qualms that Drake had watched as Howard, this man of peace, came sailing towards Plymouth. As Drake and all his men watched from their ships, Howard himself lowered the flag of the Vice-Admiral and sent it to Drake on a small boat, bidding Drake to set it upon his flagpole. Before his cheering men, Drake had done so, hoisting the banner so it billowed upon the sails of the *Revenge*. Drake noted the honour Howard had done to him. No clearer sign of Howard's respect could there have been for Drake, a man born so much lower than him.

Pleased his command, albeit under Howard, was recognised, Drake had sallied out, the agile, beautiful *Revenge* cutting through the water with speed, with forty ships in three files behind him, banners of Tudor white and green rippling from their sails, and music playing, to escort the Admiral into harbour.

Howard was a man of tact. There was no doubt of that. A council of war lasting two days had followed their first meeting, and whilst some captains thought Drake's ideas wild, Howard supported them. Spoken against conflict the Admiral had, but now he was committed to war, Howard was all in. The Admiral understood why he had been chosen. It was not only for blood; he was a good leader, and the best leader uses his men to their full advantage. That was what Howard did, and he did more, bringing men who before this time had been foes, like Frobisher and Drake, together so they might act as a team against the bigger foe of Spain. Howard gave few speeches, but he guided carefully, seeming to understand his men with but spare experience of them. Howard had sent letters to the Council praising Drake and his other captains, calling them men of the greatest judgement and experience, and supported their plans. Howard might not understand the sea as well as Drake, but he understood men. That was why he had been chosen. There were others to advise on battles and strategy; Howard's task was to unite the fleet.

Howard was, in fact, one of the rarest kind of men; one who knows his strengths and weaknesses. These creatures are curious to many who hide in fictions of themselves. Howard was willing to learn, and whilst he would not cede a scrap of his authority, he would listen. Howard was no sheep, bleating after a ram; he questioned Drake sharply, made him justify his plans, but he also respected his authority in matters of the sea. Diligent, calm and controlled, with an ear ready to hear and a mind to learn, Howard was more able for this position than even he thought, for he knew what he had and what he lacked.

Few are so honest with themselves, a great shame, for in understanding of self there is power. In recognition of fault, there is the ability to grow. Where man is most broken is where he has the most potential to build again.

And Francis Drake, son of a yeoman lay-preacher, and a man who many looked down on for his coarse ways, fiery temper, inability to accept the opinions of others and low birth, had found a lord of blood so noble it was shared with the Queen not only listening to him, but deferring to him. Drake was well aware what people thought and knew much of it was true. He *was* a hothead, his temper as scalding as his hair when roused. He had a tendency to boast, and he did not suffer the ideas of others well. Drake was brilliant, daring and the best sailor there, but he was also not unaware of his failings, but unlike Howard he had not mastered them. As the weeks had gone on, Drake had come to understand why, even had blood not been an issue, he would not have been chosen. Unite his own men he could, unite all the captains of the English fleet, he could not.

Howard was cool water to Drake's flames. The Admiral was the steady ship steering, as Drake was the guns firing beneath. Somehow, without knowledge of the sea, the Queen had selected the perfect partnership; energy, rashness and flame mated with calmness and control.

Seeing the respect Howard offered without reservation to him, Drake responded in kind. Over the past few months they had become close, working well together, with Howard's reserve and ability for contemplation complementing Drake's passion and his often rash, if uncannily lucky, ideas.

Howard had brought the other captains to him, too. John Hawkins of the *Victory*, Martin Frobisher of the *Triumph,* largest ship of the fleet, and Thomas Fenner, Drake's deputy, of the *Nonpareil*, were experienced men of the sea, but they recognised Howard's authority. In a short time, they had become a fine team.

Other captains, young and chosen more for rank than experience, were Lord Thomas Howard of the *Golden Lion*, and Lord Edmund Sheffield of the *White Bear,* second largest ship of the fleet. They were but twenty-seven and twenty-five, and included in the rolls as much for the fact they would support Howard's vote if the need came, as for their blood. Thomas Howard was the Admiral's cousin, Sheffield his nephew. Sir Richard Southwell, too, Vice-Admiral of Norfolk and Suffolk was a relative; Howard's son-in-law. His ship, the *Elizabeth Jonas*, was third largest of the fleet.

Young, inexperienced men had not been the only trial Drake and Howard had faced. Plans on how to defend England, many of them poor, had been sent by the Queen and her Council. The trouble was, many men of England had no idea of what sea and ships were capable of, and still fewer had any idea what the Spanish had planned. This had led to lunatic ideas hatching from seething brains.

First, the Council had tried to imagine they knew something of the sea, since most men with a pinch of power like to think they know all. Howard was a rare, wondrous, exception.

The Council had ordered the fleet to be divided between the east and west coasts, with Howard and Drake in command, one to watch Parma and the other for the Armada. Knowing a worse plan was almost impossible, Drake had gone to court and spoken to the Queen in person. Dividing the fleet made no sense at all, and he made her see that. Reports came that if Parma was to set out, he would send his men on flat-bottomed barges, people carriers, which had few guns. Drake had persuaded the Queen to put a few ships, commanded by Seymour, about Kent to attack Parma's men if they set out, but to concentrate the rest of the fleet at Plymouth. Facing the Armada would require the bulk of the English fleet.

The Queen had listened. She, too, was not unaware of her lack of experience. Later that month had been when the rest of the fleet and its Admiral had arrived in Plymouth.

All this may seem well, but there had been no orders to sail out to catch the Armada at sea, and only after much talk and dithering had it come. The Queen, finally persuaded by Drake and Howard that stopping the Armada before it entered English waters was a good notion, had granted permission. The men had sailed out together, making a dash into the seas. But as they reached the Scilly Isles, no sign of the Spanish had they seen. Howard and Drake had pressed the fleet further towards Spain, but nothing had they found and the wind turned on them, transforming into a perilous calm which threatened to stick them fast in open ocean. Then the wind had risen from the south-west, granting the Armada ideal conditions to use to reach England. The Queen, fearing her ships would be wrecked in the summer storms that were rising to whip the oceans, had called them home, and Howard, fearing the enemy might slip about them, reaching an undefended England, had given the command to return. At Plymouth they had reassembled.

Howard wrote to the Queen, reassuring her and her Council that the fleet had *"danced as lustily as the gallantest dancers at Court."* Howard knew how to calm his Queen, but she forbade them to head out again. Her Howard cousin pointed out that his men were better able to judge the seas than men of court. She relented, they went out again, but again were blown back.

The plan had failed, and some had criticised Drake for it, for it had been his idea, but Howard had not. They had, if nothing else, sailed together and seen the skills each possessed. Howard, although no veteran of the oceans, was a quick study, and his confidence in Drake had not diminished for their failure to find their prey. The voyages had reassured Drake, too. Howard had sued for peace once, but was willing to seek war when need came.

The other thing gained was intelligence. Drake had found a Dublin bark which had almost run into a Spanish ship off the Lizard in Cornwall. The Dubliners had told tales of the number of ships and their weapons.

Plenty of other insane plans had come from the Privy Council. Drake had urged Howard to fight many of them, but as the Queen made last efforts to stop the Armada through talks, the English fleet found themselves *"tied like bears to the stakes,"* as Howard put it as they were kept at port. The Queen had never been one for giving a straight answer. It seemed that whilst that had aided her and England often in the past, it might have become too much a habit and had become a hindrance. Between war and peace she wavered, driving her men to distraction.

Hints the fleet might be disbanded for lack of funds, to be called back if the Armada was sighted, had left many captains dumb with disbelief. The waiting time before battle had been a battle in itself. Drake, Howard, and other captains had struggled for their voices of experience to be heard against the shouts of those with *no* experience who happened to be closer to the Queen's ear.

But Drake and Howard had kept the fleet together, and the Queen seemed more willing to bend to their opinions now than to those of others. One other thing to be grateful for was that they were to direct conflicts as they saw fit. Well aware she had no idea how to organise a battle at sea, the Queen had sent word that captains of the fleet were to use their own wits and instincts to fight, to do as they saw fit. That was the way Drake liked it.

"There have been so many plans sent by Walsingham," Howard said, his fingers heading from gnarled nose to greying beard where they strayed, stroking it. "My wife says the Queen, her mistress, remains unsure about what tactics the Spanish will employ, but Walsingham seems to think you are right, Drake, and the Armada will be used to create a barrier so Parma's troops can be ferried across, to somewhere in Kent, but there are others we have heard of."

"We can guess at some of their plans, my lord," Drake said. "Others will be revealed when we face them."

"I like not the notion of running at their heels, guessing what they are up to, but I deduce you are correct. We must alter our course to match theirs, hold them away, prevent landings if they look to make them."

"We men of England are thought of as stalwart and immovable by those who know us not," Drake said. "Yet we easily become as changeable as our weather."

"Let us hope we have as much might," Howard said, looking up at the skies. "For we have powder and shot not enough."

"Her Majesty is careful with her purse."

Drake was showing tact, something learnt from his Admiral. Although he thought Howard a good man, he was still the Queen's cousin, and might relay criticism to her if he lost faith in Drake.

But supplies were short, there was no denying that. There was also no denying that some of that was the fault of the Queen. Long she had delayed, trying to hold off war with talks of peace, and her delay meant that not enough powder, food, water, weapons, saltpetre or men for the land forces had been assembled. What Cornwall and Devon could provide had been used up quickly by the enormous fleet over the past few months, and supply carts trundling from London had been delayed by summer squalls and rivers of mud upon the roads. Even as food and water had arrived and was loaded onto the ships, Howard had written, urging the Queen to dispatch more. The delays had caused rational Howard to suspect that treason was at work in the court, spies of Spain holding up the supplies he so urgently required.

Lack of food was not the only matter troubling the men. Ship's fever, always a risk, had broken out on the *Elizabeth Jonas*, spreading swiftly to other vessels. And the wages of the navy had not been paid. Although this was no uncommon thing in any land, it caused tension. Howard had told Drake that Seymour had written to him with the same complaint, and Seymour had had a reply from Baron Burghley, the Queen's right hand, saying the Crown had not even the fifty thousand needed to pay outstanding wages and costs, and certainly no more could he find after that.

Powder and shot was what worried Drake at that moment. Wages would be found, he had no doubt of that, and wages were always paid late, but there were other means of gathering money. Plunder from crippled ships might offer his men much. Fever also always came; he had lost a brother to it. But if they were to live to enjoy wages and fight off sickness, they had to beat the enemy. That would not be easy without enough powder and shot.

The trouble was, no one knew how much they needed. Certainly more than they had, but Her Majesty was not one to spend where she did not need to, so was unlikely to buy in huge reserves of powder that might not be used. The militia, Drake knew, had been trained with false fire, arming the priming pan of the gun only, so there was a spark but no fire. The Queen had sent a hasty letter to Drake when she heard he was training his gunners using targets at sea, and had cut his supplies, not trusting him to obey her and conserve powder, until quite recently. As it stood, that day they had eighteen days of provisions, perhaps two days' worth of gunpowder.

But they were close to home, which was more than the ships of Spain could boast. There was, in any case, not one war where the powder had been enough, and they were unsure how their cannon would measure up to that of Spain. They might have all they needed, they might not, only time would tell.

"Her Majesty is too careful with her coin." Howard shot a look at Drake, perhaps wondering if he would inform the Queen of this condemnation. "I would not criticize my Queen and royal cousin, for I know the war in the Netherlands has taken a toll, as has supporting our Protestant ally Navarre in France, but we are not well off with weapons. I have written, asking for more." He sighed through his nose. "Walsingham sends word from his spies. The money the Pope has promised to the King of Spain will come in two instalments. One will be paid if they land on English soil, the second will come if they take the kingdom."

"Then there are two more reasons to stop them sinking anchor on our shores, my lord."

Howard nodded. "Indeed. Even an insecure foothold upon England will grant Phillip of Spain more coin, and with that he might buy mercenaries."

"They will not step upon our soil." Fire churned in Drake's eyes as he watched men walking the ships, shovels of glowing, smouldering pitch in hand to ward off the spirits of sickness that had fallen upon them. On the galley hearths, in the ships' bilges, fires of broom branches burned. When roaring, they were swamped with wet broom, creating thick smoke. Men would leave the ship, closing hatches, allowing the pungent fug to fill the air. When fire turned to ashes, they returned to sweep it out, the vessel by that time cleansed of fever, lice and rats. Drake watched the fire, but the flames in his eyes were not reflected from the ships, they echoed from his heart. Since his youth he had learned to hate Spain. That fire had been glowing in him for years, but now a wind had blown, rousing ember to flame. He would not allow his enemy to invade England.

Howard shifted step, the grass growing damp under him. Rain had come the night before, and the Hoe was still wet. "You have read this vile work Cardinal Allen has penned?"

Drake inclined his head. "I heard what it contains, my lord."

"He wishes to persuade men of England they will be better off with Phillip on our English throne."

Drake barked a laugh. "Better off, with the Inquisition roaming, lighting fires with English bones?"

Howard grimaced. "I remember the pyres of Queen Mary. Phillip lit many. Never again will such horror walk abroad in England."

Drake looked in the direction of St Nicholas' Island, just off Plymouth. Once called St Michael's Island, the name had changed when the chapel had been rededicated. There his father had hidden when forced to flee Queen Mary and her men because of his faith. From there he had sped to Kent, grappling a living on one of the merchant hulks on the rivers, barely surviving. As a boy, Drake had lived and worked on boats shipping goods between Kent and Antwerp, until his father had sent him to work for a kinsman, William Hawkins, a merchant who dabbled in piracy.

"My father hated Queen Mary, and all of her faith," Drake said.

Howard sniffed. He was one of the few in his family who was not a suspected papist. "At least our Queen beheads or hangs those who commit treason. Her sister, Spain's whore, was crueller."

"Our Queen turns her eyes from examining souls, unlike her sister, who wanted to see the centre of all men." Drake rubbed his forehead. "But I save my wrath for Spain, my lord. I do not forget how they killed the men of my cousin, John Hawkins, when we were at peaceful anchor at San Juan de Ulua. I do not forget the men they burned at the stake in the New World." Drake shifted, his limp apparent. A wound inflicted by Spain, another reason to despise the enemy.

Spain was the centre of his hatred. Silver, gold and jewels might have been what Drake plundered, but revenge was what he sought. The name of his ship was apt.

"My royal cousin will not tremble on her throne." Howard stiffened his back. "We will ensure that."

"Our ships are greater, my lord. We will prevail."

"They will try to draw close, grapple us," said Howard.

"We will dance away, my lord."

Howard grinned at his second in command. "Done much dancing, Drake?"

"Not at court, my lord, but often on the sea. The waves make merry partners."

Drake's eyes were glittering, offering Howard hope. That was the thing about Drake. Boastful, hot-headed and impulsive though he was, he was charming, engaging, confident and fortunate. Luck was with him. It had not failed him yet. Such thoughts granted courage to Howard at times he most needed them. Few saw past Howard's stoic visage, but fear was with him, fear of failure, his own most of all, fear of invasion, for his wife, his kin. But Drake was a man to whom luck clung. There is something greatly reassuring about having a good luck charm at your elbow.

It was as well, for the weather was certainly not promising. Summer storms and gales, the like of which had not been seen for years, had struck. Although this had delayed the Armada, it had done little to aid the English fleet and the south-west wind was more favourable to the enemy than to them. And yet, standing there with Drake, Howard had the feeling luck would fall upon them. Attracted to Drake, it would rain upon the English fleet.

"There is time yet, my lord," Drake said. "A game, to pass the hours?" He indicated to men behind them playing bowls, a popular pastime in England. Knowing such a commonplace thing of ease would assure the people watching them, Howard took his place beside Drake, playing bowls on the Hoe.

The soft clink of ball hitting ball, of globes sliding upon grass and the cheer of spectators was all that was heard for a while as the sun slid in the skies.

As the afternoon sun shone dim through the racing clouds, a man came running up the hill to the Hoe. His name was Thomas Fleming and that morning he had been sailing about the Lizard in Cornwall in his ship, named after Drake's, *The Golden Hind*. Drake stopped the game as the man raced to him, word of the Armada upon his lips.

Howard and Drake knew Fleming well. They should have clapped the man in irons when they saw him, for there was a warrant out for his arrest, on charges of piracy. Instead of arresting men like Fleming at such a time, however, they had engaged him. Fleming was part of a small fleet of boats they had sent out to keep a lookout for the Armada.

Howard and Drake listened as Fleming spoke, and exchanged dark looks. The Armada was off the English coast, and the timing could not have been worse. The fleet was trapped inside the Sound, the tide against them. They could not get out.

"The seas themselves seemed to groan with the weight of ships," Fleming gasped, leaning on his knees to catch his breath. "Two miles wide it is. The skies went dark under all the sails."

Another exchange of grim glances. They were stuck in the Sound with the wind blowing south-west, favouring ships coming from Spain. If Medina Sidonia, Admiral of the Armada, wanted, he could destroy the entire English fleet whilst it was trapped in Plymouth. Drake knew the danger well enough. Attacking a fleet in port was what he had done at Cadiz and it had worked only too well. There were shore batteries with guns along the pass into the harbour, but many enemy ships might make it past, on to crush the fleet before a thing could be done. English resistance to Spanish invasion might be over before it started.

Seeing their men watching, and beacons from Cornwall igniting even at that moment on the hillside, Drake turned to Howard.

"There is plenty of time to finish the game, and beat the Spaniards too," he said, tossing the heavy ball in his large hands, a grin on his face and a swagger to his gait.

Howard almost laughed. There was nothing they could do right that moment, and if they, the Admiral and Vice-Admiral, showed signs of panic the men would fall apart. Howard grinned at Drake, knowing this false show of confidence was a pageant. "Then throw, Drake," he said, plucky spirit rising within his heart. "Though it will do you no good. The game is mine."

As Drake took position to throw his ball at the Jack, the men about them seemed to sag, as one, with relief.

The bells of all the churches in Plymouth began to peal. Seeing the beacons igniting, they sent warning to the people of England; the Armada was come.

As Howard and Drake played on, orders were dispatched from the Hoe. Captains on the docks mustered their men, readying for action not dependent on the tide.

Howard and Drake might look relaxed, but their hearts were anything but. There was only one course of action, and they took it. Nature would not aid them, so the strength of men would have to.

"The enemy are yet too distant to take advantage of the flood into Plymouth, my lord," Drake whispered in Howard's ear as they bowed down, side by side, to measure distances between their balls and the Jack. "We have a few hours yet."

"Pray to God that is so," Howard replied, standing to announce, to a cheer, he was the winner.

When the game was done, they went to their ships. At their backs, beacons on the hills lit, one after another, baskets of iron containing wood and bracken, ignited by men who had watched for weeks for sign of the enemy. All along the coast they burned, these iron towers of fire, heading for London and the eyes of the Queen.

Howard looked to the hillside, his feet feeling the sand scattered on his deck and his eyes grave. A flash of crimson fire from a blazing beacon stroked his face, light playing on his features, his expression unreadable.

Chapter Three

The English Channel
July 19th 1588

Death

Had the King of Spain possessed my eyes, he would have looked down upon Plymouth and laughed that day.

The English fleet had been caught at the worst moment, and they knew it. If Drake had underestimated the speed at which the Armada moved, they might well have been caught at anchor, and destroyed.

And so out the fleet crept, relying on muscle and wit rather than time and tide. Their pace was laborious and slow. Night was falling, the wind blowing gently and the tide coming to ebb. One gun was fired to let the captains know it was time, and out they skulked, sneaking soldiers slinking to a field of battle. Royal galleons and the largest ships weighed anchor, iron breaking the surface of the waves in a roar, then caught and hauled aboard their longboats, which would pull them from the harbour.

Longboats rowed out ahead of ships, carrying anchors attached to long, slippery cables. When the weighty cable, slimy with green weed and heavy with water, was stretched, the anchor was thrown and the huge ships were hauled to it by muscles of the men on the capstans. As it was winched along, inching painfully through water, another boat would race ahead, carrying another cable. Some ships were winched out by cables fixed along the shore, smaller ones towed behind other ships. Men on the longships and at the oars worked hard that night, sweat pouring down glistening backs, muscles screaming in the chilled night air. But they did not stop. They did not dare. They knew what would happen if they were caught.

On the docks stood the crowds, bathed in the flickering light of amber torches and lanterns held aloft in hands, as the people of Plymouth watched their sons and fathers inch from the port, knowing many would never be seen again.

Oars bent, splashing into the water, and ships began to warp out, down the Plymouth Sound, the whispering trees of the Edgcumbe estate murmuring as they passed. Wood creaking, cables groaning, anchors splashing and the sound of feet racing upon decks as men took position broke the silence of the night. Against hulls small waves broke, the impact echoing within the bellies of the ships. The lee of Mount Edgcumbe sheltered the fleet from the wind, still blowing south-west, as they emerged.

As they came into open water they could use the breeze. Waves lapped the bows, and the sound of water, rushing now with greater power, filled the ships. Men climbed like apes up rigging, unfurling sails. Guncrews ran below, hard, bare feet sure upon the slippery steps as they stacked gunpowder and checked weapons. Helmsmen watched the horizon. As they came clear of the Sound and entered the lee of Rame Head, lanterns and torches went out with a hiss, plunging the fleet into velvet darkness, the only light the moon. They could not be found now. They were free of the Sound, but if the wind backed southerly they could still be trapped by a Spanish attack.

As men of England waited at Rame Head, some hunkering down on the decks to sleep, others whispering prayers, men of Spain were doing the same not far away… or some of them were.

Don Alonso Perez de Guzman, Duque of Medina Sidonia, could not sleep. He was never easy at sea in any case. Water churning under him made his stomach sick and his head roll.

The Admiral of the Armada was no man of the sea. Until he had set sail, in fact, he had not been upon it as anything but a passenger.

Don Alvaro de Bazan, Marquis de Santa Cruz, the "thunderbolt in war, father of his troops, the unconquered" had been the man who was supposed to command. His death in February from ship's fever, although many said eleven days of doctors purging and bleeding the Admiral had not aided him, and others blamed the King for hounding him at every turn as Cruz formed the Armada, had led to changes of command. Phillip had handed the honour to Sidonia.

An honour Sidonia had not wanted.

Long had Sidonia begged Phillip not to put him in charge of this fleet. His pleas had all gone unheard. When the King of Spain decided something, it was done. Sidonia had tried pleading debts he owed, his lack of experience, and even recommended other men, but the King would not hear him. The King of Spain thought Sidonia was demonstrating humility, and said he had judged his capabilities and was satisfied.

Sidonia was not.

The new Admiral had defended the coast of Andalusia from pirates, but his tasks had been administrative, not active. He was an advisor to the King, and not an unwise one, who had called for a permanent fleet. As a young man he had been married to the King's bastard daughter, the Princess of Eboli, and the King trusted his word. Sidonia had marched to Cadiz with an army, and saved it from Drake, on land at least. But he had no qualifications as a man on sea. He was always seasick, was not in good health, had no experience in naval battles, no personal fortune to spend on the fleet, and little confidence in his abilities. In truth, Sidonia had nothing but his ancient name to recommend him for such an almighty, daunting, task as this invasion of England. But the King had insisted, and Sidonia had come, along with his misgivings.

In some ways, Sidonia thought too little of himself. He was skilled at organisation, and was utterly loyal to his country, something proved in his acceptance of the post. He was also a man of great courage, as you will see as time goes on.

Sidonia's arrival at Lisbon some months ago had not reassured him. Sidonia had come to port to find chaos waiting for him. The King, far away at the Escorial Palace near Madrid, had wanted him to set sail immediately, but finding that supplies were still short, and being commandeered upon the whims of noble commanders rather than need, Sidonia had been forced to delay.

There were not enough warships, even he knew that, and some were overloaded and some under. The distribution of supplies was baffling. Some vessels had gunpowder and no shot. Others boasted piles of cannonballs and nothing to fire them with. Seeing this, Sidonia had done what he did best; administration. Sorting supplies, bringing in more, moving the fleet from chaos to order, he had managed, although not without a few surrenders to other commanders. Nobles had claimed more gunpowder than other commanders, whether it was a sensible distribution or not. But this, Sidonia thought, was a smaller problem, for now at least all ships had some gunpowder and cannonballs, even if the distribution was not perfect. On land, Sidonia had proved himself an able commander. What would happen at sea was yet to be seen.

His captains were more experienced. As Howard had Drake, so Sidonia had his own sea dogs. Diego Flores de Valdes was his chief of staff, an experienced sailor who sailed with Sidonia on the Portuguese galleon, the flagship, *San Martin*.

Hugo de Moncada and Marolin de Juan were veterans of the sea, there to advise the Admiral. Valdes was one of his squadron commanders, along with Bertendona, captain of the largest ship of the fleet. Miguel de Oquendo and Don Juan Martinez de Recalde, a man of Spanish and Italian descent, whose speciality was naval gunnery, were another two. There was another Valdes, Pedro, cousin to Sidonia's squadron commander. The two kinsmen did not get along.

There was also Alonzo Martinez de Leyva, general of the land forces. If Sidonia was killed, Leyva was to take command. His ship was the *Santa Maria*, for some reason known as *Rata Encoronada*, the Crowned Rat. Like Sidonia, Leyva knew nothing of war at sea.

Sidonia had nine Portuguese galleons and ten smaller ones, four ships of the *flota,* the escort which took silver convoys from the New World, and the same number of Italian galleasses and Portuguese galleys. There were forty-two armed merchantmen, and in all the force had seventy-three fighting vessels and fifty freighters and lighter boats. They had two thousand four hundred guns and almost thirty thousand men.

And they had God. Of that many were certain. When one captain had been asked by a papal envoy if they would win, he had admitted English ships were better, but since God was on the side of Spain, He would intervene. "We are sailing against England in the confident hope of a miracle," he had said.

That, to Sidonia, was not reassuring. He was not light of faith, but had never believed God appeared to save people when they wished the Almighty would. God helped those who helped themselves. Drake helped himself more often than not, so if the old maxim was true the Almighty might well look with more favour on a pirate than on the Armada.

Many were also certain of what they did *not* have.

Recalde and other captains complained about the lack of heavy guns. None had enough, and most ships had cannon which would only fire four-pound shot. At close range they might do damage, but not at a distance.

Sidonia had found more gunpowder. The amount they carried now was double what Santa Cruz had gathered. But cannon, the best forged in England, Venice or the Netherlands were in short supply. And there was a problem with the powder.

"It is fine-corned musket powder," Recalde had told him. "More powerful than the serpentine powder we use for the cannon."

Sidonia had thought this a good thing until Recalde informed him that many of their guns were poorly casted, the iron brittle. This high-grade powder might cause cannons to shatter when fired; no good thing for the ships, or guncrews.

One of the military commanders had complained there were not enough cannonballs. Bobadilla had come with a grave face, saying they were sure to run out, and what then?

Sidonia had sent word out for more cannonballs, but getting little for his efforts tried for other weapons. He found a great many pikes, half-pikes, muskets and other weapons, but some of the muskets were so heavy they had to be supported on rests upon the decks. "These are only good if we get close," Bobadilla had said. "If we can grapple them. But I think the English will do all they can to avoid that."

Perhaps they would, Sidonia thought, but the way of war upon the sea was to wound a ship with guns, pull alongside, grapple and board, allowing the men to fight as they did on land. Naval battles were, in effect, land battles, with the ship bearing the feet of men rather than the earth. The English might have better guns, many thought this was so, but eventually battles would be fought hand to hand. At least with his soldiers well-armed, the Armada would be prepared for this.

Their last problem was food and water. Drake's attack on Cadiz had ruined vital goods for that year's supply of barrels, leading to a worrying shortage. They had salt-fish, biscuit and salt-meat, but the barrels food was stored in were old and leaky, and already they had had to abandon rotten stores, stinking and green, overboard.

As they had sailed out, months ago, they had met storms and feral seas. For three weeks they had been forced to hold in port as a tempest broke upon them. The sight of men who had never been to sea vomiting everywhere, ships rocking and the winds howling like ghosts lost to limbo had been enough to make all the men anxious.

And all the time Sidonia held anchor, Phillip wrote. An endless stream of commands, information and instructions had left Sidonia feeling dazed and battered as a whipping boy.

The English would try to fight them at long range, so Sidonia would have to draw them in to grapple, wrote the busy quill of the King. The English were at Dover, no, Plymouth, no, Margate, wrote Mendoza, Spain's ambassador to France. Avoid fighting the English at all, scribbled the King; get to Parma to defend his troops as they are shipped across. Gain the weather-gage, get upwind, force them to fight at close quarters, wrote the King.

Even Sidonia knew what the weather-gage was. It meant your ship had the wind, and therefore the control of any encounter with an enemy ship.

But in all these contrary instructions, there was no detail about how and when Sidonia was to meet Parma and join forces. Phillip seemed to think they would simply come across each other somewhere upon the sea, but despite his lack of experience, Sidonia thought this a plan where much might go awry.

And if he could not find Parma, what was he to do? Phillip's careful instructions, unyielding and unbending, did not allow for any other plan save one, a secret command and one Sidonia was not sure he could bring to pass either.

Letters had been sent back and forth as they rocked in the grip of the storm, waves as big as mountains crashing, slapping the ships, water crashing over their decks. Wrapped in impenetrable blankets of fog and thinking he might run mad from the howling of the wind, Sidonia tried to contact Parma, form a plan, but nothing but silence came from Parma as about Sidonia there had been nothing but the keening wind and screaming sea.

When the wind fell, they had set out again, forming their defensive crescent. This was a strong formation; an arc, known as the *lunula*, which formed a crescent with flanking horns. Upon those horns sailed warships with the heaviest guns, for the tips were the weakest point.

It took more than two weeks to sail another one hundred and sixty miles. Sidonia felt as though if he dropped into the sea and swam with a cable attached to his waist, pulling his ship, they might go faster.

Sickness was swifter. It had raced through the ships; men with swollen bleeding gums and limbs, as well as ship's fever, falling ill. Damages to the ships caused by the inclement weather had to be mended, lost spars, masts and rigging replaced, and some men had deserted. Sidonia had written to Phillip many times, urging him to put off the attack for a year and seek peace with Elizabeth of England in the meantime, saying that perhaps this ill weather was a sign from God. Phillip refused. What Sidonia did not know was that he was not alone in urging delay. Parma was doing the same from the Netherlands.

Concerned about the notion his forces and the Armada were to meet, but with no plan as to how, Parma wrote to Phillip, saying he could not simply go out to sea in his boats and find the Admiral. *"These things cannot be, and in the interests of*

Your Majesty's service I should be anxious if I thought the Admiral were depending on them… He will plainly see what with these little flat boats, built for rivers but not for the sea, I cannot diverge from the short, direct passage which has been agreed upon… If we came across any armed English or Dutch rebel ships, they could destroy us with the greatest ease."

But Phillip believed his plan would work, that God would unite his navy and army, and he urged Sidonia on, whilst never telling him of Parma's misgivings. By that time Sidonia was feeling somewhat brighter about his prospects. Having much to organise had aided the Admiral in some ways. Finding lost ships, refitting and supplying those still with him and finding food stores had all taken up his time, keeping him from worrying on the future. Soon he had written to Phillip, informing him of their work and telling him he had placed his faith in God. It was what his sovereign wanted to hear.

More weeks had passed before the Armada could leave and reinforcements arrived to replace the dead, deserted and sick, but Sidonia had not been cheered by his new recruits. They were worse than the original men, being even less trained, many raw as fresh meat. Some had arrived starving. But they had sailed when a fair wind blew, leaving the fragrant shores of Spain and her blissful sunshine, heading for the gloom of the open seas and mist-swathed England. From the ships flew their colours and trumpets sounded, ringing across the bay as people lining the headland cheered them, and prayed for them.

Sometimes, in the days that followed, it seemed to Sidonia they might never reach this country they were to claim for their King. On that first day they had gone but nine miles when the wind died, leaving them motionless in the water. When the wind returned, a ship had broken the socket holding her rudder in her haste to hoist sail, leaving the entire fleet waiting as repairs were done.

Food and water were already a problem, but although he sent letters asking for more and waited off Finisterre for four days, little arrived. By the middle of June they had travelled only three hundred miles from Lisbon and were delayed again at Corunna, where they put in to get supplies, by another storm which scattered the fleet. Sidonia had given commands that no ship was to sail home if separated; they would rejoin the fleet or wait at the rendezvous points of the Scilly Isles or Mount's Bay in Cornwall, but that day he feared captains might have fled. Storms had hit them, waves seeming to *"mount the sky"* as Sidonia wrote in another letter dispatched to silent Parma. After one night spent in a raging tempest, Sidonia had awoken to find forty ships missing, an entire squadron, and three of his own were lost too; one wrecked upon a harbour, one beached and the last had to seek refuge in France. Sidonia noted in another letter to Parma that his ships *"are very fragile in heavy seas."*

Three days after the storm ended, thirty ships were still missing and many more had been damaged. God, perhaps, was not eager for the Armada to reach England.

"We have now arrived at this port scattered and maltreated in such a way that we are far inferior in strength to the enemy," Sidonia wrote, trying to persuade his stubborn King to hold off the invasion until a later date.

Active tasks done, the fleet sailing on, Sidonia was left to his worries of the future once more, until one day a shout went up, and through the mist and drifting fog his eyes could see land; the Lizard peninsula.

Upon sight of land, Sidonia had called a council of war aboard the *San Martin*. He had seen the drifting smoke and sighted beacons, a trailing line of crimson along the misty shore. The English knew they were there and anytime now an attack would come. There was little to be done in the night, and Sidonia had sent his men away, to pray for God to bring them the outcome they desired.

Sidonia sighed. He could hear priests singing Mass for the men, preparing them for the day to come. Boys were on deck singing *Ave Maria* to the falling skies. Each morning they sang *Salve Regina*, their clear, high voices a thing of unparalleled beauty in this ugly time. Many men would say prayers for their souls this night, more might again request last rites, preparing in case death snuck upon them in battle. Before they sailed all men had confessed and had been communicated, for death could be sudden upon the sea. More than eight thousand had been absolved, these delicate rites becoming crude; lines of men waiting for blessing as they might for meat at market. All his men wore a talisman of pewter with an image of Christ on one side and the Virgin on the other. From his mast sailed the banner, blessed by the Pope. The arms of Spain, the Virgin Mary and the Crucifixion was upon it, along with the words *"Arise, O Lord, and vindicate Thy cause."*

Faith was the reason they were there, as they had been told, as the people of Spain had been told, many times. The Armada was not an attack fleet, it was a defence; defence of the faith, the true faith, against its foes. They were to deliver the faithful of England from the heretical tyrant, the bastard Elizabeth. Daughter of a witch, offspring of an excommunicate, *and* excommunicate herself, the Queen of England had no right to sit upon that throne. Phillip of Spain was the true heir, and the false Queen had shown her animosity to the world by executing priests, and then her own cousin, the legitimate and Catholic Queen of Scots.

That was the story told, but Sidonia was wise enough to know that when war is declared the other side is always made a monster.

Sidonia put his hand to his doublet, his fingers touching the hard coldness of golden ducats sewn into the lining of his clothes. Many men had brought their entire fortunes with them, so confident of victory were they. They were not alone. English exiles that had joined the fleet numbered around two hundred. Some were lords, bringing treasure home so they could work on their confiscated estates as soon as possible.

Less favoured were the English in the murky, sweaty bowels of the galleys and galleasses; captured pirates and spies, now slaves, working to row the very ships that would conquer their homeland. Fettered to oars, forced to piss where they worked; the stench of bodies and waste from the bowels of the ships was eye-watering, trailing behind some vessels for miles.

Other Englishmen on his ships were poor; priests who had fled the country, fearing execution, or nobles with little to their name *but* their names. Some were mercenaries, seeking profit.

Many were seeking money. Faith was a good reason, a moral one, for many to embark on this war, but the coin, land and estates that would fall into Spanish hands was also inviting. Gentlemen adventurers, many in service to the King's bastard, Prince Antonio Luis, had come seeking fortune and fame. They were not the best soldiers; many had arrived wearing their finest clothes and jewels, thinking Parma's troops would do most of the fighting, but all were there to claim a scrap of England, of glory, and of money.

Although hardly poorly dressed himself, Sidonia had had cause to often marvel, as they sailed, on the clothes paraded on the ships. Nobles with no martial skill had boarded, their servants and retainers all carrying chests of money and jewels, and all dressed in fine silk, rich velvet and carrying swords set with blazing gemstones, ready for a grand, glorious entrance to England, their new, conquered country. Even common sailors were well dressed. Credit had been easy to gain from shopkeepers in Spain, since the Armada could not fail. It was blessed by God and by the Pope. Medals showing Phillip's victory, the King crowned like an emperor of Rome with laurels upon his head, had been struck before they had set sail.

Bickering had broken out as nobles fought over space for themselves and their many servants, and piles of personal goods were everywhere. His captains warned these were a liability which might damage the efficiency of ships in battle, and provide hazards for men at other times, but try as he might Sidonia could only convince a few to shift them out of the way. Baffled faces stared at him when he spoke of dangers that might come. Some were so assured the Armada would win they seemed to have forgotten fighting would even occur.

But Sidonia was worried that night as he listened to prayers being sung and smelt incense rising above the salt scent of the sea and the unwholesome stench of floating weed.

That day one of his *zabras* had gone closer to the coast, to spy, and had captured a Cornish fishing boat. Terrified men had been brought on board his ship, their stumbling mumbles translated. Although their accents were broad and many words strange, the information was clear. The English fleet was anchored in Plymouth. His men had pressed him to head straight for the enemy, for trapped as they were they might be easily destroyed. Sidonia would not. He feared a trap as he feared the narrow pass into the Plymouth Sound. Drake was rumoured to be commanding a small squadron further along the Devon coast, and if that was so, Sidonia thought, *El Draque* might fly up behind them, leaving the Armada trapped in port, lambs to the slaughter.

Sidonia feared Drake. England's dragon, the most notorious and cunning pirate the world had seen, was something to be feared, as he knew. Sidonia had commanded the ground troops which came to the relief of Cadiz when Drake had attacked. Held the pirate away from land Sidonia had, and had been rewarded for it, not least with this unwanted command, but he had seen what Drake and a small fleet of forty ships, only five of them great, had done. That man was a known magician. From his nefarious hands spells could wend, weaving winds to obey his will, influencing the waves to do his bidding. Drake was something to fear, even if Lord Howard, a man only slightly more experienced than Sidonia, was not.

And engaging the English fleet or seizing Plymouth were not part of his orders. Sidonia knew English ships were faster and had wide-ranging guns. Defeating them would not be easy. Phillip had said Sidonia was only to fight the English if necessary and only attack if ships were clearly vulnerable, separated from others. Sidonia's task was to get to Parma, and if that failed, and only then, he might take the Isle of Wight. His King had been clear; Sidonia was not to use his instincts or those of his men. He was to carry out Phillip's plan. He had sent his men back to their ships and not given the order to attack.

The second problem weighing on Sidonia's mind that night was more pressing. He had still not heard from Parma. Frantic letters had he sent, all demanding a response, but none had come. The orders of his King were unambiguous; he wanted Sidonia and Parma, navy and army, to join hands and invade as a united, unbeatable force. How that was going to happen when he had no idea where the General was, Sidonia did not know. His confessor said God would join them. To Sidonia it seemed the Lord of Heaven was being asked to perform a great many miracles on behalf of Spain.

To the Admiral of the Armada that night, the world had become as hostile as the seas on which he sailed. As he stared from his window, small square panes glinting with the light of the stars and torches burning on deck, he felt the world was a vast, empty place. Commander of the greatest fleet the world had ever seen, Sidonia was. Knight of the Order of the Golden Fleece, Duque of Medina Sidonia, Count of Niebla, Marquis of Cazaza, Lord of the City of St Lucar de Barrameda and Captain General of Andalusia, was Sidonia, and yet this lord of lands and vassals felt most alone of all men; one tiny speck floating upon a boundless sea of darkness.

Sidonia gazed out. The black sea was below, black sky above. Clouds reflected upon the water, as did the stars. He could see no land. Roaming mist obscured it, as did darkness. Sidonia could see no safe port, no hint of dawn or daylight. All was endless night; darkness wrapped about him, a void as impenetrable as death, unfamiliar as the realm of dreams.

Chapter Four

Richmond Palace
July 19th 1588

Elizabeth

Out in the gardens an owl hooted, a long, clear call echoing down the winding paths. It was a lonesome sound, a cry in the darkness, one voice reaching out in hope, trying to find another.

"How many *do* we have?" I asked, turning from the window and the misty night to stare into a room illuminated by amber light cast by flickering candles and oil lamps.

Three men were sitting near the fire on chairs upholstered with crimson velvet. It was unusual to have a fire in July, but this month had been unseasonable, damp and autumnal, as though summer had forgotten to call on England. Rain had been falling for months, making the roads quagmires and swelling rivers so they threatened to burst their slippery banks. On rare days when rain refused to fall it seemed to hang in the air, becoming mizzle and fog; the fevered breath of some ancient, underworld god hanging moist and muggy upon England.

Robin, Cecil and Walsingham looked up at me, crimson light reflected from the fire and their chairs playing on their faces. They all looked tired. I was sure I did too, beneath the paint upon my face. Imminent threat of war is no place to find sweet slumber or restful dreams. They had all been working long hours, running fast on small food and little sleep. And we were, none of us, young foxes anymore. Cecil was reaching the height of his sixtieth years, with Walsingham lagging not far behind and both men were often ill. Rob and I would both reach the grand age of fifty-five that year, and the once dark hair of my beloved was now almost all white as snow. Robin had a complaint, physicians said it was a stone, and it gave him great pain at times.

Could fate have been crueller to send war at such a time? When we were all young we might have had more vitality, but age teaches something; endurance. We knew how to run the long race.

"How many are ready to march?" I asked again.

All over the country, militias had been standing by since May. Upon sight of the Armada they would assemble at designated points, ready to defend England. Some were to march for London, some for Tilbury, with Robin as their commander.

Cecil's face became unsteady, something which happened but rarely on that façade of stoic calmness. "We thought we would have twenty-eight thousand soldiers," he said, "for the main force to repel Parma and his men if they manage to clamber over the seas."

"I believe I will have perhaps sixteen thousand," Robin said. "More are promised, but how many I know not."

I swallowed. Half the number we had hoped.

I had hoped we would not need any. I had kept negotiations going as long as I could with Parma and Phillip, hoping to wriggle my way out of war as I had so many times before. It was not to be. Parma had played my ambassadors. The day talks opened, although we did not know it at the time, was the day the Armada sailed. Even then I had hoped. But two days ago I had closed talks and called my men home. War was coming, it was on my very doorstep. There was nothing to do now but fight.

But my reluctance had caused delays. I had good reason for not mobilising for war in the months of negotiations. I thought it would certainly bring invasion upon us, perhaps sooner, if Phillip heard, and I thought my people might fall to hysteria. Panic, as had been seen in many massacres of faith and war, or both, in other countries, I would not allow to occur in England. I would not have Catholics hauled from houses to be slaughtered in the streets, would not allow neighbour to turn on neighbour, brother on sister.

Yet it could not be denied that my hesitation to mobilise had caused problems. I had been unwilling to spend large amounts on provisions or men until we knew for certain talks of peace had failed. There is no sense in spending where there is no need. My men thought me lunatic for the hesitation I had shown and the poor amounts of supplies bought, but as it was I had spent too much.

Lack of soldiers was but one issue. Robin was in command of the ground forces, my Commander-in-Chief, but he was struggling. It was not his fault, but mine. All summer Robin had been urging for greater, immediate action, and I had not followed his advice and not only for reasons of concealment and avoiding panic. I had little money left. My coffers moaned, empty, starving bellies. War in the Netherlands, supporting Navarre in France, all these actions I had taken to ward off war had led to England having little left with which she could defend herself. If I called the militias too early, it would only cost more. I was not sure the Crown had the money to pay any soldiers or sailors, for any time and blood spent in service to England.

At Tilbury Robin was supposed to gather men, mustered from county militias. Tilbury was in Essex, commanding the route up the Thames and was the place we thought Parma would make for, as it would be an excellent site from which to invade London. It was also a good site for our armies to guard England.

If those armies arrived.

The camp was ready, the men were not there. Still they were waiting. If I delayed them too long, there might not be anyone present when Sidonia landed and Parma came roaring into England, but call too soon and I would drown in debt. And that was not the only issue.

"Horses are proving hard to come by for mounted troops," Robin had told me. "Some of my captains are dealing with lords who are holding back their best horses for personal use rather than sending them to us." He had raked his hands through his hair, his brow swamped with sweat. "Merchants near Tilbury have had to be threatened with grievous punishments if they do not send required provisions, and I have had to order prices to be fixed for wheat, butter and cheese to stop merchants attempting to make money from us."

He did not add that such men were seeking to make money from our desperation. He did not need to.

Desperate we were. The Armada had been planned to be five hundred ships strong, carrying fifty-five thousand men, but the one hundred and fifty we heard had set sail was more than enough. They were carrying some eighteen thousand soldiers and eight thousand sailors. Phillip's notion was this would be an invasion fought on land, not water; the strength and distribution of his troops proved that. And although we had heard different plans, the most likely seemed that this fleet would join with Parma's troops in Flanders, a force rumoured to be thirty thousand strong, and together they would invade.

Phillip's recruits upon the Armada were raw, so we had been told by Walsingham's spies, but Parma's were not. For years they had been fighting in the Netherlands under one of the most skilled generals our world had seen. Parma was brilliant, and brutal. If army and navy joined, we were in more than just desperate circumstances, we were doomed.

Even had we possessed the same number of troops as Spain, which we did not, the men of England were not trained soldiers, not even raw recruits. They were men who had never seen war. Some had flocked to my banner in the Northern Rebellion, but not a battle had been fought in that uprising. Some had gone to the Netherlands, but most were merchants, fishermen, farmers and yeomen.

The fact was, England was no nation of soldiers. For decades we had been at peace as Europe had rent itself apart. Men might have taken part in tavern brawls, local disputes, fights after games of football, but they were not skilled soldiers. I had no standing army, and the levies had not been called for so long that organisation was poor at best. Not only were there not enough men for the army at Tilbury, there were not enough for *all* the other places enemy forces might land. Despite Walsingham's men spying high and low for us, all we had was a best guess as to where the Armada and Parma might land.

High numbers of landing sites along the coast meant that towns and cities up and down England were screaming for men to defend them. There were not men enough. We had selected beaches we thought most vulnerable, securing them with wooden stakes rammed into soft sand, and shingle set up to provide obstacles for incoming boats. Earthen fortifications had hastily been thrown up to protect what land cannon and musket we could spare, but most men would be armed with knives, pitchforks and reaping scythes. We had not even enough bows and arrows to send to all the forces gathering. Bands of men to defend deep water ports, like Falmouth and Plymouth, had been assembled, in case the Armada thought to land. This had reduced the number who could march to join Robin.

Many lords of court, with lips more active than minds, were declaring our shortage of men was impossible. Estimates some years ago of men who could be called into Crown service had put the number at over three hundred thousand, but that was a simple count of every man between the ages of seventeen and seventy. Only a few hundred of that mighty number were men of war, and the estimate ignored those who could not fight due to disability or disease. Even some who had martial experience clearly could not be relied upon. Some of our men fighting in the Netherlands had been called home, but many had deserted, snatching the opportunity to go home amongst the confusion of troops returning to England. Many of our troops I could not take from the Low Countries. We were treaty-bound to keep soldiers there.

The Pope had declared England was more than ready to meet the threat of Spain. We were not. If Parma's troops landed, London would fall in less than a week.

There was even infighting amongst my men. Arguments about how best to defend certain areas had set lord against lord, which was far from helpful. The clergy had offered money to arm the militia, but little had been paid. Because no one knew where Phillip's men would land, if an immediate landing was their plan, bickering had grown, with some men protesting about the numbers sent to defend places like the Isle of Wight, as those men would then not be present to hold off the Spanish at other sites, something I thought rather an obvious point. My people were complaining about being asked to guard places that were not their homes, and nobles moaned about their servants being taken away.

It was chaos.

But some rose to the challenge. Gentlemen, Walsingham amongst them, had paid for contingents of troops and their weapons. Armed with good pistols and lances, mounted troops were scarcer than ground, but my men were paying for infantry too. Some were there to protect personal property, I knew, but at least they were ready. Some counties were joining in, reporting almost unbelievable numbers they would dispatch to us. Hampshire declared it had just over nine thousand men to send when the beacons fired, although also admitted most lacked helmets and swords. Other counties were having more problems; the commander of the Dorset militia had sent word that he thought his men would rather kill each other than the enemy.

Equipment was spare. People might boast about the effectiveness of English bows and arrows in wars long since lost to time, but they were no match for the new guns being made. This deterred few, it seemed. As many bows as we could muster, and arrows to match, had been shipped out and more were being made. Men trained with the bow from childhood. Although it had fallen somewhat from fashion, archery was one of the permitted activities on the Sabbath, and many were good with a bow.

Some lords had brought out old armour, last used in France when my father was King, and had cleaned it, polished it, and made ready for war. Kent had rallied just over twelve thousand men, with three thousand of those being trained soldiers, and the rest were being hastily drilled so they at least knew how to defend themselves. The main forces, at Tilbury and in London, we thought would eventually total twenty-seven thousand with Robin, and twenty-eight with my Carey cousin, Lord Hunsdon. The City of London had promised to rouse men, creating four regiments armed with harquebuses, pikes and halberds. Ten thousand men of London had now been armed, although admittedly my men found it hard to find ten thousand who were fit to be armed, but much of the city now had weapons. They were being trained day and night. Some men, in fact, were drilling on any available patch of ground, marching up and down, training others to jab and thrust. Ferries were being guarded, the Watch was on high alert and crossroads were being watched. Booksellers had been producing titles such as the *Art of Shooting* and *The Most Excellent Method of Curing Wounds*. It was hard to look anywhere and not see someone readying for war. A state of chaos we might be in, but chaos is not inertia. There was possibility in our turmoil. This granted some hope, but most of my hope was in the sea.

I was not the only one who knew where England's destiny would be decided. Phillip himself, when married to my sister, had said, "The kingdom of England is and must always remain strong at sea since on this the safety of the realm depends."

People thought I did not understand how important the English fleet was, because more had been spent on the army, but it was not so. I spent where I feared, not where I had hope. Englishmen are sailors all. Cut English veins and you will taste the sea upon the air. It was in us, as much as our souls.

I knew, with my most experienced troops on the Scots' border, or in the Netherlands, the fate of England rested on water. If Parma's troops came and faced my men on land, it would be a massacre.

The ships led by Howard and Drake had not enough supplies, I knew that, and we had not spent as much on them recently as we had on the army, but in all the years I had been upon the throne money had gone into the navy, building better, faster ships, boasting good cannon and swift manoeuvrability. I had faith in my sea dogs. Although some had been chosen for title and blood rather than experience, there were enough men with them, like Drake, Frobisher and Hawkins, who knew the sea and her temper. Howard had been chosen because only a noble could command the fleet, but I had selected him because he listened. His pride was not fragile, but pliant. He would listen, he would learn and his calmness would temper the fire of Drake and other pirates.

Although I placed faith in my navy, there were issues I was trying to forget. England had not fought a war at sea for generations. The navy had been seeded under my father, grown by me, but compared to other countries it was far from professional. The men who were about to form the front line of our defence came from wildly varying backgrounds, not only in blood but experience. Drake was the world's foremost sailor and most feared pirate, but others with him were men who saw sailing as a pastime, like Howard, or were predominantly merchants, traders or fishermen. Men of courage they were, but they were unlikely to be prepared for what might come. We English had small experience in naval warfare, none of our men were accustomed to sustained combat, and although a few had done battle at sea, many more had not.

And, not knowing Phillip's plan, ours was far from coherent.

The original plan had been to invade, wed Mary of Scots to Parma, and the two would claim the throne. With Mary's demise, this plan had altered and Phillip now wanted his daughter to wear my crown. We knew Parma and Sidonia would try to meet, that news was all over Europe, but detail was missing. We knew not if the Armada would try to land in a deep water port and ferry Parma's men over, or if they would brave the Channel, heading to Flanders or France to meet him. We knew not which beaches to defend or where to amass men, aside from London and Tilbury. And there were dangers from within as well as without.

"The idea of a Spanish ruler, a queen who is her father's puppet, will not be as palatable to many as Mary of Scots might have been," Walsingham had said, "but the danger of an uprising from within, led by Catholics, remains a fearsome and daunting possibility, not least because of priests still at large in England, loyal to their master Cardinal Allen." He had stared into my eyes, distrust in his pupils. "Action must be taken, Majesty, to head off this threat."

With my reluctant approval, Walsingham had rounded up many recusants he believed to be a threat, and local justices of the peace had done the same. Told to arrest the *most obstinate and noted* recusants, lieutenants of each county had moved swiftly. Fears of an English St Bartholomew's were on the rise, and I worried news of the Armada might lead to Protestants starting to murder Catholics in a pre-emptive strike born of frenzied fear.

Gaols were groaning for the weight of people within, and my pursuivants were raiding here, there and everywhere. Many serving on my ships and marching to join the army had re-sworn the *Oath of Allegiance*, but the possibility of traitors in the ranks who might try to assassinate me, Robin, Cecil or Walsingham, remained high. The bull of excommunication the Pope had enacted upon me held that whilst there was no chance of overthrowing me or my government, Catholics could rest under me as their Queen. But as soon as opportunity came, they were to rise. This was a time most testing to the loyalty of English Catholics, and although I declared boldly to my men that I had unshakeable faith they were loyal to England first, Rome second, I admit nights had passed in fear for me, thinking that my own people might rise the moment the Armada was sighted, leading to England's destruction and my fall.

"And still they have not enough powder and shot?" I asked Cecil, speaking of our fleet, which he said was woefully unprepared in terms of gunpowder.

"They have not, madam," he said.

His face held unspoken condemnation. Cecil, like many others, held me to blame for this. He was correct to do so. I had tarried too long. The fleet had not enough powder, our men not enough weapons and my generals not enough men.

"Our men of the sea are resourceful," I said, setting my shoulders back. "The ships they will assault will carry powder and weapons, too. Drake will show Howard how to become a pirate."

"Let us hope that is the case, Majesty."

"It *will* be the case," I said, fixing a glimmering eye upon him.

My tone, as much as my eye, told Cecil not to press me with further condemnations. I had been on the edge of my ability to reason for more than a year, since the execution of my royal cousin. Being told I might have condemned England by attempting to keep her free of war was not likely to aid my fragile state of mind.

But it haunted me as Mary's ghost did. Mistakes often do. And yet it was helpless and worthless to linger on that now, for what could I do? Men had been sent to buy powder and saltpetre in other lands. If they returned in time to arm our ships, they would. If not, Drake and Howard, Seymour and Wynter would have to find ways to gain what they needed themselves. My men were capable and resilient. They would find a way.

Pirates they were, and pirates do not ask for what they want. They take it.

"Edward III won at Sluys, and no one thought he would," I said, speaking of an ancient battle, the first at sea that England had gained notoriety in.

"That is true, madam," said Cecil. "Do you have orders for Howard at Plymouth and Seymour at Dover?"

Many nobles had told me I should tell my men what to do. That I, the Queen, who never had left the sands of England, should instruct men of the sea in how to act, attack and hold off this threat. My knowledge of many things was vast, but I knew nothing of war at sea, and the well-meaning, if useless, plans my Council had come up with of late had left me with small faith that they should be telling my captains and admirals what to do either. I had ceded to Drake's plans, and although general instructions were sent to Seymour and Howard, I knew now that the specifics had to be left to them.

I had put trust and faith in my men for years. I would now, at this most important time.

"Howard, Drake and Seymour have their orders," I told Cecil and Walsingham. "They have general instructions, but not specific. That way they can do as tide and time tell them."

"We are told Sidonia is receiving regular commands from the King of Spain," said Walsingham.

"Would you have me emulate Phillip?" I shook my head, my red wig trembling upon it. "No. I chose men I trust and know to lead our fleet. They will do as they see fit. Only if I think there is need will I intervene. We tried to tell them what to do and Drake and others pointed out where we were wrong. Let us put trust in our men of the sea."

Phillip, according to Walsingham's spies, was not willing to allow his men to use their initiative. Of course he had been upon the sea a few times, so perhaps had more idea than me about what could be done upon it, but he was no sailor. What he was, was an obsessive. Phillip could not bear being out of control. Unwilling to leave anything in the hands of his men, my fanatical brother-in-law had dispatched them with strict, unyielding instructions, and sent many missives flying to them as they sailed from Spain towards England. The trouble was, we were not sure what those instructions were.

The possibility they might use Ireland, as papal and Spanish forces had tried to before, was high. Scotland seemed less likely, despite letters Walsingham's men had intercepted from Catherine de Medici, the Queen Mother of Henri, King of France, saying that King James of Scotland was on the verge of converting to Catholicism and becoming my enemy. James was about to do no such thing; not only had we a treaty between us but he was being paid an English pension, which he had sore need of. If he went against me now he would never be named heir to England. Phillip's plan to set his daughter on the English throne was not about to inspire James to join his campaign. James and Scotland were on our side.

Other allies we had; words. My men had sent out proclamations to stand against those coming from Spain and Allen which stated that the Armada was here to defend English Catholics. Our pamphlets told of the horrors that war would bring, and were worded in the most graphic, hideous ways. They said English men and women would be hanged, their children slaughtered, and babies branded. Spanish wet nurses were to be brought in to suckle motherless children after their parents had been whipped and executed by Spanish forces. All threats that could be imagined, all horrors to be faced were exaggerated, on purpose. Some of my people needed firing into action, and all needed to be ready, because with war agony and loss come hand in hand with nightmares. They needed to be afraid, to stop bickering amongst themselves, to see who the true enemy was.

But as we sent our words out, so did others.

A rallying speech, written by a Jesuit, had been sent out to the men of the Spanish fleet. *"With us too, will be the blessed and innocent Mary, Queen of Scots, who, still fresh from her sacrifice, bears copious and abounding witness to the cruelty and impiety of this Elizabeth and directs her shafts against her."*

"Is it true, cousin?" I whispered to Mary's ghost that night after my men had left to continue their work. I sat at my window watching. I had every night for weeks. Yet I saw no fires coming over the hilltops, no sign the Armada was here. The beacons had not been lit, aside from a few heart-pounding accidents which had caused utmost panic.

"Do you ride the wind and drive water under this fleet come for my blood?" I whispered to my cousin. "Do you come for revenge, Mary? Are you with these men of Spain who would take the throne from me, and from your line too?"

Far away, I thought I heard laughter, mocking and cruel, a ghost in the wind.

Chapter Five

San Lorenzo de Escorial
Madrid, Spain
July 19th 1588

Death

To look upon the favoured residence of the King of Spain, you might have been forgiven for thinking you gazed not upon a palace but a monastery. Yet in seeking the quiet of these stone halls and covered walkways, the King often abandoned the noise and clamour of his court in Madrid.

It looked like a fortress on the outside, a monastery within. A huge complex of buildings, standing in the Guadarrama Mountains outside of Madrid, the San Lorenzo de Escorial had a fearsome, forbidding air to it.

It had taken over twenty years and three million ducats to build. Seven towers stretched into the sky and twelve thousand windows shone from the walls, staring down upon Spain like so many glimmering eyes. Although interior walls were painted with frescos and marble statues stood in the hallways, there was something cold about the palace. Ornaments of alabaster, paintings by great artists, decorations of rose coral and glowing red-brown hardwood from the New World could not warm the house of Spain's King.

Monks walked the echoing hallways, their cowls deep over their bowed heads. Priests talked softly in small chambers. There were more men of God in the palace than men of court. In the centre was a church, almost the largest in the world. The only one bigger was the Church of St Peter in Rome. In Phillip's church lay more than seven thousand relics of saints; hands, fingers, heads, shrouds, parts of the true cross and vials of the blood of Christ. As well as the sainted dead,

Phillip's ancestors lay there, in tombs within the church. His father, his mother, two brothers who died before becoming adults, as well as his mad grandmother Joanna *la loca*, and all his aunts. His tomb was already there, waiting for him.

If you walked through the church with me, you would find a concealed doorway near the altar, leading to Phillip's private chambers. No man to hide from death was he; Phillip could look upon his own resting place with ease from his nearby rooms.

In his small office, the King of Spain sat, working. He was always working.

It was something he had in common with his sister-in-law of England, although he would not wish to admit any similarity. Some sovereigns left the running of their country to other men, Phillip and Elizabeth did not. At his desk, the King worked facing a blank wall with no decoration upon it. The barren sight kept his mind focussed. Despite gout and arthritis, Phillip worked day and night, sending out a relentless river of instructions for his commanders in every part of his vast Empire. Phillip did not trust easy and found it hard to relinquish control. Every matter, no matter how small, came to his desk and all were commented on. He did not like to receive visitors or petitioners, most irritated him too greatly and took up too much time, so everything was set down in writing and sent to him. That way he could work in peace without the jabbering of fools polluting his ears.

Outside, cicadas sang, butterflies danced and birds trilled, delighted by the hot skies of summer. In the cool palace, the King worked on, ignoring day and night as he stared at his papers. And yet today, the hard-working King was finding himself distracted, thinking of the past.

In his library, amongst his many religious books, portraits of his wives hung. There had been four, and all had died. Maria of Portugal, Mary of England, Elizabeth of France and Anne of

Austria all graced his walls, staring down at a man some of them had loved with blind devotion, like Mary Tudor, and some felt they had barely known.

But a woman once he had thought to marry had a portrait of him. It was said she had kept it for years after their engagement came to an end when he married Elizabeth of France, daughter of the Valois line. "Your master must have been *much* in love with me not to be able to wait four months," that woman had wryly said when she heard of his marriage to the fourteen-year-old princess of France, who once had been engaged to his son.

Were it not for the fact that woman was the ruler he had just sent men to depose, the memory might have made him smile.

Staring at his barren wall, Phillip thought of other times with Elizabeth of England. Before she was a queen, he had protected her as a princess. When first they met she had been hauled before her sister, his wife Queen Mary Tudor, to answer for suspicion of treason. He had hidden in the room, trying to gauge something of this girl, for girl she had been then, who so alarmed her sister and roused equal amounts of love and jealousy in Mary. He had thought he was well hidden, but as Elizabeth left she had seen him. And caught, for a moment, by her amused eyes, he had smiled at her and a small flush had coloured his cheeks.

It was odd, for she was no beauty, even then with the bloom of youth on her face. Her hair was red as fire, her form lithe and pleasing, her eyes bright, dark, yet oddly unsettling. She was not a beauty, but she was arresting, interesting. In that moment, offering a smile to her, he had felt naked, stripped by her eyes in a way no other person had ever managed before.

Emperor and King, the essence of success and majesty he was, and yet when Phillip remembered those black eyes catching him watching her on the first day they had met, he remembered what it was to feel like a foolish lad again.

And not only then. After that first meeting there had been many games, some real and some of mind. The game of chess they had played, where she had all but said she wanted him to wed her when her sister died, and they had exchanged tokens, stuck in his mind. Walks in gardens where she hinted at naughtiness, then drew back in feigned, modest horror, played in his memory. Phillip would admit it to no one, but he had found her fascinating. At that time, he had thought she might be the bride for him, a woman whose wit and intelligence matched his own.

Then, as soon as she had her crown, one she would not have had but for him interceding with her sister to save her life, Elizabeth went back on her word.

That, he had come to understand, was what Elizabeth of England did. Slippery as a snake and sometimes just as infuriatingly clever, the Queen of that tiny, unimportant island which had always thought itself more important than it was had often outwitted him. Not always, sometimes he had taken the upper hand, but often enough.

When she had delayed taking his offered hand, and said she thought she could not wed him, he had said to his men he was relieved. Part of him was, but part would always be affronted. She had played him, and she had won her game. She had done the same to other princes and kings over the years, stringing along men so she could secure trade terms, then refusing to abandon her maiden state, *if* a maiden was what she was. But the fact she had done it to others had not made it sting less for him. Phillip did not love her, he never had, but he was not used to rejection, still less was he accustomed to being played by a woman. And so, from flirtation had come foe.

What was maddening was that she had been skilled as a girl and only seemed to improve as she aged. They had been allies, then foes, allies again and although Phillip was accustomed to the shifting winds of politics, Elizabeth of England rode them far too well. Her incursion into the Netherlands, his territory, had been enough to make the controlled and careful Phillip quite feral inside with rage, and then she sent out her pirate, Drake, to steal from him and terrorize his people.

And what was worse, was people seemed to admire this Queen who had no compunction in stealing his gold, using pirates to wreak havoc in his lands and invade his empire! She was even affecting surprise he would consider sending the Armada, as though she had not done more than enough to deserve the wrath of God, and Phillip of Spain, falling upon her and her people.

And yet, people spoke well of her.

Even the Pope, the Holy Father of the Church which was supposed to be her, a heretic's, foe, praised her, saying how Spain was afraid of her and her men and if she were Catholic she would be his most beloved daughter. Phillip had no doubt some of this was said purely for the sake of annoying him; the Pope did not like or trust the King of Spain, but all the same, it was vexing.

Phillip, of course, like most people, was leaving out his part in the games of shade and secrets he and Elizabeth had played. He had funded plots against her, and encouraged rebellions in her country to place her cousin on the throne. He had supported assassins who thought to take her life, and he too had seized ships. It might be hard to say who had started their war, so long fought without war being declared, but both were guilty of much, and both justified all they did using the crimes of the other.

They were more alike than they would like to admit.

Sitting back in his chair, Phillip grimaced. Gout pained him, and a cough that had come last winter had refused to vacate his lungs. He was in his sixty-second year of life, and there was much to pain him now. His grey eyes rested on the wall as he fingered the emblem of the Golden Fleece upon his breast, the sole ornament on his dark, simple clothing. The Queen of England dressed in gold and silver, purple and crimson, rich wigs of red and gold on her head and every visible inch of skin covered in jewels. Phillip dressed in rich cloth, but always his clothes were simple, austere.

Not only was he thinking of Elizabeth, but his ships. In many ways the two were related, and with the favour of God, soon the throne that once was his would be again. He had been named King, not consort, in the reign of his wife, Queen Mary. He had a right to rule England for that title, even had he not had a blood-claim, being a descendant of John of Gaunt. Phillip had *allowed* Elizabeth to take the throne, on the understanding they would marry, and he would rule again. When that had failed, he had thought she would retain him in grateful friendship, since he had stood aside for her, and since he had saved her life more than once. Small friendship had he had from her, and over the years hostility between them had increased.

And now they were at war. And now she would lose that stolen crown.

But there were problems. The death of Santa Cruz and the elevation of Sidonia had not been planned, and the continued delays and accidents that had fallen upon the Armada before sailing, and after, worried him. Sidonia had sent word that they should hold off, but once Phillip was committed to something he did not like to wait. Much as Elizabeth, he could pontificate on a situation for years, but when a choice was made he went ahead with fire and vim. God was with them, he was sure. How could the Almighty be on the side of that woman? Any challenges the Armada faced were but a test from on high, and in passing them they would show they were worthy of all the benefits God would bestow.

Parma was not so sure. When objecting to Phillip's first attempt to launch the Armada in the winter, the Duque, his nephew, had seemed scornful of Phillip's assurance that God would send good weather. *"God will tire of working miracles for us,"* Parma had written.

But hours on his painful knees had told Phillip that God was listening.

And whilst he knew Sidonia had not wanted the commission, Phillip believed in him. The Duque had saved Cadiz, and now he would take England. It was in his blood; his ancestors had seized their land in battle, and the family honorific *El Bueno* was accorded to them because in war they were valuable allies. When they met, Sidonia would follow Parma, which was important since Phillip's nephew was the more experienced man in war, and the Admiral had brought order to the chaos the Armada had fallen into upon the death of Santa Cruz.

Phillip also had faith Sidonia would follow his orders. That was important to Phillip. Sending out a fleet was one thing, being out of control of it was quite another. And he needed to be in control. This conflict was personal, in many ways. Faith was given as the reason for this crusade, and it was a good and true one; Phillip had said once that if he found his son was a heretic he would burn him himself. But in the secret recesses of his heart, Phillip knew faith was not the only reason he wanted to crush Elizabeth. She had humiliated him time and time again, refusing his hand, toying with him in games of politics, foiling his underhand plans to depose her and sending her pirates to plunder his shores. That a bastard could claim a throne was an insult to all those of true, legitimate blood who ruled. That a woman could play men was an insult to his sex. That a heretic could wear a crown was an affront to God and His Church. Elizabeth murdered priests, and had even killed a prince of true royal blood. Everything about her he hated, and he hated more that once he had found her so enthralling.

Phillip had cause to think invasion would work. The Tudor dynasty had begun with King Henry VII invading, so it was apt it would end with that King's granddaughter falling before another invading force. One of his advisors, an exiled English Jesuit called Robert Persons, had told him that England had been invaded sixteen times in the past, and only twice had managed to repel the invaders.

Phillip also had the largest navy in the world, and he had Parma, a highly experienced general who would have won long ago in the Netherlands were it not for that harlot of England interfering to aid the rebels.

And Phillip knew England. Although his visits there had not been of long duration when he was married to Queen Mary, he had made good use of them. He knew how the shire levies were called in times of war, and he knew they had not been assembled for a long time. He knew how hard it would be to defend all beaches and coves along the coast, and he knew the fortifications of England. Her castles were old and many had not seen battle for decades. The English had grown soft. They would not stand long against the hard iron of Spain.

Sidonia would sail through the Channel, avoiding combat with the English. When Parma had word Sidonia was there, he would send out his men on barges, protected by the Armada. Once his fleet had landed, English Catholics would rise. The Queen would fall with London, and England would be his.

Phillip had only been in battle once, and swore he would never be again, but he was not lacking in confidence. He knew what the future would be, for he had suffered few defeats in his life, and none permanent. God was with him. He, like his Armada, was invincible.

Phillip had an image in his mind, and thought it to be true. It is a not uncommon failing. People all imagine how things, particularly of the future will be, but most realise that not everything turns out as they wish. Phillip did not. Most of what he imagined would come true had in the past; he therefore thought this was the way it would always be. Fantasy, at times, is helpful, but it can also become a blindfold.

He ignored much Parma and Sidonia warned of. In the margin of one of his nephew's letters, Phillip had written one word; "*Nonsense!*"

It was not only the King of Spain, however, who was ignoring what he did not want to hear. His men were doing it for him. Phillip did not know that his advisors had been hiding some letters from him. Sidonia, writing in despair about the Armada, had been told by Phillip's men not to *"depress us with fears for the fate of the Armada".* When more letters came, his men sent threats in return, warning Sidonia that his reputation and the King's esteem *"would entirely be forfeited"* if what he had written to the King became commonly known. The most informed King of Europe was unaware he knew not everything.

But since he did not know, Phillip was filled with confidence. It was about time someone taught that bald-headed bastard of England a lesson. Phillip thought he was the man to do just that.

*

Another was wakeful that night. In Flanders, Alexander Farnese, Duque of Parma, nephew to the King of Spain and General of the Netherlands, was watching from his window. He, too, had concerns.

He had received small news of the Armada from Phillip and nothing from Sidonia. Rumour was all he had to go by, and that was wild enough; the Armada was already victorious, the Armada was wrecked, the King was merry, he was sad.

Parma was no stranger to war, or death. His birth had been marked by the demise of his twin brother, and his life had seen much action. At eleven he and his mother, Margaret of

Parma, bastard sister of Phillip of Spain, had been summoned to court, and from there had gone to England to help Phillip persuade Queen Mary to fight in France. At the age of twenty-four, Parma had fought, coming to the aid of Venice against the Turks. He had been part of the victory at Lepanto, greatest sea battle of all time, where Santa Cruz had also fought, and had been sent to the Netherlands to crush the Dutch rebellion. Becoming Supreme Commander of Spanish Forces in the Low Countries, Parma had advanced upon the rebels with valour and brutality. He had raised his men's wages, made sure they had arms, and over the years had moulded them into the most feared fighting force in the world. They were a model of discipline and order and Parma was a student of military tactics and glory in war. His favourite author was Julius Caesar.

No stranger to politics, Parma was slippery, using words where weapons failed. He had managed to keep Elizabeth of England's envoys talking, promising peace whilst his master plotted war. He used engineers to make battlefields work in his favour, and bribed and used spies where he could.

Elizabeth had sent her whore, Robert Dudley, against him, and it had done nothing to set Parma back. City after city had fallen to him, and now he was to lead his men to England, ending war in the Netherlands by cutting off the aid England sent.

At least that was the plan. Not Parma's plan, but Phillip's. Parma had held other ideas on how war in the Netherlands would end.

He had taken Sluys from the English, at a dreadful cost of lives, and had planned to capture Flushing; the perfect spot from which to launch an invasion. The Armada could linger at that deep water port, defending his men as they were ferried across to England. But his uncle had stopped his plans. Phillip wanted Flushing taken afterwards, not before. If England fell to Spain, Phillip could use the English fleet to block the

Channel and other approaches to the Netherlands. Food would be held back, the Dutch rebels would be starved until they surrendered. Make war on England, Phillip thought, and he would bring about forced peace in the Low Countries. Thirty years of rebellion would be over, and England would be a problem to Spain no more.

Parma thought it would be a better plan to take the Netherlands first, then work on England. Parma understood strategy better than his master, but his King held the power of blood and crown over him, and to that Parma had to bow, no matter how unwillingly.

Parma believed England would not fall so easily. Even if his men made it to England, something he was by no means assured of since the Channel was swimming with rebel Dutch boats and the English fleet, Parma did not think English Catholics would rise as promised. That event had been foretold many times, and never, in all the rebellions and plots his master and his servants had undertaken, had it happened. The west, east and north of England had large areas which remained estranged from the law, and Parma, student of history, knew past rebels had used marshes, forests and swamps to hide in and launch attacks from. The Commander of Spain's Forces in the Netherlands was aware, as his master was not, that England would be a longer campaign than supposed. They might, in fact, end up fighting ongoing wars in two regions, rather than conquering both in one fell swoop.

But Parma was sworn to his King, his uncle, by duty and blood.

Operations were to be suspended in Flanders, only feints would remain to distract Walsingham's spies as all Parma's energies went into the invasion of England. The bulk of the army would go to England. Barges would come to Dunkirk and other ports to avoid the Dutch fleet and their meddlesome Sea Beggars. He had thirty thousand men, but the delays of the Armada had left him with troops idle. Desertions had occurred, sickness fell. His reinforcements were not as well trained as the soldiers they replaced. In the winter he had complained to Phillip about the delay, and warned him about the winter quarters and the effects on his fighting force. By the start of summer, Parma had been in dismay about money, but Phillip had none to send. It was all in his ships.

And for the ships Parma waited. But of them he had no news.

The General was not one to despair, but he was not one to hope without reason, either.

Chapter Six

The English Channel
July 20th - 21st 1588

Death

Let the restless Queen of England, the worried Duque of Parma and the irritable King of Spain try to take some rest. Upon wings of the wind we will fly to the English Channel, where dawn was breaking on the 20th of July.

It was a misty morning; white fog twisting like smoke across the curling waves. The day before Sidonia and his men had glimpsed ships upon the sea, heading their way. Grey ghosts upon the water.

Leaning on the wooden rails of his ship that day, the 20th of July, Sidonia had seen the coast, cliffs of sand and stone, bright green hillsides and forests appearing and disappearing in the thick blanket of swirling fog. He could see the black, shining rocks of the Eddystone glowing with the first light of day, and knew that rock heralded Plymouth was not far away. Sidonia had sent his men to stack stores of gunpowder and shot, food and water, for he knew battle soon would come.

Glimpses of English ships had floated through the mist; appearing and disappearing like wraiths in limbo. Men had shouted each time sails were seen, billowing and dark in the haze of mist, and each time captains had raced to look, they were gone. On the night of the 20th, Sidonia's lookouts had spied lanterns to their south, dim glowing lights of amber in the darkness.

At dawn on the 21st, Sidonia woke to an unpleasant surprise; the English fleet at his back. They had the weather-gage.

How they had got there was anyone's guess on the Spanish ships. Last they had heard the English fleet was trapped in Plymouth harbour, but now not only were they here, but were behind them, hounds at their heels. Sidonia wondered if Drake had worked magic in the night, calling upon mermaids to haul them into the open seas.

On English ships, guncrews were working on light weapons mounted on the upper decks. In the bellies of the ships were the heavier guns, huge bronze and iron cannons decorated with heraldic beasts, positioned at the ships' waterlines where their weight would not unbalance the vessels. Shot was piled nearby; black shining cannonballs, ranging from four pounds for light guns, up to sixty for the heavy. They were clustered in pyramids, standing near piles of cloth and paper cartridges; cylinders containing the correct measure of powder for each gun. Near them were lengths of cord, ramrods for forcing down powder and shot, and handfuls of lambskin used to swab barrels between firing. Left un-swabbed, cannon could retain hot powder, leading to the gun exploding when it was reloaded, massacring the guncrew. More powder and shot were stored in lockers. Rolling shot racing about the gundeck was not a wise thing, and powder grew unusable if damp. Stores of powder were kept near the waterline, the safest place if the enemy was firing. Some powder was so powerful it needed little to ignite it and blow a hole in the ship.

The gundecks were dark, sultry and warm, even when empty of men. Close-clustered oak beams hung just over the heads of gunners who would work the cannon. The feet of masts plunged through from the deck above, invading the wooden cave of the gunners. Everything in there was black, stained with gunsmoke and powder, the only light sailing in through gunports and from small lanterns at each end of the decks.

Under the cannon were the carriages which bore them; small carts, with wheels and a base of smooth planks. English guns were mounted on squat carriages with four wheels, making them less precarious. Spanish ones were almost indivisible from land cannon, bearing two great wheels and high carriages. They rocked back with alarming speed when fired, and had unpredictable tempers.

Seeing the English at his back, Sidonia ordered the Armada's formation to remain tight, guns were fired and flags hoisted to signal this to his other captains. The crescent was the safest formation, almost impenetrable. They would keep going along the Channel, ignoring the English unless they had no choice but to fight.

Leyva's squadron of middling size galleons went to the vanguard of the Armada to defend against attack from the north. Recalde and his division went to the south. The biggest warships took position on the wings and Sidonia and his galleons were positioned in the centre of the Armada, guarding the transport ships. They would prevent English ships sailing into the heart of the crescent, breaking the Armada apart, making single ships more vulnerable.

Howard and his fleet held the weather-gage and were upwind, granting them the advantage. Fifteen ships had been left at the coast near Looe, hoping to lure foolhardy Spanish captains out of their formation by tempting them with easy prey, but the rest had gone, tacking into the wind, displaying excellent seamanship. Working through the night, they had come about to the seaward and windward flank of the Armada. They had headed past the long sands of Whitsand Bay, sailing abreast and beyond the Armada.

Both sides had a nasty surprise that morning. Sidonia understood with sudden and unwelcome clarity how fast the English ships were and how well they could use the wind. Howard and his men saw how huge the Armada was, and how tight their formidable formation.

"By God," Howard murmured. "A sea of giants is come."

At that moment, it looked as though many giants had joined, becoming one ancient god of war. As the Armada fell with ease into formation, becoming a fearsome six miles wide, colours were hoisted. Each ship displayed the personal colours of their captain or squadron. Trumpets blared into the mist and drums began to thump, a heartbeat upon the oceans. Nets stretched tight upon the decks to prevent enemy soldiers boarding. The guns were run out.

"I can hardly see the sea," whispered a man near Drake on the *Revenge*. Ships left behind to defend Plymouth meant the English fleet had not been at full strength, but as light came to the world Drake and his ships had come out to join Howard.

"Remember David and Goliath," Drake said, turning to grin at his man with a face devoid of fear. Drake knew how important it was for a captain to show no fear even when terrified. In his secret heart, Drake would admit he was daunted. Show that, he would not.

Through the mist, Sidonia saw a single ship. A small pinnace, the aptly named *Disdain*, which clearly was no threat to the Armada, had been dispatched by Howard. It had a single, important mission. With great courage did this small barque sail towards the Armada, to within hailing distance of the centre of the crescent. There, it fired a single shot at the *Santa Maria Encoronada*. It was a "*defiance*", a challenge, a declaration of war. Sidonia almost smiled. The Admiral of the English fleet was clearly an old knight, aware of the rules of war and its courtesies. This was as clear as if Howard had removed a gauntlet to slap it about Sidonia's face. "Let it go," Sidonia said to his men.

As the *Disdain* raced to retreat with haste, Sidonia's ship raised a flag to indicate it was to be left alone. Howard would perform courtesies of war, Sidonia would respond. Not all his men saw this, however. From Leyva's squadron shots fired, but fell short, smashing into the sea near the *Disdain*.

Sidonia raised his royal standard and hoisted the papal-blessed banner to the maintop. With this signal, his men knew that if the English engaged, battle could begin.

At nine of the morning, Howard gave the order to attack.

Howard and his men had experienced little rest. Many were tired. Hauling the fleet out of Plymouth had been no short order, and fighting to gain position behind the Armada was not a thing of ease either. But they had done it. They were not captured in port, helpless, and now they were in waters they knew well. A brief council of war the previous night had led to the decision that the Armada must be driven past Plymouth.

"We know not it is their aim," Howard had said, leaning back on his plush, upholstered chair. "But a deep water port such as Plymouth would make a fine base for Sidonia."

Drake had been in agreement. It was true he thought this was not the Admiral's aim, but Plymouth was his home, and he was damned if he would allow Spaniards near his home, or his beloved wife.

"We should attack with cannon only," said Drake. "Our guns are strong and load fast. Our gunners are the best in the world. If we get too close, the enemy will board us and they have the advantage in men."

"Do not get close," Howard warned his captains, nodding as he agreed with Drake. "Once grappled and boarded, we will not have the men to repulse them."

The other captains had glanced at each other. This was a revolutionary idea.

Sidonia was prepared for a normal sea battle, where ships were laid siege to like castles, and fighting was between men, as on land. It was a time-honoured practice. Great guns would fire as smaller ones shot hails of lead and iron cubes, broken shards of red-hot metal, into wood and flesh. As the ships came close, hand-thrown incendiary devices would be launched, pots filled with gunpowder and resin, which would shatter on deck, igniting and exploding. As confusion set in grappling hooks were thrown, hauling ships together. The great guns would fire at close range, disabling the enemy ship and stunning her sailors, which allowed musketeers to fire and soldiers to swarm aboard, racing up upon the deck and over the rails, and under, through gunports, deciding the battle with hand-to-hand combat. Naval battles had been fought this way, albeit with variations, since the time of Roman dominion upon the world.

Drake and Howard were speaking of using *ships* to make war. It was a concept not seen before but made perfect sense. The Armada had more soldiers. If English ships were boarded they would be overrun. But the English ships were better, faster, and their cannon were powerful. Fighting at distance would give them the advantage.

That day, naval warfare was to see something new.

From behind the Armada the English came. Sidonia made a play of making for Plymouth, trying to draw the English close enough that his musketeers and arquebusiers could pick off men on the deck. On his ship there were three hundred such men.

Marksmen scaled masts and rigging, taking position so they could shoot men on English ships, wounding those in charge if possible, and pikemen took position on deck, ready to repel boarders. Boys raced, scattering sawdust to collect blood.

Sidonia was about to get a shock.

Drake led his squadron out, forty ships strong, assailing the northern tip of the crescent formation. Howard went for the *Rata Encoronada* at a range of four hundred yards, believing her to be the *San Martin*, Sidonia's vessel. It was fitting the two commanders, alike in rank and blood, fight each other; another sign of Howard's notions of chivalry. With Howard was Hawkins, the more experienced sailor aiding the lesser. After a flurry upon the *Rata* and ships near her, Howard plunged north to support Drake's attack on the tip of the Armada. The *Rata* came about, attempting to close on the *Revenge*, but Drake danced away, firing on the *San Mateo*. The assault on the tips of the Armada's formation began.

In a line, English ships came, one after the other, firing bow-chasers, then turning, emitting a turbulent ripple of cannon shot from the broadside and finally firing the heaviest guns of the stern. Just as a ship sailed almost close enough for the Armada's vessels to grapple, she would sail out of range, her gunners reloading as fast as they could. And then another would be upon them, and then another; an unending fulmination emitted from ravenous guns.

Sidonia and his men were astounded. Their reliance upon the ancient, tested ways, firing, grappling, boarding, were so deep-rooted that there was almost no plan for reloading guns in the midst of battle. Never before had they needed to. Men were screaming in the smoke-filled, dark underbelly of the Armada's ships. Light guns on deck were toil enough to shift, their wheels and carriages designed for land, but the heavy cannon below were so large it was a struggle to haul them back in at all when fired. Some cannon needed to be reloaded from *outside* the ship. Others took an hour to pull back into position.

And an hour they did not have. Again and again the English came, firing all guns. As one vanished, another ship emerged from the bank of smoke, and another, and another. As Spanish ships fought to bring guns back to position and reload them, the English came again and again, relentless in their aggression. It was a barrage, unrelenting, magnificent and seemingly endless.

In the belly of the Spanish ships, guncrews were struggling. They were soldiers, not dedicated gunners trained solely for this task. Scouring and cleaning barrels, swabbing out hot powder, they worked in near-perfect darkness. Above them rumbled the thunder of cannon shot, the explosion of powder, the sickening crunch of metal smashing into ship. Many guns were lashed to hulls to prevent the cannon recoiling back into the gundeck, and when they rocked backwards they pulled at the structure of the hull. Carpenters worked furiously, hammering and patching with lead plate and plugs as about them men ran, pulling guns into position with handspikes and tackles. Even with all their work, some Spanish guns fired only twice during the whole day.

On English ships, below deck was no less dark or confused with noise, but their guns were better, as were their crews. It was a position of pride to be named a gunner on an English ship, and the men were trained specially for the role.

Narrow, four-wheeled carriages kept English cannon steady and could be hauled back into position swiftly, quickly swabbed, reloaded and aimed through the slim gunport. English cannon had a range of over a mile, but more damage was done close up. At one hundred yards, cannonballs could smash with ease through almost five feet of hard, sound oak. Their guns were long-ranging, more accurate and reliable than those of Spain, and their powder was better.

English crews used corned powder, less dangerous than serpentine which, if a ramrod was used too ferociously, might well blow the cannon to bits and take the crew with her. English powder was more stable; it contained glazed fragments, almost impervious to damp. Much of it came from Morocco.

Their near-naked bodies, stripped to the waist in the heat and smoke, were smothered in black ash and powder. Commands bellowed into ears went unheard as guns roared like wounded dragons. Steam from sponges used to clean the guns hissed into hot air, joining smoke, making the air thick as it tumbled into lungs. Boys ran from stores to guns carrying shot and powder, tripping over spent cartridges and swabbing cloths, racing in darkness and flame. Hands burning, skin screaming, eyes blinded by smoke and fire, they toiled like men possessed, ignoring the wounded that fell, shrieking as musket balls and cannon shot ripped through the hulls, killing, maiming and wounding. To surgeons were injured men hauled, where rocking beds of blood and flesh witnessed horrors as men tried to save lives by hacking off limbs, and cauterizing blood-soaked flesh with hot, glowing irons. The awful grinding crunch of bones being broken, the soft squeal of the saw, and the pop of dislocated shoulders being thumped back into place filled the air below deck, as did the screams of the patients.

But Drake could already see the English fleet were too far away to inflict real harm upon the enemy. Many cannonballs were smashing into sea, not ship, sending water pluming upwards in a diamond shower of spray. They had to break the formation of the Armada. Straggling ships in trouble, rigging and sails damaged so they could not use the wind, could be picked off one by one, but the English were finding it impossible to separate ships. This hard crescent was as unassailable as the moon. English captains, accustomed to acting independently, were awed by the fearsome discipline the Armada displayed. Drake continued to batter at the northern tip with the *Revenge*. Howard went south in the *Ark Royal*.

English guncrews could reload within two minutes, but knew to let guns cool between firing. Overheated barrels led to cannon exploding, rupturing, or breaking. Caution led to the English firing ten shots per hour. The only other thing holding the English back was lack of gunpowder, but they would fire throughout that day, throwing all they had at the ships of Spain.

But it is no easy feat to sink a warship; not a matter of one great shot fired and the whole vessel goes down. Cannonballs ripped into hulls, taking men's legs and arms. Splinters of wood flew, slicing faces and lacerating eyes. Screaming was heard when guns were not, but the ships were in less danger than the men. With carpenters working to patch holes, and divers going beneath where water had flooded in, with the English fearful to be boarded, therefore staying further away, the Armada stayed afloat with ease. The English could not break them apart.

That did not mean they would stop trying.

Thinking to board, the *Rata Encoronada* tried to close on Howard. Behind her came the *Regazona*, largest of the Armada ships, and the rest of the squadron. Howard danced away, his flatter sails more efficient than the *Rata's*. As he sailed off, Howard fired upon the enemy ship. The *Rata*, pushed back by wind and wave, could not get into position to face her foes.

One Armada wing was being torn apart by the English onslaught. A few Spanish ships tried to fly, and some endeavoured to get closer to other Spanish vessels. As they desperately sought to get downwind, they started to affect the formation of the Armada.

Sidonia gazed through the thick smoke. Some Spanish ships were more than two miles out of position, making life taxing for Recalde on the other wing. Recalde was having enough trouble without allied ships making it for him by ranging out of position and confusing his squadron, for as Howard and Hawkins assailed one wing Recalde was fighting off Drake and Frobisher on the other.

Recalde shortened sail and brought his ship, the *San Juan de Portugal*, to face his nimble foes, all guns bearing on them, only to receive the fire of eight ships concentrated on him. He tried to get close, he could not. Ships flowed past firing bow-chasers, then broadsides and finishing with hard fire from the stern. As ships turned, tacking back into the wind, windward guns fired as the ship came about, readying for another pass, another rain of fire. Isolated and in peril, Recalde's ship suffered more than three hundred rounds fired upon her, damaging rigging, foremast and wounding one of his captains. Fifteen lay dead below, but Recalde knew little of them. He had no time for the dead or dying as he screamed orders to his men.

Dauntless, Recalde stood firm in the water, returning fire, fighting eight ships simultaneously. Blood ran upon the deck mingled with water. Cannonball flew up, fired from below, hitting mast, rigging and sails. Shot thumped into hulls, shattering wood, sending deadly splinters flying, rippling into bone and blood and flesh. Screaming wood and wailing wounded filled the brief silences. Limbs were torn from bodies by flying shot. The smoke-filled air was shattered by tongues of red flame as cannons fired. The wind plunged in, surrounding the ships with a miasma of fog and mayhem as men shouted orders, trying to be heard in the desperate confusion.

Seemingly abandoned, or having made a perilous decision to move away from the other ships, Recalde looked not only vulnerable but potentially a fool. Yet he was nothing of the kind. Recalde had noted the English tactics. Bringing his ship to stand alone was a trap. Offering them an isolated, vulnerable target, he hoped to draw them close enough to grapple and board.

It was an act of astounding courage. Recalde knew what a risk it was. He was facing not one, but eight ships, but he also knew his soldiers were many. Hand to hand, they stood a better chance. His actions were in direct opposition to Sidonia's orders, but experienced Recalde knew this was the only way. Another ship, the *San Mateo*, did the same. When fired upon, they did not return fire, hoping the English would come close.

They did not. At three hundred yards they closed, but no further and there they assaulted the two ships for an hour. Through the fug, Sidonia saw Recalde's ship, surrounded, and he went to him. Rescued by Sidonia and his squadron, Recalde rejoined the formation.

Relentless fire sounded for two more hours. The Armada was good at remaining in position, but this method of attack, and its sheer violence was not what they had expected. Once Spanish ships had fired, they simply had to withstand the barrage of the English guns, for they could not reload in time to return fire.

Musketeers on deck kept firing, hoping to hit men working the cannons. English guncrews could take no more than a swift, cursory glance at their targets through gunports. Many cannonballs hit water instead of ships.

All that could be seen was grey smoke, fractured by red fire. The air filled with the stench of gunpowder, the iron tang of blood and the salt of the briny sea. Men went flying across the deck and crashed into walls below as ships shifted suddenly, trying to evade attack.

The men, many new and inexperienced, discovered the true horror of combat upon water. There was nowhere to run. They were trapped in madness.

Along the coast, standing upon the green hills of Cornwall and Devon, people came to watch. Normally the loudest sound heard was the occasional ripple of thunder in the skies, but not that day. Booming guns echoed over the waves, leaping up the grey cliffs. Gulls shrieked in response like souls of the dead.

That afternoon, the lonely hermit of St Michael's Chapel on Rame Head found himself no more alone as all the people of Kingsands, Cawsands, Millbrook and Rame came flocking up the hill to join him, sitting on wiry grass and gathering about clumps of coarse bracken as deer from the Edgcumbe estate fled, unused to so many people in their quiet kingdom. Three beacons blazed on the hillside, calling local men to report for militia service. Some had gone, more were watching the sea. If the Spaniards came, men of Cornwall would defend their homes first, duty be damned. They were no strangers to pirates. Their coasts had witnessed attacks by Barbary corsairs for years, plundering villages, carrying people away to become slaves. The Cornish knew how to repel raiders.

Out at sea, Sidonia had re-formed the fleet into columns, ready for attack, but was affronted when the English seemed to treat his stance with contempt. They would close a gap, fire, and dance away. Sidonia ordered the fleet to sail eastwards, away from this taunting fire.

At one o'clock, the English broke away. Their gunpowder was low. Sidonia lowered his topsail, an invitation to continue the battle, but Howard knew they were doing small damage. Howard could comfort himself with the idea that the threat the Armada posed to Plymouth was gone; they had been driven past. He knew the captains of the Armada would be unnerved by his surprise tactics. That might well make them fear what the English would do next. His ships were easily more nimble, they moved swift and sure as the vessels of the Armada struggled.

The English had fired more than two thousand shots, the Armada returning less than eight hundred. Faster and quicker to reload were English guns, that had been proved, but even Recalde's ship, surrounded by eight English for hours, was not badly damaged. He had lost men, but the ship was still seaworthy. This was not a comfort to Howard.

Consolation came later that day for the English Admiral. The Armada had been forced to hunch close together, many captains panicking, heading closer to the centre. And this caused problems.

As the smoke of the battle began to drift, and the blessed sound of water became heard again as the Armada sailed away, the *Señora del Rosario* made for Recalde's ship to assist with repairs. But because of the tight formation, confused due to crowded, close-packed ships, the *Rosario* collided with a Biscayan vessel, breaking her bowsprit and crippling her steering. She remained afloat, but the *Rosario* was now in trouble.

This was not the only disaster for Sidonia. At two of the clock every man slaving to repair his ship jumped almost from his own flesh. The *San Salvador* exploded.

In a roar of fire, both after-decks went up, men and wood flying into air then falling to sea. Flames poured from the belly of the ship. Black smoke raced into the wind. Rent in bow and stern, the ship was torn, and the *Salvador's* rudder was also damaged. On what was left of her deck lay dead men, groaning men. Limbs were scattered across the burning wood like leaves in autumn. Clouds of bitter smoke plumed into the skies and red fire licked and crackled in the ship's gaping belly. Men started to leap from the rails, escaping fire only to find the sea waiting for them, pulling their legs downward until they rested on the belly of the ocean, weed and sand and rock holding them safe. One hundred men died in the explosion, many more drowned.

The Armada stumbled to a halt as Sidonia sent men to try to pick up survivors from the sea, the water littered with burning wood and drowning men. Those of high rank were picked up first, of course. Those who survived bore burned flesh, scoured red and black; terrible burns racing, weeping, bleeding across once clear skin. The scent of cooking meat filled the air to mingle with fire and smoke and death. The wounded were taken to the hospital ships. Many would not survive the hour.

Some later said that powder brought on deck had been carelessly cared for, and a stray light ignited the ship. Others claimed that a disgruntled soldier, a German mercenary whipped earlier in the day for some misdemeanour, had lit it on purpose. None knew, but it was a grievous loss. The *Salvador* was carrying the bulk of the payload of the Armada.

Sidonia sent men to rescue the gold in her holds, taking it to other ships. They also turned her in the water to stop the raging fire within her belly blowing further into the ship. Human chains formed, the remaining crew of the *Salvador* working with those who had come to aid them. They put out the fire only just in time, for flames were dancing close to the powder magazine under the forecastle where seven tons of gunpowder lay waiting to ignite.

Towing the stricken *Salvadore*, the Armada continued. But another ship was about to enter danger.

The *Rosario* tried to follow, but her steering was in true trouble. At five that afternoon, she again ran into another ship. Sliding into her sister galleon, the *Santa Catalina*, the *Rosario's* foremast snapped, crashing down upon the mainmast. The upper deck became a heavy web of broken rigging snapping in the wind. The sails slapped down, crushing men on deck. Timber fell; men dived into the sea to avoid being killed by falling masts. Floundering, helpless, she began to fall behind.

Pedro de Valdes fired a shot, pleading for aid. The *San Martin* came alongside, and Sidonia's captain, Marolin de Juan, said the ship should be towed, but the sea was rising. Within moments of the tow being secured it broke and the ships swung apart. Sidonia tried again and failed as the seas began to rise and the wind grew in intensity. The other Valdes, Diego Flores, told Sidonia to leave the *Rosario* behind. "Any delay is dangerous," Valdes said. "You must be at the head of the fleet, my lord Admiral."

Sidonia, well aware there was rivalry between the two Valdes captains, estranged cousins, hesitated but eventually agreed. Boats were sent to take the crew from the ship but Pedro de Valdes refused, saying it would be an insult to abandon his ship to the enemy.

Valdes stayed, as did his captains, two hundred and twenty-eight sailors and one hundred and twenty-two soldiers. Fifty thousand ducats in the hold, belonging to Phillip of Spain, also remained.

It was no small victory. The *Rosario* was one of the largest and most heavily gunned ships of the Armada. She was carrying one of the Armada's leading officers as well as a third of the Armada's money. She was also carrying something else; seven English Catholic exiles.

As night approached, the *San Martin* left, unable to persuade Valdes and his captains to abandon ship. Sidonia had to catch up. The Armada was now two hours ahead. One ship, the *Señora de Pilar de Zaragoza*, was left behind to guard the *Rosario* along with four pinnaces.

As darkness fell, so did despair. The Armada had survived this first battle almost intact, but something more precious had been damaged. The *Rosario* whispered in the ears of Spanish sailors. They knew, if their ships were damaged, they would be abandoned by their commander.

Chapter Seven

The English Channel
The Night of July 21st 1588

Death

As darkness fell, Howard sat down at his table to write to Walsingham and Cecil in London. *"I will not trouble you with any long letter,"* he wrote. *"We are at present otherwise occupied than with writing…"* He told them of the battle, informing them of the tactics used. He praised his captains and their courage, and promised that nothing would be neglected in the overthrow of the Armada. Lastly, he added a note asking in the strongest terms for more powder and shot.

Howard was not the only one writing. Drake too was at his desk, quill scribbling at speed. He was writing to Seymour, guarding the seas between Flanders and Dover. Drake told the Admiral of the Narrow Seas of the chase, and sent advice to put his ships *"into the strongest and best manner you may, and be ready to assist his lordship…"* Drake told his fellow seaman that the Armada had many great ships, but not half of the one hundred were men of war.

Sidonia was also at his desk, writing to Parma. As well as informing him of the first battle, Sidonia asked Parma to send out pilots, as he was heading for the Flanders coast and knew the area not. Sidonia knew he would have to find shelter, for the slightest storm would scatter his ships and with the English on his tail they would not last long if separated.

If Sidonia saw troubles, his men were, if not happy, not despondent that night.

"There was little true damage done," said Valdes at the council of war that night. "Their turns of speed are impressive, their cannon clearly faster, but they inflicted small harm. Even Recalde's ship, battered for hours by eight ships, has taken little damage."

"It is true, my lord Admiral," said Recalde. "Yet I fear we could be picked off bit by bit. Two ships were lost today, if not directly by the English, by accidents their assault caused."

"Yet so few are dead I think God is truly on our side," Sidonia said. "If we keep in formation they cannot get close enough to harm us, and we will reach Parma."

"The *Rosario* should not be abandoned," Recalde said. "We might use it, my lord, as bait. Draw the English in with the promise of its prize and they could stray close enough to be grappled. That would grant us a close-quarter battle, as we need."

"The King was clear that we are not to attempt to engage the English unless we were forced to," said Sidonia. "We were forced to today, but to do as you ask would be to go against the ultimate plan of the King. We will go on. The *Rosario* stays behind."

Recalde did not like it, but Sidonia was his Admiral, and he had to obey. As he was rowed back to his ship that night, wind lashing his face and sea spray falling on his clothes, he thought with annoyance about the orders of the King of Spain. If captains could not be trusted to know the sea, to act on instinct, what use were they? Recalde felt his hands bound, as sure as if ropes had been lashed about his wrists. The sea was no place for set plans; men and ships had to be as changeable, as adaptable, as wind and wave to survive. This rigid plan would do them no good, of that he was sure.

Howard raised a blue flag and called his own council of war, his captains ferried to the *Ark Royal* by lantern as the light of day tumbled from the skies. About his table they talked, breaking their fast on ale and wine, dried prunes, roasted meat, cheese and bread. Howard's cabin was comfortable, with furnishings of green and yellow, plates of pewter and goblets of the same metal.

Rations were being handed to the men, of a poorer sort. That night it was a gallon of beer per man along with a pound of bread, butter and four herrings.

On the Armada they drank wine. On English ships, ale and beer was more popular. Soldiers and sailors were fed rice and bacon on the Armada, with beans, but on English ships there was a pound of biscuit or bread each day, a quarter of stock fish, four ounces of cheese and two of butter. On flesh days they had a pound of salt beef, sometimes made into pottage with oats and dried peas. The English ate better than the Spaniards.

The behaviour expected was different too. Sidonia had sent commands that since theirs was a holy crusade, God's work, there was to be no cursing, blaspheming or raging against God, His saints, or the Holy Virgin. Drake and the English captains were well aware attempting to ask this of Englishmen was not likely to be obeyed. Besides, a few curses helped men to release fear.

Men ate on deck and in any spare space they could find, their meal sloshing in wooden bowls. Some scratched their heads, already rampant with lice and the larvae of seaweed flies. Below deck, the scent of piss and shit, vomit and blood, was pungent, and the ship's rats, and the cats brought on board to catch them, were adding to the stench, and they were less careful than men about where they chose to relieve themselves.

The scent in Howard's chamber was better; fresh food and wine, along with the perfume of incense.

"We may praise our ships for being greater in speed," Howard said, plucking a grape from the bowl before him. "And in high winds the Spanish stoop like old men, as we flash past, stout and low. We have seen how easily we out-sail them."

"The problem, my lord, is we cannot get close," said Hawkins. "The closer we go, the greater damage we will do, but greater too is the risk of being grappled."

Frobisher agreed. "They need to be drawn in close, but not too close," he said as he cut a wedge of hard cheese on a pewter plate and pressed it into butter and bread, freshly cooked only two days before and still retaining its fluffy innards. Above them they could hear men on deck. Most sailors had time off when evening came if they were not working. Cards were being laid on barrels employed as gambling tables for the night. Dice were skittering on deck as men laid wagers. Small boys were snoring, jerking in troubled dreams, exhausted after a day of pure terror.

"A hard and risky feat to achieve," said Howard. "But they are driven from Plymouth, and that was our first task. The size of the Armada limits what ports they might use. Having seen them now, I can say no more than half a dozen of the sites named by the Queen's Council could be used for the Armada to drop anchor in."

"The most likely are Portland, then the Solent and the Isle of Wight," said Frobisher. "Waters I know well."

Howard gazed for a moment at Frobisher. He had no doubt the captain knew those waters. Frobisher was one of the most experienced men of the fleet, and he was also a notorious pirate, one of the most lawless of all if reports were correct. Sent to sea as a boy, Frobisher could barely read a page of a book, but he could interpret the sea. No stranger to hardship and peril, he had been held captive in Guinea and when released had become most successful at sea. The Queen had sent him on a voyage to find the North-West Passage, which had failed, but Frobisher had served under Drake, a man he liked now not a whit, and since then lived by piracy. He used the Isle of Wight as a base for preying on ships in the English Channel. Frobisher also had a fearsome and famous temper. Pirate he might be, searing his rages were, but none of that meant Frobisher was wrong.

"I agree with Frobisher," said Howard. "I think they will not attempt to turn about for Plymouth, or Milford Haven. Falmouth remains possible, and although I heard of six thousand men being sent to guard it, it is the least defendable of the possible ports."

"The Solent or the Isle of Wight itself would be best for them, most dangerous for us, to be captured, my lord," said Frobisher. "There were several thousand men sent to the Isle to defend it, and many large guns, but it would make a good base. It is the closest English deep water port to both Flanders and London. Sidonia could place his fleet in the Solent and his men on the Isle."

"A longer campaign that would make," Hawkins said thoughtfully, "which would allow Her Majesty to gather more men, more arms."

"Such a surrender would, even for tactical reasons, give Spain and Parma more time, too," Howard said, shaking his head. "And land on English soil, and the Pope sends money to Spain. We cannot have them take the Isle, even were it a strategic move to buy time. There is *no* time for England on land. You know the state of the army, if such a thing it can be called. Months would not make England's men into soldiers, and allow something like that to occur and we could face another fleet coming from Spain; more ships than we could hope to defeat."

"I simply meant time might be bought if such a thing occurred, my lord," Hawkins said. "I did not mean to purposefully allow them to take the Isle of Wight, only to examine what might benefit England if the worst happened."

"I understand, Hawkins," Howard said. "It is hard to guess what is best when we cannot see their plans."

"We need to *know* their plan, my lord," interjected Drake. "We outmanoeuvre them, that is obvious, and we are quicker with our guns, but they are large ships, not easy to sink. Their formation is swift to assemble considering how ungainly the ships are, and once in that crescent there is little we can do. We might hope to pick them apart bit by bit, as fingers to a roasted capon, but as they are, they may well be called invincible."

Drake sat back. "We need their plans, my lord, where and when they mean to land. We need to know what English waters we can use, all their tricks we know and the Spanish do not. We need information."

Howard glanced at Drake. He knew what Drake was thinking. The *Rosario* had been left behind with only a small guard. It might not be hard to seize, but that would delay them and the main Armada had to be their target. "I see what is in your mind, but it is too much to risk, Drake," he said. "You will take point tonight. The *Revenge* will lead us by lantern through the night, tailing the Spanish ships. That way, the rest of us can gauge how close we are to the main fleet, so we do not come too close. In the morning, there will be supplies of gunpowder brought out to us, so we may continue the fight."

Howard read men well. He put Drake on point that night to stop the pirate sneaking away to capture the *Rosario*.

"We will continue to engage at long range," Howard said to many a dark face.

"My lord, my men saw some cannonballs hitting Spanish ships and bouncing off," said Frobisher. "At the distance we are keeping, by the time cannonballs get to the ships they have lost most of their power."

"If we continue at long range, Sidonia will meet Parma with ease, or land somewhere," said Hawkins.

"Engage far enough away to prevent grappling," Howard said. "Close enough for damage. We will have to practise our dancing steps, gentlemen."

"I think, my lord, we fire too high, too," Hawkins added. "The guncrews must aim lower, for the hulls, to inflict more damage."

Drake said no more, but he had no intention of allowing the *Rosario* to escape. It was a huge ship, with few to defend it, and would be carrying gunpowder and shot as well as money. Drake knew they needed all of those things. Supplies from London were unreliable. They needed what was on the *Rosario*, and they needed something else even more; intelligence the men left behind were carrying. Capture the *Rosario*, and they would know where the Armada was heading.

Another ship clearly had the same idea. At nine that night as the fleet was making final repairs before setting after the Armada, the *Margaret and John*, captained by John Fisher, a privateer financed by the City of London, made for the *Rosario*. People would later wonder if Drake and Fisher had made a secret pact, for Fisher's ship was too small to take the *Rosario* alone, being only one third as large as her. The galleon guarding the *Rosario*, however, along with the four pinnaces, abandoned her, thinking Fisher's approach indicated the rest of the fleet would come. They sailed away to rejoin the Armada.

When his vessel was nearby, Fisher watched, but no sign of life could be seen upon the ship. He brought his ship in close, only to find the *Rosario* was not bereft of men after all. Valdes, still aboard, fired two shots at him. Fisher responded, then took off to a short distance away to wait.

He did not have to wait long.

The English fleet sailed into the night following the Armada at a distance, banks of fog rippling across decks lit by spare light. Men were up, working the sails, setting and stowing, suspended at terrifying heights. Even up modest masts, the climb could be forty or fifty feet into the heavens, and from there they had to clamber along the yard, pulling sailcloth out, trying to balance on the rocking timber as water assailed the ship. Fall, and they would break at least an arm or leg. Fall from the topsail, and they surely would die.

Men were at the tillers, steering. It took more than one man at the best of times; in gales there would be six or seven. And tillers were below deck. Men steered ships without sight of sea or sky. The long steering pole pivoted below deck, controlling the rudder, allowing the helmsman to stay above, but sudden surges of the sea could tear the helm easily from his hands.

They tried to keep sight of land, the surest way to navigate. The tides and currents, the phases of the moon could be used, but land was the best guide. It was harder to see by night, which was why they needed Drake's lantern.

Men hunkered down to sleep, wrapping their weary bodies about cannon and stacks of supplies, between barrels and casks of beer. Those on the upper decks slept under the cold stars, rain falling on their skin, wind brushing their faces. Men rising in the darkness to use piss-pots or shit in barrels or at the bow head tripped on others sleeping nearby, the sound of muffled curses following them as they went to offer relief to their aching bladders. One third of the crew stayed awake, on duty on deck.

They made steady progress through the glistening dark water. Above them shone a crescent moon, offering intermittent light as cloud rolled across the shadowed heavens. Silver light played on black water, shimmering as the wind ruffled across its surface.

Howard's *Ark Royal*, Sheffield's *Bear* and Edmund Fenton's *Marie Rose* led the main fleet, following the guiding light shining from the stern lantern of Drake's *Revenge*.

In the early hours, the light went out.

Ships hoved to. Howard was called from his cabin as the light vanished, leaving the fleet with nothing to follow, but soon there was a cry. The lookout in the crow's nest had seen light. It was further away than expected, but still there. Howard ordered the ships to move faster, to catch up. In the haste many were scattered.

Howard did not know he was not following Drake. He was following the light cast by a lantern on the poop deck of an enemy ship.

Drake had gone after the *Rosario*.

Sailing away from the fleet, seeing the mast of Howard's *Ark Royal*, a beam more than one hundred foot high, vanish in the darkness, Drake knew he was disobeying his Admiral, a man he respected, but he also knew he was doing what needed to be done. Sometimes what needs to be done is more important than doing what is right.

And Drake knew the temper of his Queen. For years had he sailed out to cause chaos for Spain at her command, and if this was expected, so was something else; money. The Queen liked a return on her investment. Elizabeth of England might never have been to sea, but she was a pirate. She had given him direct commands before, *expecting* him to disobey them to her benefit. That had happened when he had sailed to Cadiz. The Queen had been talking of peace with Spain, and after he had sailed had sent ships after him to call off the attack, only they had not reached him. With a glittering eye of barely concealed amusement had the Queen scolded him at court afterwards for disobeying her. Drake had lifted his hands in the air, protesting that her messengers had not reached him. And he knew why. They had been sent in the wrong direction, and with a great delay. She had meant him to burn Cadiz, but needed Spain to think she had tried to prevent it.

Sometimes orders needed to be disobeyed.

Drake knew how slow the Armada was. A fleet may only travel at the speed of its slowest ship, particularly when relying on a tight formation. He had time to get to the abandoned ship and back to Howard before dawn.

Spaniards said Drake kept a spirit in his cabin allied to the Devil. Others claimed he possessed a magical crystal through which he could see what his foes were doing. Neither of those powers of the supernatural did Drake possess, but he did have an almost unearthly bent towards recklessness. That he would wield; a weapon against Spain.

Chapter Eight

Richmond Palace
July 21st 1588

Elizabeth

My feet pounded the floor, to the fire and back again. At the hearth they turned and came about, across the room. Once at the wall I turned again, hands clenched at my sides.

I was pacing. I had been doing that a great deal of late, pounding rushes upon the floor rich with meadowsweet to dust, and wearing down the nerves of my ladies at the same time. I could see them flinch as I turned again at the hearth, but I barely noted it. They could keep still, I could not.

My women sat, hands busy with embroidery, attempting to display a state of serene calmness they did not feel. I knew they were as rigid with fear as I was from the muttered curses that flew into the air as they made a wrong stitch, or impaled fingers with fine needles from the Moorish pin-maker I employed from London. I knew it too from the creases on their brows, wrinkles formed from fear, and from powder and paint clustered in the corners of their eyes from nights of small sleep and days of no rest.

But on they sewed; stoic in the face of encroaching doom. Ladies of high birth are raised and expected to display spare emotion in times of trial. Hysterical women were always condemned, as though showing fear makes it real and concealing it is a strength. But in times of strain we cling to what we know. We think it will protect us.

What fallacies we live by, I thought as I marched on. Women who hailed from ancient bloodlines were supposed to look upon storms with a calm, collected air, knowing their men would save them. *Perhaps all this is to make men feel better,* I thought, or perhaps my women were better at pretence than me. What was more likely was they had not the wealth of experience I possessed. I knew well enough when the final days came I would stand alone.

Think not I had no faith in my men. Many times I had escaped death because of the lengths they had gone to, yet still, from a youth of fear and death, brutal lessons called. When the end came, the only person I could rely on was me.

But they will not let you fall, something of hope screamed within me. *They know that with no sure heir, if you fall so does England.*

That was true. My death would be calamitous. There was no named heir, I had always refused, knowing that to name one would be to name an enemy primed and ready to supplant me, but possible successors were readying themselves, of that I had no doubt. My choice, never spoken aloud for my own protection, was my cousin and godson James of Scotland, but there were others of less hallowed blood. One was Arbella Stuart, daughter of Elizabeth Cavendish and Charles Darnley. The girl possessed Lennox blood, making her distantly of the Tudor line. Some in England thought her a better choice than James, for she unlike him was born in England, of the line of Margaret Tudor, Princess of England and once Queen of Scotland, and, perhaps most importantly, Arbella was young enough that she might be moulded into what powerful men wanted of their Queen.

They had not had that chance with me. I was fully formed when I came to the throne, already well-versed in politics and survival and no fool apt to fall for the wiles of ambitious men. Men who had grown from childhood to adulthood in my reign had never had the chance to create their ruler and control her, but the possibility was there, now.

Because of upstart, arrogant Arbella! I thought as I reached the wall and turned again.

She was not at court, and not only because I could not stand her. Arbella was young, but possessed the effortless vaulted arrogance of ancient blood. Able to look down upon anyone she met, Arbella had been raised by her grandmother, Bess Talbot, Countess of Shrewsbury, and had been told that she would be Queen one day. Fond of Bess though I was, I was well aware of her ambitions. I did not think badly of her for harbouring them, who would not want to advance their grandchild into the highest position possible? But I was not about to welcome Bess trying to play with the succession. That was for God to decide.

Unfortunately, Bess was not the only one playing.

Cecil had often been a mortal who dared to dabble where only eternal beings should, and he had been courting Arbella. Not as a woman, he was old enough to be her great-grandfather, but as my potential successor. He had recommended her to Raleigh, paid her attention when she came to court, and it seemed to me that whilst Cecil might prefer a king on England's throne after me, he was secretly laying bets both ways in case Arbella became promising. There was also the possibility she might wed her cousin, the King of Scots, grafting the Stuart-Lennox branches, bolstering their united claim. A queen who owed much to Cecil and his family would be useful. He was thinking of England's future, and that of his line.

Just before we heard of the Armada setting out, I had offered Arbella to Parma, for his son, thinking such a sacrifice might head off war. King James had written almost before I sent my missive, demanding that the girl not be wed to anyone without his approval. She and any husband she took could challenge James's claim, so I did not blame him, although *how* he heard so swift was something I wondered about. James clearly had spies in my household.

I was almost proud of my godson, no matter how annoying it was.

Arbella, however, I was not proud of.

She had come to court that summer, and managed to irritate every single one of my ladies by pushing ahead of them in a procession to church one morning. The thirteen-year-old girl took the position of a princess ahead of the greatest ladies of court, despite the fact her present titles were nothing to theirs. When asked to step back by my Master of Ceremonies, she had the gall to inform him that the position she had assumed was "the *very* lowest that could be granted" to her.

As people stood staring in wonder at her breathtaking arrogance, my newest favourite, Essex, had saluted her with a merry grin. It was a way to save her reputation, make a breech of protocol into a mistake of childhood, but I wondered if my new young admirer was considering that a girl with Arbella's blood might make a good match with much potential for him in two years when she was of an age to wed.

When informed, I had laughed. "She is an eaglet of my own kind," I had said, thinking to salvage this unfortunate incident. If I was to use her in the future to bargain with James or Spain, I could not have them thinking she was wilful and unmanageable, nor could I let them believe she was in disgrace, even if that was where she belonged. No, for the sake of future deals, I had to pretend to support the chit. I had called her to my rooms and had her dine sitting next to me. All that night I had to pretend to be interested in conversation that was decidedly dull; one of the many trials of being Queen.

Not long after I had sent her, for her own *protection* I said, to Wingfield Manor along with Bess. I claimed they would be safer in the country as the nation mobilised for war, but in all honesty I could not stand the girl near me. She made my skin itch so all I wanted was to tear it from my bones.

Yet I am going to have to start courting the child, I thought angrily as I turned at the hearth. It was necessary, not least because others already were, and I needed to always be one step ahead. Besides, it was not beneficial for James of Scotland to rest too easy. Arbella at court, in favour, would be a warning to my godson to play nicely with England. And when I sent her away, as I was bound to, it would be a warning to Arbella and her ambitious grandmother. Balance was what I sought, with my men, my country, and especially with those with an eye on my throne.

I stopped at the window, watching misty rain fall. *Bless England and her endless rain!* sang my agitated mind. But for these summer storms, the Armada would have been upon us sooner. Clement skies and summer sun would have aided the sons of Spain. Rain would make their lives hard. They were not used to our weather, as our men were. Rain had come to England as a saviour.

I leaned against the window, then bounced back to my pacing. In some ways, thinking of Arbella, being angry at her, was a relief; something to think on other than the Armada, and Parma. When a vast shadow looms, it can be beneficial to look to smaller shades and unleash anger upon them. That was what I was doing; sending rage upon those who would play with the succession, rather than thinking on the imminent possibility that any day now we would hear the Armada had been sighted, had blown our ships from the water, landed, and were ferrying Parma's men to English soil.

I was not the only one dwelling in dark thoughts. I had heard reports that women all over the country were hiding knives in their kitchens and up their skirts, ready to defend themselves. Stories abounded that in Cornwall *fogous*, small man-made caves used in ancient times for refuge, were being opened again and paths to them from towns and villages carefully broken, so women could steal children away and hide them. Others, it was said, were making for places like Carn Brea, where giants once lived, to hide. In some places along the coast, women were standing with men who were to defend towns, not so the women could fight, but so if sailors on Spanish ships looked to the hillsides where they stood, our enemies would see a great force waiting.

These were not the only tales. Whish-hounds, heralds of doom, had been seen running on Dartmoor between the darkly twisting trees and grey, rocky outcrops. Mermaids were calling from the seas, voices as mist floating upon the waves. In Essex, a man had seen ghosts of an ancient army led by a woman with red hair of fire marching past him, her eyes blazing with crimson darkness, off to face an enemy he could not see. People were saying this was Boudicca, the warrior Queen written of in the works of Tacitus, a tale long forgotten in the time of our ancestors but brought back to English memory by the writers of Rome.

I hoped for any ghost who might aid us. For anything. Allies were thin on the ground.

Some said that due to our brutal treatment of Ireland all souls of that country would rise and fight for Phillip, save Dublin, Waterford, Cork and Drogheda. Others protested that Phillip had dismissed Ireland as a possibility, preferring to claim England rather than deal with the "Irish beggars" as he reportedly called them. Yet some rebel chieftains were ready to rise, it was claimed. The modest guard we had in Ireland, a mere two thousand men based in Dublin and the Pale, might not stand against the Irish if they united, wiping out English settlers and soldiers. Walsingham thought Phillip had ceased to concentrate on Ireland; perhaps engaging in war on so many fronts was proving too costly and taxing. My spymaster thought Spain's spies would go into Scotland, in hope of using the execution of my cousin of Scots to inflame lords, if her death could not rouse the King himself.

It was not that James did not care his mother was dead. The King was a pragmatist, like me, and saw the futility of seeking revenge. He wanted to be named England's heir, and making war would be disastrous for that ambition. Joining with Spain would do him no good since Phillip wanted the crown for himself or his daughter. It was not for lack of love that James did nothing about his mother's death. He simply knew any offensive action would be a waste, and he was not one to throw things away. James, therefore, appeared to be on our side, although how much he would be willing to risk in defence of England was another matter.

In truth, James had enough to deal with. The exiled Earl of Morton and his rebel allies had been sent by Phillip to return to Scotland, armed with money to begin an insurrection led by Catholic lords. If that happened, James and his country were in dire danger. Delays caused by tempests striking the Armada had caused this plan to go awry however. Rebellion requires a swift strike and near-perfect execution in order to be successful. Earlier in July, James had declared himself more against Catholics than ever he had been, and had sent men to find the exiles in his kingdom and arrest them. All the same, I had been forced to send money to my godson to keep him loyal. Promises were pouring from Spain, all with the aim of making James turn on me. Just as we could not afford rebellion within England, a second front marching upon us from Scotland would also spell disaster.

France would be no help. The country was tearing itself apart again over faith and politics. Navarre, the rightful heir to the throne, was being held back by the Guise who had taken control of King Henri. The Guise, now deep in the pocket of Spain, had acted upon a bull sent out by Rome.

"The Pope has declared Navarre a heretic and released his people from obedience to their King. The Unholy Father has declared him unfit for the throne," Cecil had told me some months ago.

Navarre had been fighting for his position as heir for two years, with small success despite money I had dispatched to him, the Huguenot hope of the country. Sadly, part of Navarre's failure had sprung from a desire to be chivalrous; after one victory, a great one, he had sent word to King Henri that he would be willing to support him if conditions were agreed. Navarre had then disbanded his army. Mercenaries Navarre left behind had briefly united, but had been slaughtered by the Duc of Guise. King Henri tried and failed to claim credit for this victory, but his people attributed it to Guise, and were rumoured to be ready to follow the Duc, rather than their King.

The Duc of Guise had issued a manifesto demanding the expulsion of heretics from about the King and a declaration of royal support for the Catholic League. The Inquisition was to be granted access to all provinces, Huguenots would lose their property and those who refused to recant heresy would die. The King, knowing he could not allow this, refused and started to raise an army to fight Guise.

"King Henri is aware he is really fighting Spain," I said to Cecil. "If Phillip crushes England and the Low Countries, France will be surrounded. The demands made by Guise are a foothold, Spain creeping into France bit by bit."

Despite the King's martial declaration, Guise and his armies had moved long before the King. Towns in the north had been captured. King Henri had sent word to England, asking me to beg Navarre to surrender his faith for the Catholic Church, and saying Henri himself had refused to join a Catholic League against me, so we were therefore allies. Guise sent word out through pamphlets that the King was a useless fool, and Guise was the only hope of France.

And then Guise had entered Paris with an army, claiming he was there to clear his name. He was not. His soldiers, more than two thousand of them, roamed the streets and armed the mob. Fights broke out in Paris. The King's Guard threw down their arms and surrendered, and people lit bonfires to celebrate Guise's triumph.

The King of France was a prisoner and Guise's terms were hard. The King would be *permitted* to continue to reign as long as he sent away his friends and guards, blocked Navarre from the succession and named the Duc of Guise his heir.

In the dead of night, the King had managed to escape the Louvre, saying as he fled that Paris had rewarded his love with treachery, insult and rebellion.

"King Henri has every reason to support England over Spain, and might even join with us and Navarre against Guise and Phillip," Cecil had said when we heard the news.

"But he cannot do a great deal in practical terms," I said, "for he is too busy trying to cling to his own throne to uphold those of others."

I promised Henri aid, but at that moment my hands too were tied by the tight, thick rope of necessity. I could little spare men or ships to aid France whilst Spain hunted England.

I had many reasons at that time, beyond personal grief, to mourn Anjou. Were he still alive France would not be at war over the succession, and might have come to our aid.

I was warmed to hear, however, that when Henri was informed the Armada had tarried at Corunna because of bad weather, he had remarked, "That is a fine story. It is more likely they saw the English fleet and were frightened!"

It is always nice to hear people offer support, even if they can do little in practical terms.

King Henri, my erstwhile suitor, might be an ally of the future, but he was not useful to me at that moment. Making sure we *had* a future would be the first step.

But friends we did have. Much cause had I had of late to be grateful to my decision to maintain friendship with the Sea Beggars. Hounds are loyal to them that feed them. Sea dogs are no exception.

Although the bulk of Dutch rebel troops were still struggling against the skeletal forces left behind by Parma, the Sea Beggars, their wily ships upon the oceans, had come to our aid. They were mostly fishermen, but after years of facing Spain at sea they were brave, resourceful and a power to be reckoned with. Not large ships did they possess, but all they had were fast and deadly. They knew the meres, salt-marshes and shallows about Zeeland and Flanders. Their fly-boats were swift, their men fierce fighters. Their presence would prevent Parma using many ports to ship his men from, limiting his options. The Sea Beggars were patrolling the shores of Flanders and the Low Countries, and might be called upon to fight in an emergency. At the moment, I wanted them where they were; stopping Parma from crossing.

Other allies I had approached had not been so helpful. The Swiss were allied with Spain even though many of their princedoms were Protestant, and they had sworn not to send men or arms to me. They were not sending them to Phillip, either, which was some comfort, but I knew many German and Swiss leaders preferred to keep friends with the Catholic Hapsburgs as many of their subjects shared Phillip's religion. Men of the Palatinate had spoken in support, as had their leader John Casimir, but he had no navy or men to send so his support was nominal at best.

Once I might have relied on the Danes. Their King possessed a great navy, and had always been charming in his letters to me, but he had died and his young son had claimed the throne. Hampered by careful and cowardly advisors, the young King was instructed not to risk involvement.

One last, rather desperate, attempt had been to send secret word to the Duc of Guise. This was doomed to fail before it began, but had it worked I might have stolen a powerful friend from Spain and brought France to us at the same time. Guise had no interest in supporting me, however, and his reply, that he would see me *"ruined and hanged"* and if hangmen were in short supply he would *"willingly put the rope"* about my throat himself, had left me in no doubt about his feelings.

But lack of money, more than lack of allies, assailed us.

"We have raised forty thousand pounds from the Merchant Adventurers of London," Walsingham had informed me some weeks ago. We had been gathering loans to pay for England's defence.

Even as I had felt some relief in knowing there was coin, for the moment, I knew how fast it would go. Money is always in a rush to be somewhere else. Often it is wasted, so goes seeking new friends.

Wastage was on my mind as I paced. Ramparts built to defend Portsmouth had been condemned by Raleigh and demolished, much to the irritation of my unstable temper. Surely it was better to improve than to tear them down and start again? Earthen walls had been built at great cost, complete with ditches, but my men were already despondent about the soldiers sent to defend these fortifications. Ramparts had gone up to improve walls at Great Yarmouth the year before, and I had sent money to Harwich in Essex to improve its defences, but some had to be donated by local people. I tried to remind them that it was their welfare we were trying to protect, and reasonable contribution was needed.

Money was pouring out of me as water from a broken barrel.

And many of these defences might not be needed, I thought angrily, my nape bristling with rage. Perhaps all would, perhaps none. It infuriated me that in a time when I had no money I was potentially spending where there was no need.

My annual income was two hundred and fifty thousand pounds. Parliament had handed a further two hundred and fifteen thousand to me in the past four years, and more funding had come from the reserves of the exchequer; two hundred and forty-five thousand of a possible three hundred thousand. Those reserves were supposed to be just that, reserves, but they had been drawn upon. Support to Dutch rebels had taken more than four hundred thousand over the past three years, and that was considering standard delays in payment to our soldiers. Defence of the realm for the Armada had taken almost two hundred thousand. Even with Cecil reassuring me that *perhaps* the sums were not as thought, I knew there would be little left after this whichever way the war went. Come autumn, I might have fifty thousand left, a sum that would last, at most, eight months.

Old debts were rolling on top of one another, and we were fighting for creditors to accept delayed payments. Cecil, when not busy trying to locate gunpowder, food and other materials for our army and ships, was in furious talks with bankers, trying to secure loans.

A forced loan had been inflicted on the nobility, bringing in seventy-five thousand, but that along with the money from the Merchant Adventurers was gone. Thousands had been spent on food and wages for the fleet, and tens of thousands more were needed. My country might well be ruined by war through money if not by invasion.

Pressures of money, debt, and the looming possibility I would soon be deposed and my country would fall were upon me, the weightiest cloak ever I had worn. Were I not careful, I would shatter; a sheet of glass thrown to the floor.

First we must ensure we have a future, I told my feet as I paced up and down. *When we have a future, we can worry about how to fund it.* I almost laughed. If Phillip won, at least I could take satisfaction in the fact he would inherit all my debts.

"We should send for Master Tarlton," Blanche said, looking up from her needle. "He would calm Your Majesty."

Tarlton was my preferred player. A master of humorous face-making and witty ridicule, he was my favourite fool, and a good player who was part of my personal company *The Queen's Men*. My men toured the country and had a famous name, as they should do since only the best were allowed to enter. Tarlton was the only man who could always make me laugh.

But even he, that day, would have failed.

"He is not in London, Blanche," I said. "It is a good thought, old friend, but nothing will calm me today."

She rose, dusting down her dark gown. Like all my ladies, Blanche wore black and white so I would shine in gold and purple against their black background. Unlike many, she did not resent it. "Let us walk in the gardens, Majesty," she said quietly. "That way you can wear down your restless spirits and not unnerve those of your ladies."

"I am making them nervous?" I kept my voice low.

"How could they be otherwise? They are here, their husbands, fathers and sons with the fleet or army. Their hearts beat with the same terrors as yours." She put her hand on my arm. "Let us to the gardens go. There, amongst the flowers walking will not seem strange, and your ladies may be able to lose some restless energy as you do."

I nodded. Blanche was wise.

It was warm but not bright in the gardens. Skies hung heavy, threatening rain, but the air was warm, close, clinging. There was a scent of sweat and incense on the air, rising from worried people and braziers burning sweet scents to ward off sickness. Many of my fine flowers, usually a blaze of colour by this time, looked under-grown and sad. Unseasonable wetness and small sunshine had led to my glorious gardens becoming puny and pitiful, but I could not mourn that. Bad weather had held back the Armada, after all.

I thought about what we were to face even as I tried not to. There is a sense of irony that often the thing we try hardest not to think on becomes all we can think about. In truth, my mind was dazed, reeling from horror to horror like a girl racing through a castle bound by evil, seeing demons at each step. Much of me wished I was a man, not because I had any desire for a shaft but because then I would be allowed to *act*, to take to a ship or grasp a sword in my hand, to *do* something, rather than being left a woman sentenced to inaction by my sex.

It had not always been that way. Remembering the tale of the marching ghosts, I remembered the mention of the warrior Boudicca in Tacitus. I had read that work, finding it most different to other accounts of my country, such as the *History of the Kings of England* by Geoffrey of Monmouth. He had said nothing of this woman, who had been royal, and had led her people into battle.

Was life ever truly that way? I wondered. Had women once been seen as no different to men, been allowed to be soldiers, to lead troops in war, like men? It seemed a thing impossible, and yet it was there, in a book of history written by a master of that art. Perhaps there had been a time when women were not encased in the slavery of sex, had been seen as equals, had been allowed to march out, shed blood for their people.

If that had been allowed, the time of Queen Boudicca was superior to mine, no matter if it was called barbaric by men of Rome. Inaction in such a time as this was torture. As a man I might die on a field of battle or drown in the sea, but at least I would not be stagnant, immobile, unable to move, act or fight because I had been born of one sex and not the other. What more helpless and useless state could I have been thrust into? Everything in me rebelled against it.

I knew I could not be risked. I was needed to hold together the threads of my country. I was the mind to England's body. This I knew, but never had I resented my position so wildly. All I wanted was to do something, *anything*. Trapped in my palace, trapped in my mind, I thought I would run mad.

That night, tired in body if not in mind from my walk, I made ready for bed. Women plucked pins from my wig and gown as I stood, arms raised, in the centre of them. We were all trying to pretend this was but another day. Inside me something was screaming. Something wanted to run free. I could not let it. I had to maintain the calm shell of the Queen over the feral, lunatic creature rearing up inside me.

They slipped my nightgown upon my skin and wiped the paint from my face. This took some time, so thick did I wear it now. Water infused with lavender caressed my skin, and the scent, one Kat had always worn, rose warm and sweet into my nose. It was the smell of childhood, of a safe pair of arms holding me tight against the horrors that night could bring.

My heart ached, missing my friend. When I thought of Kat always I was sent backwards to the first moment of mourning. That is what grief is, often not a constant, but a visitor who comes over and over through life. As soon as you think grief is gone, back he comes. Perhaps it is good. Not all that hurts us is bad. Grief reminds us how deep our hearts are, and what bravery we have within us, in daring to love another. Grief is a measure of love and courage.

I bathed in my hip bath, hot towels about its rim, fragrant water and flowing rose petals lapping against my old bones and tired skin. They dried me and dressed me in a nightgown of lace-trimmed cambric and a cap, slipping it upon my balding head, keeping it warm. Perfume of my own making was dabbed on my skin; a mixture of sweet marjoram and powdered herb Benjamin, which smelt like perfumed sugar. They brushed my teeth with wood ash and powdered cuttlefish bones, a mixture made in an effort to restore whiteness to my yellow teeth. They gave me cloves and cumin seed to chew to freshen breath and to relieve the pain I felt in my gums, now swollen about my aging teeth. I would not allow more to be pulled, although some needed to come out. Instead, doctors treated me with infusions of spurge, marjoram and parsley. I found spurge most effective. It removed almost all pain when applied directly to the tooth.

I climbed into bed with Blanche. Bess Throckmorton, Helena, Kate Carey and Mary Radcliffe slept on pallet beds on the floor. The risk of assassination was great, so many stayed. Those not in my chamber went to nearby rooms. I think they knew they were safer with me, although soon a time might come when that was far from the truth.

I barely slept. For hours as Blanche twitched in restless dreams I lay awake, staring at the walnut bedposts and hangings bearing my arms. Draughts blew, making the coverings shift. I thought I heard a sigh in my ear, as though the ghost of my cousin, Mary, was also awake, waiting on news of invasion and my downfall. Would she smile to see my ghost rise, taking its place beside her? Only a year had we been apart. Would my fall into disgrace and death, the obliteration of my people, my plan for England, comfort the woman I had murdered, the prince I cast into death? I knew not, but there was some sense within me that the ghost of my cousin was not merry that night. Oddly, I found that comforting.

As dawn came, a fire that was not the sun blazed upon the horizon. The light of beacons, rippling up the coast from Plymouth, reached London.

When I woke, men came, one message only on their lips.

Our ships were upon the seas. The Armada had arrived. Fighting had already begun.

"God, in your mercy," I whispered, "hear my prayer. Save my people and I will sacrifice anything, even my own life, even all that is dear to me. Take what You wish from me, but save my people."

Chapter Nine

The English Channel
July 22nd 1588

Death

The Queen woke, sitting in her nightgown, spare paint upon her face and a red wig hastily placed so men would not see her bald head, as her men told her much. Along the coast, almost at London, messengers on swift horses rode, a relay bearing letters from Howard for Cecil, Walsingham and the Queen, and from Drake to Seymour.

But if one man was about to hear from Drake, another was wondering where the hell he was.

As dawn started to break on the 22nd of July, Howard had been roused from his bed with disquieting news. The light they had been following, the one they had hastened after, scattering the fleet, was not the light upon Drake's ship. It was mounted on the poop deck of an enemy vessel. They were far too close to the Armada, and there was no sign of Drake.

Muttering curses, Howard closed his eyes. He knew where Drake had gone. Back to the *Rosario*, leaving Howard and his captains following the wrong light; something that could be fatal for them and England. Howard and his two companion ships were close to Berry Head in Devon and they were right up against the rearguard of the Armada. The rest of the fleet he could barely see; of the nearest they could spy only masts on the horizon. The others were nowhere in sight.

Sighting Howard's ship right behind him in the dim blue light of dawn, close enough for culverin shot, Admiral Hugo de Moncada, commander of four galleasses, sent word to Sidonia requesting permission to attack. Three English vessels, the flagship amongst them, were isolated, he wrote, and his oar-powered ships with powerful bow guns could ignore the wind set against them, race upon the English using manpower and oars, and attack. Moncada could achieve a significant rate of knots at a short distance. He might force Howard to engage, and board him.

The crew manning the boat which carried his message to Sidonia could not paddle fast enough, thinking finally they would fight the slippery English bastards, but Sidonia, remaining true to Phillip's command not to engage, told Moncada not to attack.

Howard, naturally, had no idea the ships of Spain had been told to let him alone. Orders were barked out, ringing over the splashing rain and keening wind. Hands, chilled by early morning wind, struggled to grasp rigging and rope. Men teetered on the sails, unfurling them. Heeling about into the wind, the three ships escaped.

Although safe, Howard was concerned. The next deep water port was Torbay, and the English fleet had become scattered in the night. It would be hours before the rest of the fleet caught up. Devon and her coastline were undefended. Howard's face was grim as he sent ships off to find Drake.

It did not take long. Howard was a clever man, and could make an educated guess as to where the pirate had gone. Drake's ship was spotted near the *Rosario*. Another vessel, the *Roebuck*, was with him.

Drake set out to rejoin the fleet. His task, self-appointed, had been accomplished. During the night he had sailed to the *Rosario* and sent a message to the captain to surrender. At first, Valdes had refused, but when he was told it was Drake asking, he was flattered such a notorious man would have come for him personally. Sending some English Catholic exiles away secretly by boat, for they knew what would happen to them if caught, Valdes had accepted a gentlemanly invitation to dine with Drake aboard the *Revenge*. Over a supper of wine and meat, Drake had offered generous terms. All lives would be spared. Valdes's men would be taken as prisoners of war, to be exchanged or ransomed in the future. His ship would be seized along with his treasure, but, Drake assured him, these terms were more generous than anything any other would offer. Valdes accepted, kissing Drake's hand and commenting warmly on his humanity and mercy. Valdes's commander had abandoned him, so what more could he do?

When Drake boarded the ship he found much to please him. Fifty-five thousand ducats as well as gold, silver, gems and fine clothes were taken to the *Revenge* along with a chest of jewel-hilted swords intended as gifts for the English Catholic nobility. Captain Jacob Whittan, commander of the *Roebuck*, towed the *Rosario* into Devon, transferring hundreds of captives so they could be shipped to prisons; the first human prizes of the engagement. Two English exiles that had remained on board were sent to the Tower of London as traitors. Forty of the best prisoners went to the Bridewell.

Drake also had all their powder and shot. This, too, was taken to port, where it was unpacked, sorted and loaded onto boats which would head out to reinforce the English fleet.

When he reached Howard's ship, Drake knew he had some explaining to do. Howard sent for him to report immediately, but Drake had handy, politic lies up his sleeve.

"Just after midnight, my lord," he said blithely to Howard's grim face, "We sighted unknown sails to starboard. Believing them to be Spanish vessels secretly working windward as we did at Plymouth, I ordered the lantern doused and we set after them. I thought it my duty, my lord, and did not think that taking the entire fleet off-course would be a good idea. Only the *Roebuck* and two pinnaces came with me. When we caught them some hours later, we found they were not Spanish, but Hansa merchant hulks. I turned to rejoin your lordship, but at dawn found myself, quite by accident, upon the *Rosario*. Since we were there, and we are all in need of powder and shot as well as information, I took the opportunity. At full strength, the *Rosario* is more powerful than my ships combined, but she had no sails left and the mast and bowsprit were clearly damaged. I thought she would be easy to seize, and we could use her powder."

"It is a good thing you are a fine sailor, Drake," Howard said, his eyes not breaking contact. "For your career at court will surely fail."

"How so, my lord?"

"You are a terrible liar," said the Admiral.

Drake came very close to smiling, which perhaps was Howard's aim; a jest to trick Drake into revealing himself. Only with great control did he manage to hold his lips down and affect surprise.

"You put the entire fleet in danger!" Howard shouted, no more able to restrain his temper. "And what if they had landed at Torbay in the night, or blown my ship from the water this morning? You took a grave risk, Drake, and only luck meant it paid off! The fleet is scattered because of you."

"I took a risk, my lord," he agreed, "and for good reason."

Howard listened as Drake told of what he had found. As he came to the end, Howard was nodding. "I did not discover their plans, my lord, but their powder I took, and I saw their guns. We are right to attack at a distance. The guns are great, but they are also not secure. Two high wheels, like land cannon, make them hard to manoeuvre, and slow to reload. One of the men, a soul of Portugal, also told us that they have few provisions. Their food is bad, their water and wine short. Their bread is ridden with worms and their fish is rotten."

Drake looked his Admiral in the eyes. "This is good information, my lord, and the captured ship will make the people of England merry when she is towed in. They will see we are taking ships, see small victories. They need cheering as we need powder."

"Were you any other man," Howard said, "I would court martial you for your rash actions." He glanced at Drake and barked a short laugh. "But since you are not any man, but *Drake*, you escape punishment this time." His unwilling grin turned into a scowl. "But mistake me not, this cannot happen again."

"It need not," said Drake.

"Frobisher is not merry about what you did; he thinks you a pirate."

Drake hid a grin. Frobisher did not like him, but what he liked even less was another man getting the treasures of a fallen ship. Frobisher was a pirate the same as Drake. When *he* stole something it was honourable, if Drake did the same, it was piracy.

"He wants a share of the loot you stole," Howard said, confirming all Drake had thought. "And it will take time now to regroup, meaning the Devon coastline is unguarded." He narrowed his eyes at Drake. "No more games, Drake. It is not just for me, or for you, or for the Queen that we must stay together, but for England. I know you are a pirate at heart, but for the rest of the time you serve under me you must be a man of England first. Be a captain with the wiles of a pirate, not a pirate wearing the clothes of a Vice-Admiral."

"I understand, my lord."

"I hope you do. If the Spanish had landed in the night, or do so today, and we are not there to stop them, the loss of England and its people is on your head." Howard regarded him with a glimmering eye. "I will leave my report spare of details about this incident, unless England falls, in which case all will know what you did. Pray other captains do the same. Your story, poor though it is, will suffice. I need my men together, not tearing each other apart with bickering."

Drake smiled, slightly abashed. Being scolded by Howard was almost like being told off by a grandfather of whom you were most fond. "I will not disappoint you again, my lord," he said.

"See you do not." Howard sniffed. "Captain Valdes is still on your ship?" he asked. Drake inclined his head. "Will he tell us of the Armada's plans?"

Drake shook his head. "I questioned him, and he offered up tales I know to be untrue. He will not betray his country."

"I would not either, were the situation reversed," Howard said. "Relay what you know to the other captains about the guns and the layout of the ships. We will use the information you gambled so much to gain."

It took a day to regroup, but it was not a lost day. After one of the clock, believing her crippled and slowing the fleet, Sidonia gave the order for the *San Salvador* to be abandoned, the remaining crew on the fire-blasted vessel to be taken to other ships. The ship was too badly damaged, water pouring in faster than pumps could take it out, and her crew too few. The badly injured were left behind.

Sidonia, had he been more experienced, might have ordered her scuttled, but he did not. The *Salvador* was one of the great ships, carrying much in the way of munitions. When the ship fell behind, one hundred and thirty barrels of gunpowder and more than two thousand cannonballs tumbled into English hands. When Lord Thomas Howard and John Hawkins boarded, they found her deck fallen into itself, the stern blown out and the bodies of fifty men blasted into death inside, corpses reeking with the scent of death and burned flesh. The sight was so repellent that they did their work fast and Captain

Fleming, he who first warned of the Armada, towed the ship to Weymouth. There she was stripped of munitions, which were shipped back to the English fleet, arming them well for the next battle.

Dignitaries of Weymouth were, at first, happy to see the *Salvador* in their port. That emotion wore away swiftly. They had to employ crews to keep pumping her out to stop her sinking, and no one had told them what to do with the prisoners on board, many of whom were injured and, since surrounded by corpses, blood and flayed flesh, were running swift to sickness. Problems only multiplied when, in the night, people of Weymouth came and stole away rope, rigging, casks and cable, seeing the ship as salvage, which they had a right to claim.

On the hillsides of Cornwall, the militia were ordered to march east to reinforce their neighbours in Devon and Dorset. Some did, many did not. The harvest was almost ready to gather in, and they had done their part. Many marched home rather than to war. Those who went to war walked into a rainstorm, and on foot, struggling through water and mud, they were far behind even the slow pace of the Armada. Perhaps those who went home had the right idea, for whilst they would not be there in battle if men of Spain landed, it was unlikely the marching militia would either.

The English fleet came together, finding each other on the water, and once Frobisher had been convinced that skinning Drake alive was not the best thing he could do that day, the captains talked.

"If we keep the weather-gage, which we need in order to use best our speed, all we will do is drive the Armada up the Channel to meet Parma," said Drake.

"What if we harry from upwind?" asked Hawkins. "As it sails eastward, we could attack, and there are many waters coming in the Armada's path which offer potential for traps. We know the dangers of England's coves and currents, the Spanish do not."

"Frobisher, you know the waters we are approaching best," Howard said. "Tell us of them."

Frobisher was more than happy to.

*

Across the water, Sidonia ordered the formation of the Armada to alter as they sailed towards Dorset and the Portland Bill isthmus. The Admiral had seen fresh sails on the horizon. Howard had sent for reinforcements. Concerned that Seymour would come from the front, sailing from Dover, and they would be trapped between him and Howard, the Armada divided, two flotillas of warships protecting the hulks. The rearguard, commanded by Leyva who was to relinquish command to Recalde when the *San Juan* was repaired, had forty-three ships, and the smaller vanguard led by Sidonia had twenty. With the panic of the previous day in mind, where ships had fled position, causing collisions, written warnings were sent to all ships stating that the commander of any vessel which strayed from position would be hanged.

Sidonia was concerned. He had maps of the English coast, but his charts of the waters were few. As Sidonia stared at the sea, willing a ship from Parma to appear, Howard dispatched another letter to Walsingham, urging for reinforcements. *"I pray you, send out to me all such ships as you have ready at Portsmouth with all possible speed. We mean so to course the enemy as that they have no place to land."*

As night came, the wind dropped. Both fleets, held still by the lack of wind, were off Lyme Bay on the Dorset coast. Men tried to sleep on the deck amongst gun batteries. Lords, captains and admirals went to private sleeping quarters, with soft pallet beds. A few men had hammocks, but they were not common.

That night the men slept, cloaks wrapped about them if they had them, exhausted as under them the sea curled and fish swam. Some dreamed of their wives, hoping that if they died their wives would know, that comrades on board would see them fall and carry the news home. If a woman lost her husband to the sea but had no sure news of his death, she had to wait seven years to remarry, leaving her to fend for herself and any children on what little she could earn, in the few jobs open to women. Many sailors' widows starved, or had to turn in desperation to prostitution.

Men closed their eyes, hearing the hiss as charcoal cooking fires were doused to prevent fire. Some men sang softly in the darkness, songs of love and home, of hope.

Sidonia walked on deck that night, the package of secret instructions hard against his breast, concealed in his doublet. His leather shoes padded softly on wooden boards as the ship creaked and moaned. He wandered past men shivering in their sleep, trying to ward off rain by huddling against meagre partitions erected to shelter them.

The Isle of Wight was not far away, and Phillip's instructions had been clear. If Parma and Sidonia could not join hands, the Isle of Wight should be taken. It was not strong, not well defended, and would prove a perfect invasion point to take England from, and to ferry Parma's men to when the time came. It would be a safe port, yet it was *only* to be used if the first plan failed, which it had not, as yet. As Sidonia walked, watching the servants of lords huddle under fine cloaks ruined by gunsmoke and fire, he wondered if he should keep to the original plan. Ships carrying his desperate letters into the sea had not returned. Perhaps captured by Seymour or by the Sea Beggars, they had brought no news to him, and perhaps not delivered any to Parma. He had been told Parma would be ready as soon as he arrived, but he did not know that.

The sealed instructions in his pocket were for Parma, in the event they did not meet. They told the General what he was to do if Sidonia was forced to land in England without him. They laid out demands for peace negotiations with Elizabeth: Catholics would have freedom of worship; the English would return all towns and cities seized in the Low Countries and Phillip would have financial compensation for all losses incurred. Phillip had believed that if Sidonia landed, Elizabeth would be forced into these measures, since her ground troops were too weak to resist. Then, Parma's troops would come to ensure England's fall.

Sidonia believed he should capture the Isle of Wight. The English fleet had done small damage, but if they chipped away at his ships they might well reduce the Armada to dust. Taking the Isle of Wight was possible, and would grant him a port from which he could use his soldiers, up until this moment almost useless, and from which he could contact Parma. It would buy time.

Sidonia might have laughed had he known that in Turin people were saying he had already sailed up the Channel and met with Parma. The gossip in Prague was somewhat different. There people said the Armada had been struck with plague and had fled back to Corunna.

As dawn came, spindly fingers of silver stretching into a sky of cobalt blue, a light north-westerly began to blow. Portland Bill was close and for the first time the Armada had the weather-gage.

Sidonia walked on, the creaking of wood and the groan of water beneath him his only companions.

Chapter Ten

Richmond Palace
July 23rd 1588

Elizabeth

I blinked as dawn's fire entered the chamber. I had ordered the shutters taken down. Often, I did not like to get up early unless I had worked through the night, but I had not slept, and had awaited the coming of the light with weary impatience. Messengers were surely on their way now; they would have ridden from Plymouth upon sight of the Armada. I was hoping they had collected letters from Howard and Drake on the way. I needed to know what was happening. Was England already lost, or was the war won? Sometimes, that night in particular, I had wished I had wings that I might fly to the sea and spy my ships. Being closed up inside a room, waiting for news in a helpless, fraught and suffocating manner was torture.

The world seemed still, but it was not. I was. Alone, I was motionless; frozen like ice, solid as marble. Like one of the beasts atop striped poles in the gardens I was stuck. I was still, stagnant, trapped as about me the world was quaking, trembling, tumbling.

Phillip's face came to me, a picture of him in youth, when married to my sister. I thought of his proposal, made when my poor sister was still living, hanging on to life as much for love of him as fear of death. I thought about how I had agreed, then tarried, holding him at bay until he married Elizabeth of Valois. And I wondered just how much of this conflict was because I had refused his hand so long ago. Oh, I was sure my pirates pilfering and England's martial incursions into the Netherlands had set rage deep into his prideful heart, but all arguments start somewhere, usually somewhere personal and private. Many men do not handle rejection well, and my rejection of

Phillip had been most public, most shameful. When this happens to common people women are called names, or they are bullied by the rejected man and his friends. Sometimes they are abused and sometimes they are killed. Phillip and I were princes, so the game went deeper and higher. The punishment would be more hurtful, more lasting. Phillip had failed to bed me, to subdue me in marriage or politics, so now he meant to destroy me and my country.

I leaned back on the perfumed sheets, breathing in. I needed a moment to pull courage upon my face. Until now, our games had been covert, just as our games had been when we courted. Now they were out in the open. The King of Spain had lost patience for subtlety.

Craft wings of wax, dear brother, my mind whispered as I opened my eyes, *and fly close to my English sun.*

"You look pale, Kate," I said to Kate Carey as I saw her haunted face in the light from the windows. Long shadows drifted down pinched cheeks, and her eyes looked bruised, purple and grey puffy bags hunching under them.

"I am well, madam," she said, offering a brave smile.

I rose and padded to her, my feet soft on the rushes, herbs breaking under my heels, releasing sweet scents into the air. "You are not," I said. "How could you be? Your husband upon the sea, your father leading the armies defending my person?"

"I am proud of them both, Majesty," she said.

"And worried for them." I took hold of her chin and turned her face to mine. "See my eyes, cousin," I said. "I, too, fear, as I too am proud. No shame lies in showing either emotion. If we fear but stand to face the fight, only then can we say we have courage."

Kate nodded and offered a braver smile.

My Carey cousin had been with me since before I came to the throne, although not all the time. The eldest daughter of Lord Hunsdon, my cousin, was Kate, although if rumour was to be believed and Hunsdon, son of Mary Boleyn was my bastard brother, Kate was my cousin *and* my niece. Whatever blood bonded us was strong, either way. Her family and mine were joined, not only because of the strange dalliances of my amorous father, but in the defence of England.

"Have you heard from your father?" I asked.

"He has thousands, he believes, madam, all ready to defend you with their lives."

She spoke such words to comfort me. I knew many had deserted. Some called too soon, some told to defend lands not their home lands, some just not willing to fight, knowing the odds were against us. Many had not come when called, preferring to stay at home to guard their own families and lands. In some ways I could not blame them.

My men, much like Kate, thought I knew nothing and had no intention of telling me. They thought it better I believed all men of England ready to fight and die for their country. But I had ears everywhere. Not for nothing were my gowns embroidered with eyes in thread of gold and pink, silver and crimson. My father had ordered carved men to be placed upon the beams, overhead in his palaces for the same reason that I ordered my ladies to embroider eyes on my gowns; sometimes it is good to remind courtiers that the monarch is watching, always.

Concerned though I was about desertions, I understood my people. They, like me, had faith in the sea to keep us safe, and in God. There was a reason, people supposed, that England had been kept safe thus far, and would be now. We were God's chosen. I wondered how many in Spain also believed this. Phillip certainly thought God was with him.

In truth both of us thought the Devil stood on the other's shoulder.

That day, the militia was to mobilize. Rusty England, groaning like an ancient gate, was about to swing open, ready for action.

Tilbury was ready. The old blockhouse had been strengthened and Robin wrote he had erected a sea of tents. Two ditches circled the camp, with drawbridges for our troops to use. Across the Thames was a similar camp and cannon from the two would fire across the river at any enemy ships sailing up the Thames. Robin had also been inspecting batteries at Northfleet, Erith and Greenhythe in Kent, but had reported platforms for guns were still being built. With Essex, Master of Horse for the army at his side, Rob had not stopped moving for weeks.

Robin had been up and down the south of England, riding like the wind, inspecting defences. Some places had not adequate fortifications, he wrote in hurried notes. I could see, with a pang hitting my heart, how tired he was by looking at his writing. It had never been tidy by my standards, but of late his writing had become as the scrawl of spiders. Yet nothing stopped him. Robin was not well, and was fifty-five, but he toiled with the energy of a young man. If we survived this invasion, I was going to have to send him to the country to recover.

The thought of Robin brought fire to my soul. So long I had loved him now that the feeling was familiar as the hand of a friend held in mine. We had loved and fought, been torn apart, hearts broken. And we had found our way back to one another, meeting on another path, finding friendship once more.

The best of love is this. We offer ourselves, a sacrifice to love. We give all we can, and lose much, yet our lives are enriched, brightened beyond measure, by that daring, that courage.

Through loving Robin I had come to know myself, the depths of my soul, the strength of my heart. I knew myself, for loving him had tested me in all ways I thought possible, and many I had never considered.

Orders went out as I rose for lord lieutenants of all counties to mobilize their forces. Men were to set out for Stratford, Tilbury and London. Six thousand had already amassed in Kent. They were told to stand ready to repel the Spanish wherever they landed, and send word to nearby forces if ships were seen.

Mercenaries had been suggested to bolster our numbers, but even had we time to employ them we had not the coin. "Our militia has some training," I had said to my Council, which was true. Since a decree some twenty years ago, men of all shires had been trained a little. Whether it was enough had yet to be seen.

There were Trained Bands, and almost three thousand had experience in cavalry fighting, perhaps eleven thousand as foot soldiers, but this was a slim number in all, and weapons were still short. Firearms were expensive and few possessed them. Crossbows were more common, and their rate of fire, much like the longbow, was faster than guns which took much time to be reloaded. Powder growing damp was also a problem for guns, especially in misty England.

Men had been making longbows at a furious rate, but there were still not enough of the weapons which had won at Agincourt and Flodden so long ago. Those who had bows had been out using them. Fields to the north of London, in the lordship of Finsbury, had become a site of archery once more as it had been in the time of my father. Although many had flocked there to build houses in recent years, the pull of tradition was too strong to ignore. In what spaces there were in Finsbury Fields, men had built targets, bringing their sons out to shoot, practising for aiming at Spaniards.

Lack of weapons was haunting me. Of almost two thousand men mustered in Surrey I had been told only three hundred would have bows when they reported to their captains. It was meant to be law that every man over seventeen and under sixty who was not lame, maimed, noble, of the clergy or a judge was supposed to own a bow and keep four arrows in his house. Clearly, many had disobeyed this law for some time.

In truth, archery had been slipping away for some years. In battle, cannons and guns were more frequently employed, but I wished then, very much, that men had kept to the law. We might be better armed if that were so.

Amongst the nobility weapons were more common, although some of the armour men had was only for jousting, and some was only good for decoration, to wear in portraits on which descendants would gaze in admiration for their ancestors' warlike appearance, never guessing the armour was useless and never once had been used in battle. But noble men had swords and daggers. They were carried as symbols of status, but at least they had sharp edges and points. Men of towns carried a dagger and a club for protection, and even outside of towns most men usually kept something to defend themselves with. Men worth between ten and forty pounds were required to provide weapons when the militia was called, and some were bringing arms to their commanders. Lords, who were to keep cavalry, weapons, and armour for Crown use, were supposedly bringing theirs too. It was as well, for weapons of the Crown were slim.

Devon and Essex had been sent most of our arms, as we thought those places at most risk, but other counties were relying on men showing up with weapons, bringing pitchfork, scythe and daggers if they had no swords, bows or guns.

All the cannons of the Tower of London had been taken out, shipped to the coast and to Tilbury. More had been loaned or purchased from private citizens. Some were ancient. Carts were shipping cannon and powder to Tilbury and London, but they moved slowly, the roads wet and muddy, sometimes only crawling ten miles a day.

"Our ability to shift weapons about if the enemy lands somewhere we have not thought of is limited, Majesty," Cecil had said.

We had to take our best guess.

Men were posted at Dover and other points along the coast, watching for ships. A relay of fast horses had been set up at key positions to bring news fast to London. Preparations were underway to demolish bridges and to flood roads if word came the Spanish had landed. Men were driving pack animals and livestock away from the coast, so men of Spain could not consume or use them if they stepped on our soil. Commands had gone out the night before to all county commanders, identifying which strategic points were to be held and which abandoned. Specific places were given where supplies could and could not be stored, and landmarks were named where our forces could rendezvous if we needed to retreat.

I had taken an almost unwholesome interest in this. No soul of the sea was I, but I had read enough of the tactics of Caesar and other generals of history to understand strategy. Warfare in England had always been more a series of skirmishes and sieges than grand battles. If our ships lost, if our army failed, we would be fighting as the Irish fought us; rebel tactics using surprise, using territory, hoping to win in a long fight of many years. In view of that, Windsor Castle had been chosen as the site I would flee to if Parma and Sidonia landed. My men were urging me to go there already, but I would not. Run the moment the Armada was sighted, and I would infect my people with terror.

Blanche came, a goblet of wine doused liberally in water for me in her hand. Although I preferred small ale, wine with water was a pleasing substitute. I did not drink a lot, unlike my men who would happily drown in ale and wine if left to their own devices at feasts. I did not like the foggy head some welcomed. Years of fear left me wanting sharp eyes and responses, but a little did not cloud the head and yet steadied the nerves. I was in need of steadiness. I drank it down.

When I was dressed, there came a knock to the door. Thinking it was news of the Armada I leapt from my chair, dropping my embroidery on the floor. But it was not news, it was my physician.

"You sent for me, Majesty?" Roderigo Lopez asked, bowing as he stood before me.

"Actually, I did not," I said, casting an eye at Blanche whose face was suspiciously calm and collected.

"Now I am here, however, perhaps there is something I can do?"

I eyed the doctor with no small measure of suspicion, knowing that this timely arrival had been engineered between him and Blanche. She was worried about me, I knew, and Lopez was the best physician ever I had had. Usually I distrusted doctors. They were all too eager to throw noxious concoctions down my throat, using me as some test subject, which pleased me not, but Lopez was different. He had worked for Walsingham before me, and had aided him with his persistent complaint of the waters. He had also tended to Robin and Essex. Lopez, unlike other doctors, was willing to listen and had sampled many of the potions I made myself, declaring them to be of great worth.

People at court did not like him. He was not an Englishman for a start, hailing as he did from Portugal. The second reason was he was a Jew. Officially, he was a *conversio*, his father having been a *marrano*, a Jew forced to convert faith in Spanish lands, but I was well aware Lopez, like many Jews living in England, practised his original faith in private. I had never minded what people got up to behind closed doors in terms of religion as long as in public they adhered to the Protestant faith of England, demonstrating a united front. And Lopez was a fine doctor. That was how I measured his worth, not on faith but abilities. He was one of the few men who had permission to enter my bedchamber, as I trusted his character. And he had been rewarded with the monopoly on importing aniseed and herbs to London apothecaries. This was something else people did not like.

I cared not a whit. Lopez and I followed the same teachings, bowing to ideas born in the universities of Bologna, Padua and Paris that an excess of anything was poor for the humours. He approved of my slight diet, my habit of watering down ale and wine, and we shared notions on cleanliness. Some doctors threw their hands up in horror when I bathed more than once a month and almost fainted to hear I kept my windows open even in winter. Lopez agreed fresh air and a clean body were healthy. We had both studied the works of the Stoic philosopher Epicurus, and agreed with his teachings that in pleasure is the greatest good, but the way to attain pleasure is to apply moderation to all things: a little ale was fit for the stomach, too much brought on unhappiness with sore heads and bellies; a little good food was beneficial, but too much led to indigestion and portliness. Live well, but modestly, was the counsel of Epicurus, thereby attaining a state of tranquillity, freedom from fear and absence of bodily pain.

Lopez had cured Walsingham's stones of the kidney, and I was fairly sure was working for Walsingham as a double agent, which was another reason I trusted him. Walsingham was not a man to trust where it was not due. If he was using Lopez to gain intelligence on the King of Spain, the best place for this useful and skilled man was right next to me; a front for his work.

Besides, I liked Lopez.

"Can I make anything up for you, Majesty?" he asked, his dark eyes roaming over my pale face. "Perhaps a draught to aid slumber?"

"You think I look tired, doctor?" I asked, a teasing note in my voice. I found Lopez really rather attractive. He had the dark looks I warmed to in men, and I found his intelligence added to my affection.

"Your Majesty teases," he said, smiling. "For you know you are the spring rain, beautiful and refreshing, but times are hard, and my spies in the bedchamber have said sleep flees you again, for the great love you have for your people."

"I thought the bedchamber contained only *my* spies," I said.

"I am the guardian of your health, and in that respect alone do your ladies share information, Majesty, and all for love of you."

I knew that to be the truth. Were they passing on secrets about my health or anything else, *to* anyone else, they would be dismissed or imprisoned, and they knew it.

"I admit sleep is no friend to me, as you know it often is not," I said, "but no draughts, even mild ones. I need my wits."

"I understand," he said. "I have a few tonics for strength in body and mind, and to calm the nerves but not dull them. I will instruct your ladies which are which, and when you want them they are here, ready to use, or not to use, depending on how you feel."

That was what I liked most about my doctor. Many doctors insist they know best and batter you into consuming vile potions. Lopez trusted me to know myself.

"Leave them with Mistress Parry," I said. "If I need them I shall take them."

"And if your good Master Raleigh, Captain of the Gentlemen Pensioners, thinks it safe, might I recommend a walk in the gardens?"

"Raleigh is not at court. He is in the West Country," I told the doctor, thinking of my Water.

He was in Cornwall, entrusted with the defence of that county and Devon, which would possibly be the front line of Spain's invasion. He had not been merry about his command, thinking he should have been in Drake's position, but no matter how fond I was of Raleigh, I knew he was no match for Drake at sea.

"You are more soldier than sailor," I had said to him, and it was true. He found being on a ship taxing, and did not sleep, as he had often told me. Although tied by blood to sea dog families like the Gilberts and Drakes, Raleigh had more experience as a soldier, from his time in Ireland. His largest contribution to the fleet had been to send his ship the *Ark Raleigh* to me on loan. Renamed the *Ark Royal*, Howard had taken it as the fleet's flagship. Raleigh was concerned that, sent west, he would see little action if the Armada and Parma landed near London. He wanted to place himself in the thick, in a position of command preferably at sea, where he could reap glory.

But I needed men where most they were needed, not where they wanted to be. At times, in the lead up to the Armada being sighted, I had often felt I was commanding a great gang of boys playing war, rather than grown men.

And my faith in Raleigh's soldiering abilities was well-placed. Unwilling though he had been to go, he had done a good job in the south-west of England. He had sent reports about men and arms he had mustered and positioned. From Cape Cornwall to the Tamar, Raleigh had men and guns ready.

His appointment as Lieutenant of Cornwall had not aided his popularity at court. Many hated him, and only more so now for this prime position in my army. But Raleigh knew the West Country, it was the place of his birth, and he knew how to use the terrain if the need arose. He sent reports which warmed me, saying where the Tamar might be forded, what towns needed the most men, like Newbridge. He knew better than others where Cornwall was weak and strong, and upon arrival on the tip of England's foot had set to work, ensuring the poor plans laid out by people who did not know the territory were put right. At the end of many of his letters was his motto; *Nec mortem peto, nec finem fugio, I neither seek out death, nor flee from the end.*

When Lopez left, Cecil came with reports.

Men had started to dribble into Tilbury, reinforced by three hundred gunners and pioneers. The force Hunsdon had was better than Robin's, but still not what we had hoped.

"Sadly, madam, false alarms are breaking out everywhere, hues and cries raised with no purpose, and London is busy, half the merchants sealing their shops and houses with wood, and the other half still trying to trade." Cecil sighed, passing a weary hand over his sweating brow.

I smiled at him. I had no doubt much was carrying on as normal. Some merchants would not miss a day's wage even if the end of all days was upon us. In Cheapside some traders would still be there, people wandering through the sea of timber stalls buying meat, vegetables and herbs. Moneylenders might be busy, with men needing coin to purchase weapons, some being sold from the Tower armoury. Other merchants knew they could charge higher prices for their stock, since they might be one of few trading that day. Some men do not hold back from turning profit, even or especially in times of war.

And some had tasks to do that could not wait because of war. Some would carry on as normal in the hope it would hold off the enemy.

The Conduits, Little and Great, would have people still flocking to them with leather vessels in their arms, queuing for water. Taverns and inns would have men in them, drinking ale and beer, some using tobacco in long white pipes, an act called *drinking* the smoke. This herb had come from the New World. It was a common sight now to see soft white smoke mingle with that coming from fires in inns. People claimed the brown herb held much benefit for the health, but I held with those who said it made the breath stink like the piss of a fox, and some doctors said it was harmful, causing sterility and fevers. It was also expensive. Pipes had small bowls, and were often shared between men.

Preachers would be in the streets, shouting the evils of Spain at the people, calling on them to repent before death came. From prisons the voices of inmates would still be heard crying out through grilles on the walls, begging for bread from passers-by. At the edges of the city people would be just starting to gather the first apples from orchards dripping with the lingering rain of the night before, and with fat, juicy fruit.

Kitchens would be preserving food, worried cooks toiling over thick, fragrant steam to make dinner for their masters that night, listening to rumours of the Armada as they came to the door on the lips of maids bringing in eggs from the gardens and fish and meat from markets. Livestock still had to be tended, fires still needed to be lit. Life demands that it go on, even in the worst of times.

"We are to keep ten thousand men in London to defend you, madam, and send the rest to Tilbury or the south coast. We think to muster twenty-seven thousand at Tilbury eventually, and two and a half thousand horse."

"And you have that number?"

"We will." Cecil sounded more confident than he looked. "The Earl has a certain ten thousand at Tilbury, and more are marching to him. There is a sad lack of provisions, and we have told men they must bring food and drink." Cecil checked his rustling stack of papers. "At your command, most militia are to serve in their own counties, and those counties will pay for their food, training, wages and weapons."

"Men defending their homes fight fiercely," I said.

"And the boom to bar the Thames, built by Giambelli, is up, madam. It is made of around one hundred small ships, their masts bound with chains and tethered with cables. They are fitted with gunpowder set to explode if required. If the Armada comes sailing up the Thames, we will destroy and disable their ships with this."

I nodded. Fedrigo Giambelli was an Italian who had made a name for himself in the Low Countries by creating fireships which, although a common feature in naval battles, had been rammed with so many explosives that his had been dubbed *Hell-Burners*. At one battle Giambelli had terrified the seasoned troops of Parma and even injured the formidable general himself when the shock of the explosion threw Parma to the ground. In that battle, metal and fire had rained from the heavens, killing almost one thousand men.

At my request, he had come to England to use his considerable skills in our defence. In addition to his trap of ships crafted into a boom across the Thames, he had advised on other defences. Cannon had been positioned along the banks of the Thames to fire from land. The other Thames defence was a galley at the mouth of the Medway which commanded the Thames approaches. William Borough, the captain, was really there simply to give advance warning of the Armada, and would fire shots to signal if they were sighted to give Giambelli time for any last tasks on the boom. Borough would hold the Medway for as long as he could, then block the channel by scuttling his ship.

"What of the Armada, and our ships? Does Howard send word?" I asked.

"This morning the first letters came," Cecil said. "The fleet were almost caught in Plymouth, wind and tide against them, but managed to warp from port, heading into the seas. They have engaged more than once, but although our ships are faster and, Howard writes, have superior guns, they are doing little damage. Three Spanish ships have been damaged, two captured, but we have lost none."

"That is something," I said. "What of fortifications on the south coast?"

"Castles and gun batteries are being manned, but with many of the able men called to the militia there are old men serving where younger should."

"As long as they can light a fuse, I am satisfied for the aged to serve their country," I said. "But if a force lands this is the worst time, or the best for them." It was almost harvest. An incoming army would find plenty to feed themselves with.

"We will burn crops, rather than let Spain take them."

"Light not the fires too soon, old friend. When we send those ships flying home, we will need food to last through the winter." I grinned at him.

Cecil returned my smile. "People are working to rebuild old fortifications," he went on. "Ditches have been cleared and deepened, people are working on London's city walls, the older parts especially, and the men of Yarmouth write they have completed the great wall, now forty feet wide, and topped with a rampart. They say it will withstand any battery."

He paused, his face becoming unsure. "What is it?" I asked. "This is not the time for secrets, Spirit."

"Walsingham greatly fears a Catholic rebellion from within," he said.

"He does every other Tuesday," I said dryly.

"It would be a time for one, if ever one there will be," Cecil said. "The Pope's bull of excommunication and his later revision of it said that Catholics of England could wait until your overthrow comes, but when it comes, they are commanded to rise. Many will think this the time, madam. The danger is greater than before."

I nodded. Although most of the time I would fight such ideas to the end, I could see the sense in this thought. Most Catholics had no wish to overthrow me, I knew. I was their Queen even if Rome was their faith, but the Pope's commands had been explicit. Many might well think this was the time they were destined to rise against me.

"What does Walsingham want to do?" I asked.

"He wants to send men into the houses of known Catholics on more raids. If lords of each shire are told to increase their raids, they will, knowing the threat posed to us."

"I want no hysteria leading to killings," I said. "Nor do I want more people in gaol than I already have. If raids increase, they must be done on sure evidence that the house and people within are a threat. Only the most dangerous will be rounded up. The law-abiding will be left alone. No petty squabbles are to be settled using this as an excuse, and no religious madness, Cecil. Send my officers out with clear instructions."

"It will be done, Majesty."

"And no abuse. I want peaceful Catholics protected. I will not have mob rule running free, pulling people from their houses to be murdered in the streets. No Bartholomew's in England, Cecil. The people are afraid, and fear makes men do rash and strange acts. The Watch are to be on their guard for abuses."

"Do you not think the enemy without and within should be watched first, madam?"

"I think the enemy of madness, in whatever form it comes, needs our attention, Spirit. I want no dangerous ecstasy falling upon England. Rebellion would be perilous, indeed, but crazed slaughter of our own people in an attempt to ward off that threat is just as bad." I rose, thinking I would take Lopez's advice and walk. I was growing twitchy.

"Keep the peace as we prepare for war," I said as I stood. "I will not have us fall apart at the moment we need to stand together."

Chapter Eleven

Portland Bill
July 23rd 1588

Death

At Portland Bill, off the Dorset coast, the wind had shifted. The calm of night was gone, and the Spanish ships had been handed the advantage of the weather-gage, many said by God. Sidonia felt it was time; thus far the English appeared to have stolen all favours from on high.

A stiff north-east wind blew, but as men called down information on the English fleet from the topsails, Sidonia knew the English would already be altering tactics based on the change of wind.

Howard, too, was thinking of his fellow Admiral. He thought Sidonia would head for Weymouth, a deep water port. But something else he knew beyond mere supposition. His men knew the wind. Off the south coast of England, summer winds hold a tradition as deep and ingrained as those people keep. At dawn, a land breeze blows, fading to calm as the sun rises. The wind then swings, coming about, and south-westerlies blow from sea to land, the ocean reaching out to caress the shore. These winds continue until evening when the sea breeze roams from its mistress, the land, and the wind calms again. Then the land, missing the sea, reaches out with the hand of the wind, making a land breeze fall upon the waves. Sidonia might have charts of the water, but he did not know the temper of the wind. Howard and his men did. And they would use it.

Sidonia was having problems with one of his captains. He had sent orders for Hugo de Moncada to assault the leading English ships that would come against them. Moncada refused. Perhaps still irritated that he had not been permitted to attack Howard when the English Admiral had been at his heels, Moncada declined the honour, saying he should be set against Howard and no man lower than the Admiral. This led to a delay.

Scenting hesitation on the wind, Howard took action. He sailed to the landward side of the Spanish fleet with his squadron, hoping to gain the weather-gage and drive them from Portland Bill, but his way was blocked, defended by the squadron of Bertendona on the *Regazona* and Sidonia on the *San Martin*.

That was when Sidonia unleashed the formation of the Armada. The wind in their mighty sails, the crescent opened forming a line, bearing down on the English squadron, using the favourable wind to drive their huge, powerful ships.

Howard swung into attack at close quarters, much closer than before. The distance between enemy squadrons closed so tight that muskets could be used. Volleys of gunfire sounded on each side. The pop of muskets firing and the great boom of cannon filled the air. Soon the clamour of battle was upon them again, like a nightmare that comes one night and returns ever after, haunting the dreamer. Blazing darts, shards of ship and hull flew into faces, and impaled breasts and throats. Signal fires sent up by captains went unseen; all was smoke and fire. Under them the waters shook, and above the heavens bellowed with the echoing howl of guns.

Gunners worked in a dark chaos, their only view of what was going on outside brief snatches of sight through gunports. Cannon fired, rocketing backwards as fire and smoke burst from their dark mouths. They were hauled back, men screaming orders which went unheard under the din of guns firing. As they swabbed and reloaded, eyes pouring with tears from the pain of the smoke, their mouths and lungs full of ash, their heads full of terrors, another ball was loaded, and it began again.

Men on deck could see the crimson and grey burst of cannon shot from below, smoke erupting from enemy ships, the plumes of crystal water rocketing into the skies as shot missed, hitting the sea. They heard the dead, dread thud of shot battering into wood, into hull, fracturing oar, whizzing through sail. There was the cracking lash of severed stays whipping the wind, the awful grinding crunch of masts damaged, threatening to fall, the gasping wheeze of sails punctured, whistling in the wind.

And under this was screaming; men shrieking orders, boys screaming in pain, the gurgling groans of the injured, the wretched rattle of the dying.

Howard returned from the landward side, tacking to come about the southern flank along with Hawkins. Behind them came many vessels, pursuing the *Ark* as she turned seaward, swiftly opening the space between them. As they came seaward, the battle fell into a disorder of skirmishes.

Ships of Spain did not move as the English did. Their slow pace was terrifying to their men. A ship under attack less than a mile away might take half an hour to reach. Many Armada ships were not skilled at sailing into the wind, their forecastles too high. Slaves below deck rowed hard when commanded, trying to achieve speed at close quarters as shot whipped into their ships, their bodies and oars, destroying their seats and sending arrows of wood flying into their lips, their throats, their thighs. From above they heard the sounds of battle, but they could see nothing but the oar in front of them.

Spanish ships tried to grapple, but each time the English ships pranced playfully out of the way. And still guns pounded, and still smoke rose and still men screamed. Soldiers, standing in line at battle stations, armed with pike and musket waited for a time they might do something, might act, but they remained where they were, useless in this battle.

The sun headed high into the skies. The wind started to change. Swinging to the south-west, it sent both fleets heading for Lyme Bay.

Battle raged in the centre, the *San Martin* and Howard's *Ark Royal* in the core of the chaos. On the two flanks more battles were being fought. On the landward side, cutting to St Alban's, was Frobisher. His huge *Triumph* and her squadron of armed merchantmen of London had taken up position on the tidal race by five of that morning, south of Portland Bill. Any attempt the Armada made to head to Weymouth would be blocked by him.

Moncada and his galleasses went against Frobisher, who seemed to have run into difficulties. To watchers on the hillsides it looked as though Frobisher and his merchant ships had dropped anchor, unable to shift. It seemed the captain was waiting for the weather-gage so he might rejoin battle on the westward side.

But Frobisher was not in trouble.

Frobisher had sailed these waters for a decade. He had often based himself on the Isle of Wight, using it to launch attacks on ships sailing between the Baltic and the North Sea, between Spain and the Mediterranean. He knew the coast, the rocks, the tide, the perilous banks of shifting sand, and most importantly the two large bays that Portland Bay becomes, containing strong eddies on both flow and ebb tides. The Bill has sharp, steep slopes that continue under the waves. Frobisher knew this.

And he knew the Portland Race.

The Portland Race is a tidal rip, perhaps the mightiest on the south coast of England. From the tip of Portland Bill it runs along the steep, underwater slopes towards a bank of sand, grit and broken shell hidden underwater to the east, called the Shambles. Here, the water becomes treacherously shallow.

The Race achieves seven knots at peak tide, the eddy moving at one knot in the opposite direction. The invisible line separating these flows is sudden; one moment the current runs one way and a second later it flows in the opposite direction. And the Race, like all water, keeps her secrets well, for there is no sign on the water's surface of the power and flow lurking beneath. This was what Frobisher would use when it was time, but first, he would use the current to hold ships away from the main battle, and inflict damage.

Knowing the force of the current was dangerous to the low-waisted galleasses, Frobisher watched them come, holding in the eddy where he looked immobile. His ship had been selected for this role, as the *Triumph* was the best ship in the English fleet to avoid the risk of being boarded, for it had high fore and stern castles, built to repel men, like ships of the Armada. But Frobisher did not intend to be boarded.

Positioned in the eddy, looking motionless and trapped by still, calm water, Frobisher appeared a snared hare; a tempting, easy prize. The Spanish came, but their galleasses struggled immediately in the changeable waves, vortexes rising in the water where competing currents of the Race clashed. Spanish captains watched the high cliffs nearby and the water beneath, fearing it was shallow and they would be beached. But just offshore there was deep water, which Frobisher knew. Galleasses swept into the powerful, erratic current, struggling against its potent vigour. They were thrown back, time and time again, their oars no match for the water. Pitching and tossing, ships swinging dangerously side to side, they were swamped with water. The current swept them away from Frobisher, and each time they came back, trying to get to the *Triumph*, Frobisher and his armed merchants unleashed a rain of cannon fire, cutting through soldiers gathered on the decks, battering hulls and slicing through sails. The return fire of the galleasses did little.

To Sidonia, it looked as though Moncada was refusing to engage the enemy, but Moncada could do nothing. Plunge towards Frobisher recklessly, and his vessels would be swamped.

For an hour and half battle had raged and the wind was still backing. As the tide ebbed, Howard led a squadron of the Queen's galleons and merchantmen into the fray, sending out orders of a fresh assault at close quarters to aid the *Triumph*. Howard thought Frobisher was trapped, for although Frobisher had shared his plans the night before, Howard was not as well-versed in the seas as his man. He thought Frobisher was truly in trouble. Sidonia, seeing Howard's move, made to intercept with sixteen ships. Recalde suddenly found himself alone yet again, surrounded by the enemy and fighting more than a dozen ships with no aid from the fleet. Realising his mistake, Sidonia sent ships back to aid the *San Juan*, but the Admiral sailed on to confront Howard.

Sidonia went after the *Ark*, splitting the English fleet in two. Howard had been forced to go about, turn east towards the sea. The wind was with Spain, and the English Admiral was struggling leeward. Now was the time for Sidonia's attack. But he could not close; his ships were too slow even with the wind in their sails.

By chasing the English Admiral, Sidonia lost the advantage. Had Sidonia sent ships after Frobisher, Howard would have had to turn and fight on Sidonia's terms. As it was, Sidonia ended up surrounded.

Howard slipped away, but he could not outflank Sidonia, nor could he aid Frobisher as more ships broke away, sailing to attack him. The two flagships veered close and the *San Martin* turned to Howard's *Ark*, lowering her topsail; a challenge to fight Admiral to Admiral. To the broadside of Howard's ship, Sidonia was offering a chance to grapple, to engage hand-to-hand, to decide this battle as gentlemen. Howard did not accept. He delivered a ferocious broadside into the *San Martin*, and his line of ships did the same. Each ship, the *Ark*, the *Elizabeth Jonas*, the *Victory*, the *Leicester* , the *Marie*

Rose, the *Dreadnaught*, the *Golden Lion* and the *Swallow* flew past the *San Martin*, firing all guns. The English squadron came about, thundering a second then third broadside into the *San Martin* as Sidonia's men struggled to respond. English fire was continuous. The Spanish answer was a stammer.

Fighting alone for more than an hour, Sidonia and his ship were lost in a fug of gunsmoke. Sidonia could only use one side of his ship's guns, and he was alone in a tumult of noise and mayhem of smoke. Howard pressed closer and closer. Hoping to do more damage, he dared to dance almost within grappling distance. Five hundred shots were launched at Sidonia's ship, but his men, fighting with unwieldy cannon, could only return eighty. Sidonia's flagstaff fell, as did one of the stays of the main mast.

The papal-blessed standard billowing from the topsail was tattered as a pauper's tunic. Sidonia knew he was in trouble, his masts were badly damaged, yards splintered and the rigging had ripped, hanging over the ship like the cloak of death. The ship was taking on water, fast. The dead and dying were sprawled across the deck and spaces below. Iron joined ash in the wind; a scent of blood and fire dancing in the skies.

Out to sea, Drake appeared from the pall of black smoke, his squadron launching a vicious, downwind attack on the Armada. Like an eagle they soared into the fight, using the wind, which was rising as the heat of the sun rained upon the sea. From westward they came, assaulting the Spanish fleet so quickly and brutally that ships were forced to give way. Under the onslaught, the wing faltered as vessels tried to hide behind each other. Some went to Sidonia's aid, clustering about his ship, trying to shelter him. Collisions were heard, ships rocking and crashing into one another. The wind shifted, sending men to scale rigging to unfurl sails. Ships pitched and tossed as men dodged shot and musket fire raining through the sails as they tried to do their desperate task.

The wind was in the south-west, pushing both fleets away from Portland Bill, across Lyme Bay. It allowed Oquendo to lead a line of galleons to his master's rescue. Frobisher chose this moment to rejoin the fleet. Using the Portland Race, he pulled clear from his assailants. As Frobisher returned, the English fleet pulled back from Sidonia and from battle and stood out to sea, shifting with such speed and grace that Spanish captains stared in awe.

"It is as though we remain at anchor, as the English are granted wings to fly," Valdes muttered.

It was five of the clock, and for almost twelve hours they had fought. Howard and his men had driven Sidonia and the Armada past Weymouth.

Portland and Weymouth were beyond reach to the Armada now. The wind had turned against them, but ahead was the Isle of Wight and the Solent. These, both Admirals knew, were vulnerable and worthy targets. Howard thought Sidonia would head for the Isle of Wight. It was what he would do. The Isle was not large, but neither was it small, and it would be easily defeated with the thousands of soldiers Sidonia had.

Battered but not yet broken, the Armada resumed the crescent formation, heading east towards the Isle of Wight as aboard the damaged vessels carpenters worked with furious haste to repair holes. No ships had been lost. The Armada had been assaulted and herded once again, but not defeated.

And behind them came English ships, almost undamaged, and as they came, they continued to snip and lash at the tails of the enemy, their guns snarling; dogs upon the sea.

From Howard, pinnaces and barques raced to shore to collect more gunpowder and shot. Fresh supplies came out from Weymouth, Lyme and Portsmouth, many of them barrels stripped from the *Rosario* and *Salvador*.

As the two fleets headed east, captains were ferried across to meet their Admirals.

"We cannot close!" Recalde cried, infuriated. "Each time they slip away, as though we are standing still and they are dancing."

Sidonia glared, well aware what Recalde said was true. There was small chance they would destroy or drive off the English fleet before they reached Parma. Even when they had the wind, Spanish ships could not close upon the English. All the way to Parma, the enemy would be on their heels, biting chunks from their ships as they came. The English could outflank them with ease, and gain the weather-gage without any issue, it seemed.

"And their cannon, how do they fire so many shots in so little time?" asked Moncada. "Their guns are more accurate, and have more power than ours; they are three times as fast! And ours are unreliable."

That, too, was true. On the *San Salvador*, another ship bearing the same name as the one abandoned, gunners had been killed as cannon exploded whilst they were reloading. Fire waiting inside had ignited the new powder cartridge, and it had blown the cannon to bits from the inside, but although this was a mistake, self-inflicted harm, other cannon, the iron brittle, had ruptured under the force of powerful gunpowder. Men were dead, others badly burned. Doctors on board the ships were fighting to keep ahead of the wounded. That day had been the first that all Sidonia's captains had reported lost men.

"Yet small damage again was done to our ships," said Sidonia. "My ship, surrounded and alone for more than an hour had but a few holes to be plugged and a flagstaff missing."

"But they bite, my lord," said Recalde. "They bite again and again, chewing at us. They were not badly damaged either."

"We must continue on course," Sidonia told his men. "The English mean to delay us, but they will not succeed. As we sail, we will take formation as a block, with a van and rearguard."

"What of Parma, my lord?" asked Valdes. "Is there word?"

"There is not," Sidonia said.

"We must consider capturing the Solent," said Recalde, who had studied charts, spare though they were, sent by Phillip. "General Parma may be delayed or under attack by the Dutch. Until we have word of him, we remain insecure. If we have to wait for Parma's barges off the coast of Kent, we will be vulnerable. We might face assault from east and west. It would be better to hold the Solent, my lord, a defensible anchorage protected from the vile English weather, and attempt to land on one of the beaches of the Isle of Wight. We could re-provision there too, for we are lacking food and water."

Sidonia had thought the same. "If the Isle looks promising, we will take it," he said. "Watch for my signal."

On Howard's ship, the mood was also not bright. The way they saw it, although the Armada had been driven from Portland and Weymouth, this day had been a victory for Sidonia. They had done no more than harass the Spanish ships; even drawing in closer had not inflicted the damage needed.

"We cannot get close enough," said Drake. "For an hour you assaulted the *San Martin*, my lord, and although the wounded will be many, the ship itself continues on. My assault into the Armada battered them, but no more ships have fallen into our hands."

"And each day that passes brings the Armada closer to Parma," said Howard, fingers thick with grime running through his beard. "If we cannot splinter the fleet, they will keep on course and we will have failed."

From both fleets that night messengers headed out, over the moonlit water. Howard sent men begging for more gunpowder and shot and Sidonia dispatched another pinnace into the sea, in another desperate attempt to contact Parma, telling him he *must* have his troops upon their boats and ready to sail, for with the English on their tail the Armada would not be able to tarry long before they assaulted them. Howard's letter warned that without more powder and shot the English fleet could not possibly succeed.

Both Admirals slept little that night, fear, like the moonlight, drifting upon their faces.

Chapter Twelve

Richmond Palace
July 24th 1588

Elizabeth

Grey light crested over me, chilled yet carrying a promise of warmth. In my nightgown and a fur-lined cape to protect me from the early morning mist, I walked in the gardens of Richmond.

Guards lined the paths as at my heel my women walked. Some ladies wore furs like me, warding off the crisp early morning air, but my clothes were sparer than theirs. Not scandalous; the nightgown I wore was long and thick, as was the cloak, and often I received visitors in them, as many people did, but I liked to feel air on my skin.

I needed to be outdoors. The close confines of the palace, the hangings about my bed… during the night they closed upon me like a fist. I often felt this way within buildings, as though the terrors of my youth became as one with the bricks of my houses. At times I felt them suffocating me; a pillow pressed against my face in the dead of night. That morning I was even more aware of the feeling of something of dread closing, doom drawing close, the icy breath of Death upon the nape of my neck.

They did not want me outside. My Council, Cecil and Walsingham, even Robin writing his many notes from Tilbury all warned me to stay inside, to stay safe. I ignored them. Stay inside and I would fall to madness.

An hour amongst the flowers, air and paths and I returned to break my fast and to be dressed. Washing in rose-scented water, I was dried as the ceremony of dressing began. At that time more than others, it felt I was donning armour as I was sewn inside my glorious clothes, as though I were putting on a helmet as paint and powder was plastered on my face. Perhaps all women feel this way at times, that the clothes we wear and the mask we put upon our face protects us from a world that judges the woman hiding beneath, that we may become another person by wearing certain clothes, one able to deflect all condemnations and slanders. Perhaps men feel that way too; armour, after all, is heavy and often hinders men in battle as much as it protects. Perhaps we all seek to hide, transforming the outside shell so the fragile one within will rest safe, hidden from the world.

As I was sewn into my gown, so it was tight about my lithe willow-waist and small breasts, I thought of the men flying about England, gathering munitions to send to our ships. News had come of the first fight off Plymouth, and of the next day. But information is a slow traveller. Rumour is faster; she jumps ahead like a Turkish charger, bounding out of mouths. Some said Drake was dead; others claimed the fleet was lost. From reports heading up the coast, we knew this was not so, yet still it entered men's minds in London, leading to messages of doom flooding through the capital.

As they dressed me, I sipped ale brewed with malt and water, flavoured with mace and sage. It refreshed my tongue and senses. Blanche offered me mead, but I refused the honey-sweet drink. It was too strong.

I wished I might read, but I knew attempting such a feat would be useless. Reading was one of my greatest pleasures. I turned to books when I wanted to escape the world and when I wanted to understand it, but I knew there was no sense in opening a book. I would be doing the author a disservice, nothing of words or wisdom would I see. I could see only the sea in my eyes.

"What a useless thing it is to read!" I had exclaimed at Blanche that morning, throwing a book I had been vainly trying to read across the room. "For all a person reads in a tome will be lost upon death, so where is the sense in reading? It is a fool's game."

Blanche, knowing how I loved many books more than people, had eyed me steadily. "One might say, madam, that all we do in life, then, is senseless."

"One might," I grumbled.

"Many of the most foolish things in life are what makes it rich," she said. "We dare to love, knowing all life is transient. We dance knowing we might slip and crack our bones. We eat, knowing we will be hungry again in a matter of mere hours." She smoothed the front of her gown. "The greater the fool we are willing to be, the richer and more varied is the life we will have. Perhaps the happiest of us all is one who can look back when the shadow of death falls to say, 'Fool I was, and happy to have been so blessed'."

In silence I had gone, feeling like a scolded child, picked up my poor book and restored it to a shelf. I should not be punishing my library for my present state of terrified agitation.

If anticipation of a welcome event is the true source of happiness, as often I had thought, waiting for something ill is the root of all misery. It is so easy to imagine only the worst outcome, and at that time there were many for me, personal and political; the overthrow of my country, the arrival of a gloating Phillip of Spain, or potentially worse, merely his daughter. If Isabella arrived it would be another insult to men of England, demonstrating that Phillip did not consider England worthy enough to come in person.

My people would be subjugated, the faith of England destroyed, forced to bow once more before the skirts of the Bishop of Rome. I would be cast into prison, a fate I had avoided since I was a young maid, but this time I would be old, shorn of all the clothes and paint, trappings and adornments which I relied upon now to present a fortified, magnificent pageant of immortality to my people. I would no more be their standard. They would have nothing to believe in if I was paraded, bare-headed and naked-faced before them. The lie I told of youth and eternity would be unmasked. They would see the old woman I had become.

With my humiliation would come that of England. Our country would have no will, no chance, no choices. England's men forced to surrender, her children captured for the faith and whims of a foreign prince; and her women? We were, none of us, unaware of what happened to women when a foreign army landed. As though the subjugation of the female body may come to represent that of the nation, women are raped and brutalised. That fate was in the eyes of many of my ladies. They, like me, would rather have died.

Death might come for me at last, perhaps in a prison cell, perhaps on a block like my cousin. Would I burn for my faith? I doubted Phillip would trust any conversion protested by my lips in an attempt to survive.

And yet, here we all were, going on as normal, pretending today and yesterday, tomorrow and what would come after were as they had always been. What else could we do?

The machine of government, too, continued. Hatton, my Lord Chancellor, went on with his work, hearing cases in chancery each Monday, Tuesday and Friday, using lawyers more proficient than he to counsel him. Hatton was the symbol of my royal justice and called himself not only the mouthpiece of the monarchy, as others did, but the *conscience*. He was a good Chancellor, protective of my reputation and of that of my Church. He was also a good administrator, handy in these days of chaos where so little order lived.

Despite the still-prevailing disorder with our armed forces, with men marching to join Robin, Hunsdon sending men to the coast and every scrap of useable armour and weapons being gathered, even from farmer's fields, Walsingham's men seemed more ordered. Known Catholics in many shires, particularly about London, had been rounded up and sent either into prison or house arrest. The chief suspects amongst Catholics, including men of high birth, had been sent to Ely. Lord Vaux had been one of the few who had not been sent, because his health was so poor. I had insisted all who had been detained be treated with dignity. Right though I thought this, there was another reason. If England fell, it might be well to have imprisoned Catholics remember they had been treated fairly.

The other possibility which might bring about internal mayhem was not so much an organised rebellion as a massacre. To my mind, this could erupt from either side of our religious divide. Protestants riled by the stench of terror floating upon England might decide to start killing Catholics before they turned on them. The same was true of Catholics. It was all so easy; just a flip in a mind and friend would become foe. As much for the danger they presented as the danger *to them* were Catholics held away from the rest of the people.

Foreigners had also been told to stay within their homes, under risk of imprisonment.

The English were a curious race when it came to people from other lands. Foreigner could mean a man of another country, or just of another town. Men of other countries were more often named *aliens*. Some welcomed our new adopted children, refugees from war-torn lands, and understood they had brought new skills, trades and benefits to England. Some blamed them for stealing away English jobs and homes, which was ludicrous. Most had come with their own trades, ones not seen in England before, and many more had built their own homes. People like having someone to blame for the troubles in their lives, and the easiest person to blame is a stranger, for on his back they can heap all their woes and grievances with the world without need for sense or reason.

There were many unhelpful suppositions about aliens, even from the friendly. The French were foppish dandies who spent all day fanning themselves with lace and eating cream. The Dutch were boorish brutes who could not be trusted. Italians would much rather stab a man through the eye than speak to him, and Turks, too, lusted for blood as a man in the desert longs for water. Moors were creatures of incurable carnal sensuality who chatted with the Devil most days. The Flemish were unendingly intoxicated.

Not only for men of other countries was slander invented; the Cornish were terrible cooks and made undrinkable beer; those from Devon were ignorant bumpkins; the Welsh were thieves all and the Irish unsalvageable in their perpetual poverty. My favourite slander was one aimed at the Polish. They ate honey all the time, it was said. Quite why that was a crime, I knew not.

I sighed, knowing many of my adopted children would be unhappy, thinking I did not trust them even though they had done nothing wrong. Trust I wanted to have in all my people, but I could not. If rebellion came England was lost.

If we could get through this, hold off the Armada without my people turning on one another, it would be a double miracle. England was a tinderbox. One spark and we would destroy ourselves without the need for Phillip to lift a finger.

Another reason for the foreign citizens of England to stay inside was their stories. Now that all knew the Armada was here, hearing tales of the bloodthirsty acts of Spain might not be helpful. Some fear I needed in my people, but not too much. Enough to fight but not enough to fight *anyone* was the level of terror I wanted in my kingdom; no easy balance to strike.

"But I have always been good at balance," I muttered.

"Did you say something, Majesty?" asked Kate, pausing as she dressed me.

I shook my head. "No, nothing."

Kate's eyes flickered to Bess Throckmorton, who was under my arm, pinning a sleeve to the rest of my gown. I could not see Bess's eyes, but I knew they might hold confusion. It was not unusual for my ladies to find me talking to myself, but always it unnerved them. It was not the only trait I kept that worried them. My eyes, short of sight, often might seem as though they were fixed on one person when I was, in fact, staring at a blur behind them, thinking of something else. Robin always said that when I stared at someone it was as though I could spy into the core of their soul. John Dee had told me this was an effect of the fading power of my black eyes. They had never been strong at long distances, and were growing weaker with age. *Perhaps it will make the end easier,* I thought, *if, like a seeled hawk transported for hunting, I cannot see what is coming.*

As I stood, dressed and ready, Blanche arrived with a note from Robin. "I read here that the Earl has almost seventeen thousand men now," I said to my women, "as well as six thousand at Sandwich, also under his command." I glanced up at them. "He says many are men of experience, good soldiers."

I had been relaying messages to my ladies as I received them, where I was able to without compromising security. Numbers can be comforting, particularly when they grow rather than fall. As my men shied away from telling me the whole truth, however, I did the same to younger women in my household. They did not need to fear more than they already did.

Cecil and Walsingham came that morning. "Seymour and Wynter send word that they are holding fast near Dover, but the weather is not aiding them," said Cecil. "They need more supplies. Seymour says they will run out of food at the end of the month, and they need more powder and shot too."

"They are not engaging the enemy at the moment, are they?" I asked, my heart leaping in panic.

"There has been a slight engagement, but nothing continual," Cecil said. "I have a report here to inform Your Majesty of it."

My heart was still racing, but blood flooded as warm, soothing water through me as relief entered my soul with his words. "Food we will endeavour to find, although London is almost stripped bare, but powder and shot must go to Howard and Drake."

"The seized ships have been stripped, I have been told, and that powder and shot is on the way to them."

"I told you our men would find ways to get what they need." Perhaps my tone was too smug, for Cecil did not look pleased. "Send what we can," I said.

It would be little, I knew. The harvest was approaching but was not gathered in. London was almost bare. Water was easy enough to find but barrels were growing short. Ale took time to brew and spoiled with fair speed.

"Seymour complains he needs more ships," Cecil said. "He has been forced to send some vessels to guard cloth merchants on their way to Stade, but for want of provisions has had to dispatch other ships to port."

"Check with London merchants to see if they have any ships to send, and of the ones in port get them stocked with anything we have and sent out again." I paused. "But enough of his complaints. What of this engagement Seymour spoke of?"

"He writes that they chased two ships which emerged from Dunkirk. The ships would not strike their sails when challenged, so he and Wynter went for them, teeth bared. They turned out to be French ships operating with permits from the Governor of Calais, but the chase Seymour gave them when they refused to strike sail was magnificent. One crew abandoned ship, as it was stuck in a sandbank. The other struck sail in fright after Seymour and Wynter brought down their mainmast."

"Even if the ships were peaceful, that will give Parma something to chew on," I said, thinking with satisfaction that the General might understand now he would have a hard task shipping men across the Channel to us.

"We are having problems with Parma," Walsingham interjected. "It seems, in order to disguise the amounts of his troops and their exact position, he has scattered them. My spies know not their numbers."

"But when he brings them together, they will be in large barges, not in warships," I said. This snippet of information had been floating about for months. "And the speed and violence Wynter and Seymour demonstrated in this attack will tell Parma how vulnerable his men are."

"Let us hope that is the case, Majesty, and is enough to put him off."

"But the spring tide is coming," Cecil warned. "That will offer a favourable crossing from France or Flanders."

"What weapons and men does Robin have now?" I asked. I did not want to think of the benefits being offered to Parma by the weather.

"Seventeen thousand men, perhaps two thousand horse. They have just over a thousand muskets, eight hundred halberds, three thousand pikes and one and a half thousand bows."

Cecil reeled the numbers from his list. "But food is a problem, as is beer."

Beer *was* a problem. Soldiers sent into Spain by my father had mutinied when their beer ran out. "Send out orders again that troops marching to Tilbury *must* carry their own provisions, including beer," I said. "And enlist every ale wife in London to brew more."

"There are issues about strategy," said Cecil. "Norris says all effort should be concentrated on Canterbury, as it is the most defensible town and will keep the enemy from London. Sir Thomas Scott disagrees and says troops should be drawn along the Downs, keeping to the shore, so the Armada will see a great show and think our forces larger than they are. Others think contingents should be set all through Kent to make an attempt at resistance if Parma comes."

I closed my eyes for a moment, bewildered. Long had I studied history, battles included, but I was no soldier. Games of politics, battles of wits I had played for years, but I was not experienced enough to make these kinds of decisions. That was why I had selected men who had fought in war to make such choices for me. That they could not agree, and no man could follow another, was likely to send my fragile senses into as much chaos as England was in.

"Robin and Hunsdon are the leaders of the army," I said. "These decisions must be made by them and the Privy Council."

Eventually the Privy Council made the choice. Forces were to be concentrated at inland points. From there they could march *en masse* to defend key areas, as and when soldiers from Spain arrived.

When Cecil told me this, I nodded, but I was disturbed by his wording. *"As and when soldiers from Spain arrive"*…

It seemed there was no more "if".

Chapter Thirteen

The Solent and the Isle of Wight
The English Channel
July 24th 1588

Death

"Today, my lord, God will smile upon us," said Sidonia's servant as he entered the Admiral's cabin bearing a platter of bread, fish stew and cheese. He struggled to keep the pewter plate and bowl steady as his body attempted to roll with the ship.

Sidonia smiled. The sight of food was not welcome, his belly was still troubled by the water and the listing gait of the man carrying his breakfast was not aiding matters, but the thought that the day was blessed was good. It was Saint Dominic's Day; Sidonia's personal patron saint, and one of his distant ancestors. In Spain the date of that day was the 4th of August. In England, where they followed not the new calendar of the Pope and stuck doggedly and heretically to the old one, it was the 24th of July. Sidonia wondered which calendar God chose to follow. Perhaps the Lord of Heaven would bless him, bestowing the grace of his patron saint that day, but if God was with the English, as He seemed often to be in this fight, perhaps not.

Sidonia hoped he could rely on Saint Dominic even if God was clearly of two minds about the outcome of this mission. The saint was also patron to astronomers, and had founded the Dominican Order. A man who much aided the poor and abstained from meat was Dominic, who had been born of a barren mother. She had gone in desperation to the Abbey of Silos, and there had a dream of a dog bounding from her womb carrying a flaming torch, which seemed to set the earth afire. The Dominican Order, *Dominicanus* in Latin, were sometimes called *Domini canis* as a play on words; dog of the Lord.

Sidonia hoped the dog of the Lord would aid him that day against the English sea dogs.

"The men are greatly cheered this morning," said Sidonia's man, placing the plate before him and pouring wine, not soured as the wine other men on board drank, into a silver goblet decorated with the arms of Sidonia's family. "They say, my lord, we will be victorious, for the Saint watches over you this day."

Sidonia hoped that was correct. He had been thinking that they should attempt to anchor in the Solent and take the Isle of Wight. Not knowing what Parma was doing or where he was, Sidonia feared that the fleet would reach Margate only to wait for no purpose. A fleet at anchor was vulnerable. Even he knew that. And he knew of the Solent. Phillip's charts, imperfect though they were, had shown him much of this stretch of coastline. The Solent would be safer than Margate.

The chalk cliffs of the Isle of Wight were steep, and Phillip had written that if they thought to take it they should come from the eastern side, which was wider than the west. The western approach to the Solent, a twenty-mile-long strait between the Isle and English mainland, was rocky and narrow, a danger to ships. The eastern passage offered a place to secure anchor and was sheltered from the weather. There was good fishing there, too, Phillip had said. It had been used in the past. The French had sailed into St Helen's Roads, the eastern side, in 1545, leading to the loss of King Henry's flagship the *Mary Rose*, and Phillip himself had gone there when he came to marry Queen Mary.

The Solent, although shallow compared to some ports, was deep enough for Sidonia's ships, and although it varied in width, the slimmest part being two and a half miles wide and the fattest five, it was sheltered and had a strange tidal system which extended the tidal window, allowing deep-draught ships to linger long within its waters. Once inside the Solent, English ships were less likely to come after them as they would be sailing straight into the entire Armada with but small space to manoeuvre and escape. There would be no more English ships dancing about, speedy in the wind, if they followed him into the Solent.

But there was danger. Waiting on hostile land and with his ships moored between two patches of English territory waiting for news from Parma was not without risk. Even if they took the island, there would be resistance, and Howard and his pirates knew these waters too. They might guess he would try for the Isle.

But Sidonia's spirits lifted as he ate, his belly quietened by food. With no experience he had led men across the seas and had faced the English fleet at the cost of only a few ships. Keeping to tight formation had kept the ships together and they had escaped with only a few bruises from what was, quite clearly, one of the most advanced fleets in terms of ships and guns that the world had witnessed. Although the captains of the English fleet had a disadvantage in that they were not as disciplined as his men, so sometimes their tactics seemed disjointed, the ships of England were to be feared. Many experienced men might have done worse than Sidonia.

And today he might take water from them. Today he might feel earth beneath his feet once more. The thought of that was almost as sweet as the thought of going home.

Sidonia dipped bread into his stew as he thought of the day before. As the Isle of Wight had come within sight, the English had pounded his rear-guard. Drake's ship, now easily recognisable to them all, had headed in particular for one ship, the Gran Grifon, flagship of a squadron of hulks.

The Grifon had been falling behind in the night, exposing her in the dawn light as an easy target. She bore thirty-eight guns, but was a slow, clumsy craft. As the sun had shown her face, her captain had made a fraught attempt to rejoin the fleet, but Drake, tasting blood in the air, was already on him. Drake brought his ship to point blank range and fired. More ships joined him, and they went at her like dogs, firing forty shot into her. The starboard wing of the Armada, led by Recalde and Leyva, had been forced to come about and join the fight.

The *Grifon* had been unable to steer or even move properly. Her rudder was smashed, her guns failing, and her masts and rigging were in poor shape. Men littered her decks. More men fell in that spare hour than in the entire day of fighting the day before.

Sidonia and Oquendo had raced to her rescue, throwing rope aboard to tow the *Grifon*, causing the English to retreat. It was thought Drake's rigging had been slashed, the worst damage he had seen in this conflict. The fact it had been inflicted by a hulk rather than a warship was a touch shameful, and the *Grifon* had taken worse damage in return. Sixty had been wounded, but the English had retreated again to the sea at the beamside. Sidonia struck sails to indicate conflict should continue but the English drew away, maintaining fire from a distance. They appeared to be preparing for something.

Sidonia suspected they were preparing to see them off the Isle of Wight.

When the French had come some forty years before, they had occupied the Isle, so it was possible to seize, and Phillip's intelligence held that it had not many defenders. The English would try to drive him away, but Sidonia thought the Isle was their best chance. His men agreed. The Isle should be captured, and after that they would reach Parma. It was the last place they could stop before Flanders.

With the English holding out at sea and the *Grifon* being towed, Sidonia had sent up flags and fired guns to signal for the Armada to re-form, and they had sailed on. From his ship that day he could see the Isle, and that was not all. Smoke was rising from beacons about its green hillsides, calling men to report to militia bands all over the Isle. There were small boats on the water, ferrying from England to the Isle, no doubt carrying men and munitions. As the Armada sailed east, her new goal in sight, the wind fell to a small breeze, making their progress slow. Sidonia's one comfort that afternoon had been that if the wind was not with him, it was also not with Howard. The English advantage in speed and nimble footwork relied on the wind, and there was little to be had.

As they had come to the Needles, the wind had gone completely. The two fleets had drifted, only a few miles apart but helpless to reach one another. And yet still little boats ran from the Isle to the mainland, powered by oar and muscle. God had granted the Isle of Wight time to order its defences.

As dusk came that night Sidonia had seen that some ships were rowing out to the English fleet. Although he knew it not, they were carrying men who had organised the defences of Devon and Cornwall. Now they were not needed there, they came to aid the fleet and catch a scrap of glory. On boats that came to Howard that day were the Earls of Oxford, Northumberland and Cumberland, Robert and Thomas Cecil, and Sir Walter Raleigh, merry to finally be in the thick of the action.

As night drooped a weary eyelid over the skies, one man, Robert Carey, son of Lord Hunsdon, and Howard's own brother-in-law, was so keen to be in the fight that he did not notice he had sailed out to meet the Armada rather than the English forces. Finally noting in the dawn's light that he was, in fact, racing towards the enemy, his ship turned, and fled.

Some men were not there to fight at all, but simply to get a better view. Sir George Carey, Captain of the Isle of Wight, along with the Earl of Sussex acting Constable of Portchester Castle and the Lord Lieutenants of Hampshire and Dorset set out on boats that morning so they could see what was happening.

Carey had, all night, been riding about the Isle of Wight, checking guards, watchmen, and troops on the headland and beaches. They were to watch and listen for the sound of soft oars in the water, he told them. His main camp was on full alert and patrols were moving across the Isle. He had only three thousand men to defend the Isle, so was hoping Howard would not let the Armada close. This done, Carey had taken to the water, joining other men being ferried out to watch or join the fight.

Howard was in spare need of more men, as few had been lost, and was chagrined to find many of these ships carried no supplies. Still, some fresh men might be good, he thought, for ship's fever was taking some of his sailors, and more were weary. He did send back a contingent of musketeers sent to him, for them he had no need, their weapons of small use to him.

That morning Howard ordered his men into four divisions, each with twenty-five ships and each with purpose. One of the great problems Howard had understood that they had in battle was one captain not knowing what others were up to. There were signals of smoke, shot and flag, but no signal that could convey *every* part of a plan that came to a captain as battle went on. Even signals of flag and gunshot could be obscured by the smoke of battle. Frequently, as Howard had seen, all his men were individuals working to their own plans rather than as a coordinated mass. They were skilled, brave individuals, but as single men standing not as one, they had no hope against the Armada. Howard wanted to limit the chaos he had seen hovering at the edge of their battles and skirmishes. He wanted to instil more discipline. It worked, after all, for the Armada.

The plan for the Isle of Wight was therefore more coordinated than any they had fought thus far and for good reason. They had a time limit. By fall of night the tide and wind would push the Armada past St Helen's Roads and into the Narrows. There was no port for them there. If Sidonia was to take the Isle of Wight, it had to be today.

"We will chase them off, so they cannot anchor in the Solent or land on the Isle," Howard had said to his men the night before, watching a gull preen itself on the outer sill of his cabin window. The gull hunkered down, curling its head about to tuck it between its wings, seeking slumber. "The tide will be in Sidonia's favour from seven of the clock until noon. That is the time of danger, the time he may race into the Solent. After that it will be against him."

"The ships of Spain are not good for racing, my lord," Drake said. A number of men, including Howard, chuckled.

"Tomorrow the sea will have had three days of peak spring tide," said Frobisher. "If we drive him past, it will carry him away even if he has the wind."

"So we attack at first light," Howard said.

Frobisher was promoted, granted a commission as a squadron commander and took the inshore waters as Drake took the seaward wing. Howard and Hawkins claimed the centre.

But as first light came there was no breeze. No wind to use.

Wily Sidonia had set two ships behind the main fleet that dawn, the *San Luis de Portugal* and the *Santa Ana*, the first a royal galleon and the second a merchantman. They were to linger behind as bait, splitting the ships that would fight Sidonia for the Solent. And the English were tempted, but without wind they could not sail upon them to attack.

Hawkins, who was closest, took a risk and towed his ships into range using longboats, only to find three Spanish ships, powered by their formidable oars, bearing upon him. Moncada finally had a chance to use his oars. The *Rata* was towed in behind, bringing her guns upon Hawkins. Musketeers on board fired upon the longships, hoping to kill men before they could row and tow the ship into position.

The *Ark* and the *Golden Lion* were towed into range to support Hawkins. Their longboats too came under fire from musketeers on the Armada, but the English ships used their forward guns and bow-chasers, offering cover for the men heaving upon oar and pulling on cable. Musket balls spattered into water and drummed into the longboats as men heaved English ships into battle formation.

As the ships closed, the longboats hauled the ships' broadsides about to bear upon the Spanish ships. Fire sounded and one English ship had to undergo hasty repairs, but its carpenters toiled and pumps heaved, and the ship was saved. Howard and Lord Thomas Howard were doing better. A Spanish ship began to list, heavily damaged, and another lost her lanterns. A third had, "Its nose blown off!" shouted young Howard, cheering with his men as he watched a galleass's prow shot away.

The wind rose, blowing from the west. Using it, Armada ships rescued the *Santa Ana* and the *San Luis*. Frobisher sailed shoreward as Drake and Hawkins took the seaward wing. Howard sailed to the centre, going for the *San Martin* which was advancing in support of Moncada, with all his guns. Sidonia took fire from many English ships. His mainstay was cut through and men on deck fell, but his rearguard came charging in.

Howard and his men were now using only heavy guns. They could not waste powder on lighter ones; the heavy had more chance of causing destruction. But if they were taking no risks with powder, the English took all others they could. They closed on Spanish ships, not firing until the last possible minute, hoping to inflict real damage.

And there was something else they would do. Frobisher was to be used as bait.

As Sidonia's rearguard came in, Howard and Hawkins retired from the centre of the battle. The fleets were closing on the eastern approaches to the Isle of Wight. If the Armada reached the approach whilst the flood tide was running they would enter with ease, carried by swift flowing water, and behind them the English would not be able to follow. If they did, they would be trapped, fighting at close quarters and would not last against Sidonia's soldiers. Yet if they held off, Sidonia could put men to boats and land on the Isle.

But in two hours the tide would change. In two hours the opportunity would be lost.

Howard's men knew there was a Race there as at Portland, called St Catherine's Race. Some of those waters were more perilous than Portland, for the Isle of Wight possesses rocky cliffs and deep waters common to the West Country combined with the shallows and shoals of the eastern coasts.

Frobisher and his squadron kept inshore. The tide swept the fleets east. The current was faster near the shore, throwing Frobisher to the north and east of the Armada. On the seaward wing, Drake and Howard sailed, waiting for their moment. The *San Martin* became isolated for the second time that day and the English lashed her with gunfire. As the wind came up, Oquendo came to aid Sidonia, but he found the current of the Race so powerful he could not come alongside the *San Martin*. He had to put his ship in front of her. Most of Frobisher's squadron escaped the Spanish attack, but Frobisher's *Triumph* remained, apparently trapped, to leeward. His ship moved strangely in the water, it looked crippled. Guns fired to signal he was in distress and ships near him shifted away, apparently abandoning him.

Sidonia went for him.

What Sidonia did not know was he was about to fall for the same trick, again. The *Triumph* was not moving oddly because it was crippled, but because of the clashing waters of the Race and eddy. Sidonia sailed for him, delaying the passage of the Armada into the eastern approaches to the Isle. As Sidonia came, Frobisher lowered his boats to tow the *Triumph*.

Sidonia was still after Frobisher, certain that finally he would get close enough to board, for the ship was being towed, but the *Triumph* was pulling into the swift current. Frobisher cast off his towing longboats and piled on sail. Then, into the current went Frobisher, using it to sail away. As Frobisher emerged, the *Bear* and the *Elizabeth Jonas* went for the Spanish flanks, gnawing hungrily with their guns.

Frobisher flashed away so swift that it seemed Sidonia and Recalde, on the *San Juan*, were standing still.

"That must be the fastest ship in the fleet," a man near Sidonia said, staring open-mouthed at the *Triumph*.

Yet the *Triumph* was nothing of the sort. It was one of the slowest, being top-heavy and aged. It was Frobisher's skill and knowledge that allowed his swift escape, not his ship.

Frobisher joined Howard in the centre, attacking the base of the rearguard, driving it east. At the same time, Drake and Hawkins took on the seaward flank of the Armada, aided by Fenner on the *Nonpareil*. Their swift attack, like the one used at Portland, came from the open sea and smashed into the Armada with ferocious speed and strength.

Although Fenner's ships had to do much of the work, as the *Revenge* was still damaged from the day before, the Armada was driven into itself, towards the *San Martin* squadron. The English isolated one of the galleons and battered her. The *San Francisco* came to protect her, but it too came under fire. The seaward wing of the Armada was lost in confusion, being driven along by Drake and Fenner and falling to disorder. Ships flocked about the *San Martin*, dangerously close. The formation was falling apart and they were teetering close to the perilous shallows of the Owers Bank. The tide was turning against them. The wind joined in, pushing them away from the Isle, into the shallows.

Sidonia swiftly realised they were all in danger of being beached. Pilots were shouting. They could see sandy, shoal water not far away, and jagged black rocks. The invincible Armada was within minutes of being wrecked.

"By God," Sidonia said. "*El Draque* is driving us onto the sand."

That was just what Drake, Hawkins and Fenner were up to. If English guns could not destroy the Armada, English soil would. Using wind and tide, which were pushing the Armada as sure as English ships were, Drake was trying to beach them.

Firing guns to signal the danger, Sidonia led his group south-south-west, the only safe route of escape open to him, trying to gather scattered hulks as he went.

If Sidonia had not chosen to take action in that moment, the Armada would have been lost. His quick thinking saved the ships of Spain.

But he could not make it to the Isle, he knew that. They had been driven off and now all there was for miles were shallows and sea cliffs, too dangerous to anchor in. They were upon the open sea with few supplies, ships full of injured men and no safe haven in sight. As Sidonia heard church bells pealing on the Isle of Wight and the distant whisper of men cheering all along its hillsides, his heart fell. They were at the mercy of the English fleet, the sea, and the weather if they stayed out upon the water.

The last refuge was Calais. The French officially were neutral but the Duc of Guise, now more in control of France than the King, was allied to Sidonia's master. They would be allowed to anchor there, and from there he could reach Parma. Guns fired to signal the ships to follow. The Armada sailed away, heading for France.

"You have to say," Drake said that night to Howard, cutting slices off a tough, leathery apple, "Sidonia has shown admirable courage." He looked out of the window. Beacons had been lit on the Isle of Wight, calling the men of Sussex to their rendezvous points. Bells were sounding in the darkness, ringing out over the sea. The English fleet was following the Armada, but they had made no effort to engage. They had not the powder.

"I thought he would be easier to defeat. Not the Armada, but his ship, certainly," Howard agreed. "He is even less a man of sea than me, but at every step he has rushed in to aid his men, and stolen many a victory from us. And he seems to see our tactics, no mean feat for a man who knows nothing of ships, the sea or our coast."

"Perhaps he was not so badly chosen, after all," said Drake.

"He was chosen for his title, like me," said Howard, "but he has wit and intelligence."

"Also like you, my lord," Drake said, slipping the apple into his mouth and offering a grin to his commander. "Although you own more of both virtues."

"Thank you, Drake," said Howard. "For your praise."

"Not praise, honesty," said Drake. "You were chosen well, my lord. The Queen was right to place faith in you."

"And now she must place more," Howard said, rising from his chair to stretch his back. Every part of his body was weary and aching. He had wrenched his neck more than once and his spine was in savage rebellion against him. "They will go to Calais. That is the nearest friendly port."

"And there may be Parma, waiting," said Drake.

Drake cut another slice of apple. To Howard, the smooth crunch of the knife sounded like the swing of a sharpened blade slicing through flesh.

Chapter Fourteen

The Sussex Coast
July 25th – 26th 1588

Death

That day, ships set out from the English coast to replenish Howard and his men with munitions. Both fleets were off the Sussex coast, held by the calm, unmoving wind as carpenters worked to rebuild the damage done from the day before. Via letters rowed out from Walsingham and the Queen, Howard was offered musketeers again, selected from the best trained men in Kent. He had refused them before, but now was thinking they might be a good idea. The time had come to engage at closer quarters than they had dared. They might soon be in need of soldiers.

Not far from Howard, Seymour was awaiting reinforcements. He had been worried about his squadron, thinking it too weak. They had had perhaps twenty ships left, some having been sent back to port for lack of food. Eight ships hired in London headed out to him that day carrying rumours that Parma had marched with all his men to Dunkirk.

At the same time, boats were flocking to Howard and his men, carrying supplies. Where powder and shot could not be found waste metal had been provided, so cannon could fire molten shards at the enemy. "It is better than nothing," said Drake when he saw the barrels of scraps.

That night, Howard summoned his men. "We will not engage again until Dover, and only if they look to try for Kent," he told them. "We have more shot and powder, but barely enough to do true damage. Therefore, we must pick well our battles." He looked his men up and down. Wearied by battle and action they were, but he was proud of them. "But there will be reward," he said.

Howard knighted his men; Hawkins, Frobisher, Lord Thomas Howard and Lord Sheffield became knights that day, along with George Beeston, the eighty-nine-year-old captain of the *Dreadnought*. Drake, already knighted by the Queen, looked on.

Knights of the sea rose to stand on the deck of the *Ark*, faces shining with pride. Battered and weary they were, but new courage sang in their hearts. Howard understood his men well. As dusk fell, they went back to their ships and their men cheered them, the sound of voices singing and shouting as ale and beer were handed out, fresh and good from provisions dispatched from the mainland.

There was good cheer for good reason. The Armada had been driven off. Most of the Spanish ships could not sail into the wind, and with the English holding the weather-gage only an east wind would allow them to return. That east wind was a rare guest in the Channel during summer months. Danger remained that Parma and Sidonia would meet, that an east wind would blow, but Seymour had sent word he was on his way and for the first time that meant the English would have more ships.

It was a time to celebrate. The war was not over, danger not gone, but they had won a victory. Howard was sensible enough to know that men need small successes on the way to great ones. It keeps them striving towards the goals they seek. It keeps hope in hearts.

That night the wind rose, filling the battered sails of the Armada. Like a wounded leviathan they sailed in formation for the French coast, sighting it by ten of the clock the next morning. Sidonia, warned not to anchor in the Calais Roads, since strong currents might sweep the fleet into the North Sea, sending them sprawling towards Seymour and Wynter, dropped anchor at four of the afternoon four miles off the port of Calais. They were twenty-four miles from Dunkirk, the nearest point, so it was thought, where Parma might be waiting. Howard took his fleet to Whitsand Bay, just out of cannon range. That afternoon Seymour and thirty-five ships arrived to reinforce Howard.

The French were supposed to be neutral, but Sidonia sent messages to allies of the Guise, knowing they would reinforce him. At the same time, he wrote to Parma. *"I have constantly written… and not only have I had no reply to my letters, but no acknowledgement of their receipt… I am extremely anxious at this, as you may imagine, and to free myself of the doubt as to any of the messengers have reached you safely, I am now despatching this flyboat."*

Informing Parma that the English were at his heel, able to attack whilst he was in a position to do them no harm, he urged Parma to send word and ships. If Parma could dispatch fifty ships to help defend the Armada in the shallow waters they lay in it would be a great help, and they could then sail together and claim a port close to England. Well aware the Armada was supposed to be protecting Parma's men, not the other way around, Sidonia sealed the letter with hope as much as with wax.

At three of the clock that very afternoon, English envoys in Flanders had received news of the engagement off Plymouth, fought days before, from their Queen, and packed their bags, leaving Parma and his insistence that talks of peace were still possible behind. Parma, having no knowledge of the Armada, thought this a negotiating tactic, and asked them to remain, but they would not hear him. Parma put aside munitions for the Armada, and started to send commands to his scattered men. If the battle at Plymouth was indeed true, the Armada was coming, but he had no word as to when. He left Bruges for the coast, thinking to supervise gathering forces.

On Howard's ship, captains were discussing tactics.

"We need to close, and to isolate," Drake said. "The *Gran Grifon* should show us that when we draw close enough we can do much damage."

Howard nodded. The *Grifon* had been towed away, but in the short space of time she had been isolated and set upon, they had all but torn her apart.

"But our ships, too, were wounded in that encounter," said Hawkins. "Drake's ship was one."

"That is something we may have to risk now," Howard said. "We have harried them up the Channel, kept them from England, but now they may meet with Parma. He may have good ships, hidden from Walsingham's spies. We hold the advantage of numbers until Parma arrives. We should use it."

"Then we must strike quickly," said Frobisher. "Risk our ships for a final victory. If we drive them from Calais, or manage to destroy them, the only other port nearby that might accommodate them is the Scheldt below Antwerp."

"That passage is narrow and difficult," Drake said. "They would need Flemish pilots to guide them in, and without Parma they will not have them. The Dutch Sea Beggars guard those waters and although we have little news of them, other than that Lord Seymour brings, we do know they will not allow the Armada to pass into those waters unharmed if they see them."

"The Dutch would trap them in the Scheldt," said Hawkins. "They know the sandbanks and shallows. They could attack, escape and come back, and they could destroy ships one by one if they try to emerge."

"The Dutch are wolves upon the sea," said Captain Beeston. "They might be strong enough on their own to hold the Armada in the Scheldt."

"What if that is the plan?" Seymour asked.

"What mean you?" asked Howard.

"If the Armada were to reinforce Parma's troops, rather than the other way around, Spain might win the Netherlands," Seymour said. "The Queen was forced to pull three thousand troops from the Low Countries to defend England. The soldiers of the Armada would bolster Parma's forces, and might see him to a victory over the Dutch. With England's ally fallen, we would stand alone."

The men looked grim but Howard shook his head. "It is an intriguing idea," he said. "And a clever one, but nothing gathered by Walsingham and his spies suggests that is the plan."

"They might make a new one, since the present one looks set to fail," said Seymour. "If the Netherlands fell, the Sea Beggars would have to retreat or surrender, leaving Parma and Sidonia free to use the Low Countries or Flanders as a base to attack England from."

"Parma might well think of that," said Howard, "but the King of Spain wants England first, and he is not a man to alter plans. He is rigid as a corpse."

There was a pause. Howard could feel concern drifting from his men's minds. Allowing them to think about what might come was unhelpful.

"We must attack now, before Parma arrives," said Howard, rubbing his brow. "We cannot guess at what might come next, but must instead respond to the largest threat. That is that Parma and Sidonia will meet and launch from here to England."

As Howard's men spoke deep into the night, Sidonia awaited the food and water, shot and powder coming to be loaded onto his ships. He waited, too, for favourable news of General Parma, hoping he was close, ready for war and to sail.

Parma was none of those things.

Chapter Fifteen

Richmond Palace
July 26th 1588

Elizabeth

In and out my needle dipped, silver slicing into white cloth and out again, pulling bright blue thread through, turning to assault the virginal cloth again. It is a thing remarkable that continued onslaught might bring about something beautiful.

I sometimes welcomed the task and office of embroidery. It was a battle no man ever fought, being a womanly pastime. Occupying hands and eyes, leaving the mind free to think, it is a meditative art and a personal one. When I was just five years old, one of my first gifts had been a shirt I sewed and embroidered for my little brother, Edward. I had embroidered book covers for translations of works I had undertaken to please my stepmother, Queen Catherine Parr. My ladies and I sewed basic garments for the poor, grander ones for my Chapel Royal, a space many complained was far too Catholic. Even though its ornaments and adornments were spare compared to those my sister had used, people often moaned about the Catholic airs my Chapel adopted.

Often I turned from embroidery, finding it too sedate, but I needed occupation. I had walked already that day, and could not find the rest to read. Without needle and cloth I might have driven my ladies into madness, pacing the floor, waiting for news.

I was trying to find a solution to my financial woes. Parliament could be called to raise money through taxes, but that would take time, and the people had been sapped as it was. Calling Parliament now, with fear riding the wind of England, and discontent rife, might force people to think Phillip *would* be a better monarch for England. I could force the gentry and nobles to grant loans, indeed I had and would again, but I did not want to do so right now.

If we were conquered, all this would be in vain, but if not we had to find a way to survive, and all the men serving England aboard ship and on land at this moment were expecting to be paid. I had no idea how I was going to achieve that. Money was needed for Scotland to keep James on our side, for the defence of Ireland against the Pope, for Navarre if ever France was to be our friend again, and I dared not pull out of the Netherlands. Pirates like Drake might bring me coin, but would it be enough? I hoped they would pillage the Armada, bring me some return on my investment of men and munitions in this war.

The other option was to raise loans from overseas. German and Genoa bankers might lend to England, they had to my father, but again, time was an issue.

The last possibility was one I liked the least. I could sell off my own properties. This would reduce my status as Queen, and royal revenues from estates, but it might be all I could do.

I had worked so carefully to restore the coinage and bolster the depleted coffers my forebears had left behind. In peacetime, my efforts had worked, but war takes more than just life from a country. It drains it of blood and money. Monarchs before me, my sister and father being prime examples, had sent their people into war and wrecked their treasuries without seeming to care, but I did care. The financial stability I had brought England had been something I had been proud of. Now it was slipping through my fingers, sand in the wind.

People would say that I, the Queen, spent lavishly. It was not actually true. I was more like my grandfather than my father or siblings had been. A cursory glance at my accounts would make a fool think I was a wild spender, with no care for my subjects as I indulged my own pleasures first, but it was not so.

I had to pay for the entire government of the realm. Feeding my court, the centre of control, took more than one third of my income in a good year. In a bad year where crops failed, it could cost a lot more. I paid few wages to my ladies, but all courtiers were provided with candles, firewood or coal, ale and wine and food at my expense. Whilst the wages of my royal officials amounted to more than seventy thousand each year, I spent no more than twenty on my horses, carriages and barges which were not only used by me, but my men. In that twenty thousand too was money spent on my clothes. Clothing was important. I was the symbol of England and had to appear regal and rich at all times, but my clothing was a pageant. Most of my wardrobe was made up of gifts given by nobles on progress or at New Year. My ladies *never* threw out cloth that had ripped. They mended gowns, sleeves, kirtles and undergarments each day, and when items could no longer be worn by me they were given as gifts, or made into altar cloths. Candle stubs and unused firewood were collected to be redistributed, the waste wax formed into new candles. The kitchens took what could be salvaged from one feast and put it into another; roasted meat of one day becoming the base of pottage for the next. There was no waste in my household.

Two thousand went yearly in alms to my people, and four thousand to dignitaries visiting from other lands. My houses and palaces took fifty thousand to maintain, but court entertainments stole less than five thousand and many of my jewels had been gifts, had been inherited, or I had bought at low prices from cast-off collections of other princes. Pearls from my cousin of Scots, sold off by her son before she died, were a worthy example.

Other princes spent far more on themselves than me. Most of my coin went into wages and the maintenance of palaces, where officials of state lived and worked.

My financial woes were not unique. Many lands suffered when countries they were in conflict with closed ports to merchants trading goods. Even Spain, who had vast lands to draw wealth from, was not in a good state with money.

Two things I had done had impacted England most. The first was war in the Netherlands. Wool was England's primary export, as it was the finest in the world, and in the past it went to Antwerp for sale. Conflict with Spain had crippled a great deal of this trade and although other markets had been found it had taken a toll. This problem was not all of my making, however. The Dutch and Spanish had been fighting for years and the fall of Antwerp as a trading port was caused by ongoing war. Had I not intervened, the city would have only fallen faster.

The second was my habit of granting monopolies on certain goods to courtiers as favours. This, however, was done so I would not have to hand them money and estates. The cost of rewarding loyal men, and men must be rewarded to keep them loyal, would have arisen in any case.

But in my court and country I had been careful with money. Frugal and mean some called me, thinking summer progresses where my men paid for my court, and my habit of accepting and expecting gifts along the way, were not fitting for a queen. But I thought they were, and such measures had allowed me to rebuild the treasury, until now. I had been prudent, but war is a greedy god. When he comes to dine, never is anything left upon a table.

I once said never by violence would I be constrained to do anything. But perhaps by money I would. I had no idea how I was to pay for this war, for the soldiers and sailors fighting even at this moment, *and* retain enough to keep England going, her officers working, her Queen upon its throne.

That night, I went to my private closet to pray. "Bow down Thy ear, O Lord," I whispered. "From the bright sphere above, behold and see Thy handmaiden. Hear my petition, as I hear those who come begging to me. Protect my children from the dangers of the sea and the swords of our enemies. Hold them close in Thy heart, so the peril of the waves and the danger of deep water cannot touch them. In Your bounty and grace, hold my men to Your breast and keep them safe, as You keep England in the same place, close to Thy eternal heart, where all goodness is to be found."

I might well have added, "and protect us against our want for money", but I thought my worries on coin too crass for the Lord of Heaven to hear.

Chapter Sixteen

The English Channel and Calais
July 27th 1588

Death

"So much for France being neutral," Drake said to Howard as they stood on the deck of the *Ark* in the spindly, grey light of dawn. Under them the ship creaked and metal squeaked as stores of food hanging from rafters in the bowels of the ship shifted, rocking with the waves. Always there was noise on board ship; the groan of planks, the sound of the ever-shifting sea kept separate from men only by the width of wooden planks. Ships moaned and sighed as the sea carried them, and when it held them still.

The two men were watching ships ferrying back and forth from the Castle of Calais to the Armada, unloading stores. The castle was the headquarters of the Governor of Calais.

"The Governor lost a leg fighting us," Howard said, leaning on the rails of his ship. The wood, once painted green and white, was black with powder. "It is no wonder he would support the Spanish, even if he has not been commanded to by the Duc of Guise."

"You know this for sure, my lord?"

"I make a guess, Drake, but I think I am correct. Guise controls France now."

"At least there is no sign of Parma, my lord."

"A miracle in itself," said Howard, shading his eyes to peer into the distance. From his position, the men loading Spanish ships were little more than ants upon the ground. They were not alone. Upon approach, it had been easy to spy people along the shore, watching for the Armada and the following English fleet, waiting to see if they would witness a battle. The cliffs of Dover had been lined too, crowds of English men and women trying to see their fighting men at sea. Horror calls to the human mind. The eyes may not wish to see, but the mind gives them no choice, sending them to stare upon that which terrifies and disgusts, as though to look away will allow fears to come to pass.

The English fleet were not far from the Armada, but not too close to Calais. Not only was the Duc of Guise largely in control of war-torn France, although Navarre, the Huguenot successor was hanging on grimly, but Calais had only been taken from English hands thirty years before, in the reign of Queen Mary. Before that time, it had been an English stronghold, England's gateway to Europe, and the last vestige of the once glorious empire of England stretching from Aquitaine to the Scots' border. But when Calais fell to the French, the French had poured back in, and they remembered English occupation of this part of their now-territory with grim recollection. Anti-English sentiment was strong in the city.

Despite this, men of the port, some of them English spies and some Huguenot sympathisers, had sent word that the supplies granted to the Armada were not offerings of friendship. Sidonia had been told he must buy all he needed. It was said that merchants had taken advantage of his need, and the supplies were costing the Admiral twenty times what they were worth. It was rumoured one egg was costing Sidonia five pennies. It would not be a problem, perhaps. Sidonia had set sail with a great deal of money, but it would not be welcome.

One other slice of news had been even more welcome to Howard's ears. The Governor had refused to send articles of war to Sidonia. Only food and drink was heading to the Armada, not shot and powder. The Governor might be keeping friends with Spain, but he was also being careful not to antagonise England.

"Spanish officers will dine well tonight," Drake said, shifting and revealing his limp. Drake reached down to massage his leg; the muscles had become tight and angry with continuous action.

Drake knew the best supplies would be kept for nobles on board. Sailors and soldiers would receive mean rations from the depleted stores the Armada already possessed. Although Howard and his commanding officers got the best food, and many would say their brains needed it, English rations were always more generous than those of Spain.

"Aye," said Howard, but his eyes were lost. Not long ago they had seen a ship approach Sidonia's fleet, only for it to be fired upon by the Armada itself. The guns had ceased when the Spaniards realised it was not an English ship. It was probable the ship was bringing news from Parma, but what that news was Howard could only guess. Their spies told them Parma was not in Calais, and did not seem to be camped nearby, which was good, but no one knew where he was. Howard did not know whether to rejoice or not.

"They cannot get to Flanders," said Drake, watching Howard's troubled face and knowing where his mind wended. "They have not the galleys to stand against the Dutch flyboats."

Howard nodded, eyes on the shimmering water. That was true. He had heard that Santa Cruz, whilst still alive of course, had petitioned Phillip to release galleys from his Mediterranean fleet which guarded against attack from the Turks. Phillip had released some, but had not been generous. Four galleys had sailed with Sidonia, but all had been turned back by the storms that hit before they entered English waters. Galleys were a match for the flyboats used by the Dutch, but the only ships Sidonia had that might work now were his galleasses, and they were a risk to release as they were needed to defend the rest of the fleet. Without releasing them,

Sidonia could not reach Parma, if Parma was in Flanders. If he did risk his galleasses, he risked the Armada.

"Ships are to come from Portsmouth to reinforce us with more powder today, I hope," said Howard. "And Seymour thinks Sea Beggars are along the Flemish Coast. Justin of Nassau commands them. Little did Seymour see of the Dutch, but if they *are* in position no ship from Parma will get out of Flanders, and the Armada needs deep water to anchor in. If Nassau is in place he can keep Parma penned up in the shallows, where the Armada cannot land."

"But we do not know the Dutch are in position, and Parma may launch from Flanders or march to Calais." Drake leaned on the rail next to Howard.

"That he may," said Howard. "If the Dutch are in the seas, Calais may, in fact, be the General's only option." Howard's face grew grimmer. "We are going to have to do something, soon. If we can rip them out of Calais, and scatter them, send them into the seas about Flanders, then our ships might be able to crush them. If we allow them to sit here, we are just waiting for Parma to arrive."

"We outnumber them, for the first time, with Seymour's ships now here," Drake pointed out. "And the *Rainbow* and *Vanguard* Seymour has brought are the newest and finest ships of the fleet, some would say." Drake sniffed, a trifle dismissively.

Howard grinned as he glanced sideways. Each man was protective of his ship, Drake not least amongst them. He would always claim the *Revenge* was the best ship. But it was true the large galleons Seymour had brought with him were new and powerful. They had seen little action and were fresher than Howard's fleet.

"But you would be the first to say attacking a fleet in port is not as easy as it sounds," Howard said. "And although we will have more munitions soon, I wonder if it is enough."

Whilst Howard and Drake could only guess at what the unfortunate ship, arriving that morning only to be fired upon by the Armada, carried for Sidonia, the Admiral himself was about to find out.

"News from General Parma, my lord!" The excited servant looked fit to tumble to his knees with joy as he raced towards the Admiral, a roll of parchment clenched in his fist.

Hands shaking with relief, Sidonia broke the red seal of Parma, and opened the letter. His relief did not last long. He was, in fact, swiftly horrified.

Parma was not ready to sail. He was not close by, but in Bruges. Not a barrel of beer had been rolled onto his barges and not a single man had walked aboard either. He would not be ready to meet the Admiral until at least a week had passed.

Sidonia could hardly believe what he was reading. Phillip had sent his nephew many instructions, but all of them general, not specific, Parma wrote. Phillip had seemed to think that Parma's troops could sail out to meet the Armada on the sea, which they could not, Parma explained, for few cannon did his ships have. His barges were for carrying soldiers, not for fighting and Parma had told Phillip repeatedly that he could not sail out without the defence of the Armada. Parma said he had told the King of Spain this in January of that year, and the idea of his boats defending the Armada was impossible. His forces were the ones who needed to be protected, for they would not be able to cross the forty miles from Dunkirk to Margate, braving the sea, the flyboats of the Sea Beggars and the English fleet without help. The General wrote that he had been told the Armada would clear the Channel of English ships, granting passage for his men.

Sidonia stared for a long time at this part of the letter. He had *specifically* been told he was not to engage the English unless it was unavoidable. It seemed the King of Spain had been saying different things to him and Parma.

Parma wrote he was aghast that rather than clearing the Channel, Sidonia had arrived in Calais bringing the entire English navy, unharmed and well armed, with him.

Parma had perhaps two hundred craft that could ferry his men, but only a dozen were flyboats. The Sea Beggars had more than four hundred vessels, of varying size and weaponry and they were positioned all along the coast. They vastly outnumbered his fleet and he had fought them before. The Dutch knew those waters well, and knew how to use them as a weapon. If he set sail from Flanders, his men would be drowned within hours.

And Parma was not confident about many of his vessels. He had been forced to conscript Dutch carpenters and shipwrights, many of whom had no love for him or Spain, therefore the wood some had used had been rotten and the workmanship poor, on purpose. Some vessels were simply not seaworthy, and many had sprung leaks as soon as they were lowered into the water. Others started to take on water when loaded. He was confident of forty of them, but most could only hold two hundred men, which would mean more than one trip across dangerous waves, guarded by the Dutch and English.

Parma was also short on good pilots and seamen.

He had sent word, and complaints, to his royal uncle, he wrote, but they had all been ignored. He had wanted to take Flushing, a deep water port the Armada could have used, and from which a true invasion could launch, but had been told to hold off. Had he been permitted to do as he wished, wrote the General, masking complaints against his uncle with flowery language, the Dutch rebellion would be over by now and they would have been able to bombard England using not only his forces and the Armada, but all the captured ships and forces of the Dutch and their Sea Beggars.

But the main point hit Sidonia hard. Parma *could not* sail out to meet Sidonia upon the waves, something Sidonia had been told the General most assuredly could do, and there was another problem.

His armies were scattered.

In an effort to confuse Dutch and English spies, and because he had no idea the Admiral was so close, Parma had held his armies back from embarkation points to fool the enemy into thinking the plan was to invade from the Low Countries. His fleet was split between Sluys, Dunkirk, Nieuport and Antwerp, the last being where Parma's flagship was moored. At Dunkirk there were fifteen and a half thousand men, and at Nieuport were five thousand. Other units were moving towards other ports. It would take time to call them to Dunkirk or Calais.

He did try to cheer the Admiral. Other preparations Parma had made. He had defences ready to build walls and temporary forts, which had been loaded onto ships. These pre-built forts would have wooden beams and pikes jutting from them. He had made portable bridges, which they would use to advance through Kent as it was likely the first thing the English would do if they landed would be to blow up bridges or flood roads. He had bundles of faggots to be issued to men, which could be used as shields for those who were to be in firing positions. If they could land in England, Parma was certain he had the troops, defences and plans to succeed. But the question of how they were to get there remained.

Excusing the fact his men were not ready to leave, Parma said he had received one letter from Sidonia after the 10th of June, asking for a point where they could meet, but clearly the Admiral had not had his letter in response. The officer sent to inform Sidonia that they could not meet on water had likely been killed by storms or by the English, he wrote. No other letters had he had from Sidonia.

The Admiral knew then that not one of his dispatches sent from the time he left Spain until now had reached Parma. All must have been intercepted, blown out of the water by English or Dutch ships.

With a hopeless heart did Sidonia read how Parma was grieved to learn the Admiral had no *"place of safety in case of necessity, whilst the winds that have prevailed for so long still continue"* and the weather was causing Parma problems too. *"The wind will prevent our boats coming out, even if the sea is clear of the enemy's ships. But I trust in God that He will aid us in everything, and allow us shortly to send good news."* Winds were rising off shore. If Parma and his men set out on their flat-bottomed barges, the Dutch would need to do little work. The weather would be enough to drown the soldiers of Spain.

The General would leave Bruges immediately, he said, and send orders to his men. He would need at least three days to gather his troops, but it could take up to fifteen days. If he set out upon the sea his men would have to run the gauntlet of Dutch flyboats before they reached Sidonia, and when they got to him they would be no help in aiding Sidonia to fight the English fleet. The Admiral, therefore, needed to wait and needed to prepare his ships to battle the English, defending Parma's men as they were shipped across.

Parma was deluding himself about the time needed to depart, although he did not know it. He had sent commands and was accustomed to his orders being followed, but he had not heard of the local trouble his men had run into. The ships were not ready, despite his orders. Common people were making sure there were obstacles in the way of gathering food and many of his seamen, a great number of them Dutch, worked listlessly on purpose to slow his preparations down.

Sidonia sat down to write a reply, trying to hasten the General. Lack of shelter, strong winds, and the English fleet not far away were all dangers. *"I therefore beg you to hasten your coming out before the spring tides end,"* he wrote. He could not stay at Calais and it was a thing impossible to keep sailing along the Channel. The English fleet was hardier than any of them had imagined. *"It is impossible to do any damage, hard as we may try."*

As his servant took the reply and closed the door behind him, it was all Sidonia could do not to fall to the floor in despair. If Parma did not find a way to rally his men and march soon, Sidonia did not know what he was going to do.

Chapter Seventeen

Richmond Palace
July 27th 1588

Elizabeth

"This is news which pleases me," I said.

I even managed a smile. Cecil had just reported that Anthony Browne, the sixty-two-year-old Viscount Montague, who once had served on my Council but had been asked to leave because he was a known Catholic, had volunteered himself and his retainers in my personal defence.

Montague was one of those lords whom I had always known to be Catholic, yet had kept close as long as I could, for I believed he held Queen and country above faith. He had once been my ambassador to Spain and Lieutenant of Sussex, but had lost those posts too because of his faith.

But now, in England's hour of need, Montague had hoisted his colours for all to see. Hearing gunfire off the coast of Portsmouth, he had sent word to court, saying he wished to defend me personally against any and all peril. He was not under any obligation to make such an offer. Catholic lords who had been spared being placed under house arrest had not been asked to provide retainers for the Crown. Walsingham believed there was a danger they might send informers and assassins into the ranks, attacking me, Robin, or other men. Montague was volunteering out of loyalty, not requirement. The fact that one of his brothers was actually aboard an Armada ship made this offer only more remarkable. Blood and faith were not as thick as loyalty to his country, for Montague.

"You will proclaim this news to my people, that they might see how the hearts of loyal Englishmen are bent," I said to Cecil.

"A good strike against Spain and Rome, who say all Catholics of England cannot rest without my blood on their hands. This shows their lies for what they are."

"We will use Montague's offer to our best advantage, madam," said Cecil.

Not all lords of England were pleasing me. The Earl of Arundel, son of my executed cousin Norfolk, was still in the Tower of London after his part in the Babington-Ballard plot had come to light in the year just passed. It had recently been found he was not only hearing Mass inside his cell, but was encouraging priests imprisoned in the Tower to pray for the victory of our enemies. He should not have trusted fellow prisoners so easily, for it was one of the captured Englishmen from the *Rosario* who sent this information to the guards and then to us.

John Snowden was a Catholic exile, come to invade with the Armada and captured with the *Rosario* by Drake. Thinking to save himself from death, he betrayed the Earl, whose rooms were close to his. Snowden said he had received encouraging messages from the Earl, as had priests and other captives. Snowden had passed some on to Walsingham. We had, therefore, a confession from Arundel written in his own hand. The incautious Earl had been handing out promises as well as notes, swearing to make the priest who sang Mass for him into the dean of St Paul's when the Armada was triumphant. He mourned that his brother, young Thomas Howard, was serving as captain on one of my ships, and had said he hoped to God he would soon hear the Mass again in England.

"What a fool," I said. "As fool as his father, and as arrogant. Do you think such traits run in blood, as red hair flows through my family line?"

"Fortunately, there are better Howards in the world, Majesty."

I smiled. I was proud of all I had heard of my Admiral. I had been wise to choose him. I had also heard young Howard, Lord Thomas, was doing England good and noble service.

"Shift this priest, Master Bennet, from the Tower to another prison," I said to Cecil. "And arrange for Arundel to be questioned."

"Walsingham is already on the Earl," Cecil said.

Arundel saddened me. He had been popular at court after his father's death and had supported my marriage to Anjou. In the past few years he had taken himself away from court and, like his father before him, had dabbled in Catholicism. Perhaps it only came to mean more to him because of the death of his father. His wife, Anne, was also a dabbler, and there were rumours she was offering her husband's money to Jesuits. I hoped this was not so, but women got away with a great deal more in terms of religion than their husbands. The law reduced married women to vassals of their husbands, but it had some unwelcome side effects. Married women owned no property, so fines for recusancy could not be handed to them. A husband could not be punished for his wife's criminal acts, so arresting him instead of his wife was against the law. Proceed against spinsters and widows my men could, but, ignored by law, married women had grown powerful in the very obscurity that was supposed to strip them of power; flowers blooming in darkness.

People often accused women of being flighty creatures, like birds or butterflies, but those who bend the wind to their wishes slip through many a narrow passage. Women like Lady Arundel were using laws which had long rendered them obsolete to become powerful.

But if some were disloyal, I was happy with others, who, like Montague, put their country first. Catholics only recently imprisoned for recusancy, like Lord Vaux's servant, Athony Carrington, had publicly sworn the *Oath of Supremacy* and taken positions in regiments of the militia. Sir Thomas Tresham, Vaux's brother-in-law, was another who had volunteered. Vaux himself was still under house arrest, but he had been speaking about the villainies of Spain to many. I was hoping I might restore him to the House of Lords. His son, Henry, had died in gaol and with him Vaux's passion for rebellion seemed to have perished too.

"Do we know where the fleet are?" I asked.

"Chasing the Armada along the Channel, heading east," Cecil said. "Madam, there is something that must be considered. The last missives said Howard thought they might make for Calais. If they do, there is a risk that is where they will meet Parma."

"You want me to move to a more secure location," I said, reading it in his eyes.

"If you are lost, madam, so is England."

"I will not go to Windsor," I said. Windsor was secure indeed, a mighty fortress, but it was far out of London.

"It would be the best place, madam."

"For me, not for England," I said. "If my people hear the Queen has fled London, there will be panic. The people will think the danger is imminent. I cannot allow that, and how could I face my own mirror if I fled now, as so many cannot?"

I shook my head. "If there is word they are at Calais, we will move the court to St James's Palace. That is easily defended."

Cecil did not look happy, but he nodded. "As you wish, Majesty."

Chapter Eighteen

The English Channel, near Calais
July 28th 1588

Death

That day, there was a lull. The breeze was perfumed with the scent of wood smoke from fires carefully contained on ships, and with the tang of ale, as men took the time to rest and replenish their weary bones. The sun was dancing on the slick surface of water below, light rippling and bending, dancing on the darkness of the ever-shifting seas.

The wind was low, and the Armada anchored at Calais, supplies still being loaded. Howard and his men had been reinforced with gunpowder and fresh recruits, many of them merchants and sons of noble houses, but they needed a new plan. They were also low on food.

As Howard called his men to his ship to talk, lips were moving all over the world, spreading false rumours. In San Sebastian in Spain, one of Walsingham's agents, Edward Palmer, a Catholic priest, heard that Howard and Drake had been captured by the Armada. Bells pealed in the nearby church as people traded frenzied gossip on the streets. Drake was in fetters, a prisoner of war and would be brought back to Spain to answer for his crimes. The Isle of Wight and Plymouth had been taken, it was said. Parma's army were in England, marching upon London. The Queen had fled so fast her famous wig had fallen from her head, revealing she was bald as a plucked hen.

Towns all over Spain held feasts and dances to celebrate. Men raced down the streets on horseback, spreading the news, crying out that *El Draque* was a dragon no more, but a broken bird, wings clipped by the guns of Spain. That night there were bonfires, and people made merry about them, dancing and mocking the Queen of England, that bastard heretic harlot who had thought she could withstand the greatest Empire and King in the world.

The King of Spain, safe in his palace, heard the rumours but was warier than his people. Had any of this happened, Phillip thought he would have heard the joyous news from Parma, or Sidonia. The last dispatch he had had from Sidonia seemed to indicate the Admiral was having problems communicating with Parma. There had been no news of the capture of any town, island or deep water port.

In Rome, Ambassador Olivares was troubled too. The Pope was holding daily Masses for the success of the Armada in public, but in private was refusing to hand over the promised coin. Olivares had made speeches, reminding the Holy Father that he himself had pushed the King of Spain to launch an attack, and warning that if money was held back victory might not come.

Sixtus merely shrugged.

Sidonia, worry now a cloak he wore continually, had a new pin to ornament his cowl. He was concerned about the current. He had been warned not to stay long at anchor for good reason. Some of his ships, held by two anchors because of the strong spring tide, were in peril of being carried by the current into the North Sea. The Dutch were out there, as he knew from Parma's letter. The English were also not far away. Sitting directly in the path of the current was not welcome, but he knew not where else to go. He was also risking his ships being beached when the tide ran the other way.

Sidonia knew how his ships felt. From Phillip there had been clear directives on his mission, but from Parma had come news of others. Sidonia felt pulled in two directions, by his King and General Parma, and at the same moment held fast in the middle, disabled by the realities of his present, rather hopeless, situation.

Sidonia might have to do something drastic. He could order the Governor of Calais to allow the Armada to enter the port, or face his guns. Calais had cannon, but they would not hold out long against the Armada troops. Such rash action would grant Sidonia a port to which Parma could march, but such a reckless, brash offensive was not part of his instructions sent by Phillip, and France, or rather the Duc of Guise, was allied to Spain. His master was unlikely to welcome an act which might amount to a declaration of war.

But it was too much to hope the English would simply lie in wait for the Armada to emerge. Sidonia knew what they might attempt, it was not an unknown tactic and he had taken steps to prevent it. But with all that was in his heart and soul he prayed, prayed they would not do what he thought they would.

But if Sidonia could not hear Howard and his men, I could. Death hears all.

"Against the whole, we can do but little damage, their discipline in formation is too great," Howard said to the men gathered about the table in his cabin that afternoon. The groaning of the sea against the ship's hull sounded, a constant dirge; the lament of the mermaid. "And Parma might arrive at any moment. We must assume the General and the Admiral are in constant contact now."

"We need to separate them, my lord, pick them off ship by ship," Drake agreed. "When they stand as one, our ships cannot wound them, but ship to ship we are more than a match."

"And we have more vessels, for the first time," Frobisher added. "So more than one of ours can go against one of theirs."

"The biggest ships will require many of us," said Howard.

"The tides are turning," said Drake. "The spring tides and westerly wind are growing. That will allow ships to sail straight at them."

"But if we are caught in harbour, surrounded by them, it will do no good," said Howard.

"I was not thinking of us, exactly, my lord," Drake said, offering a slow grin. Other, more experienced captains, had already grasped the answer unspoken and were nodding. "We need to separate them, and strike terror into them at the same time. The mightiest discipline can be shattered when men fall to fear."

"And what do you suggest?" Howard asked, his eyebrows raised.

"Fireships," said Drake.

Chapter Nineteen

Calais
Midnight, July 28th 1588

Death

You would think men of the sea would fear water; liquid death that closes, cold and suffocating over a struggling man, bearing his body to the belly of the sea. You would think that would be their greatest fear, especially since most sailors had no idea how to swim. You would think that skill, prevalent amongst men of Africa, would be something all sailors would learn, but what good would it do in most cases but to prolong the agony of death? If a ship sinks out at sea, few men would have the strength to swim to shore.

But water is a friend and foe to men who ride oceans, much like the wind. Sailors know its barren, harsh side as they know how it aids them, taking them out, taking them home. Water is not the greatest fear of men of the sea.

The great fear is fire.

If a ship catches fire, men are trapped, surrounded by wood, gunpowder and cloth. If fire sweeps through a vessel, men have two choices; drown or burn. Fire means that I, Death, am coming. There is nothing left to do.

And for that reason, men use fire against each other. It causes panic, bad choices, and terror. These things are heralds, calling to me.

That afternoon, a pinnace had swept from the English line. A small ship, it had caused no fear to the Armada, but sailed towards them, circling the *San Martin* and firing four shots from its bow and stern chasers. With only the *San Lorenzo* getting two shots off at the pinnace, it turned and sailed back to the English fleet, leaving Sidonia baffled. What had been its purpose? Was it a challenge to fight from Howard?

But its purpose was not to raise a challenge, as Howard had at the start of this campaign. It was to gather information on the arrangement of the Armada.

That afternoon, other ships had raced from the English fleet to England. They had gone to ask for ships, sacrifices to offer up to the gods of fire in return for victory, but even as he sent them Howard knew he could not wait for ships to come from the merchants of London. They needed to act *that* night.

At midnight, eight fireships would be sent on the westerly wind towards the Armada. Their cannons would be left on board, packed with powder and shot, and their hulls and decks would be stuffed with materials quick to catch fire. They would be sent into the Armada. Their purpose was not to destroy the ships, but separate them. If the warships could be isolated and disabled, the rest of the Armada would have no choice but to surrender or flee.

It was not a new tactic. Fireships had been used many times, and for good reason; they worked.

The idea being Drake's, he was the first to offer one of his ships as a sacrifice. Other captains followed suit. It was not entirely an honourable offer. They would be compensated for loss of vessels, so if captains picked ships that were old they might well make a profit, earning back more than the ship was worth from the Crown.

When the fireships had done their work through the night, at dawn the fleet would attack.

As evening came, men were readying the fireships. Other men were summoned to pray, for in the morning there would be battle.

As night fell, a gown of darkness billowing on leaden skies, the wind rose. The skies were heavy with cloud, obscuring the radiance of the moon. Light rain, mizzle, fell and tarried in the skies. The wind was blowing high. As the tide grew in power, ships of the Armada strained against their cables, rooted deep in the sea attached to anchors. The night was hushed, wind and wave the only sound.

The attack came with sudden speed. Skeleton crews manning the fireships cut the cables tethering them, and on the wind they sailed, straight for the Armada. The tide was running at three knots, and the wind was in their favour. Men stooped in the dark holds, flint and lengths of glowing cable in their hands. As helmsmen made true their ships' courses into the centre of the Armada, bowsprits pointing into the wind and the natural direction of the strong, spring tide, men beneath deck struck flints and laid lights to cloth, powder and wood. The holds were full of brimstone, pitch and wild fire. Tar barrels were tied to the bows. On deck men lashed helms to hold the deadly course true. Men raced up from below, ready to escape the boats of fire.

It took less than ten minutes for the fireships to reach the Armada.

At first, the light of the moon not their ally, Spanish lookouts had not seen ships separating from the main body of the English fleet. As the ships caught light, red flames bouncing upwards from the dark belly of the water, there was first not the cries of alarm you would think of, but a second of strangled silence.

Their eyes drawn to stare at fire by the ancient call that masters the hearts of all men, sailors of Spain hesitated, the lure of fire holding them fast, stopping their minds and lips. The brutal, blinding flames were hypnotic.

But with swift speed did fear break through fascination. That is the task of fear, to make men move, to push them from danger.

There were shrill cries of alarm. The high wind carried the tongues of flame swiftly, lapping dry kindling, cloth and powder. Pitch, bundles of faggots and tar fed the fire, as greedily it ate, licking rigging, sail and wood.

Within moments the ships had become fast-moving castles of flame.

Roaring towards the Armada with the dark night behind them, light blazing from open gunports like the eyes of demons, flame snaking up mast and rigging like swift-moving serpents, these were infernos of raw, brutal power and terrible beauty. With the wind behind them and full, flaming sails unfurled, the fireships came, swift as death.

Spanish lookouts saw men scrambling from the fiendish ships, dropping into the water as smaller boats rowed out to bear them back to the English fleet.

On his ship, Drake smiled. The idea had been his, which was one reason to rejoice, but he had another. In his first martial encounter with ships of Spain in the New World, fireships had been used against him and Hawkins, separating their fleet and sending them fleeing. It felt apt to do the same now to the Armada. Revenge has a long memory. It lets go of nothing.

The ship he had volunteered was named after and captained by his brother, Thomas. Loath though his brother had been to lose her, he had agreed. The ship was sent in memory of their other brothers, Joseph and John, killed in action long ago whilst fighting Spain.

Against the black night's sky, the red ships, crimson flames flickering and lashing out like dragon breath, were apparitions of pure horror. Gaining speed, they raced upon the Armada as an impenetrable bank of flame. Sidonia barked orders. Pinnaces, prepared in advance for this situation, were sent to take hold of the ships, tow them away, but the ships were moving fast, and had been chosen well. They were not small ships, but large. Only two did captains of the Armada manage to tow away, the ones at each end, leaving the main body of fire still sweeping towards the Armada.

The pinnaces tried again, but as they came close to another fireship, cannons blasted them back. Guns on all fireships began to explode, firing recklessly into the night. Shot and fragments of metal screamed out, flying in all directions, scattering the pinnaces. Panic swept Spanish ships. Men fought to hide from the firing guns, dodging shot, flying plough-chains and soaring red-hot metal shards as they struggled to save their ships. Burning with all the fury trapped in Hell, the fireships, consumed by flame from mast to waterline, roared into the heart of the Armada showering crimson embers upon Spanish ships. The cruel, capricious guns fired at will, their aim erratic and wayward. Forked tongues of flame lashed out, hungry for a taste of Spanish sail.

Sparks began to take hold of sails, and rigging ignited on the ships of the Armada. Men ran to extinguish the flames. Buckets of piss and water were being thrown. Everywhere, men were screaming with fear. Orders were not being followed.

A signal gun fired from Sidonia's ship, telling his men to flee, but many were already on their way. Cables were slashed, anchors abandoned. The Armada scattered, each ship looking only for itself, trying to escape the fire.

In red darkness, ships could be seen fleeing, putting out to sea, vanishing into the darkness. Many had left their anchors in the sea, with no time to reel them in. Men scrambled aloft, set sail to shift the bows about, for they had been lying head to wind. Ships swung to broadside with aching slowness, then came about, the wind astern. Men leapt again to adjust the sails to use the wind, as helmsmen, blinded by smoke and bright fire and darkness, tried to navigate ships through the tangled confusion of the Armada. Some ships were still in place, some in motion, some shifting position, most racing away. Ships that managed to break through the web of chaos shook their sails out and gathered speed downwind.

The sea had become Hell; red fire, panic and confusion. Dark skies filled with stars and clouds and flames reflected upon the water. The air itself was afire.

Although it was hard for Howard to tell if he had his chance to destroy them, it was not hard to tell for Sidonia. He had seen abject chaos unleashed. And to chaos, the discipline of the Armada, its greatest weapon, had been lost.

The fireships ran through the Armada, coming aground on the shore, burning bright, lashing the skies with smoke and with flame. The fireships had not caught a single ship, but they had done their task. The formation was broken, the ships were gone, scattered.

At a distance, amongst the sound of the sea and shouting of men, Sidonia heard an almighty crash. At least one ship had run into another somewhere in the darkness.

Alone, only four other vessels still with him, Sidonia's ship remained. The ships with him retained their anchors, shifted position and moored in safety. Looking to one side, he could see Recalde's ship. The other vessels were ghostly in burning light and thick darkness. All Sidonia could fathom was their number. He sent a fast pinnace after the fleeing ships, ordering commanders to re-form in open water and await his command. Without anchors to hold them, he knew many would not be able to obey him, even if they wanted to. All he could do was remain, hoping the fleet would come to him.

What Sidonia and his fleeing men did not know was that the Dutch had been busy. They had stolen from the sea all markers, buoys and navigation points that would aid men to read the waters.

Still in position, but almost alone, the Admiral stood, as from his deck he watched his fleet vanish into the dark cowl of night.

Chapter Twenty

Calais and the Flemish Coast
July 29th 1588

The Battle of Gravelines

Death

Dawn came. The bitter, clinging stench of burned, wet wood, cloying as blood, hung upon the air. Fireships smouldered on the coast of Calais, smoke curling into grey morning skies, the last of their crimson light glowing in fading darkness. Only ruptured remains stood; the blackened bones of sea dragons upon the sands of the shore.

As the sun rose, Howard peered across the grey seas and white, curving waves, ready to issue the order for attack. A mile away, he could see just five ships at the Calais coast. The *San Martin* was there, along with the *San Juan , San Marcos, San Felipe* and *San Mateo*. They were the great warships of the Armada. Feral skies loomed. The wind was rising. The five ships were struggling to hold steady in the current, and the weather was threatening wildness to come.

Only one other ship was in sight, the *San Lorenzo*, but she would be no help. She was the crash Sidonia had heard in the night. Battering into another ship in the chaos she had lost her ability to steer. Crippled and broken, she was drifting to the cliffs.

All the others, all of the vast fleet, had been dispersed.

Pinnaces were racing upon the wind, sent by Sidonia to gather the Armada, strewn across the sea. Some ships were in sight. Knowing he could not rely on them re-forming in time to aid him, Sidonia gave the order for the five ships to sail north, and to hold the English off for as long as they could.

From Howard's ship a signal gun fired. Trumpets blasted, clear and true, ringing across the water, shattering the peace of the morning. Sidonia shivered to hear them. English ships hastened to pull anchor and unfurl sails, men racing up rope ladders, their feet curling like those of apes as they flashed quick to the sails, balancing on rigging and mast to untie them. The one hundred and fifty ships now in the fleet began to move. Drake led them, an honour granted by Howard. The wind was with them as was the tide. With allies of weather and water with them, the English set after Sidonia.

Howard went with a squadron after the crippled *Lorenzo*, driving her under the ramparts of Calais Castle. As the ship ran aground, screams from the holds broke out; slaves rowing the broken vessel were drowning as the ship ground into rock and water. Her starboard cannon buried in the mud, her lower decks awash with water, the *Lorenzo* was dying, plunging into the inky water.

Howard could not get within cannon range, so dispatched longboats and pinnaces loaded with men to board the stricken ship. He was after money and gunpowder. Pinnaces swarmed about the *Lorenzo*. Although the ship was broken, soldiers within were not. They had the advantage in a fight, positioned much higher than the attackers below. There were three hundred soldiers on board as well as four hundred and fifty slaves. The English only had one hundred men. But many soldiers jumped into the thrashing sea, knowing with their vessel shattered and aground there was little to die for but vain glory.

Some put up a fight. Howard's men, many of them, were wounded in the struggle that followed. Moncada died, struck through both eyes by musket fire, and as he fell so did his ship. As the English piled aboard, teeming over the ship's rails and swarming in through open gunports, slaves made to escape the same way. Some made it to the port of Calais, swimming about rocks and malevolent waves that sought to steal their lives. Their aim achieved, Howard's men stripped the ship of all it had. Plundering the ship kept Howard away from the main battle for a while.

Whilst Howard plundered, Drake led the assault on the five ships left in port. Sidonia and other captains raced downwind, hoping the tide would reunite them with the rest of the Armada before Drake fell upon them. But Drake, the south-westerly wind in his sails, came for them hard, fast and strong. Through the North Sea straits they sailed, encountering the five ships just off the shores of Gravelines. With the numbers in their favour, and experience under their belts, the English were ready to take greater risks. Capture the flagship, and the morale of the Armada would be compromised. Seize Sidonia, and the war might end that day.

The English ships veered close, engaging at closer range than ever they had dared, the lure of plunder and victory in their minds. Sidonia, knowing they would try this, sailed away downwind, taking them to the banks of Dunkirk, hoping to wreck them upon the jagged offshore rocks.

By nine of the clock, Drake was closing on Sidonia. Both ships held fire until they came within a whisker of each other, and then guns on the *Revenge* boomed, bow guns then broadsides roaring. Smoke seemed to carry flame, burning air and lungs. Red-rimmed eyes, blinded by smoke and wind, struggled to see in the arid blackness as guncrews toiled, loading, firing, reloading, and firing again.

The *San Martin* responded, broadsides screaming at the *Revenge* in defiance. Shot of all sizes sailed through the air from one ship to the other, and from ships behind Drake and Sidonia. On the *San Martin*, sails, rigging and spars were struck by flying balls and chains, as hull-shot from lighter guns caused disarray to fall upon men dodging their fire on deck. Heavy cannon on the *Revenge's* lower gundeck pelted the hull of Sidonia's ship. Thirty- and sixty-pound shot, fired at close range, ripped into the four-inch oak planking. Balls of metal blasted into cabins and gundecks, sending a thousand sword-sharp arrows of wood flying. Into face and breast, arm and leg, darts plummeted. Men screamed, lips drawn in snarls of agony as they were blinded, as blood flowed from a thousand tiny cuts. Those unfortunate enough to be in the way of the shot itself had their legs torn away.

Shot burst into the lower decks still smouldering, glowing red hot, burning the floor, bringing the promise of fire. Buckets of water were heaved over them, water racing to join with blood, ash and debris washing across the floor.

After Drake came Fenner on the *Nonpareil*, firing bow then broadsides into the *San Martin*. Then the rest of Drake's squadron followed, each ship firing, raining destruction, guns reloading and firing three times as fast as Sidonia's.

Drake wheeled about, leading his squadron to pursue other Armada ships out to sea. Some were just in sight. Frobisher continued the attack on the *San Martin*, but was not merry with Drake. "That man is a pirate!" he screamed to his first in command over the hollering guns. "Any time he scents plunder, he is away!"

Frobisher thought Drake a coward, but Drake was not. Most of his career at sea had been a series of great risks taken against a strong enemy with but a small band of men to support him, and he had just opened fire at a range the *San Martin* might have used to grapple him. Pirate Drake was. Coward he was not. Spanish ships were coming. He thought to head them off before they got to Sidonia.

Frobisher sailed upon Sidonia with the *Triumph* at close range. He, too, was no coward. With great guns he blasted the *San Martin*, as his squadron assaulted her bow, stern and flanks. After him came Hawkins, leading his own squadron with the *Victory*. Seymour was at the rear, attacking the *San*

Martin's tail, along with Wynter in the *Vanguard*. Sidonia was rapidly becoming separated from the rest of the ships.

But to the aid of their commander, Spanish ships came. The *San Marcos* plunged into battle, and Hawkins's *Victory* engaged her, along with the *Marie Rose*, the *Dreadnought* and the *Swallow*. On the *San Martin* forty men had fallen. They lay heaped on deck. A fifty-pound shot crashed through her belly, below the waterline. Sidonia was in true danger of sinking.

The *San Felipe* found herself surrounded by seventeen English ships, taking heavy fire to stern and both sides of the ship. The captain, Don Francisco de Toledo, steered his ship into the middle of his attackers, seeking to board them. It was an act of courageous lunacy. He ran his musketeers out; the ships were so close short-range guns could be used. Behind piles of corpses men sheltered, taking aim upon their foe.

Shot pouring from cannon was joined by volleys of musket fire peppering the English ships. Men fell on both sides, coughing up blood from punctured lungs, grasping their hearts, shot through and torn. Smoke poured into the wind, whipping about the ships as guns fired, and blasts of red flame rocketed into the air. The *Felipe* plunged again, trying to get close. The English ships danced away, refusing to be grappled. The *Felipe's* sails whistled in the wind, torn to bits, her hull groaned with pain and hundreds of men were in heaps upon the deck, dead, face down, their own blood mingled with water washing over their faces. Five of her cannon were blown clean off their carriages and her foremast shattered under the rain of shot. Her upper deck blasted to bits, her rudder disabled, and her pumps broken, the *Felipe* fought on. She was all but lost, but like a wounded sea monster still she roared.

Along with the *San Luis* and the *La Trinidad Valencera*, which had returned from the open sea, the *San Mateo* came to the *Felipe's* rescue. The *Mateo* was also in trouble, grievously wounded, but she would not abandon her sister upon the sea. English ships tailed the *Mateo*. As an English ship swung alongside, a foolhardy sailor jumped over the rails to the Spanish ship, and was swiftly cut down by men on board.

The *Felipe* and *Mateo* were in poor shape, the *Maria Juan* was sinking. An Italian ship was more blood than wood. From all ships men were plummeting from rigging and sail, from deck, splashing into the grasping sea. The water was crashing with debris, sail, rigging and bodies. The air was thick with smoke and burning tar. Ash and pitch lay greasy upon the water. Sea foam, pink with blood, rose and fell upon the surging waves.

Spanish ships, disabled, defenceless, sallied still into battle, defending fellow ships with their crushed and broken bodies where they could not with guns.

The most astounding acts of courage are not those taken when a man enters a fight knowing he will win. They are crafted when men enter, knowing they will lose. And that was the situation the rest of the Armada was in, but they were coming. Many of them were not great warships, many were hulks, merchantmen and smaller ships, but to aid their brothers they came.

The wind was harsh and the sun strong, but out at sea, demonstrating astounding skill since the wind was against them, Spanish ships had rallied and resumed their defensive formation. From chaos they crafted order. More and more ships of the Armada came together in the heavy seas, seeing how dangerous the assault on Sidonia was. They returned to him at great danger to themselves, for the pride of Spain. Into a ragged crescent they went, racing upon the wind to save Sidonia. As they neared him, the crescent arched out, drawing Sidonia and English vessels into its belly; the maw of an almighty dragon gaping open, threatening to snap shut.

It was a clumsy formation, but it was there and no other fleet could have done better. Taking a vicious pounding from

English guns, they came about Sidonia; their discipline inspiring and skill formidable.

They began to make a fighting retreat, but the English hung on like rabid dogs. As Wynter attacked the starboard wing, four Spanish ships collided, their grappling hooks, long useless, lashing them together.

Spanish sailors fought to free their ships, hacking at entangled rigging and grappling ropes with axes and knives as the English kept firing. The thin, crisp sound of sails rupturing sliced into the air. Rigging plunged down from above. Blood ran on deck, and men slipped in it, falling, thumping to the floor. Shot whizzed through the wind as musket balls cracked into cheek and eye. Far below deck, men stood chest-deep in water trying to plug perilous holes in the hull as more water rushed in, eager to carry their ship away to the ocean floor. Divers toiling in freezing water were underwater much of the day, battering cloth, lead plates and debris into holes the English tore.

Watchers on the shores of Calais could only stare in awe and horror. They could not believe the rate of fire, the viciousness of the attack, or the skill and courage displayed by both sides. As the hours drew on, the ships became obscured by smoke, moving as ghosts through the water, blasts of crimson light illuminating the battle with sudden radiance, then vanishing as smoke wrapped around them once more. The only way to tell ships apart was the rate of fire. It was the greatest battle ever seen, many said, greater than Lepanto, than Sluys. From the shore of Calais and that of Flanders and England the sound of the guns could be heard, thunder in the skies.

As the echoes of English guns faded from one ship, another began firing, a steady rain of shot pouring from them, effortless as breathing. The Spanish ships responded with hesitant shots. As Spanish ships heeled over in the water, the English fired hard, aiming at exposed timbers of the waterline. Heavy guns blasted the bellies of ships as smaller ones rained fire upon the deck, the masts, the sails, the rigging and the swarming men. Soldiers waiting for orders to board were mown down by shot and crushed by falling timber. The English fired scraps of iron, where they were short on shot. Missiles of molten metal whipped into cheek, eye, throat and thigh. Cannons were blasted from their carriages on deck, hurtling through the air, smashing into men and mast and then sailing into the pounding sea.

Don Pedro Enriquez screamed as his hand was blown away, but Don Felipe de Cordoba had not a moment to let out a sound as his head was ripped from his body by fast-flying shot. His friend, Pedro Estrada, stared in dumb horror as a white spray of brain burst from his comrade's head, splattering upon his shoes.

On Drake's *Revenge* a gentleman attempting to take rest had his bed shot away from under his back, and on another ship dinner was rudely interrupted for the Earl of Northumberland and Charles Blount as a cannonball burst through the hull, slicing off the toes of a man sitting with them. Men died, but not as they did on the ships of Spain.

As the battle went on, some guns fell silent. Spanish guns which had been damaged, or were deemed useless as they took too long to reload, were abandoned. Musket and arquebus fire took over, puncturing the air with the softer, small sound of bullets. As the *Santa Maria de Begona* and the *San Juan* came close to boarding English vessels, many English captains ceased to bring ships so close. Great shot slammed into hulls and easily sailed into the tough flanks of the Spanish ships. Peppered by so much shot, the ships were becoming softer, easier to damage. The Armada was in danger, all its ships had rigging and sails flapping, masts broken, and all were taking on water. Decks and holds groaned under relentless fire. Ships hung low with the weight of water, and bodies of the dead. Men on deck were glancing at their shot-riddled masts, waiting for the dreadful, long crack and creak that went on forever as masts fell like trees in the forest.

But courage did not flee the sons of Spain.

They had no hope of boarding the English ships. They knew English guns were better, their vessels faster, and they knew they were close to defeat. Yet the Armada fought on. The Spanish did not fail in fellowship or bravery. No ships fled, no matter how broken, no matter the danger. Again and again they sailed into the attack, coming to the rescue of comrades, displaying such reckless courage that Howard and Drake could not fail to be awed.

The *Regazona* came to the rescue of her sister ship. The *Regazona* had no cannon left, but into the fight she sailed, nothing to defend her but musket fire against the English ships swarming about her sister. From her decks blood poured as though the ship herself was bleeding. Musketeers fired on deck as the ship swung in to aid her sister.

Again and again the *Regazona* took position in the fighting line, nothing but small arms to attack or defend with, displaying breathtaking courage.

On the *San Mateo*, half the crew was dead or wounded. She had no guns left and was dangerously low in the water. As Seymour and Wynter attacked her and the *San Felipe*, the *Mateo's* crew hurled broken masts, sails, even dead men overboard in an attempt to keep their fractured ship afloat, to continue the fight and continue to aid the *Felipe*.

On the *San Martin*, Sidonia could hardly see a thing. The smoke was thick as soup. In the heat of battle, Sidonia himself climbed the mast to try to see what was happening to his ships. From there he saw the *Mateo*.

Even though his ship was broken, her rigging in shreds, her belly shot through so badly that she was in danger of sinking,

Sidonia knew the *Mateo* was close to going down, and he knew he must save her. He ordered his own boats, which might be needed at any moment to rescue him and his men, to make for the *Mateo* so they could rescue her crew. When the *Mateo's* captain refused to abandon his ship, Sidonia sent his diver to the *Mateo*. That diver was sorely needed on his own ship to plug holes, but Sidonia sent him to the *Mateo*, to see if she could be saved.

She could not. Men were taken off, those few still alive, and the ship sank deeper and deeper into the green-grey waves, carried away from the fight by the tide. Last seen heading into the sea, towards Zeeland, the *Mateo* was lost.

The *Felipe* was, too, in grave danger. Her guns were destroyed; the ship was ready to surrender to the sea. Seymour pulled alongside in the *Rainbow*, and shouted terms for surrender, but was answered by a bold gun shot. Seymour fell, crashing on his deck, wounded but not dead. The *Rainbow* sailed away as men of the listing *Felipe* mocked them, shouting they were cowards and "Lutheran chickens".

The *Doncella* came alongside, taking three hundred men off the *Felipe*. But the *Doncella* herself was sinking, and captains of the *Felipe* decided they would rather die on a galleon than a hulk, and went back. The *Felipe* drifted away, to the Dunkirk shore.

She was not alone. The *Marie Juan,* blown apart by Captain Robert Crosse on the *Hope*, was sinking. The two captains were shouting terms of surrender to each other as the ship lurched, her broken belly gasping in the throes of death. Boats went out to save the crew but only one boat had filled before the ship went down, men leaping from her into the sea, others clinging with desperate fingers to the mast and rigging.

The battle had raged for nine hours. The Armada was broken. Its formation was shattered, ships were sinking, so many men had died that the waves churned red and the sea was choked with floating corpses. Men bounced on waves, face down with wood, torn sails and fragments of rigging hitting them. Some floated face up, glassy eyes staring blankly at the heavens above as though asking God why He had allowed them to die. The belly of the ocean was awash with cannonballs and corpses. Men sank to the sea floor, limbs tangled in drifting weed as past them floated balls of iron, bubbles drifting from their tails. Ships were listing, dragging dangerously low in the water. Smaller boats could be seen upon the waves as men tried to save themselves and their comrades by abandoning ship. Howard was on the Armada's rearguard with the *Bear*, *Bonaventure* and the *Lion*. Near him was the *Vanguard*, with Captain Wynter, still screaming orders to his men despite being almost crushed by the recoil of one of his cannon.

The weather was growing worse. The wind keened strong, howling through broken ships as thick rain fell. And still the English came, five squadrons firing into the mashed wood of the Spanish ships, driving them towards the Banks of Zeeland.

These were evil waters, where skulking low-tide off-shore sandbanks could wreck ships with ease. So low were they that fishermen rode into them on horseback. The English knew these waters. For years they had crossed the sea, shipping wool to the Low Countries. Drake had worked here as an apprentice to his uncle, and knew how to navigate the snaking, sinuous channels and malicious mudbanks, the hiding sand, the shifting waterways. Into this treacherous place the English herded the Spanish, pushing them closer to the deadly sandbanks with each volley of shot.

Then the English broke from continuous fire, knowing weather and sand might do their task for them.

The Armada soldiered on, pumps toiling relentlessly as ships tried to stay afloat. Exhausted men headed out to undertake repairs. But their captains were worried.

The Armada could not pull clear of the looming sandbanks. The wind was blowing northerly; even the lightest, most manoeuvrable of the ships could not pull away. Into the shallows they were thrust, unable to pull anchor for many had none left after escaping the fireships.

Night fell, not an easy one for any of the men. Stars shone as white fire upon the waves. Banks of cloud shifted, alarming those watching on board as they caused momentary blindness.

All firewood was soaked. When night came rations were handed out, cold and meagre, spoiled not only from weeks at sea, but by fire, smoke and salt water. The gundecks of all ships were cleansed, fallen timber, rigging and sail swept into the sea along with the flesh and blood of the fallen. Blood mixed with the water until it flowed blue once more, clean. Water is God's element. Enough can wash any horror away.

As men tried to sleep, the groans of the dying and the scent of blood washing up from the surgeons working below filled the air. The waves crashed on, relentless, uncaring, as men settled into nightmares of fire and death and blood.

Beneath the sea, men fell and floated, bodies washing down to the bottom, their passage made gentle by my hands. Carefully I carried them to their resting places on the sand and rock of the ocean floor. They had fought well, with pride and most certainly with honour. On the sea bed, men of Spain and England lay, arms about one another, like children curling up together to sleep in safety and warmth. In death they were enemies no more.

There they rest, bones sinking into sand, hands and skulls a playground for little fish. The last terror of life gone, the world opened her arms and reclaimed them, so as their blood became part of the sea, so bones became part of the soil and sand feeding the heart of the ocean. From the turbulence and terror life provides, I took them, for in death there is no fear, only calm, cool ethereal darkness, like the boundless sea, closing over mind and soul, bringing the long hush of drifting eternity.

Chapter Twenty-One

The Flanders Banks
July 30th 1588

Death

By dawn, no attack had come, and Sidonia knew why. Howard, only half a league away, had no need to attack with guns when the weather would vanquish Sidonia and the other ships for him. Sidonia stared down at the shallow, deadly sea. They were perilously close to the banks of Zeeland, wind and tide thrusting them closer all the time. They could go nowhere but the sandbanks.

Sidonia's men had told him to flee in a pinnace, but he would not. Others had suggested surrender, but when Valdes had said this Oquendo had threatened to throw him overboard. All men took instead to their knees to pray.

By four of the clock that day, the tide was running onshore and the Armada seemed doomed. There was only eight fathoms of water beneath them, a slim gap between keel and sand. Sidonia knew if a miracle did not occur, they would be grounded, beached as the English swarmed upon them. The whole Armada, this almighty force, might be crushed upon these sandbanks, what men they had left slaughtered.

Sidonia's ship was falling towards the sand and Howard and his fleet manoeuvred with vexing ease, keeping the Spanish ships between their guns and the coast of Zeeland. The waves were large and choppy, revealing the dangerous sandbanks below. Sidonia was forced to send commands that ships that could were to weigh anchor, and those who could beat upwind were to come to him. Many could not, since their anchors were lost off the coast of Calais, and some chose not to, knowing the danger they would face. Many ships sailed on, close to the wind.

Sidonia, almost on the sandbanks of Zeeland, with few ships near him, leaned over the rail of his ship to shout to Oquendo on the *Santa Anna* not far away. "Señor Oquendo, what shall we do? We are lost!" shouted the Admiral.

"As for me, I am going to fight and die like a man!" Oquendo screamed back. "Send me some shot!"

Sidonia thought the end had come. It seemed there was nothing for him to do to save his fleet, or himself.

But perhaps God was listening, and if the Lord of Heaven had been in a Protestant frame of mind of late, that day He altered His thinking.

A storm rose out of nowhere. Wind rushed from the south-west, bringing a squall that came thrashing through the skies. Swollen raindrops plummeted, the fall of rain so intense that no man could see further than the end of his arm. All hands went to the sails to trim them. Men, some fifty foot in the air, some one hundred, balanced on slippery poles, blinded by wind and rain as they worked on the sails. The blackened skies loomed upon them so barely could they see their own hands in the ominous gloom. Helmsmen controlling the ships tried desperately to avoid collisions in the mist of pouring rain. For half an hour the tempest raged, and when it cleared, Howard and his men could see the Armada.

Their sails were unfurled, glorious wind filling them they snapped and flapped like birds preparing to fly. Sidonia and his men were sailing as fast as they could to the north-east, away from the shoals. They were already out of cannon range.

The Armada, shattered though it was, resumed formation, ships coming alongside each other like brothers in battle carrying wounded from the fray. Sidonia shortened sail, inviting the English to attack again.

On his ship, Howard laughed. "They lack nothing in courage," he said to one of his men. Howard's face was grey with water and gunsmoke. Ash collected in the wrinkles about his eyes had turned black, painting his skin.

"They do not, my lord Admiral," his servant agreed. "I saw ships fight yesterday that had no guns and hardly a man left alive on board. Yet to save their brothers they came."

"Worthy opponents," Howard agreed. "And now their Admiral invites attack."

But Sidonia was hoping the English would not attack. The shortening of his sails was a last act of defiance, a final brag. They had hardly any guns left, only small arms. Had the English come again few ships would have survived. Sidonia shortened sail to boast he was not beaten, but he was. He was hoping Howard would be running low on shot and powder.

And Howard was. So were his captains. They had hardly anything left, but their ships had not taken the thrashing the Armada had. Howard issued an order to follow the Armada. They were broken but not beaten, and there was still a danger to England. If they could see the Armada away from the shores of Zeeland, away from Parma, the danger was lessened.

The English fleet pulled out into the water, rations of bread and beer handed to all men. As some slumped, exhausted, onto deck and in the holds to eat and drink, carpenters and riggers, sail makers and doctors worked, trying to repair ships and men. To those beyond aid, chaplains offered the last comfort of God.

On the air, voices of all the priests on the Armada were heard, trying to offer last comfort and rites to dying men. Bodies were slung over the side. There was small time to offer the dignity of a funeral when so many were dead. Men working to repair ships wheezed and coughed, lungs full of smoke, gunpowder and ash. Sidonia's captains reported many were collapsing as they worked, keeling over as water rushed into the bilges and rain lashed them upon the decks.

The Armada sailed away and behind her came shadows. The English fleet, hardly damaged, followed Sidonia and his men, their pace gentle and their ships effortless and sleek in the silky blue-grey water.

Chapter Twenty-Two

Richmond Palace
July 30th 1588

Elizabeth

I had never seen my men move so fast. It was dizzying to behold.

Meetings, insane in number and haste, were going on daily at Richmond. Men arrived each morn as chilly blankets of mist slowly burned away, leaving the skies glowing, blinding-white and grey-gold. They came by horse or water and entered the palace, racing from meeting to meeting in the halls of court. The threat of the Armada, now docked at Calais, had unleashed a terror into plain sight that many had kept hidden all this time.

"If they have deserted, dispatch men to haul them back!" I almost screamed at Cecil in one early meeting that day. "Tell Robin or Hunsdon to send men to drag the Dover militia back into formation!"

From the four thousand supposed to be at Dover, we had twenty-two companies of one hundred men each left. The rest were on the run.

From Cecil's face, I already knew what the answer to my furious demands would be. We could not spare men to go after those who had deserted; it would leave another area of fragile coast undefended, and might not bear any fruit in any case. We might, in fact, lose only more men. They might think their brothers-out-of-arms had the right idea and follow suit.

I knew why most had gone. They were going home, to defend their own families, their own villages. Everyone in England now knew the Armada was at Calais, so close to Parma and his troops that the General might have spat and hit Sidonia's sails. Invasion was imminent. Where should men want to be at such a time than at their gate, holding death away from their parents, their wives, their children?

But in other ways, desertion was nonsensical. Allow troops to land, anywhere, and England was done for. *No* home would be safe. A matter of days, and we would all be fighting to protect our gates. And divided and scattered we would lose.

"Eight hundred Dutch musketeers are ready to be sent to reinforce Dover," Cecil said, hoping this would make me feel better. It did in some ways, but the fact the defence of England had to fall to men from other countries was not entirely heartening. I had also heard that some people of Kent were rejoicing to hear of any successes of the Armada. Some were saying the Spanish were better than the people of England.

Another matter was our defences. Never had I heard my men speak at such speeds; lists of fortifications that surely *would* crumble within days sped from their lips like the rush of a cascading waterfall. Works on ports, castles and defences that should have been completed weeks ago were being rushed through. Sweating, groaning men were toiling day and night to build walls, banks and ditches. And my officers were making war upon each other; preparation, perhaps, for when the sons of Spain poured into England.

"Send someone possessing sanity to Sussex and Winchester," I said, speaking of the Earl of Sussex and Marquis of Winchester, who, Cecil informed me, were so busy fighting between themselves that they might not have noticed the enemy marching upon them. "Hampshire must come together, not fly apart. Tell them it is my *pleasure* that they reconcile themselves to better behaviour and in such times as these, unkindness between my men helps us not at all!"

"They want one thousand more men," Walsingham said, mopping his grey, wrinkled brow. I was worried about Walsingham. He looked sick. He was ill again and the stress of the situation was hardly aiding him. His eyes had fallen to continuous weeping, as though he already mourned the fall of his country.

"We will send what we can, but with men deserting posts all along the coast, there are few to send!" I grasped shaking hands into fists at my sides, willing them to stop trembling.

"Seymour has powder, but needs more food," Cecil said later as we strode along the hallways to another meeting. Gunpowder, all we could scrape together, was being carried on the fastest wagons that could be found to the coast to restock Howard, Seymour and Drake, but food was becoming a problem just as large. "The closest provisions that can be sent are from Rochester or London storehouses," he went on, his steps close to mine as he winced, gout plaguing him. "Since the closure of the Maison Dieu in Dover, the old monastic building, there is no storehouse at Dover."

I grimaced, feeling another subtle dig at me. I had allowed that victualling establishment to fall out of use. At the time I sent that command, it had not been needed, and was an added expense I could not afford. Now, it was something that might cause starvation to fall upon our ships. *So easy is it to see what should have been done when we glance from present to past,* I thought. "Send whatever can be gathered from Rochester and London by boat to Seymour," I said, not breaking step. "And have the Lieutenant of Dover gather women to brew ale and beer for the ships."

We entered the Council chamber and immediately men began to speak on top of one another. The brawling of voices created a din that polluted my ears and threatened to mash my brain into mush. I held up a hand. "Gentlemen, speak one at a time or nothing will be heard. Little time do we have. Let us waste it not."

I sat down and they followed, taking seats rather than standing, flustered, hopping from foot to foot.

"Drink," I told them, indicating to cups of ale on the table. "All of you are racing about and I doubt you are taking time to succour your bodies. While you have this chance to fuel blood and brain, use it." I turned to Walsingham. "The Essex militia," I said. "I hear they are on the march at last?"

"Four thousand men are on their way to Tilbury," he said. "The Earl reports they are bold men, ready to fight."

"They are carrying food?"

"Some are, Majesty."

"They were all told to. Much of our supplies are even now heading out to sea and the storehouses of London are groaning bare."

"We will gather all we can, Majesty."

I paused. I could taste panic on the air. Like sweat it rose, threatening to overcome my men. We had heard of guns firing off the coast the day before, so knew there had been fighting, but there had been no letters from the fleet. For all we knew, our ships were at the bottom of the sea and Sidonia and Parma were loading men ready to sail to England and slaughter us all.

"I want each of you to concentrate on your work," I said sternly. "I feel the heat in your spirits, but panic will do none of us any good. When you feel fear rise, stop, breathe and then go back to your work. Keep England moving, keep our men marching and keep finding supplies. That is your task, gentlemen. Concentrate on it."

Nodding heads about the table calmed me. I could sympathise with the situation they found themselves in. For decades I had been dealing with the doom-laden fug of panic. It settles, sending your own body out to attack itself. Breathing rises to furious speeds, and darkness falls, threatening unconsciousness. I had faced danger of assassination, invasion and death many times. For some of the men before me, this was the first time they had been threatened so intimately. At least now I could pass on the wisdom I had learned after years of dealing with sudden assaults of panic.

I looked to Walsingham. "Your spies in Flanders," I said. "What news do they have of Parma?"

"Little," he said. "Parma has closed his doors to all he distrusts, which now includes most men of the world. Some write that his forces are scattered, some think they are ready to set out." Walsingham paused to dab his sore eyes. "In honesty, madam, we are blind. We must prepare as though he means to set out and is ready to. That is the only course of action."

"The Dutch Parliament has answered our call to arms," Cecil interjected. "Justin of Navarre has twenty-four ships along the Flemish coast, blocking Parma from crossing the Dover Straits. There are another thirty-two ships off Sluys, perhaps one hundred around Antwerp."

"That is wonderful news," I said, breathing out and at the same time thanking God that I had aided the Dutch rebels in the past.

"What is less wonderful is that some Dutch leaders fear Parma will use their absence to attack Holland and Zeeland," said Walsingham. "I have reports some Dutch commanders have stopped reinforcements being sent to the fleet of Navarre."

"But at least there are ships in position to defend England," I said. "And my royal godson has written. King James declares he will do anything and everything in his power to defend England, his ally. He says we are bonded by blood and religion, and offers us his forces and his own person. He will come not as a stranger, but as my natural son, willing to hazard his life and Crown in my defence."

Although this cheered some, many looked infinitely suspicious. An army of Scots marching into England for our defence was a good thing, but what if James should use this moment to make a play for the throne, stealing it from the hands of Phillip, using the King of Spain's assault on the south to claim the north?

"I will call on my royal brother only if Parma lands," I assured them. "But I believe in the honest goodness of my godson. He is our ally, and if he offers himself to England as a son and soldier, we must trust that is what he will be. The word of a prince is sacrosanct."

They nodded, but I knew they were thinking of all the times I had gone back on my word.

"Orders are to be sent to Sussex," I went on. "Tell Lord Brockhurst not to stand his troops down yet."

"It is thought the Armada will not attempt to land in Sussex now," Cecil said. "They would have to turn about and face our fleet head on." He paused. "And the troops held there are an extra cost, if not needed."

"I am aware of the cost," I said. "But have Brockhurst hold a few more days, until we have sure news."

"More gunpowder is on its way to Portsmouth to be sent out to Howard and Drake," said Walsingham. "And ten lasts have gone to Kent."

"Why is gunpowder on its way to Portsmouth?" I asked. "Kent is surely closer."

"It was dispatched before we had news of the fleet's movements, Majesty," Walsingham replied. "To recall it and send it out again would take longer than allowing it to get to Portsmouth and from there be carried by boat to our ships."

"Hunsdon reports he has almost twenty-nine thousand infantry and four and a half thousand horse to defend Your Majesty," said Cecil. "They will concentrate on the western edge of London, with some men sent to Richmond, and another ten thousand of the men of London to support them."

"The hospitals are ready for wounded?" I asked.

"As ready as we can make them, Majesty."

"I must show myself to the people," I announced, watching faces become grey and horrified.

Cecil hesitated to speak, but could not stop himself. "Majesty, that would not be a good idea."

"My people need to see me, to know I am well."

"One fortunate shot by one traitor and England would fall with you, Majesty," Walsingham said. "There are high and strange tempers upon the wind. Men who have lost their wits or whose faith is awry might take a chance now, as they would not at another time."

I closed my eyes. I knew I was right, just as I knew Walsingham had a point. Danger was high indeed, but I had ruled all these decades by showing myself to the people, talking to them, being amongst them, approachable as a friend. In this, our hour of danger, it was only more important they saw me and drew strength from me, the emblem of England. Hiding me away in a palace was akin to a lord riding into battle with his standard tucked under his arm. If men could not see the banner calling them to fight, how did they know where to go? I should be with them at this time, not simply just near them.

"Many of us would feel better, madam, if you in fact moved to Windsor," said Cecil. There was a rumble of agreement from about the table.

"I say I wish to go out and you suggest I become only more locked away?" I asked. "I will not to Windsor go. I will remain in London. For now, I will not go amongst my people, but I will not remain hidden away for all time, gentlemen. I am England's Queen. If men see me, they are reminded what they are fighting for."

That was not the first or last meeting of the day. By the time I went to my rooms my head was spinning. Words, thoughts, information and images of what would come, what was occurring now and of the past all came, swimming in my mind, a miasma of confusion.

I sat down on a cushion before the bare fire, watching wind whip rain past the windows, lashing them with grey streaks of water. Blanche joined me, and in silence we sat. I did not call for music, nor tried to make any myself. I did not pick up my embroidery.

As the hours passed more of my ladies came. Like soldiers they flowed to me, their commander. None carried words, only hushed stillness, and together we sat, our eyes on the windows or lost staring into tapestry, as silently we all prayed for ourselves, our men, our children, and for England.

Chapter Twenty-Three

The Escorial Palace, Madrid, Spain,
and
The Coast of Zeeland
July 31st 1588

Death

"This news is asserted in France to be true..." Phillip's quill scratched the paper as he wrote to Sidonia. The inner sanctum of his stark room echoed with the sound of monks singing Mass from the chapel; a haunting, lonely sound.

Had Phillip looked from a window he would have seen members of his court wandering along covered walkways which protected eyes and skin from the fierce sun, or standing beneath billowing banners, tumbled by the soft breeze, which carried his motto *The World is not Enough*. But Phillip did not look from a window, nor to another wall where a portrait of the Holy Virgin hung, her gentle eyes resting on his back. His eyes were on the page he was writing and his body on a stool, on a floor which stood above his own tomb in the church. Here he worked, and here he would rest for eternity. The King of Spain was a creature of habit, in life or death.

"... I hope to God that it may be so and that you have known how to follow up the victory and make the most of it, pursuing the enemy actively without giving him the opportunity of reforming and pushing on until you join hands with my nephew, the Duque..."

An excited missive had reached Phillip that morning, inspiring this letter of congratulations and yet more advice to Sidonia. The letter, sent from France some days before, had been from Phillip's ambassador to the French Court, Mendoza. The ambassador had written that a great engagement had been fought off the Isle of Wight, the Armada had sunk fifteen English ships, including Howard's, and survivors had fled for the cover of Dover. Drake had last been seen in a tiny boat, heading east. This had been seen by witnesses, Mendoza wrote, and he had sent a letter to Count Olivares in Rome, who was presently attempting to extract the money promised to Spain from the Pope. Such a glorious victory might mean the wholly tight-fisted Father of the Church might part with some coin.

A note from a lesser person planted in Mendoza's household, one of Phillip's spies, said the ambassador had been so delighted with this news he had taken his sword in hand and rushed into the Notre Dame shouting, "Victory! Victory!"

The ambassador had also built a great bonfire in the courtyard of his residence, wrote the spy, but was waiting on confirmation before lighting it.

Phillip was, by nature and due to practice, a careful man, but eyewitnesses reassured him. There was, however, a hint in his letter to Mendoza that he was not entirely convinced. *"As you consider the news to be true…"*

Phillip had fair reason to distrust his ambassador. For many months Mendoza had been blithely lying to King Henri of France, telling him the reason the Armada had been sent was to clear the Channel of the English corsairs, as Elizabeth would not control them. Ambassadors were good liars, and Mendoza was also just a little too eager to believe any rumour that brought harm to or defamed England. He had not forgotten or forgiven being thrown from the country by the Queen like a soiled handkerchief tossed into a fire.

As he came to the end of his letter to Sidonia, Phillip wrote, *"I confidently look for God's favour in a cause so entirely His own, and expect your valour and activity will have accomplished all I could desire. I anxiously await news."*

The last part was truer than most things ever he had written. Never had he wanted news more. The thirst for knowledge of the Armada was dry upon his tongue, aching in his belly. The delay of letters coming from France was intolerable, even though this one had taken less than a week to reach his hands. The trouble was, he did not entirely trust Mendoza's report. He was not alone. Many men thought the ambassador prone to exaggeration. Phillip did not like embellishment. Facts should be plain and true, not gathered from wayward, flighty gossip.

As the day drew on, Phillip became less and less certain. The Venetian ambassador at Phillip's court was sceptical. He had been heard asking why, if this battle had been fought and the flagship captured, had there been no rejoicing in France? Why had no ambassadors been dispatched from King Henri to congratulate Phillip? This was something Phillip, too, wondered.

He had also had another letter from Parma, complaining about the same problems Phillip had been hearing for months, but with no indication Parma had heard from Sidonia.

Another concern Phillip had was money. When he had sent a fleet to Lepanto, supporting forces of the papacy and Venice, the cost had been almost ruinous. Only more had been spent on the Armada. Although he hoped for swift victory, Phillip was well aware he might be entering a long engagement, open warfare falling to the disorder of skirmishes as Parma attempted to claim England. Phillip's wealth from the New World and the Indies had been plundered by Elizabeth's pirates, and what was left spent in the Netherlands and on the Armada. England thought Phillip's coffers bottomless, but in truth the silver and gold on each year's *flota* from the New World was already spent, mortgaged against existing debts for his vast empire. As soon as money came, it went. His armies, court, palaces, informers and officials in his empire took all his purse could offer. He had borrowed one million in gold from the bankers of Genoa at close to twenty-five per cent interest, and had even pawned his wife's jewels. The King of Spain might appear rich, but his coffers were as barren as his writing room.

Heading that afternoon to his private oratory to pray, its walls lined with glimmering white marble and sea-green jasper, Phillip took to his knees. It was painful; gout plagued him, making the extended periods of prayer Phillip undertook torture. Candles lit the interior spaces, light flickering on the painting of *Christ and the Cyrenian*, by Titan on the wall.

He bowed his head to pray, but whilst his lips moved through the familiar words of the psalms, his mind was in France and on the Armada. Stafford, English Ambassador to France, and a spy in Phillip's pay, had sent word which had arrived at the same time as Mendoza's letter. Stafford had spent much money printing a pamphlet which denied this rumour of Sidonia's victory, for he said it was of no help to Spain if false news was put abroad. Stafford said claims of success had been shouted about Paris, but no confirmation had anyone received. Phillip had no doubt Stafford had printed the pamphlet also so the ambassador could salvage his relationship with England. Up until the last moment Stafford had been sending missives to Elizabeth and Walsingham claiming the Armada had not set out at all, something which now was shown to be untrue.

Phillip also suspected the ambassador in other ways. Lists of English ships, their men, firepower, supplies and weaponry, had been handed to Mendoza, but many thought they were exaggerated, making England appear stronger than it was, perhaps as a way to put Phillip off the enterprise. Phillip wondered if Stafford's tales that the Armada had not set out had been too outrageous, on purpose, and if this pamphlet decrying the gossip was another feint. Perhaps Stafford was working for Walsingham and Elizabeth again, a double agent. Which side the dubious ambassador was on was anyone's guess.

Mendoza had sent another letter, hard on the heels of Stafford's, which reached Phillip that afternoon. Handed to him whilst he was still upon his swollen knees, it said Catholics of France would not allow Stafford's pamphlet into the streets, knowing it was false, but Phillip had much cause to wonder, and to curse the slowness with which reports came to his hands. His one comfort was to think they were just as slow to reach the Queen of England, but even that was a false hope. She was closer to this action than he was.

Wilder tales were being told by that night. Drake had been captured, Drake had been killed, Parma had landed, the Queen had fled. And yet, of all this, Phillip had no confirmation. Something nagged, gnawing his nerves, telling him that had such victories occurred, Sidonia would have sent news by now. Some of the rumours of triumph had begun more than two weeks before that day. Surely a messenger would have reached him by now, carrying news from Sidonia or Parma?

What Phillip did not know was that battle had indeed been fought, but his men had not won. Technically, no one had, as the death shot had not been fired upon the Armada. Driven to the Dutch coast, but not wrecked upon the sands, saved by the intervention of God, the Armada was sailing up the Dutch coast, tailed by the English.

Drake and Howard were dispatching frantic messages to England, to tell the Queen of the battle, but also of their lack of supplies. If they had more shot and gunpowder, they wrote, they could destroy the Armada completely. The Spanish ships were badly damaged, their men exhausted, weak and many wounded. The squall had saved them, but the warships and hulks were all leaking, their sails and masts were broken, and they were limping in the sea. It would not take much to finish them, but it would take more than the English fleet had.

Some Spanish ships were so low in the water that the waves were at their rails, pouring onto their decks. Howard and

Drake could see men on every ship repairing sails torn in so many places they were more thread than cloth.

On his ship, Sidonia was staring at lists of the dead, disbelief in his watery, tired eyes. His men claimed only six hundred had been killed, but Sidonia could not believe it. He thought the true total might be closer to six thousand. They had brought eighty-five surgeons with them, and all were working at a rate unprecedented, hacking off torn and broken limbs, stanching them with fire, trying to save lives. Many men had bled to death or been drowned in the sea before ever reaching the surgeons below decks.

And for all those who survived blood loss, limbs hacked away and the fire to cauterize them, many more would fall to pale, hollow shock and to fever caught inside their wounds, festering their blood and carrying them into the arms of God.

The night before, the welcome shores of their homeland in sight, fourteen Dutch men who had been forced to serve the Armada had dropped into a cockboat and fled. When men heard, others deserted, dropping into the sea to swim for shore rather than waiting for death to come for them aboard the ships. One party of Portuguese deserters took a boat and made for the English fleet, offering information on the Armada in return for sanctuary.

Behind the fleets, on the shore of Flanders, the *San Mateo* and the *San Felipe* washed helplessly along in the current, grounded on the very sandbanks that had failed to capture their friends, and were quickly surrounded by the Dutch Sea Beggars. Men left on the *Mateo* fought the Dutch for two hours, but finally yielded. Nobles and officers were saved for ransom, the common men were slaughtered.

You might be tempted to think ill of the Dutch for this. Do, if you wish, but understand that all captives taken in war are treated thus by all nations. The rich are taken for ransom, the poor die. Men are easy about casting those with little money into my arms.

Claiming the ships as prizes, the Dutch took the *Mateo* and *Felipe*, and stole away the *Mateo's* banner, sending it to Leiden so it could hang from the choir of St Paul's Church. Sir William Russell, English Governor of Flushing, sent men to the wrecks to capture his own prisoners and took one hundred Spanish men away. Sixty were sent back to Parma, to inform the General of the battle and to show him what happened to those who attacked England.

Parma was having problems all his own. Gathering his scattered troops was not easy, and many were in a state of mutiny after a winter of no action, held in cold barracks with small pay. Hearing of the losses at Calais, he knew there was no way he could meet Sidonia now. The fleet had been driven off, were heading right into the path of the Sea Beggars, and without Sidonia he could not get his soldiers out. He wrote, he said, to inform Phillip *"in order that Your Majesty may adopt such measures as you consider advisable in Spain and elsewhere to prevent this misfortune and the presence intact of the enemy fleet from leading to further evils."* The Armada, he wrote, had last been seen heading north, with the English behind it, and his only consolation was spare. *"This must come from the hand of the Lord, who knows well what He does and can redress it all, rewarding Your Majesty with many victories…"*

Warning that if he was not sent money soon his army would desert and mutiny, Parma ended his letter, hoping that his uncle would finally listen to him.

The only one who could turn this about for Spain now, as Parma suggested, was God.

Chapter Twenty-Four

St James's Palace
August 1st – 2nd 1588

Elizabeth

I sat on my barge, the grey, silt-ridden waters of the Thames beneath me. Skies above were glowing soft, subtle pink and tender lilac. There were no clouds, just colour.

No water had I ever sailed on that was rougher than the Thames. On ponds and lakes I had drifted, along rivers had I sailed, or been rowed. Never upon sea had I been. Yet, though all those waters of my past might be considered places of greater safety than those men used now to defend England, not always had they been for me. On progress, visiting houses of friends, I had been taken on water for pleasure, indeed, but more than once I had thought I would sail towards death on water. When I was taken first to the Tower, suspected of treason, I had thought my last glimpses of the world would be snatched from a boat. When I was taken into house arrest in the country, I had thought I would lose the world once I left the river, done to death in the quiet secret of the country, a pillow pressed upon my face, hands about my slim throat.

My eyes strayed to the bank, to the timber-framed houses, lath and plaster filling the walls; tiles upon their roofs to prevent fire and great beams holding up the upper floors. Small glazed windows watched me from the houses of prosperous yeomen, and larger, diamond-paned windows shone from rich homes where people were rising from beds of warm feather-down and sleek linen. Inside, servants would already have cleared away hay-stuffed mattresses from the places they slept and worked in during the day. The shutters were down, stored near windows. Maids had lit fires for their masters hours ago, swept out old rushes, strewn new, and prepared breakfast. Women heading to market watched for *fraters*, men who stole from women bustling to and from stalls.

In poor houses, the walls earth and cob, there were no chimneys but only a hole in the wall to let out the smoke trailing from cooking fires. Labourers renting a room in another's house were heading out, walking past women selling cherries and plums from brimming baskets, gathered from gardens just that morning, dew glistening upon skins of purple and scarlet. People were breaking fast on meat or fish, some just on bread and butter with perhaps a lick of pottage from the night before, flavoured with eel or herbs. Soon, when autumn leaves cascaded from the skies, the poorest of my people would gather acorns to tease out flour to make bread. In little gardens nestled beside houses women were gathering chervil, lamb's lettuce and edible carrot. In the waterways maids plucked watercress, as in open fields prigmen stole clothes left to dry upon hedges. Servants and wily housekeepers kept an eye on open windows, knowing men named hookers were on the prowl and having seen valuables by day would return by night, to hook them through the window. These were the houses of my people.

Today I was upon water so they might know I had not fled. I wanted them to see that I was with them still.

I thought of the Dover militia deserting. Raleigh had sent word to say some men of Cornwall had done the same. I thought of troops heading for Robin, and of all the food we did not have to send to them. I thought of the forces of my Carey cousin, Hunsdon, four thousand horse and almost thirty thousand men, heading for St James's Palace on the western edge of London, where I was also bound. In a few hours I would be surrounded by two thousand of Hunsdon's best men. I had refused Windsor again, and was headed into London. My people would know I was with them in our time of terror.

I thought of the Dutch flyboats off the coast of Flanders and King James's promise he would aid us. I thought most of

Howard, Drake and Seymour, of guns heard off the coast, and of the silence that came after.

Did silence herald victory or defeat? The intolerable waiting for news was like a hand slowly tightening about the throat of England. Panic was rising, leading to my Privy Council ordering that the citizens of London were to turn out to church to say prayers for the defeat of the Armada. Prisoners captured from the *Rosario* had been carted through the streets, people hissing, booing and throwing pebbles and rotten fruit at them. It was a means to attempt to control, or at least divert, the terror and impotent rage growing in the streets. The people could not wait for news much longer. Soon there would be trouble. There would be blood.

We are creatures not made to withstand anticipation. If we suspect something ill is walking towards us, often we make something ill happen rather than wait. Curious it is that we would force darkness upon us faster as a method to withstand the terror of the approach of darkness. Yet the human heart and brain seldom make sense.

I wanted to hold off panic. The best way I knew to achieve that feat was to display myself. Not all was lost if the Queen could be found.

I heard cheers from the banks as we sailed. We were easy to spot. Not only was my royal barge painted in bright colours, but the river seemed empty that morning. It was still busy, of course, boats ferrying people and livestock back and forth were legion upon the Thames, but there were few moored ships. Most had gone to join the fleet. Those that were left were the few foreign merchants still here, unloading goods of soap and timber, rye and barley, beans and malt, spices and cloth at a furious rate. Other captains appeared more languid, clearly thinking they might as well stay within the Thames rather than seek to take ships out to sea where they might be mistaken for an enemy ship and attacked.

Smoke was rising into the grey skies, a pall of fug laced with the scent of wood, sea-coal and spices. Along dark alleyways it raced on the breeze, past men carrying sacks and children playing. In some streets, lighters were still wandering, offering a glowing ember for lighting lamps and candles from their cords and iron baskets of fire.

And like smoke, from alleyway and town house, from market and inn people came, drifting to the banks. As they saw me, they shouted. I lifted my hand, standing so they could all see me. So they would know they were not alone.

*

Into my farthingale, fifty yards of whalebone formed into a cage for the skirts, I stepped. Over it my ladies draped a gown of royal purple and blazing gold, decorated with serpents and doves. At my breast, Blanche pinned a great gold pelican with eyes of amber; the symbol of self-sacrifice.

I gazed into the mirror, the burnished surface of bronze reflecting my face in lights of glowing amber and russet-gold. Upon my head was a wig bearing locks of fire, piled high with curls falling, brushing my neck. Peals were laced through the scarlet tresses and more shone from my waist and throat. My face, neck and hands were painted violently white with ceruse, a mixture of white lead and vinegar, and dusted with powdered alabaster. My lips were red as blood, painted with beeswax and the dye of plants, and my eyes were lined with kohl. I was become marble and flame, impenetrable, eternal, mesmerising.

From my shoulders rose a vast crest of lace, like the feathers of a peacock on full display, supported on a frame of delicate stays so it loomed behind me, a white backdrop to my face. About my throat was a ruff with a simple looking design. In reality it took hours and formidable skill to starch the lace into the winding weave of knots.

In the centre of my hair, surrounded by a small crown of gold, was the ruby of the Black Prince. In many mouldings and pieces of jewellery did I use this heirloom. It was the size of a chicken egg, and if legend was correct it had been handed to the Black Prince, son of Edward III, by the King of Spain in thanks for restoring him to power. Henry V had worn it upon his crown at Agincourt, and Richard III had carried it upon his at Bosworth. That crown, my grandfather had supposedly found in a hawthorn bush, taken into his hands, and placed upon his head when he won the war for the throne of England.

And to battle I marched that day, my armour on face and form, finding my opponents in the Council chamber.

"To the south coast I will go, on the morrow," I told the horrified group of men, all staring at me as though I had escaped from the Bedlam. "I cannot sit here anymore," I said. "I must show myself, I must be near my soldiers. If they see their Queen stands with them, no more will flee. If they see I am undaunted, it will give them courage."

Walsingham was the only one who looked faintly interested in my plan. In truth, although what I said I believed, my plan had presented itself in my mind as much for the fact that I, like most people of England, could simply not sit still any longer.

I needed to *do* something. Anything. I needed to slake the fear I felt in action, and I truly did believe the people needed to see me. If a standard cannot be seen in battle, men fly.

"Madam, it is too dangerous to place you at the south coast."

"It is too dangerous not to," I retorted.

We argued for hours, and I lost that battle, but evidently not the war. Cecil came to me later with a letter from Robin. Cecil had sent a man to Tilbury, and Robin had written back. "If you wish to inspire the men, and your people, Majesty, do so at Tilbury. The men there are like to face Parma's troops, if fortune looks on us with disfavour. They are the ones we need inspired by your presence."

"You will ensure my people *know* I am going to Tilbury," I said. "And it will not be done quietly. I want all the people of London to see their Queen, unafraid and out in the open, no longer hiding in soft palaces. I want all the people of England to hear of this trip within hours of it happening."

Cecil nodded, for he could see I would not be argued with.

"And I will speak to them," I said. "I will tell them of my heart, this English heart that beats with blood of Wales, the blood of the Kings of France, Dukes of Normandy and Anjou, men of war, princes who conquered."

I sat down that night and began to write. Oftentimes I relied on my mind to present words as they came when I spoke in public, but not this time. Look back through history and you find that the most inspiring leaders are not those who wield a sword best, who killed the most men, or who were strong in body. It is the orators who inspire, those who use words well lead.

This speech would be remembered, one way or another, for the rest of time. If all else I said was destined to be forgotten, I would ensure these words were not.

I was speaking not only to the people of England, but to the future.

Chapter Twenty-Five

The Firth of Forth
August 2nd – 3rd 1588

Death

Thirty leagues east of Newcastle, the seas were screaming.

From the sides of Armada ships, mules and horses were being pushed over, into the water. Rearing and bucking in air, then waves, horses screamed, their terror-stricken cries fading as beneath the waves they went. The sea was black with bodies, thousands of them. Hooves lashed water, bucking into the air. They tried to swim, tried to follow the ships from which they had been cast. They crashed into one another, forcing others down. Waves made by wind were joined by those made by the horses and mules as they thrashed, desperate to survive.

Sidonia turned his face away, unable to bear the hideous sound. The cries of the horses seemed like those of men who had died in battle not long ago. The water was full of ghosts for Sidonia that day.

There was nothing he could do. They could not keep the animals on board. There was no water for them, little food, and the ships could not take their weight. Many Spanish ships were low in the sea, broken at their hulls, taking on water faster than pumps could remove it. The less weight, the more chance they might stay afloat.

Racing now for the Firth of Forth, all Sidonia could hope was that the English were as low on supplies as he was, and would turn away, allowing them to escape. But the English were closer to home; ships might come from any port to restock, or even to join them now that victory was so close. He could see even at a distance that the English fleet had taken less damage.

In the meantime, there was dark business to settle. Sidonia fired his cannon three times, calling captains to his ship. None came. He sent his own boats to round them up and shouted at them when on board they walked. Had they not heard his signal?

His men said they had, but had thought he was signalling that his ship was sinking, so thought they should hasten to safety.

It is likely they knew his signal was not a wise thing to respond to.

For there were crimes to punish. When defeat comes, men must have someone to blame, and usually someone other than themselves. So few admit accountability in this life. In the first days of August, twenty captains of army and navy were arraigned for cowardice in the Battle of Gravelines. Accused of not keeping station within the fleet, some were reprieved, some sent to the galleys to row with slaves, and some were hanged. Don Cristobel de Avila, captain of the *Santa Barbara*, was strung from the masthead of a pinnace, his corpse paraded before other ships as a grisly warning.

It was the afternoon of the 2nd of August when they reached the Firth. The wind was blowing south-west, bringing rain along with it. Sidonia gazed upon the shores of Scotland from his cabin with a heavy heart. Rain was drumming the ship and swirling mist raced swift across the sea. Candles were burning low on his table, shadows flickering upon the rocking walls of wood. From below, the scent of festering flesh was creeping through the decks; the wounded and dying were moaning below.

He and all his men had decided they would make for home. Spain had to be reached, and the invasion had to be abandoned. But they could not go back the way they had come, running the gauntlet of Sea Beggars and the English fleet all the way along the Channel. All they could hope was that in heading about Scotland, then Ireland, they might lose Howard and his men, and make it home.

It was a hope not without some basis in logic.

"If they make no move to land in Scotland at the Firth, here is where we leave them," Howard told his men that morning. "We have not the supplies to keep running behind them, and as long as they cannot land and gain aid from Catholics in Scotland, England will stay safe. We cannot chase them forever."

His captains agreed. Low on food they were, and sickness was spreading. Ship's fever brought on board at Plymouth had grown stronger, fuelled by the tiredness of men, ill scents roaring through the hulls, and the fetid food and water they had left to eat. Burning wood to smoke out spirits of sickness did little; more men were falling to fever every day. They could not chase the Armada about Scotland without destroying themselves. If they tried, they would become a phantom fleet, lost to sail on the waters forever, seeking a victory they would never achieve. Sometimes winning is as much about knowing when to stand back, as it is about knowing when to step forward.

Two pinnaces set out that day, shadowing the Armada to make sure they did not land. They would follow them about Orkney and the Shetland Islands, but after the Firth, Howard was sure they would not attempt to land. At two of the afternoon, Howard set off a signal gun and the English fleet turned for home. They needed food, they needed water, and they needed rest.

"They will head about Ireland," Howard said. "Of that I have no doubt. Their thoughts are of home, as are mine." An image of his wife, Kate, floated into his mind. Her smile, her warm arms, her red hair.

"Some will try to land in Ireland, my lord," said Drake, busy at that moment attempting to dig out dirt and grime buried deep in his fingernails.

"I have sent warning to Walsingham," said the tired Lord, rubbing his eyes with gritty fingers, still thick with the scent of powder and fire. "If they go not there, they will head for Denmark."

"I wish we could follow, finish all we started."

"We have done our part, Drake. England is no more under threat." Howard looked up, smiling wearily at his Vice-Admiral. "The wolf is chased from the door, and I want to see my wife."

Howard had sent letters to English ports before signalling for retreat, asking for supplies so they could continue the hunt. No responses and no supply boats had come. Either his letters had not got to port, or there was nothing to send, or supplies were still being gathered. Howard knew they could not continue without them, so the order was sent, and they were heading home.

Drake returned Howard's smile. He, too, was looking forward to a soft bed and the softer arms of his wife. Every muscle in his body ached. He felt as though he had been beaten with a dirty club for hours and then thrashed again through the night. His hair was infested with lice, and his clothes had worms eating them. And Drake was in a better state than most of his men.

Below deck on most ships, men wrestled with fever. Sweat ran down their bodies and they could not keep cool even with the damp, chilled air of the Scottish sea sailing over them. The most unfortunate had lost control of bowels and bladders, spilling shit and piss onto the floor, so it drifted across the belly of the ship, washed out by other men with barrels of water. Rats pestered, leaping upon them to chew hair and clothes, stealing food from barrels and bowls. Wounded men worked with dirty bandages covering eyes, faces, arms or legs, blood, caked dry, holding filthy dressings to wounds. Drake's men were burned black, many carrying weeping burns inflicted by gunfire. Those who could, worked, toiling with small provisions in their bellies, and smaller strength in their limbs.

On the outside of the ships, paintwork once glorious in shades of green and white, was black as night, stained by smoke and ash. Their pennants were faded, torn and limp. Most men, too, were in little but rags, their clothes torn to shreds then burned in fighting.

They had won a great battle, but this war they could not finish.

Seymour's squadron had been dispatched first. They were fresher, in a better state than most of Howard's ships. To the Downs they were headed, between the Kent coast and Goodwin Sands, where they would maintain a patrol in case Sidonia tried to come back, or Parma tried to make it to England. Seymour had resisted, thinking Howard meant to pursue the enemy fleet and keep all the glory for himself. But the Admiral did not. He was going home.

It was not a full victory, but it was all he could do. Howard, like Drake, would have stayed on to finish the enemy had he had the supplies he needed, but they had done enough. Their task had been to keep England safe and for the moment she was. Howard was not ashamed of all he had done. Blown Spain from the water he had not, but he and his men had faced a vastly superior force in terms of size and number, and they had seen them off. His concern now was his men. No ships and few men had they lost, only one hundred were dead if the tallies were correct, but if fever took hold they might lose more than Sidonia.

On the *San Martin*, Sidonia thought he might fall to his knees with relief when he was informed the English fleet were heading away. That he managed not to was only due to the pride still beating in his heart. Some would later question why he did not turn about, but there was no way he could return the fleet to the Channel, and there was no safe harbour to head to and wait again for Parma. They could have gone back, turned about, for the wind favoured them, but Sidonia did not suggest it and none of his captains did either.

They had to get home, as well as they could, with as many ships as possible, making a retreat, but not a complete disaster of this mission.

Tighter rations were inflicted on the Armada ships. Eight ounces of bread and half a pint of water, with the same of wine a day, was all they could spare if they were to make it back without stopping. But if the English fleet had gone, there was another enemy to face.

The weather.

On the morning of the 3rd of August, Sidonia woke to the ship rolling and quaking. Rain, fog and heavy seas battered them as they endeavoured to sail about Scotland. The North Sea was bitingly cold, even in what was supposed to be summer. Winds blew, gathering into swift, fierce gales, with gusts that struck like cannon fire. Rain fell, lashing faces, broken masts and sails. Spanish ships rocked like babies in a fearsome cradle, listing one way and then another. Men fell overboard, left behind in the sea. The pumps were worked day and night, men toiling into states of collapse in an effort to keep ships afloat. The *San Martin* was taking on water at an alarming rate. A hole in her hull at the waterline refused to keep the patches carpenters and divers tried to stick to it. Cables were all that was holding the ship together. Strung under the keel, three great cables had been secured to her masts, binding the broken vessel together. The *San Juan* could not hoist her sail on her mainmast. The Levant squadron were in danger, floundering and falling behind. Many hulks were trailing far behind too. Each time Sidonia waited for vessels to catch up the danger of the great ships sinking, torn by wind and rain and battle, increased.

A supply hulk sank, and meagre provisions gained from passing Scottish and Dutch fishing boats did not stretch far about the gaping hunger of the Armada. Rice had been sent to the vessels, handed out from the hulk that had gone down, but there was little of anything else left. They had enough water for three weeks, if they were lucky.

But luck did not seem to be with them. They had few charts of these waters, and the sun was hiding behind banks of churning cloud. At night the fog was so dense they could not see the Pole Star. Guiding by the coast, its rocks black and jagged, the Armada drifted on, weaker by the day.

Two days later, despite the protests of many of his captains, Recalde most outspoken of them, Sidonia ordered ships to put up full sails. Ships too damaged to keep up would be left behind. There was no other choice. Some of them had to make it home. If they crawled along as they were, none would.

Ships that had taken the smallest beatings set sails to full, leaving the wounded behind. Shamed, Sidonia took to his cabin, his ears echoing with the screaming of horses and men, his mind haunted by the choices he had made.

Chapter Twenty-Six

St James's Palace, Westminster Palace
and Tilbury
August 5th – 8th 1588

Elizabeth

At my table I sat, watching rather than eating the food before me. More so now than ever the fear of poison was on the air. All dishes had been tested before coming to me, my loyal women and Gentlemen Pensioners each trying a little of all foods and drinks. Deemed safe, they had been set before me, and yet had they been laced with poison indeed, I could not have had smaller appetite.

It was a goodly spread. Livering pudding, hog liver mixed with egg, currants, nutmeg and pepper, sat waiting for me beside golden, roasted rabbit in parsley and verjuice, roasted mallard in mustard and honey and onions, along with a mixed *sallat* of boiled vegetables glistening with oil, sugar and salt. Gingerbread, a favourite treat of mine, had been ordered from the kitchens by Kate and Blanche. They knew before I sat down that I would eat little, but sweet things I would try at least.

My *converso* Jewish musicians were playing and all eyes were watching, so I nibbled. I was, in truth, barely tasting a morsel.

I was thinking of a letter I had had from Robin that morning. I had sent word that I meant to go to his camp at Tilbury to see the troops and show myself to the people, and Rob thought it a fine idea. *"Good, sweet Queen,"* he wrote, *"Alter not your purpose if God give you good health."* Telling me a house had been prepared for me, its chambers as nicely furnished as St

James's Palace, and that my troops were eager to see and die for me, Robin was enthused about the planned inspection.

It was probably for good reason. Poor Robin had not had an easy time in gathering men, or keeping them at Tilbury, and shortages of food, which all commanders complained of, making me wonder *where* we should send the meagre supplies gathered, had not aided him. Rob had also had problems with old weapons he had been sent, and with horses, many of the best being kept back by lords who thought they might soon have need of a speedy mount.

Robin had gone on to warn me about the route. I should not go near the coast, he wrote, in case a Spanish ship should capture me. To Havering, where I had a house, I should go, he said, then on to Tilbury. He would like me to spend two or three days with him and the men, so I could bolster their spirits, remind them what they were fighting for; not me, but England.

I wanted to spend days with them too, and with Robin. Many times in our long friendship we had been apart, but now it felt like the end of days, all I wanted was to be near him. Death brings life into focus, at times, shows us what is most important. Worried for my people, my country, our future I was, but in my private heart, the heart of Elizabeth rather than the Queen, all I wanted was to be with Robin.

Plans were being made for my journey, but still we knew nothing of what had happened at sea. Guns had sounded all the way from France, sweeping across the ocean to Dover. They had ceased, but no ships had come home. I feared for our men, feared more that they had failed and England was soon to hear the step of Spanish boots upon her fragile sands.

Warnings were coming in about the amount of troops we might soon see. Robin wrote that Sir Thomas Morgan had estimated Parma had forty thousand men, and others told of the different ports they meant to use, some saying Margate and others Dungeness in Kent. It was rumoured France was to send food to them, but in all honesty with the English harvest only days from being ready for picking, our invaders might not need French aid.

My men did not want me to go to Tilbury. They wanted to cart me to Windsor, protect me and surround me, keep me as a flag to wave if troops landed and the long battle on land began. Not the first battle; that would be quick. Robin and Hunsdon would fall with their men, London would be taken. But if that happened my men would not surrender. Like the Empress Maud I would find myself hiding in castles and battling through sieges as I tried to claim back my crown. England had seen war like that many times. Years would drift into one another as we fought skirmishes and laid ambushes. I would be a queen in name without a throne, fighting on as my country was assaulted and without Robin, for if Parma came, Rob would fight and die in one last glorious battle.

But I would hide no more. I had refused Windsor again and told them I would go to Tilbury if I had to walk there in bare feet wearing only my petticoats. Seeing I meant what I said, they surrendered. To Tilbury I would go.

I gazed over my table and felt nauseous. It felt a crime, with men calling from the sea and land all about England in desperate need of food, not to eat the fine fare presented to me, but I could not stomach a morsel. As the Queen, it would be a horror to court and country if I was not always served as a monarch should be. It would be an affront to England, to our power as a country, and yet looking at all the food before me I felt sick. My table groaned and I could not eat. Men on our ships and guarding Tilbury and London were howling for want of food, and they had nothing. I, who had everything, wanted none of it.

And yet what could I do with this food? It would be spoiled by the time it got to anyone but beggars outside the palace gates. I could not ship all the court's food off to soldiers and sailors, there would be riot amongst the nobles. I picked up a sliver of rabbit flesh and put it to my lips, attempting not to retch. Everything tastes foul when you feel sick.

You will feel better when you are trapped no more, when you are with your men, I thought. I supposed that to be true, although I knew one man would remedy my sickness better than others. At times he himself had been the sickness which plagued me, but at many times he had also been the cure. A little of what makes us sick may make us well, some books of physic claim.

Robin, friend and enemy, loyal-heart and betrayer, love and brother. In a bond that had lasted all our lives, he had been all those things to me and more. If this was my last stand, I wanted him there with me, forming a memory that we might each take to the grave, to the trials of the future; that might warm us when the nights become long and cold.

*

On the 7th of August, I left the Palace of Westminster, in whose small quarters I had stayed overnight, and made for the water and my barge. Marching at my side were the Gentlemen Pensioners, my personal bodyguard, wearing half armour and helmets with bright feathers in them. No less carefully was I dressed. Tudor white and green shone from my body like fire. My wig was chosen to resemble my natural hair. Sometimes I wore gold or jet tresses upon my head, since if I was going to wear wigs I might as well have variety, but not that day.

That day I had to wear my blood upon my skin, my hair, on my face. I was a Tudor, daughter of Henry VIII, granddaughter of Henry VII. That day I was the child of England and of Wales.

In nine-oared boats, we set out upon the ebb tide, sailing through London as church bells pealed all over the city to announce that the Queen was on the move. The banks of the Thames were lined with people, crowds waiting, cheering, children being lifted onto shoulders to wave at me. Green reeds fluttered near them as though the Thames, too, was waving at me. I lifted my hand and when the boat was steady enough, stood, so they could see me. My white dress burned in the pale radiance of the sun, flashing glinting lights of silver and gold upon the faces of my people. Green ribbon on my sleeves flew in the breeze, snapping like hounds and my green kirtle shone, revealed by the split front of my gown, glowing like the green fields of England.

Each time I lifted a hand, the roar from the banks grew louder. Any moment there might come signal fires, a rider on a frothing-mouthed horse, or the clash of bells sounding across England, warning that Spanish troops were here. That I was not only in London, and not hiding in the country, but was outside upon my boat, upon the Thames, as though I were on progress or travelling as normal between my palaces, was something inspiring to the people of London. I, their Queen, was there. I was undaunted. I would be their courage.

We sailed to the sound of silver trumpets meeting pealing bells in the skies like angels and soldiers singing a chorus for God.

As we reached Tilbury, more bells were heard from nearby churches; silver spikes of heavenly sound hitting the heavens and crashing to earth. I marvelled at the sea of tents spread out around five acres with an earthen bank surrounding it. The scent of horse manure, piss, shit and sweat was pungent, but there was too the smell of cooking, the iron of armour and the soft perfume of hay, a scent of lazy summer, piled in places for horses and bound up elsewhere for men to use as targets for arrows.

A raised causeway ran from the river leading across a flat area of marsh and to a hill where the tents stood. At the water I was met by two thousand infantry and one thousand cavalry; a sea of soldiery. Horses snorted, breath pluming scents of grass and hay over the still soldiers, clearly chosen as the best of the troops. I stepped from my boat to see Robin standing, smiling at me. My heart leapt. He looked so handsome in his armour, a soldier as always he had wanted to be.

Through lines of men we rode, Robin holding my white gelding steady as we passed cheering soldiers crying blessings upon me. Robin's head was bare, his now-white hair caught, tousled in the breeze. The noise was immense, voices shouting, rising up to float amongst grey and white clouds. I stopped my horse to talk to men, ask where they had marched from and thanked them for coming to my aid and that of England. Such was their passion that I had to send messengers ahead, asking that they pay me not such "idolatrous reverence."

"I little deserve it," I said to one. "Your commanders are the ones who must be thanked. And all my thanks are due to them, and to you, for the service you do this day for England."

"We are, all of us, honoured to serve, Majesty," he said, bowing clumsily, hampered by his leather armour.

I took my horse to them, inspecting the infantry, admiring how well turned out they were in their shining armour of steel and leather. "God bless you all!" I cried, and many fell to their knees, shouting, "Lord, preserve our Queen!"

As I passed, pikes and swords, ensigns and banners were lowered in respect, and as I went by they came up again, ready for war. "God bless you all!" I cried again before giving way to a priest who said a service of intercession for us and for England.

That night was spent in the Lieutenant's cabin, a most comfortable residence just as Rob had promised. The next morning I rose early, words I had prepared blazing in my mind. I dressed with care. Taking inspiration from my sister, I had prepared a costume for that day. My gown was white and green, but over my breast, rather than silk and fur or feathers,

I donned an armoured breastplate of polished silver steel. A back plate too I wore. Dressed as Pallas Athene, I walked out and mounted my horse.

"You are magnificent," Robin whispered as he helped me adjust my stirrups.

Sitting in my saddle, I felt as though ghosts had come to me. My grandfather and father, my sister when she gathered her troops to claim her throne, were with me, and a phantom more ancient; that of Boudicca. Essex was where that warrior Queen of the ancient Britons had made her last stand, and here I, a Queen not trained to fight except with words had come, following steps laid upon the grass of England centuries before.

As I rode towards the troops, four men including Robin and Essex beside me and a page carrying my silver helmet before my horse, there was at first a hallowed silence. The soldiers took in my war-like garb, and watched my cousin, Ormonde, walk before me, the sword of state in his hands. In silence I rode to them, the clopping of hooves the only sound as a queen of England once more came before her men as a soldier, ready to fight.

And then, mouths opened and the cheering began. Men started to clap their hands, a round of applause so thunderous it shook sky and earth. There was a heart beat echoing from my chest, through the blood of my horse, meeting the noise my soldiers made. And from earth it rose, taking to the wind to fly.

My Pensioners, their feet beating the ground, accompanied by my musicians thumping drums, and by the colours of my troops flying overhead, marched behind me. The snapping of banners in the breeze, the crisp noise of trumpets blaring and the beat of the drums joined the calling of the sons of England as they saluted me that day. "I thank you all, good men of England!" I shouted from my horse.

"God save the Queen!" they screamed, filling my heart and soul with boundless joy.

The air was cloying and misty, warm and wet, but it stopped not my men. They performed a parade before me, then a mock battle, which I cheered on as though I were a lad watching his first tourney. When they were called back to their lines, it was time for me to address them.

My white gelding walked with sedate grace, my armour flashing in the early morning sunlight, glancing upon the faces of the men gathered to hear me speak. Light played on young faces and old. Eyes narrowed, trying to see me better. Upon me the sun shone, illuminating my aging face with white light reflected from my gown and my shimmering breastplate.

Before them I pulled my horse to stand. Messengers were to race between companies for those who could not hear me, for there were seventeen thousand ground troops standing there, and more than four thousand on horse. But I was accustomed to speaking to many, I did so in the House of Commons and Lords often enough. I lifted myself up, using my stirrup to push myself higher, and I breathed in, preparing to send my voice as far as I could.

I gazed out over them and lifted my voice.

"My loving people," I shouted, "I have been persuaded by some that are careful of my safety to take heed how we commit ourselves to armed multitudes, for fear of treachery." I stared at them with my back straight and horse still. "But I tell you that I would not desire to live to distrust my faithful and loving people!"

I cried out the last words and as they rose into the air so did a cheer, hearty and strong from the men gathered before me. My heart rose inside me, a bird ready to wing from my chest.

"Let tyrants fear!" I cried, to another deafening roar. "I have always behaved myself that under God I have placed my chiefest strength and safeguard in the loyal hearts and goodwill of my subjects."

I pressed my horse to walk forwards so I came close to them. "Wherefore I am come among you at this time not for my recreation and pleasure, but being resolved in the midst and heat of battle to live and die amongst you all, to lay down, for my God and for my kingdom and for my people, my honour and my blood even in the dust.

"I know I have the body of a weak and feeble woman but I have the heart and stomach of a king. And a King of England too! And take foul scorn that Parma or any prince of Europe should dare to invade the borders of my realm!"

The voices of the men, my children, the sons of England rose into the skies, touching the hands of God.

"To the which, rather than any dishonour shall grow by me, I myself will venture my royal blood; I myself shall be your general, judge and rewarder of every one of your virtues in the field. I know that already, for your forwardness, you have deserved rewards and crowns and I assure you in the word of a prince, you shall not fail of them. In the meantime, my lieutenant general shall be in my stead..." my arm swung to Robin on his horse "... than whom never prince commanded a more noble or worthy subject."

Robin's face shone with pride. He looked so young, almost a boy again.

I drew myself up. "Not doubting but by your concord in the camp and valour in the field, and your obedience to myself and my general, we shall shortly have a famous victory over these enemies of my God and of my kingdom."

There was a deafening cry of "*Huzza!*" It rained over me like the warmest summer storm.

As we rode along the line, Robin leaned in to me. "The weakest of them here could match the proudest, strongest Spaniard that dared to land on England's shores," he said. "So inflamed are their hearts, by you, Majesty."

"This day, Robin," I said. "I could stand against the armies of the world and fear them not." I looked about, lifting my hand to my men. "For with the courage of my people I am armed, and with their love I am protected."

I saw messengers flying out. Cecil had arranged it. Within hours, perhaps days, all of England would hear my words, and they would know at this, our darkest most desperate hour, the Queen of England was with her troops, promising to die with them.

And I would have. Had Parma that moment marched towards my children, my Robin, I would have stolen a sword and faced him myself. Such was the courage my men granted me that day, I would have happily died amongst them, a prince of England, a warrior born of the line of ancient kings, and queens.

Chapter Twenty-Seven

Tilbury
August 8th – 9th 1588

Elizabeth

That afternoon I went to Robin's comfortable tent, where commanders of the army came so I could speak to each individually. They knelt and kissed my hand as I spoke to them of their needs, the restrictions on what I could provide, and thanked them for their service. To those I knew, I said they were a credit to their houses and blood, and those who I knew not I spent time asking of their lineage, and told them England was proud of them. Young men with hearts of fervent fire left, cheeks burning with pride, and all the time Robin was smiling at me, pleased that I was, indeed, inspiring his men to lust for action.

That night we sat down to dine in the tent. Rob had prepared his rations well for me. Although he provided simple meat and pottage, there were apple fritters with saffron, *moye* of mashed apples, sweet butter and cinnamon, and leached almonds seethed in cream, isinglass and sugar. Pottage of cherries on toast came after. Knowing my preference for the sweetness of life, Robin ensured there was much on offer.

"Your men, they have enough to eat?" I asked.

"Wagons are coming now, Majesty," Robin said. "We are supplied better than we were."

That made me happy enough to eat. I found out later it was a lie as much as it was the truth, a feint typical of my Robin. They had more supplies but not enough, and to feed their Queen with honour many officers had stripped shares from their rations. But, not knowing this, I ate well that night. Not feeling sick to think I had much and my men nothing.

It was as we ate that there came a noise at the tent door. All the men at table leapt up, hands on their swords in case I required protection.

A messenger entered and fell to his knees before me. "Majesty," he said, panting, his face dripping with rain and mud. "News from Flanders. The Duque of Parma has set out. His men are bound for England this very hour."

I stared at him a moment, then touched his shoulder. "Thank you," I said.

"Majesty, we must take you to Windsor now," Robin said. "My men will guard you all the way."

My face pale, I turned to him. "I will go nowhere," I said.

"Majesty, the danger…"

"Is as yet far off," I said. "After all I spoke of this morning, you would have me flee from my men the moment there is word of trouble? It would cause panic, and undo all the good work we have done. My sister did not fly from London when Wyatt's rebels entered, sacking shops and streets. She stood with her men. My cousin of Scots raised an army and rode with them. I will not run now, like a scared girl. I will stand, a Queen, with my men."

"Majesty…"

"In the hour of need I will not desert my army," I said. "I will stay, as planned, overnight. This news will spread, and my men will know I am still with them. There is time enough on the morrow to leave, if that is deemed necessary. Tomorrow, I will be guarded as a queen. Tonight, I will stand, a soldier, with my people."

"Majesty, this note says fifty thousand men are coming…"

"I will stay," I said.

I would not hear another word. I urged the men to sit and finish the meal, and they did, but glances cast my way told me they were both proud of me and scared for me. I took to my chamber early, but not before taking a ride about the camp, so the men could see me. Some stared in dumb disbelief as I trotted past, the golden light of blazing torches revealing their Queen was indeed still with them despite the news that Parma was upon us. Some cheered. Some, too astounded, merely managed to salute.

"But they know," I said to Robin as I entered my house. "They know I am here."

"If you can show such courage, it behoves soldiers trained for war to demonstrate more," he said, kissing my hand. His dark eyes met mine as he lifted his head. I felt the rush of all we had faced together flow through my blood.

"You should leave, come dawn," he said, touching my face with a gentle hand.

"I thought I was offering courage to the men?" I said.

"You are, you have done, but in order that other men can be inspired in the future, you must live," he said.

"You think this the end," I murmured.

"All ends are beginnings," said Robin. "Life is not a length of rope, but a coil wrapped about, knotted so none can find the end. And for England's coil to wind onwards, her Queen must survive." He kissed my cheek. "And that is as well, for England's beautiful Queen has always been a master in the art of survival."

I smiled and stroked his cheek. "I think her Commander always had a talent for that art too." My face fell grave. "Do not talk only of my survival, Robin. You must live, I need you."

"I am a soldier."

"The best soldiers see the end of battle, no matter how it falls," I said. "Promise me you will not risk yourself. If Parma comes, this will be a long, hidden fight. I need my men. I need you."

"I am not eager to die, Elizabeth," he said.

"Then rush not towards the hands of Death," I said. "Live, even if we fail. Fight another day with me."

Robin grinned. "To fight with you has been one of the greatest pleasures of my life."

"Fight *beside* me, then," I said, but I returned his smile. I put my head against his, our brows resting. Through his skin I could feel the thump of his heart, the warmth of his blood. "I love you," I said.

"I love you, Elizabeth."

I stood a long time at that door, watching him as he rode away on his horse. It might be the last time I saw him, for whilst Robin would promise he would survive I knew he would not. I did not want to leave. Trees were black shades against skies of cobalt blue. Birds were shifting tree to tree, cawing as they settled. Somewhere far away a fox screamed, her voice shrill, cutting the cooling air. Eventually Blanche touched my shoulder and I jumped. I glanced at her, then back at the doorway. I knew not how long I had stood there but Robin was long gone, not even a shadow in the night to show where he was.

That night I wrote to King James. *"Now may appear, my dear brother, how malice joined with might strives to make a shameful end of a villainous beginning,"* I wrote.

I stopped, listening to the noises of the camp outside. My window was open. I do not think a soul had gone to sleep, not with news that Parma was coming on their minds. There was the far-off barking of dogs, the crackle of fires. On the wind was the scent of wax as men polished armour, hoping to make leather sturdy for battle and to withstand the changeable weather. Clouds of biting winged beasts had fallen upon the camp, so braziers had been lit to see them off, and stop their stinging, gnawing mouths chewing on my men. Patrols clanked along, the sound of their feet on grass and gravelled paths snapping in the air.

Light rain was falling. I had no doubt the conditions were worse out to sea. I prayed as I wrote to James, for Howard, for Drake, hoping they were still alive, but I held little hope. If Parma was coming, that meant my sea dogs had fallen.

Long into the night I wrote letters, to James, to Cecil, to Walsingham, to friends. Head bowed over the oaken desk, amber candlelight flickering and sage smoke burning at the open window to keep biting winged beasts out, I wrote on, hoping to lose myself in work if I could not surrender to sleep.

Hours passed. My hand clasped the back of my neck. It felt like agonized iron. Hard and painful was my flesh. *Is it age alone that makes us unyielding as we tally more years?* I wondered. Youth always seems so flexible. In age we stiffen, as though Death has a hand upon us already.

Cool air washed in from the window. Rooks were still cawing in the trees. I gazed from the diamond panes to see men marching. As I could see them, they could see me. My men knew the house I had been granted and they knew the room I was in. That night they saw the light in my room, those closest saw my figure, a black shadow sometimes rising, walking back and forth to stretch muscles and straighten her back, and they knew I was with them.

At midnight, another messenger came. When he entered, it took me a moment to realise it was George Clifford, the Earl of Cumberland. So covered in rain and mud was the man I almost had not recognised him as the one I had named *Rogue*.

"What news?" I asked quietly. "Is Parma landed?"

He looked astonished for a moment. "Majesty," he said, smiling, "Parma is nowhere near you, and if your men have anything to do with it, he never will be. The beaten hound is hiding in his kennel, and your sea dogs are on the tail of his wounded pack."

Cumberland told me of the Battle of Gravelines, of fireships and guns, of wreaked ships and the sea swimming with bodies. He himself had fought in it, and although he was humble about his actions, I could see he had fought hard and well.

For a moment, as I came to understand what he was saying, I could barely breathe. Parma was not on his way, neither was the Armada. The Armada was beaten, fleeing about Scotland, trying to find a safe passage home. Our men were after them. For a moment I wondered if I was dreaming, but never had my dreams been as sweet as this.

"God be praised!" I cried loudly. "Where is Howard now?"

"Chasing Sidonia and his limping ships up to Scotland, Majesty. Drake is with him, but they are low on supplies."

"Get to the Earl of Leicester," I said. "And have him spread this most welcome news about the camp. I want the men rejoicing at this hour. I will to London go, and I will see what supplies may be dispatched."

"For by God's singular favour," I wrote, continuing my letter to James, my heart pounding with relief and joy, *"having this fleet beaten in our narrow seas and press with all violence to achieve some watering place to continue their pretended invasions, the wind has carried them to your coasts where, I doubt not, they shall receive small succour and welcome… You may assure yourself, I doubt not, but all this tyrannical, proud and brainsick attempt will be the beginning, though not the end, of the ruin of that king."*

With news of England's safety in mind, I agreed I could return to court. We left that night, making for St James's Palace, the cheering of men sounding behind me into the night. My army turned out, knowing I was going now only because all was safe.

The next day the men held a public fast in honour of God, and I ordered that they were to be disbanded, sent home to their families, and to crops. The harvest was upon us. If not gathered in, all food and fruit, grain and vegetables, hay and straw would languish in fields and run to ruin. They had done their part, and we had not the food to feed them or the wages to keep them standing by.

More news came. After drought for so long, now a steady wash of rain seemed to fall. Howard had chased the Armada to the Firth of Forth, but was heading home, knowing the danger was passed. There was scant food or water on his ships, and he had, in fact, chased the Spanish fleet without having any gunpowder or shot to use against them. I laughed when I heard that. Howard was a good card player; he knew how to make a bluff convincing.

None of us were sure what to do with supplies that had been found. Some were sent to ports, but we did not know where Howard, Drake or the other ships were. Send food to one port and they might come to another, wasting precious supplies. The feeble lines of communication between land and sea were always against us. I found myself wishing I could shout along a cable sent to Howard, and he might hear me.

They came home, arriving at ports in Kent and London on the very day I went back to St James's Palace. The Armada was crawling home about the dangerous coast of Scotland and the perilous cliffs and rocks of Ireland.

"You have saved England," Cecil said that day.

"Men of England saved England," I replied.

Chapter Twenty-Eight

The North Sea and
St Paul's Cathedral, London
August 19th – 20th 1588

Death

As news of the defeat of the Armada spread through London, the people of England let loose their joy and a celebration was prepared at St Paul's for the following day. At the same time, Spanish ships headed about the stormy coast of Scotland.

As people danced about bonfires in London, toasting the Queen and the defeat of Spain, on Spanish ships hungry, thirsty, exhausted men toiled day and night to keep sails unfurled and to keep them from being torn asunder by lashing wind and whipping rain. Wine was growing sour and the water stank like musk, spoiling in leaking barrels. Through confusing weather they sailed, rain pouring, wind striking, then mist rising as if from nowhere, harrying them, separating them and sending ships perilously close to rocks and shallow shores.

In Spain, Phillip was hearing outrageous reports. A battle had been fought off Newcastle, he was told. Phillip had been forced to seek this city in his old maps. He was not cheered to find it was in the north, but any victory would be welcome. It was said that after Gravelines, where they had suffered defeat, the Armada had changed tack and off Newcastle Sidonia's fleet had sunk twenty English ships, capturing another twenty-six, and had invaded England through Newcastle. Mendoza had lit his waiting bonfire to celebrate when he heard Drake had been captured boarding the *San Martin*, and had been seized by none other than Sidonia himself.

The King of Spain was cheered by such news. Sidonia, who knew the truth, was not. There had been no invasion, and there would not be now. They were battling not men of England, but the weather of Scotland, trying to get home.

On the morning of the 19th, the tangible blanket of drizzle cleared for a moment, offering sight of the horizon. To Sidonia's eyes, it was grey and hopeless. Many ships had fallen behind, unable to keep up with the larger and less damaged ships as they had let full sail out, into the wind. The damage many ships had taken, along with a great loss of hands, had crippled them. He could see that the *San Juan de Sicilla* was missing, along with its captain Levanter. In the night that came after, another thirteen vessels vanished, becoming mist upon the waves.

Counting on the morning of the 20th, Sidonia could see only one hundred and ten ships still with the main fleet.

What damaged morale the most was when it was found that the hulk the *Santiago*, carrying the wives of all the officers, was one of the missing vessels. Little did they know that the ship was nowhere near them, and at that moment lay wrecked upon the coast of Norway. Perhaps those on board were more fortunate than many, for they were rescued and thirty-two survivors ended up in Hamburg. Another ship lost to the same shore did not fare so well. Few made it from the water alive.

Another problem for the remaining ships was a fundamental lack of charts. They had not planned to sail about Scotland or Ireland. Although Frenchmen amongst the fleet told Sidonia to command his ships to give Ireland a wide berth, as it was an untamed land where their ships would be looked upon as plunder, Sidonia knew many ships would not last all the way back to Spain without water and food. Scotland was allied to England, and was Protestant. Ireland was still largely Catholic and there had been many rebellions there against English rule. To him, and to other captains, it seemed safer.

Sidonia wrote to Phillip, to explain that his mission had failed. *"The Armada was so completely crippled and scattered that my first duty to Your Majesty seemed to save it… Ammunition and the best of our vessels were lacking and experience had shown how little we could depend upon the ships that remained, the Queen's fleet being so superior to ours in this sort of fighting, in consequence of the strength of their artillery and the fast sailing of their ships… Your Majesty's ships depended entirely on harquebuses and musketry, which were of little service unless we could come to close quarters."*

Sidonia wrote they were headed about Scotland, trying to make the journey as short as possible. Provisions were scanty, he said, and rations had been reduced, causing suffering to his men. Three thousand were sick, and that was without counting the numerous wounded. Sidonia prayed in his letter that God might send good weather, for on that their salvation depended.

As Sidonia and his men were battling rough seas and the prospect of capture on the way home, Parma was wondering where his letter of the 3rd of August had got to. He had written, asking the Admiral to come back and escort his army to England. In his secret heart, Parma knew it was already too late. The letter had been written in part so if his King asked, he could say he had tried his best to salvage something of the invasion. Reports of Gravelines had come to him, but at least he could tell his King that this chaotic mess and ignoble retreat was not his fault. He had asked Sidonia to return, the Admiral had not. Instead of waiting, Parma began preparations to stand his army down. Much like the Queen of England, he could not afford to keep them.

Sidonia, meanwhile, was back to fighting the vile weather. Gales bearing winds of over forty knots had been assaulting his remaining ships on all sides, and then a batch of light winds came, carrying strong north-westerlies with them. Narrowly avoiding wrecking their ships upon the coast, or sweeping further into the North Sea, the Armada struggled on.

But as they came to the tip of Scotland, gales struck again, battering them as they sailed into the North Atlantic.

A sea tempest blew one night, and by morning the *Trinidad Valencera*, the *Gran Grifon*, the *Barque of Hamburg* and the *Castillo Negro* had vanished. They were not seen again.

As the wind swung about, allowing them to clear the Fair Isles and Orkneys, the Armada ran into thick fog banks. Black rocks loomed with sudden menace from swirling grey mist, and tidal rips and whirlpools terrified the men. There was no sun by day, and by night strange, glowing green lights filled the air and reflected upon the sea, sending the men into dangerous lunacies, their minds telling them this was doom falling upon them. They were making barely fifty miles a day, ships struggling against every wave, every breath of wind, and many times almost sunk by tempests and squalls.

Ireland was starting to look not only tempting, but their only chance for survival.

As the Armada struggled to stay afloat, a celebration of thanksgiving was being held in St Paul's Cathedral. One notable absence was the Queen, who had been informed the danger of assassination was too great for her to attend. Another service would be held, said her men, but since the defeat of Spain had been heard only in the past three days they feared some desperate Catholic renegade or heartsick priest would take the opportunity to fire a gun at her if she came before her people. The Queen argued a while, but her men prevailed.

So as men celebrated at St Paul's, the Queen was absent, and had other matters on her mind.

Ships had begun to return. The same winds that had attacked the Armada had scattered much of the English fleet too. Ships had separated, making port where they could. Reports were flying in that ship's fever was rife upon many vessels now in dock on English ports. Howard's division in particular had rampant sickness in their holds.

The men had not been paid, so could not be sent home, and those stricken with fever could not be allowed off the ships in case sickness spread into England. Held on board, the hale for lack of wages and the sick for surfeit of disease, more men fell to sickness. Letters were arriving from Howard and Drake, asking for more and better food, as well as the sailors' pay, so the well could be sent home. The government, not understanding why hale men could not stay in port, sent little, leaving the captains to provide for their men from their own purses.

"Why should that surprise them?" the Queen was heard to ask one afternoon. "Robin paid for many of his troops from his own coffers, as the Earl of Essex did in Ireland. When men are offered the chance to serve England and distinguish themselves in combat, they pay for their men."

Although this was true, many knew it was not the reason. The Queen might be dressed in gold and silver, but there were little of those metals left in her treasury. The Queen of England, it was widely rumoured, had not a penny to bless herself with.

As reports of sickness flooded in, so did complaints. Lack of supplies was the main one. Many English captains bewailed the lack of gunpowder and shot, saying more should have been sent whilst battle raged, for then after Gravelines they could have continued the pursuit and finished the Armada off, making a glorious, and complete, victory. It was admitted that not all shortages were due to the government; there had been many misadventures where supply ships had failed to reach the English fleet, and some shot had been wasted by the English ships themselves. But most captains held the government accountable for the short supplies.

As they turned on the government, captains did too on each other. Seymour was soon heard saying that he should not have been sent to watch Parma's activities as the rest of the fleet went after Sidonia. Had Howard not separated the fleet, Seymour said, they might have finished them off. Frobisher was busy moaning about Drake, saying he was no better than a pirate, his pursuit of the *Rosairo* had set the fleet into danger, *and* Drake had kept all the profit for himself. Accusing Drake of cowardice in the Battle of Gravelines, Frobisher began to sound hysterical, wailing that Drake was claiming he alone had done good service to England when he was little more than a traitor.

Even stoic Howard seemed vexed when he heard that the triumph of England was being attributed to the skill of Drake, as though only one ship had sailed against Spain. To hear some people speak, you might have thought no ships were even present, just Drake, a lone man walking on water, blasting the Armada from the sea with the power of his mind. News that the Pope was heard to say that *Drake* and *his* fleet had seen off the threat, without mention of Howard, hardly aided matters. Howard was prepared, more than any man, to admit the skill of his Vice-Admiral, but believed *some* acclaim should belong to the commander of the navy.

As her men argued, the Queen was staring desperately at rows of figures, showing the debts and payments now needed to be sent to men of England. Always had she known the cost of war, but never had she feared it as she did then. Even the act of issuing promissory notes for wages struck terror into her heart, for she had no idea how the amounts due could be paid. Captains asking for food up and down England failed to appreciate that the harvest was late being gathered in because so many had left the fields to enter the militia. That meant buying imports, which were more expensive. There was also no structure within the country that could deal with getting supplies to where they were needed. Most produce was grown and sold locally. To put together a system of carts taking supplies to all ports was a grand undertaking, and would not be completed in time even if she had been able to afford it. Most men with wagons were using them for the harvest. They had little inclination to grant them to the government, for they knew they would not be paid.

In the dark hours of night, when her soul was bared naked to the blackness, the Queen knew wages would not be paid, that many would die of sickness, and most importantly, that she was letting her people down.

But the Treasury was almost bare. Calling Parliament would raise taxes, making her men less able to pay for their sailors and soldiers themselves, and any money would take time to gather, and would not come in time. Thoughts of imposing a loan on the gentry and nobility had arisen, as had the loathsome thought of selling her own estates, but those ideas too would take time to show any fruit.

"The coinage could be debased, madam," Cecil told her, although from the look on his face the man might have been suggesting he cut off his own head to finance England's debts.

"My father and siblings did such a thing to England, but I will not," the Queen replied, her face grim and pale. "We are wounded, indeed, and many are weak and dying, but to debase the coinage will cause only more suffering. It would aid the present but cripple the future, and if this war was fought for anything, Cecil, it was fought so England would *have* a future."

"Men are dying on those ships."

"The sick cannot be allowed off them. As we seal up houses stricken with plague, the same must be done with the ships. It cannot spread into England, or more will die." She shook her head. "We must find loans, and that will take time, or we must steal what is needed from Phillip of Spain. Either way, the money we need is not here, and will not be here in time to save the men who served us."

"The people will hold the government responsible, Majesty. There could be riot or rebellion."

She turned to Cecil. "And therefore we must tell a tale, old friend. One of victory. The people must see the good that has come and turn their eyes from the bad. It is not right, but it is all we can do. There is no money, but we must ensure there comes no unrest within England for our failure."

She turned to the window, her eyes hollow and dark. "Make the people see the story we need them to see," she said. "And we, like them, will ignore the rotten core. It is not as I would treat my people, my children, but it is all we can do now; spin a story of triumph, keep the future secure in peace, keep England going on, pretending we are not paupers in the street like the brave men who served us who now we are letting down."

Despairing of aid reaching their men in time, Howard, Drake, Hawkins and Frobisher diverted money stolen from the Armada to pay men and send them home. Many died on the way, collapsing in hedges and ditches, too sick to carry on.

And there I found them, gunpowder still stuck in the creases of their eyes and under fingernails. I stood over them as they stared up at the last skies of summer, faces pale and sick, eyes drifting with fever. I took them into my arms and carried them away, knowing many families would never know what had happened to their fathers and sons. They would suppose they had died in battle, an end many people seem to think nobler, more meaningful, than falling into the mud at the side of a road, left to rot as horses trot past and carriages roll along, ignoring the stink of a body falling to decay, eaten by animals of the wild. If wives and children thought of their men dying to save England in battle perhaps it brought more comfort than the truth, but all who died then died for their country. Some fell to sea and shot upon the waves, others died because the country they battled to save had nothing left with which to aid them.

All these are sacrifices, as they are all betrayals. All are acts of heroism, as they are acts of desperation.

Some knew it. As Elizabeth and her men tried to paint a picture of victory glorious enough to turn the eyes of the people from the dying, unpaid, starving men of the fleet, some saw through it. Walsingham wrote to Cecil that *"our half-doings breed dishonour, and leave the disease uncured,"* when he wrote of the escape of the Armada, and added they would come again, and again, for now their hatred of England was only greater, and now England was weaker in men and money than it had been before. His illness returned, sending him to bed.

"They are destroyed," the Queen said in response to Walsingham's letter. "Their purpose is dead. What need is there to send all Spaniards to the tomb of the ocean? We drove them off, defended our gate. We have done all that was needed. More is just lust for blood."

Inside the Cathedral, gentry and nobility gathered, listening to a sermon of celebration, thanking God for England's victory. Wynter, promoted to Admiral of the White, the second highest position in the navy, for his actions in the Battle of Gravelines, stood beside his son, who had served with him on the *Vanguard*. He, like Drake and Howard, had sent his own money to pay for food and drink for his men. Proud though he was of his promotion, he prayed to God to deliver his men from death. As men poured from the Cathedral that day, crowds outside had amassed in their thousands. The setting sun shone, glowing red upon the water of the Thames as though all the blood of all the dead had flowed into London that day.

And there was but one cry on the lips of men and women outside.

"God is an *Englishman*!" they shouted over and over, throwing hats and flowers into the air. The cry spread through London, along waterways where boats ferried people back and forth, along to the playhouses of Southwark and the clustered inns of Cheapside. It was sung in markets and along cobbled streets. From the earth it seemed to rise.

In her palace, the Queen stood at her window, and nodded as she heard their cries. Happy to hear them she was, yet sad too. She and her men had sent out a story, and the people had accepted it. They, like she and her men, would turn their eyes from reality, from the dying men, the sickness, the lack of pay, from the betrayal of England. She had fooled them. It was what needed to be if there was any hope of England carrying on, but tricking her people in this matter was not an easy thought.

And yet the Queen did herself a disservice. Accountable she and her men were for the betrayal of England's sailors, but no country treats those who fight for them with honour, unless they are noble. It always has been that way, and always will, for people want to believe the stories spun of glory and greatness in war. They do not want to be reminded of the agony and horror. They turn their eyes from the dangerous ecstasy that falls at times upon those who have been in battle, as they look away from lost limbs, wounds, and mutilations. They want their soldiers and sailors to be not men who suffered and died, but heroic knights who blazed out the last of their life in a shower of honour, falling with the name of their country upon their lips.

But it is for guilt they turn their eyes away. For knowing they had a part in sending men to fight, for the horrors those men witnessed or did themselves. People do not want to glimpse the darkness they thrust their men into. And in time they turn away for further guilt, for not stretching a hand out into that darkness, to pull their sons back.

Had the Queen's people wanted to see the reality, they would have. The truth is most people do not want to see the truth. It is too hard, too harsh, too difficult to live with. Those who could turned their eyes away, preferring to see the story spun about them. Within the web they lived, refusing to see what lay beyond.

I, who brought an end to agony for men of England will tell you this; death is often not clean, not dignified, not glorious. The men who died for England whether on ship, shore, or broken as they tried to get home, deserved their story told as it was; the courage they showed lauded, the horror they saw witnessed by eyes other than theirs. All stories have power. The one the Queen and her men spun was good, but not great. For great tales, there must be honesty. Memory must play clear and sharp, omitting nothing. For in the true tale there was good and bad as there are in all things, as there is in death and life.

Chapter Twenty-Nine

Whitehall Palace
August 26th 1588

Elizabeth

In a room overlooking the grounds of Whitehall I stood at the window, watching a review of the troops. My eyes travelled over shining armour and leather breastplates, over Robin's soldiers, to look at the palace beyond.

Whitehall was vast, the largest of my palaces. The great gatehouse overlooked the tiltyard, its barrier in the middle shining in the sun's gentle light. The tennis court stood empty. Usually Essex and Raleigh would be upon it, competing to see who the better man was by outdoing each other. Through the gatehouse was the entrance to my gardens, where a courtyard stood surrounded by formal flower beds, roses blooming in dusky sunlight, glimmering soft white and blazing red. Past all the houses that made up Whitehall was the old Palace of Westminster, with the Strand connecting Whitehall and Westminster to London. The Strand was always full of lawyers and clerks wandering, black robes billowing in the wind snaking down London's streets, hands clasped behind their backs as they talked of suits and fines, cases and crimes.

Yet none but my captains speak of my crimes, I thought.

At Whitehall's centre were the private apartments and the grand great hall, outdated even when it was built, of York Place, the original building about which my father had created the rest of the palace, stolen from Wolsey.

He would not have called it stealing, of course. Wolsey would not have dared either, since the palace had been taken from him at the time of his fall when his estates and fine goods were snatched by the Crown, payment for treason, which to my father was another word for failing to deliver what he wanted.

Looking at the original structure, the heart of the new palace formed from the old, I had a feeling of unease. I knew I was doing the same, building up a grand picture of strength and might about the heart of something stolen, betrayed, when all that heart had done in truth was try to give good service. Was I the same as my father? The way I was treating the people of England, particularly those who had served on ships was much as my father had treated Wolsey. For the sake of the future, I was ignoring pains of the present. My father had ignored all the good Wolsey ever did in order that he might punish his once-friend for failing to deliver freedom from a marriage he wanted not.

Wolsey had done ill enough in his time, so perhaps deserved to learn humility by falling from grace, but the men of England had done nothing to deserve their present treatment. Perhaps I was worse than my father.

There were reasons. I had no money, no means to make this situation better, and therefore had to do what I could to mitigate the damage. All rulers find themselves in such situations at times. But reasons are not excuses. What I was doing weighed on me. I pretended, played the part as men fawned, mewing that I had brought England to victory, and I accepted their praise. But I had done little in this conflict. The men whose suffering I was ignoring had saved England. That was the truth of it, and yet I could not do anything with the truth. The story had to serve. Suffering had to be ignored. Whilst this time seemed my most glorious hour to many, it was far from my finest moment.

Perhaps the truth was that at the core of all a ruler does there is a reminder of the ill they have inflicted. Whitehall seemed to whisper this, the voice of Wolsey's ghost reaching out, wafting across the years, murmuring that betrayal was at the core of all the wonder we Tudors displayed to the world.

A sigh escaped my lips as I watched musketeers march in parade beside harquebusiers, followed by two hundred light horse. My men looked magnificent, uniforms of orange glistening in the light, white silk facings shining like silver. The dragoons bore an ensign with '*Hazard*' embroidered upon it, as the cavalry carried one of red damask, a golden veil upon it, as though it were a favour of a lady.

"You are not unhappy with your men, surely, Majesty?" a worried voice at my elbow asked. I turned with a smile.

"Not with them," I said to Robin, placing my hand on his arm. "Not with them and not with you."

He looked pleased, although baffled about the sadness of my air. But he said nothing. Robin was pale and thin, the troubled times had taken a toll on his health, but there was also pride in him, more than I had seen for years. Hard though his task had been, he had risen to the challenge and although his men had not been tested, not needed in the end, some people of England were speaking well of him. That was as much a victory for Robin as the Armada was for England. Long had he been despised. Perhaps this was the start of a new time. Some had even cheered Rob as he rolled through London in a coach, a troop of light horse and his household with him, like a king-consort. Perhaps in time people would see him as a beneficial influence, as I did.

"There will later be a joust, Majesty," said young Essex, standing not far away, as usual.

"So I have heard," I replied, bestowing a gentle smile. The young man had done well too, and had put together this entertainment, open to the people of England as well as court. Essex had led the first wave of the parade of troops, coming to my side to see the rest.

Essex had already challenged Cumberland to a joust, and I knew there would be mock cavalry battles as well as shooting displays. I was proud of my men, and that would be all that was seen in public, but in my heart I could see both the glory of what had been achieved and the cost of it too.

I had been trying to avoid meetings with captains of the fleet, knowing they would ask for money I did not have. Howard and Drake I had seen and praised, Wynter I had promoted, but many more had come only to the fringes of court. Celebrating in front of my people, selling them the tale of victory for the sake of survival, I had turned my face from the needy. It was something I would always regret.

And although these troops were here for me and the people to see, they were rare now in England. A day and night after my speech at Tilbury, I had commanded the ground troops cut down to six thousand men, the rest to be sent home. A week later, they had been reduced to one thousand five hundred. The camp at Tilbury was all but gone. A skeleton of the main body had been retained in case Parma decided to try to come to England, or the Armada returned. It was a risk, for me and for England with the Armada still sailing about Scotland, but for the sake of my purse and the harvest it had been done.

At the same time I had started to disband the navy. Hired ships were discharged and others were laid up. Howard had written to say that sickness upon the ships was horrific, men dying daily. For the sick, there was little to be done. Few doctors would go aboard to treat them, and amongst the crews there were fewer still that could tend to the sick. I was told ships of five hundred who had lost only a handful of men in battle had lost two hundred to illness after. Some had fled ashore and died in the streets, leading to panic in port towns for fear sickness would spread. In addition to food and water, captains were asking for clothing, as many men were now in rags.

Cecil, his face grave, had informed Howard of the state of the Treasury, and said at least if men died we would not have to pay them, for England could not afford the lives it had bought its freedom with.

Howard, although shocked, had gone on to tell Cecil the cause of the sickness was the beer the men had been given. Why my Howard cousin stuck to such an idea many had no idea, for all knew it was bad smells on ships that bred sickness, not poorly brewed beer. From his own purse Howard paid for fresh beer from Dover, certain it would cure his men. It did not, although it may have made some deaths merrier.

Howard printed licences to allow his men to beg sustenance from houses and churches near their ships, Drake and Hawkins sent food and drink. And I sent complaints.

"That money, stolen from the Armada, was supposed to be used for the wages of the men!" I said to Cecil. "Spending it on food and wine is wasting money that would have allowed those men to be discharged. Send word to them to cease."

My captains protested that wages were supposed to come from the Crown. I maintained that all commanders who take to sea or land in military action paid for the wages of their men. I was right, in some ways. That had often been the case with ground troops, but with the navy there had indeed been an understanding, never written down, that it was my responsibility to pay the sailors.

I said to them that the navy was always paid late. That was the truth; barely once had wages come to sailors on time, and they knew this well. The reason it was pressing this time was due to sickness.

But in desperation, we do strange things. That included bickering in private with my men about who was supposed to be paying for what. Money is a vile creature. When we have little, we can do little. When we have much we think ourselves poor. It makes honest men into villains and creates entitled, spoiled infants out of grown adults. I was as guilty as any, perhaps more so, for I knew the tricks of money and still fell to them.

One of the quarrels was about 'dead-pay'. One of the standard corruptions of our times was that commanders and captains of army or navy would claim money for troops that did not exist anymore. They would request pay for dead men, and pocket that money. Some years ago, it had become official practice that if ninety-five soldiers or sailors were provided, the government would pay for one hundred. Keeping dead-pay at around eight per cent of the wage bill seemed the only way to rein in corruption, for stopping it was apparently impossible. I was fighting dead-pay at that time. I had not the money to pay living men, let alone dead or fictional. Captains of the navy were pleading against this, which said to me they were attempting to claim more dead-pay than usual.

Matters like dead-pay also made me suspect some were asking for more food and drink than was needed. I had no doubt a great deal was, but captains selling off produce was not an unusual occurrence. Walsingham had men watching the ports to check that supplies were going where we were told they were.

Some money had been paid out to the wounded, allowing them to go home, but we were still short on much. We had sent out ideas on how to gather more money, but until any of those seeds came to fruition my people would have to trust me. Many had given their lives for England, it was true, but I too had risked my life more than once for my country. And more than this, I had sacrificed friends, kin and my principles to save England. I had palaces and good food, it could not be denied, but I too had given much, sacrificed much, and like England I had to survive.

That meant not all my men would.

Looking at Robin, my heart knew this was not the only evil I had allowed. I had wanted to honour Robin. Captains on ships had been knighted, and had spoils from vessels they had plundered, but Robin had not been rewarded. It was not his fault he had seen no action. He had been ready to give his life for England.

I had asked for Letters Patent to be drawn up, investing Robin with the title of Lieutenant Governor of England and Ireland. But Walsingham and Cecil had objected. I knew they would. The position I was thinking of honouring Rob with would have granted him more power than any other English subject in my time or the past. It was a sign, not only of my gratitude for his good service to England, but that finally I had forgiven him.

It had been a long time coming, that feeling that I could look upon Robin and not see the shadow of Lettice between us. Longer still had been the feeling that I wanted to wound him as he had wounded me. For a long time I had thought that when those feelings departed I would have nothing left, just a gaping hole inside me, a void where once love had been. But that was not the case. Love had returned, bringing friendship with it. At this time of crisis he had always been with me, in spirit if not in person. His letters had come daily. He had supported me. Robin had returned; the stranger who had hurt me was gone.

Sometimes I thought our relationship, one of a lifetime, was like the sea as it ebbed and flowed. There had been storms and times of gentle wind and water. And like the unknown, deep depths, there was much of possibility and discovery in our friendship. There was so much that people, gazing but upon the surface of the water, failed to see beneath; the winding, twisting waters of our souls, joined and bonded, in future and in past.

I had wanted to tell Robin this, but it is hard to find words for such feelings. I could say I had forgiven him, but it was almost as if that no longer mattered. As though his betrayal was a drop of water, gone the moment it meets the ocean.

Struggling to find words to describe what I felt, I had thought of this honour, this position of trust absolute. It would be a sign to my people and my other men of how I trusted Robin. But Walsingham and Cecil had objected, most violently.

"There have been times in the past when Your Majesty has noted what power can do to the mind of the Earl," Cecil warned. "Times when he has stepped above his authority and done as he wished."

"As many of my men have," I reminded him. "*You* being one of them."

"Majesty, I have long been the Earl's great supporter," Walsingham said, "but I like this not. Handing such power to one man is something you have always avoided, Majesty, and for good reason. You would make the Earl Viceroy of England, king in all but name, and a threat to you."

It was true this might turn Robin's head, that in wanting to honour him I might make him a monster. It was also true I had always refused to create such an imbalance of power amongst my men. Walsingham and Cecil thought it was too much, that I was setting up a man second only to me in power. If I died, they feared Robin would make himself Lord Protector of England, and from there would try to rule as King.

I inclined my head. "Very well," I said. "Robin shall not have this honour."

Even though Rob had not known, and therefore had no reason to feel upset, I was. To try to find another way to show the people the trust I had in him I dined with him each night, and was with him each day. In the days after Tilbury we were inseparable, closer than we had been for years.

"You are eating little," he said to me one night, gazing at me across the table.

"I have always been a slight eater."

"More so now, and without cause. Usually you fail to eat when worried."

"There is still much to worry about," I said.

In truth I could not face the food, heaped upon my table in a show of magnificence. When I thought of men starving in England, my stomach wished to show solidarity. Yet there was no choice but to come to table each night. If princes of other lands heard I was served poor fare, which I might have preferred for the sake of my conscience, they would look down on England. Kings who failed to live as Kings were always thought badly of by other princes and by their own people.

I looked up at Robin, his white hair silver in the candlelight. "This is not the end, Rob. Phillip is humiliated, or he will be when he hears of Gravelines. He will send more ships, and he has more money than me. England is a pauper. This is not the end of war, but the beginning. We have to fight on, and our men are sick and broken, our coffers empty. I fear much."

"There is always much to fear," Rob said, leaning forwards. "There always will be. That is why it is important that along the way, as we dance from the arms of one disaster and dodge another, we celebrate the good."

"The story of victory has been spun to be greater than it was, for the sake of survival," I said.

"And yet, within the tale there is much that is true," he said. "England has shown the world what she can do. She opened her mouth to roar, and men of other lands trembled."

"Think not I am not proud of my people," I said. "But we have created this story for them, and for other princes. They see only the worthy in it. I see the whole."

"That was your task, granted by God." Robin set down his goblet. "You found your way to the throne not by right of blood but wits. You have kept your throne using your mind. The people see that not. To them, you are an emblem, an icon of holy power. And that is what they should see. For men need to believe. They need to place faith, to have something to stick to, cling to and hold to through the tempests which assault them. They honour you for you are that symbol. They stay with you because you do all you can to protect them."

"There are many I am not protecting."

"You cannot save them all, protect them from all things, but you do all you can, and that they see. They do not see your fear, your worries, the nights you lay awake wondering if what you did was right. You have made a story of *yourself*, Elizabeth, and told it to the people. And in that story they believe. You see the whole for you are inside it. Your people see what they need to, in order to believe in England, in you, and in the future."

"You believe stories are better than the truth?" I asked.

"The truth is a story. Ask four men to look at a street and each one will describe a different one. What matters is that we work inside a *good* story, one that will aid us, build a better future for us and our children. You have told a good story, of yourself and of this dangerous time. Your people see what good has been done. That is what matters. That is what they will remember."

Perhaps Robin was right. Only those inside stories, who create them, can see the bad and the good, and those on the outside to whom the stories are sold see the good alone. Deception is part of the role of a ruler, for if the truth was always told panic and rebellion would come. Perhaps the truth is that the choices we make as life trips along only become more clouded. We see so many options unfold, and a hard truth is learned, that sometimes in order to do good we cannot always do what is right.

Pure moralists would disagree, and perhaps in soul-honest truths spoken before God they would have a point. But the world is a strange and devious place, and so we must at times be strange and devious to survive in it.

The next day Robin went to Buxton. He was to take the waters for he was unwell.

"Restrict your meat a while," I said as we parted. "You eat too much. The belly loves it in youth, but age cannot digest it."

"You would remind me of my age?" he asked, a teasing smile on his lips as he kissed my hand. "It is cruel, Majesty, when women may paint their faces and grow hair like maidens, to taunt men who must age and have the world witness it."

"And yet never are men thought ugly for growing old, whereas women become hags the moment they are past five and twenty years," I said. I reached out and touched his cheek. "You are one who never ages in my eyes, Rob. Always you are that boy, with dark eyes and hair, smiling at me as he tries to avoid doing his work."

"As you are to me always that wry girl, hair like fire and eyes snapping. You started to scold me the day we met, and never have you ceased."

"*Semper Eadem*," I said.

"That you are," he said. With a grin he mounted his horse. "I will send word from Buxton of when I will be back at court."

"Drink well of the water, Rob," I said, pressing a vial of medicine I had made into his hands. "And come home soon."

He rode away and I went back to the palace. For a moment I thought I saw a shadow on the path, but when I looked there was nothing.

Chapter Thirty

Whitehall Palace
September 1st 1588

Elizabeth

"I welcome the notion," I said to the men before me. "But what of ships? I thought our navy were lacking provisions, men and arms?"

"They are, Majesty," said Cecil. "This will take a great deal to achieve, but it might be money well spent. An investment, if you will."

I nodded, pondering what I had been told. My captains and my men of Council had been in many meetings of late, trying to find solutions to our perilous lack of coin. Complaints about non-payment of wages were rising, and we needed money to pay for the debts of war and for government of the realm. No money did I have at the moment, but my men had formed plans about how it might be found.

Although in England we knew how poor we were, how broken, other countries did not, it seemed. England's image in the eyes of the world had never been higher. The King of France had been heard praising my valour and prudence, as though I alone had taken to ship and fought Sidonia personally. King Henri had reason to, of course. England's victory had made Spain look weak, and threatened the power of the Duc of Guise, his adversary. My erstwhile suitor had every reason to rejoice in our triumph.

The Pope had joined in, declaring that were I Catholic, he would hold me as his most beloved daughter, and even Protestant as I was, there was no denying my courage, high spirits and hardened resolve, all of which had brought England to glory. Everyone was waiting to see what England would do next.

My men had the answer.

One idea was to send our ships out to meet the Spanish fleet sailing with treasure from Peru. Drake was keen on the idea, seeing that not only would it bolster my treasury, allowing England to pay her men and support the entire country, but it would strike another blow at Phillip, who, when he heard of what we had done would be sure to try to invade again. Drake wanted to stop Phillip before he considered sailing out.

But there were problems. My navy had only just seen action and many ships needed refitting. The silver fleet coming from the Americas usually took to the water at the end of September, although since many of Phillip's ships were floundering in our waters this might cause a delay. But he would not delay too long, it was too risky. There was little time to do all that needed to be done, and this voyage would consume the last of the money I had. It was a gamble, but early reports from men dispatched to try to secure loans in other countries were not promising, and money was not about to simply sprout from the ground just because the need was sore. A gamble this was, but perhaps the only one we could make which had a chance at reaping reward.

But Drake, now standing on the heights of his power and influence since all of England adored him, had proposed an even more ambitious notion. "If Lisbon were captured, Majesty, and Dom Antonio taken home," he told me, "the people of Portugal would rise. The port was used to launch the Armada. If it were in the hands of friends, it could not be used again."

Drake's plan was to attack the silver fleet, and at the same time send ships to Lisbon to seize that port. Inciting a rebellion against Spanish rule in Portugal, whilst at the same moment stealing Phillip's treasure, would make England rich and less vulnerable to attack all in one go.

If England had a foot in Portugal, with a King friendly and grateful to us upon the throne, another possibility opened. We might establish a port in the Azores. Those offshore islands connecting sea routes from the Americas to the east would be valuable. With Spain ruling Portugal it was a dream, but with Dom Antonio on the throne it was possible.

The combined assault was a daring plan. Even if rebellion sparked in Portugal but failed to lead to the overthrow of Spain, it would be advantageous. Phillip would be kept busy, granting us time to recover. And Phillip would have to call soldiers home from the Netherlands, also a circumstance to our advantage. If the Azores were captured, England would rule the Indies. If we took enough of Phillip's silver, he might become harmless as a dove as we became rich and powerful in more than just name.

But it was a gamble. The return might be large and quick, but the possibility of failure was always present. And yet even to this, my men had an answer.

"More than two thirds of the money will be provided by shareholders, Majesty," Drake informed me. "If the Crown could offer twenty thousand pounds, as well as siege artillery and six ships for three months, I and others will raise forty thousand, and twenty ships to complete the fleet."

Drake understood the dire finances of England. I was grateful not only that he did, but that he did not make me say it aloud. Thinking about the lack of coin was enough to rob sleep from me. Talking of it made me panic.

"If you would give five thousand pounds now, Majesty, you will not be asked for more until other shareholders have contributed," Drake went on.

"What of the troops you will need?" I asked. "I cannot pull men from the Netherlands. We do not dare free Phillip in such a way."

"If we can be granted your commission," Drake said. "We will raise six thousand men from England. Only two or three thousand would be needed from Your Majesty's forces in the Netherlands."

"Would that damage our treaty with the Dutch?" I asked Cecil, looking at him.

"It would not, madam. There would still be sufficient men in the Netherlands, and I think once the situation was explained Dutch leaders would support our plan. If Lisbon were taken, Phillip would have to draw men from the Netherlands, making victory easier for the Dutch."

Drake, in fact, had such hopes the Dutch would comply that he wanted to ask them for transports, siege weapons and gunpowder.

The idea was, in truth, a business venture. As shareholders had supported Drake in piracy, they would now in war. I liked the idea. One of the added benefits was that if all went well the conflict in the Netherlands would be over. I had always wanted its end to come with a restoration of the rights of the Dutch nobility, even if Phillip continued to rule in name. This plan was not the mad glory many of my men had desired for the Low Countries, victory brought about by flame and sword, but it would be a sensible end. If Phillip's purse was crippled, as his fleet was now, with loss of territory added to this brewing stewpot of shame, he would have no option but to negotiate.

"Lisbon and the restoration of Dom Antonio must be the second objective," I said. "We must concentrate on what we need most, here and now, and that is money. You will have the coin you need from me, the ships and men, but the first priority must be the seizure of silver ships in Galicia, Biscay and Guipuzcoa. When that is done, Drake, you may go on to Lisbon and intercept shipping in the Tagus. You may attempt a landing *only* if you believe that Dom Antonio has sufficient supporters to bring about rebellion. That man talks a great deal of how deeply he is loved, but others say different."

I had little trust in Dom Antonio, truth be told. He boasted, but I saw little to substantiate his claims. I did not want to risk a doomed war, or failed invasion.

"After Lisbon, you will go on to the Azores," I went on. "But ships of war in Biscay and the other places must be the first priority."

They could not set out immediately. Not only did ships need to be refitted, but men had to be gathered and troops from the Netherlands called home. It was thought February would be the earliest date of departure. They would intercept the silver fleet upon the waves. With my money in hand and promises for more along the way, my men left.

Sitting in my chair in the afternoon, with Blanche at my side, I went over the recent papers. "Ireland responds to the Armada, madam," Blanche said, handing me a paper as she peered at me over the rim of her eye-glasses.

Looking at it, I felt satisfaction. The Armada, what was left of it, was limping about the coasts of Western Ireland, and having no easy time of it. English cannon had wounded ships so badly that some could not navigate, and others had problems manoeuvring, their sails and rigging almost destroyed. Sickness had struck them as well as death in battle, and the ships that had been seen were reported as scarce of men. Many ships were being driven onto the Irish coast by the wind, and with few having anchors they had no way to hold in the water. Some, it seemed, were having to go to shore since they were so low on supplies, and they had no happy reception.

"Perhaps they thought they might be welcomed by the Irish," I said, still reading. "Or might rescue some scrap of honour by establishing a base there."

My troops in Ireland and the Irish themselves had seen to it that the men landing did not succeed in whatever they had planned. Captains of the Armada might think Ireland would welcome them, but the people of Ireland had had mercenaries and foreign soldiers on their shores before, and no good had come of it.

Driven in by howling gales, black rocks ripping the bellies of ships and breakers thundering, vessels that had tried to land or had been forced to were wrecked. Reports of torn ships, drifting rigging and lengths of timber washing up, told of how many had been smashed upon deserted shores, but many had been seen in populated places, and the people of Ireland had claimed great prizes from Spanish ships. Ships were being plundered, I had no doubt. I sorely needed the money in their holds, and would have to send men to gather what they could, but I could not blame the Irish for pouncing on such booty. For many of them, what was in the holds of those vessels would be more money than they would have seen in a decade, and looting wrecked ships was a common practice amongst those who lived near shores in any part of the world. Allied to the Spanish in terms of faith they might be, but the lure of so much money would cut a great deal of ties. There was, also, another reason.

"They will not work to save them," Blanche said. "The sea must have its dues."

I nodded. It was a belief of old; if the sea claimed a life, a life was what it took. If a man risked himself to save someone drowning at sea, the sea would claim a life by other means, stealing from his family, or himself. Some even buried the boots of drowned men on the shore between high and low tide, to stop corpses rising up in death and escaping the sea.

Keep them bound to the water, and no others were in danger, so the superstition went.

In the report in my hands I could see that some Spaniards had tried to get to shore carrying goods and valuables, some too weighted down to make it, and others had been stripped by waiting crowds gathered on the beach. If they were allowed to leave after they had been robbed, English soldiers would hunt them down and kill them. Ireland might sound like a good place for the Spanish to go in theory, but it was not. Death was waiting there.

There was, however, the possibility that this would ignite fresh sparks of rebellion in some hearts, or that money claimed from the Armada might fund such a notion. I made a note to send to my Lord Deputy, and asked Blanche to copy it to dispatch to all lieutenants of English counties, saying they were to have men ready to march for Ireland at short notice if we had need of them.

The next report was about Spanish prisoners in my gaols. Some were dying of fever, either contracted on ship or in the prison. "Send a note to the lesser prisoners that if they convert to Protestantism they may be set free," I said to Blanche. "Spanish men will not take up the offer, I am sure, but men of other countries who sailed with them might, and send word to Parma. I will ransom prisoners, as many as he likes. We need a full list of the names of the noble ones in particular. He will want to know who we have."

"Drake sends a missive," Blanche said. "He would like to keep Pedro de Valdes as his personal prisoner rather than sending him to the Tower as Your Majesty asked."

"Valdes would be safer in the Tower, from himself if not from my people," I said. "I hear he is an arrogant, annoying man who, despite being a prisoner, walks about like a potentate."

Blanche was watching me, waiting to see what I would decide. "Fine," I said. "Send word Drake may keep him, at his own expense. He did capture the man, so I suppose there is an argument to be made that Valdes is his trophy of war. But I expect the captain's ransom to come to the Crown."

"Of course, Majesty." She made a note on her paper and turned to the next. "Howard writes of an idea to support the sailors, Majesty," she said. "A benefit fund, money taken from the pay of men serving on royal ships each month, put towards a fund that will care for sailors if they are disabled after service. He asks for your permission to investigate how this might be established."

"He may work on it," I said.

A pang of conscience struck, not only about the men of my navy, but Howard himself. Sore torn was Howard by the treatment inflicted on his men. I knew he thought ill of me for it, as I knew he understood why it had to be done. This was his way of trying to find a solution. It would not aid men dying now, but it might aid the children of England in the future.

Amongst the papers and reports was a personal message from Robin. It said nothing important. He had reached Rycote in Oxfordshire, where he and I had often stayed with Lord Norris, and he had written on the 29th of August to me.

"I most humbly beseech Your Majesty to pardon your old servant to be thus bold in sending to know how my gracious lady doth," Robin wrote, *"and what ease of her late pain she finds, being the chiefest thing in the world I do pray for, for her to have good health and long life. For my own poor case, I continue still your medicine, and it amends much better than any other thing that hath been given to me. Thus hoping to find a perfect cure at the bath, with the continuance of my wonted prayer for Your Majesty's most happy preservation, I humbly kiss your foot.*

From your old lodgings at Rycote this Thursday morning, by Your Majesty's most faithful and obedient servant, R. Leicester."

There was a postscript which made me smile. I had sent a token to Robin, a little jewel known for its healing properties, and he sent thanks, having received it the moment he had finished the letter.

"I hope the Earl is well?" Blanche asked.

"He is not hale, but hopes the waters will do him good," I said. "As I do. He threw himself heart and soul into this conflict, and it stripped a lot from him. He needs time to recover."

"As you do," she said.

"I am well enough. If I do not sleep at least I eat. That is more than many in England can say. All I hope is that Drake and his men get their ships ready with speed, that we might take what we need for England from Spain."

I already had more faith in the plan to plunder the silver feet rather than restore Dom Antonio to Portugal's throne, but Drake was certain both could be achieved, and I felt a debt to him and other fleet captains. *Let them try, at least,* I thought. Walsingham was in favour of the Portugal plan. Thinking Phillip would attack again, and harder, he wanted the King crippled for good.

"Essex sends word from York House," Blanche said, "on that matter."

"What does *he* have to do with Portugal or the silver fleet?" I asked. I had leased York House, traditionally the residence of the Lord Chancellor, to Essex. The young man was frequently using it, for it was grand and wondrous.

"He wants to sail with Drake," Blanche said.

"He will go nowhere," I said. I liked Essex, but he was a hothead. I wanted men sent on this mission with a clear purpose. If Essex went, he would be seeking glory and that would lead to rashness. He had been sorrowed not to see action when the Armada came and, I was sure, wanted to make up for that in this expedition.

"Should I send a missive saying that, Majesty?"

I shook my head. "I will tell him. That young man carries high pride. I will explain this to him in person, or pride will make him do rash things."

"As you wish, madam."

"Is there anything else?" I asked, rubbing the corners of my eyes, staining my fingertips with white paint.

"Just one more, Majesty," said Blanche, handing me a note.

I looked down to see that Davidson, once joint Secretary with Walsingham and the man I had largely blamed for the execution of my cousin of Scots, had been set free. I had ordered this some time ago, and forgotten in the confusion. Davidson would leave prison with money, for Walsingham had quietly seen to it that Davidson's salary had been paid whilst he was incarcerated.

"That is well," I said. "And with that, let there be an end."

As I walked to my garden to take some air, I felt my cousin at my side. In a whisper which spoke in my heart, I knew it was not the end. Mary was always there, reminding me of every wrong I had done. She had more crimes now than even her death to reproach me with. Now, she could bring all the ghosts of all the men I had failed, and parade them, an army of shadows at my back, creeping upon me.

I shivered and walked quickly down the path as though by doing that I could escape the sins that walked in my wake.

Chapter Thirty-One

The Escorial Palace, Madrid
and
The Coast of Western Ireland
September 3rd 1588

Death

In Phillip's palace the King's private secretary, Mateo Vazquez, stood, trying not to hop from foot to foot as he nervously watched his master. The King habitually spoke low and quiet, and never wasted words. A cough had plagued him for months, making him even more succinct, but even when hale Phillip was not one to speak if he could write. Yet today his quietness was more hushed than ever. Bad news had come.

The King's face, grim and stoic as always, had barely altered when Vazquez had handed him the letter from Pedro Nunez, written and sent the day before, reporting the Battle of Gravelines. But Vazquez was anxious. Hints of disaster had reached them, but this letter told the truth. Gravelines had been an English victory and the wild tales of invasion at Newcastle were false. The Armada was defeated. The English had won.

The letter Vazquez had handed his master carried, along with this poor news, a warning in the form of a tale about King Louis IX. This long dead King, now named a saint, had led a holy enterprise and yet God had seen fit to cast plague upon his armies leading to their defeat and Louis's capture. Nunez appeared to be indulging in a little lecture; that those who suppose God is with them are not always correct.

Hearing quill scratching paper, Vazquez looked down to see his master scribbling something in the margin. Phillip was a man of ink; all that passed by him, and all important information did, carried his notes and amendments. It is the way many choose to think they have control over the world. They write it down, make lists, they craft order; a plan to follow.

Wordlessly, Phillip handed the letter back. Gratefully, Vazquez escaped the room. When he looked down to read Phillip's note, he saw the words of his King. *"I hope that God has not permitted so much evil for everything has been done in His service."*

News soon leaked out. People in the streets wore black for mourning, and Phillip remained inside his palace, humiliated, but telling his men he meant to fight on. The war was not done. He was not done.

"And if victory comes not from God," Phillip whispered that night to his confessor, "I hope to die and go to Him."

Some thought death a more possible fate than winning against England for the King. Phillip was troubled by gout and when sickness came he wore it long, like a winter cloak too warm to take from cold shoulders.

That was not all gossips said. Although some spoke of how the English must have been aided by demons, others questioned it. Why would God, the most powerful being of all, be unable to vanquish the forces of darkness, they whispered? Perhaps God had *not* been on the side of Spain. Perhaps God was indeed with the enemy, an Englishman, as men of England now claimed.

As the people of Spain waited for reports of their ships and sons, they heard the Pope and the King of France were lauding the triumph of England and Elizabeth. The shame of defeat was bad enough, but to hear those who should be united in faith to them celebrate their enemy was worse. They also had fear. Alone and unaided England had chased off the invincible Armada, the greatest fleet the world had seen, and now Spain wondered what England would do next.

Rumours erupted. Drake would come for Spain. England would invade. Demons would run loose in the streets. Pigs would dance, horses would fly, and the moon would fall upon the earth. The minds of men are addicted to stories, and when tales are fuelled by drama, grief and terror, they become only more in thrall to them.

As the bodies of his men, thousands of them, washed ashore along England, Ireland and Scotland, Phillip held his breath, waiting for details of the total losses of men and ships. The King of Spain swore this was not the end. His faith had been shaken, his pride had been battered, but he was not lost to his destiny. Not yet.

At times, when only his confessor could hear him however, another man, one not so sure of himself, seemed to speak. Phillip would continue the fight, but his spirits were low. To see less misery and disgrace, gladly he would go to God, he said, but if God would rain grace upon him, he would continue on.

"Please God," Phillip whispered, "I do not think I am mistaken. I think this was the fate for which I was chosen. Do not let me be mistaken."

Others were not so sure it was his destiny. The money from the Pope never arrived. The Holy Father had been clear. Land on England's sands, and the full amount would be paid. That had not been achieved, so no money would there be.

At times, Phillip thought he could hear the Pope giggling all the way from Rome. Sixtus had never liked him, had always been suspicious of his ambition. The Pope had supported the Armada with words, but money was what Phillip needed.

Phillip had sunk his fortune into the Armada, and much of the Armada had sunk. Phillip could only guess at the state of

England's coffers, but he knew the condition of his. The richest King of the world was poor. He had gambled, and he had lost. England was celebrating, his allies, the Guise, had been weakened in France as King Henri sought terms with mighty Elizabeth, there was no knowing what Drake and his men would do next and there were worrying reports of the sultans of Morocco and the Ottoman Empire. Up until that moment they had traded with England but not seen that country as a seat of true power. There were rumours they might offer alliance with England in an effort to crush Spain and her dominion over the Mediterranean.

The King of Spain had weak friends, strong enemies who were uniting and no money. His Armada was falling apart all along the Irish coast. His glorious plan was ruined.

And the world was laughing at him.

*

As King Phillip mumbled to his confessor, the Queen of England heard ghosts whispering at her back, and the Earl of Leicester set out on the long road for Kenilworth, the Armada struggled on. Some ships were still rounding Scotland, others wrecking upon the coast of Ireland. Strong winds and perilous, changing tides took ships reeling, dangerously close to beaching on small islands. Rocks, black, deadly and ominous, loomed from the water, vanishing under white, crashing waves, then appearing again. Like snatching hands the edges of rocks seemed to reach for ships, eager to haul them into the sea.

Four ships long separated from the Armada had been sailing together for two weeks when one foundered. Two hundred and fifty-six men made it from the ship before it sank, leaping onto boats which heaved through the surging ocean, taking them to safety.

On what was left of the fleet still with Sidonia, discipline had to be enforced with harsh resolve. Falling asleep on watch, a fate which threatened many since all his men were exhausted, led to the perpetrator being lashed to the mast, weights bound to his body to inflict agony. One poor soul who had fallen asleep more than four times out of sheer exhaustion was left to hang in a basket from the bowsprit until he starved or fell into the sea. Thieves would usually be cast off at the next port, but now, no port in sight, they were threatened with loss of hands. Murderers would be bound to the bodies of their victims and cast overboard, but there were few of those at that time on the Armada. Chance, fever, starvation and fatigue were claiming enough. There was small need for murder to come calling, unless it was over rations.

What the English had not completed, lack of food brought about. Hundreds at least had perished in battle, but more were dying now. Men were tired and weak. Fits of lowness took hold of their flagging spirits. With only salt-meat or rice to eat, symptoms got only worse. Limbs became swollen and black. Scars that had healed years or decades before broke open and once-fractured bones broke anew. Teeth cracked and tumbled from reddened gums. Men stared in horror at handfuls of them. Blood began to flow in little gory streams from eye sockets and nostrils with no sight of any wound that might have caused such injury.

Later men would learn that if they drank just a little lemon juice the symptoms of this hateful scourge would vanish as if cleansed from the body by the hand of angels. But at that time sailors knew not what caused this sickness. Without fresh fruit, death was certain.

But they had no fruit. Soon all they had was sour wine, plain rice and biscuits teeming with worms. Meat and fish stored in leaking barrels had become rancid, and the sea was too rough to fish for more. Men took to eating rats, roasting them, salivating over their glistening brown-golden flesh as though the vermin were fine sides of venison. In starvation, all food becomes as the nectar of the gods. Some started to gnaw leather belts and jerkins, and boiled straw in seawater to make unpalatable pottage.

Starving, exhausted and dying they sailed on, warnings ringing in their ears that they should not attempt to land in Ireland. But many, too desperate to heed the threat, decided to try. Death *might* be waiting on those shores, some said, but certainly He was aboard their ships.

They failed to understand. I am everywhere, always; in everything, waiting in each shadow. Sometimes men feel me keenly, when the end becomes obvious. That is when they understand how close I am. But always I am there, with them.

The end of life is a fate all creatures come to, just as they come to life. I am not a thing of evil. Men fear death because they fear the unknown, because they tremble to stand alone in that last moment of life, teetering on a void opening into darkness.

Not monster or demon or thief am I, but a guide, a friend, a hand reaching out from that chasm of the unknown as darkness falls. Men need not fear to die alone, for I am there. That is why I am there; to let them know they are not alone.

I am the hand reaching out to touch your shoulder. I am the one who lets you know you are not alone at the moment you fear loneliness the most.

There is someone with you in the moment of utmost terror and confusion, someone who will take you to where you need to go. And there is no need to fear that place. It is cool and calm and there are friends waiting for you.

Life is where men stand alone. Death is where all become as one.

Chapter Thirty-Two

St James's Palace
September 4th 1588

Elizabeth

Behind me the door slammed. I locked it, turning the key as though I could shut out the world. My shaking hands held the key for a moment as I leaned against the door.

In a moment, all had altered.

The morning had passed with reports pouring in.

"Fitzwilliam and your other commanders in Ireland are hunting them down," Walsingham had said. "We think there are one thousand Spanish abroad in Ireland, in the marshes and forests mainly, but our men are chasing them, and killing them on the spot."

"Are the Irish sheltering any?"

"Common soldiers and sailors, no," Walsingham had said. "Some nobles have reached the houses of Irish lords, and some of those lords have sent them on ships to France or Scotland in secret. More have turned them over to us."

"I want *all* those men. They can be ransomed and we need the money."

"Orders have already been dispatched, Majesty, and more ships have washed up in Devon. It seems the Armada is stretched out, ships all along the coast. The *San Pedro el Mayor* has been captured and the men imprisoned, although my officers write it was hard to stop local people from slaughtering them upon the beach."

"Tell local officials to keep prisoners alive, and feed them at their county's expense," I said. "These men are shipwrecked mariners, since they were only attempting to go home when their ships were wrecked. That means, therefore, they are not prisoners of war, and not my responsibility to feed."

"But they will be ransomed, madam, as prisoners of war?"

"They will."

Any saving or profit I was grasping for in those days.

"And I want the valuables from all ships that wreck upon our shores," I said.

"We are trying, madam, but it is a hard task, as you may imagine."

"Reinforce the Earl of Huntingdon at the border of Scotland," I said. "If men are making it from Ireland to Scotland there may be forces or individuals trying to cross into England. Send word to King James that the reinforcements at the border are at his disposal if Spanish forces land in Scotland. He may use my men to repel those of Spain."

It will also remind him not to reach accommodation with any of them and invade England, I thought. It was a remote possibility, but it is always good to think of what might come. James knew we were standing our armies and navy down, and no doubt he knew what a vulnerable state we were in. If he was ever to try something, this was the moment.

"The King has sent a message of hearty congratulations on your victory, madam, and further offers of support. He also asks when he will be named your heir."

"Offer my thanks for his congratulations, but say I am too busy at the moment to look into the succession. Until the Armada is gone, not only from England, but Scotland and Ireland, I can think on no other matter." *Hopefully that will encourage James to capture ships quickly and send the men to us,* I thought.

"Dutch leaders send word," Walsingham went on. "They ask for a share in the credit for the defeat of the Armada, and a share in any coin taken. They say that since they guarded the coast, Parma could not set out, and so they helped England."

"Their help is deeply appreciated," I said. "But their aid was *owed* to England in return for my past support of money, munitions and men, sent over the years. I allowed the Sea Beggars to use English ports for their activities against Spain, risking the wrath of Phillip by doing so. I sent an army to aid them. They helped us, but they did not fight at Gravelines. At Gravelines this war was won, by English ships and English men."

"They suspect Parma will turn his anger on them," said Walsingham, "and beg you do not turn your face from them now. They ask for your continued assistance."

"That they will have," I said. "And that you may tell them."

I had sat down to dine with relief, thinking I would have a quiet hour before the barrage began again. And then a messenger had come. As he spoke I had stared at him, hearing and not hearing.

Over me words washed like water. I could not understand what he was saying. I knew it could not be true. It could not.

Robin was dead.

Struck down with ague and fever on the road to Kenilworth, he had taken to his bed at one of his hunting lodges near Woodstock. There he had died at four of the morning.

He was almost alone when he died. Only Lettice and a handful of servants had attended to him.

When the messenger finished talking, I had stood from the table without a word, walked to my private rooms, closed and locked the door. I should have said something wise and clever, as I had when Seymour died, as I had to honour so many friends who had passed from life, yet there were no words in me. There was nothing in me. On top of my body, apart from my soul, there rode a consciousness but beneath it all was blank. My mind floated, insubstantial and wraith-like, above my own self.

Ghosts are not only of the dead. At times, we of the living become them.

How could Robin be gone? All my life, since we were children he had been at court if not at my side. Even when separated by his betrayal, or by the roles we were each called upon to play for England, I had felt him with me. Within my soul Robin lived, yet with this news it was as though that constant presence was ripped from me. All that was left was a shell, a barren expanse where nothing grew, where no water flowed or sun shone.

The world stopped. Time. Thought. Memory. All was still. God had taken a breath and the world had paused. Distantly I heard voices and a hollow sound. They were knocking on the door. My friends; Blanche, Kate, Bess… their hands were softly knocking on wood, beating out a tune which echoed in my soul. "Madam," they were saying. "Madam, please let us in, let us comfort you."

They were far away. Everything was. Separate from all things in that moment of pure grief, I could not answer. How can the dead speak to the living? Robin was gone and I seemed to have followed, our souls joined even in death. As he escaped into the afterlife, I was trying to go with him.

Robin had been a part of me, vital as heart or lung. Part of my mind had shut down, collapsed upon itself, and another part was blank, unwilling to accept what I had been told.

I could hear voices growing more urgent, but I could not answer. I just sat there, staring at the wall, sitting on the floor. My gown was spread around me, my face was painted with white paste. I reached up and pulled the wig from my head, pins popping, flying as arrows about the chamber. I felt one strike my cheek, a stinging smart, and yet although I knew pain was present, I felt it not. Numb was my flesh, my thoughts. Dead was all within me.

I heard them whisper, telling each other that I needed time. But what was time? The ticking of clocks held no meaning. The passage of hours, days, weeks, what was that to me? Everyone says that time cures sorrow, but it does not. Time is not a cure, only a remedy, allowing you to see that even the worst loss can be coped with, that you can learn to carry the grief. But it is not a cure.

The only cure for death, is death, for life is where we carry all we have seen, done, lost and found. Death is where we surrender it all, hand to another to carry.

In that moment I wanted to die. I wanted to leave life, this world of light and brash, painful moments. I wanted the calmness of death, where I would find Robin, take his hand, and once more know the comfort of his friendship.

From outside, from the streets of London, I could hear people celebrating. It took mc a moment to remember why. This time of England's greatest achievement was the moment of my most personal loss. And it was then I knew. I was to blame for Robin's death.

I had whispered to God, had asked Him to save my people, and in return I had sworn I would give anything. My prayer on the day we saw the beacons burning from Plymouth. That day I had said it.

"God, in your mercy," I had whispered, "hear my prayer. Save my people and I will sacrifice anything, even my own life, even all that is dear to me. Take what You wish from me, but save my people."

God had heard me. Robin was the price, the cost of saving England and my people. Robin's death was my fault. I had offered him up, a sacrifice, and God had taken him. I had thought I had given all I could to England. I had risked life, happiness, even my own soul, but now something else had been taken.

In offering my people a future, I had snatched it from my oldest, closest friend.

I stared at the walls, seeing nothing. "This little room," I whispered, "shall be where my heart is kept, from this moment until my last." Down went my eyes to watch the key in my hands.

The sun came up and went down, night came and the moon rose. Stars sparkled in the sky of night and seemed to in the day as I stared at the wall, not eating, drinking or sleeping. I rose only to piss and walked like a dead person rising from the grave. On that floor I stayed, a corpse with a mind yet still living until one morn I looked up to see people in the room. They had broken down the door. I had not heard a thing. I saw faces and recognised no one.

"Majesty," said a man, kneeling beside me. "Come, you must rise."

My eyes were dazed, glassy. The man shone like an angel; his white hair and kind, worried eyes watching me carefully. "I think you are Cecil," I said dully, my mouth barely opening to allow me to speak.

"I am," he said. "I and the Council have broken the door down, Majesty, for you must rise. You must drink and eat."

"You are Blanche," I said to a woman at my side, who was trying to make me stand. Her aged face was rough with grief and fear, but rather than speak she nodded, helping me to stand. Her eyes brimmed with tears; drops of water, so beautiful, so clean, which fell down her soft, wrinkled cheek. I reached out with a trembling hand and took one on my fingertip. I stared at it for what felt like hours.

"Water," I said. "Like the ocean."

How many tears did the ancient gods cry to make the ocean? Who was it they lost that caused such grief? Was it our God who brought the seas into being, weeping for someone lost so long ago that only He could remember them?

Dully I looked up. There were many people there, all staring at me, fear etched deep into their faces and riding the air flowing into the chamber from the broken maw of the door. I searched for the face I was seeking and saw nothing. He was not there.

"Where is Robin?" I whispered. "Where is my Eyes?"

They did not answer. Hands lifted me up, carried me away to be washed and dressed. Like a doll I let them handle me. Like a dead woman I was washed, ready for burial.

They forced ale to my lips and I drank. They put me to bed and made me eat broth. Darkness fell and morning came. Perhaps I slept, for I opened my eyes to shards of light glimmering through shutters on the windows and found women at my side.

Blanche was in bed with me, her arms not about me, but fallen as though she had held me all night. Ten other women were on the floor, sleeping at my side, trying to protect me in my dreamless slumber, trying to show me I was not alone.

Chapter Thirty-Three

Richmond Palace
February 1603

Elizabeth

"And yet I was," I say to Death. "There were people all around me when from that chamber I emerged, weak as a newborn, legs shaking, mind wandering from the pain of sorrow and from not eating or drinking for days. Friends came, their words and hands gentle as they tried to show me others were there, and I was not alone. But I was."

I stare at the floor. Time, that false promise of how sorrow may be assuaged, fails again as I think of the day I lost Robin. Sharp as the first moment of loss the pain comes.

Sometimes I think time is not as we are told. That the passage of life is not measured by minutes passing, hours fading, days and nights rising and falling behind us as we walk onwards, ever onwards, on this path between the moment of birth and that of death. Time is how we measure life, our achievements, our failures. They all fit in, slotted like papers in a chest, showing all we have done, experienced, become.

Yet when we remember points of life that struck hard, for good or ill, time has no meaning. When sorrow comes, we go back to that first moment, that moment of loss when something we needed more than anything goes, drifting from us like smoke in the wind.

And with sorrow comes questions never answered. How is it that life, this solid, hard, real substance leaves and what is left is air and ash? The breath departs, the chest falls, the body seems to shrink as the life within it departs, goes somewhere we cannot see or reach but only desperately hope is there, so one day we might go there too, and find all those we loved waiting for us, never really lost, always just waiting.

Life offers time to us as a balm, as a crutch, so we may learn to carry grief, but when sorrow falls we are reminded that time is meaningless. Life is not measured by the passage of time. Time stops with sorrow. Each time we remember the fallen, the glorious dead as our ancestors called their heroes, time fades and we are once more mired in the past, in that first moment of loss, and the grief and pain are as strong as they were then.

And we are alone.

"We know we are alone," I say to Death. "We know it, and we ignore it, too afraid of what it means to face the truth. But sorrow is the greatest truth, telling us that all is impermanent, all we love will fall, all we build will crumble, that we will die as will those we dare to love, and that at the end, when all the song and dance and noise of the world is gone, there is only one person, and that is us."

I look up. Death is at my side. I did not hear Him move, but rare is the time man hears the step of Death, even when he is expecting Him. It is another truth we ignore, so we can live. I stare into the darkness of His hood. If darkness could wear an expression, I would say He looks kind. And He shakes His head.

I understand.

In grief and in life we stand alone, no matter how many friends, how much kin, support and kindness we are offered. It is a hard truth, but a truth. After a while, others do not want to hear of grief. They want you to carry on, to be healed, be whole. Yet once broken, we do not heal as we were. Cracks are always there in our soul. The most honest thing a person can say is that they are broken, not whole but always healing.

Others may try to aid us, and they should, but sorrow is personal. Only you can know how you loved another, what they meant to you, what you lose when they are gone. People try to share this, try to explain to others, try to connect to the grief of another, and they should, that is one of the only ways to bear the weight of grief, but the weight remains.

It should remain. So often we try to exclude sorrow, try not to show it, as though by doing so we dishonour ourselves, as though in showing weakness we are saying we have no strength. But strength is not the absence of weakness. It is just the opposite. Strength is feeling the weakness within and managing to carry on.

In sorrow we stand alone because we must. We can do nothing else. Because we are shown in the moment of loss that we too will die, there are battles we will lose, people who will be taken from us, and if we are to carry on, we must carry on relying on ourselves. The only person who will remain with you throughout life is yourself, so it is not a bad thing to learn you are alone. However much we fear it, learning to be alone and be in company with yourself is a valuable lesson. If we can be alone, we can face life, and death, we can be enough.

But in the last moment, the moment of death, we are not alone. For He is there. He comes, a last friend, standing with us as now He stands with me.

Chapter Thirty-Four

St James's Palace
September 1588

Elizabeth

"Reports are that a great deal of ships have been wrecked upon the shores of Ireland's western coast, Majesty," Walsingham said, his voice calm but eyes keen as he searched my face for signs of life.

He had come, as many had, delivering reports of the Armada as it struggled home and of what the people of England and those of other lands were saying. Men came daily, bustling in with news of the Low Countries, Spain and France. They were all trying to entice me to carry on, fearful I would retreat into my little room and lock the door again. They hoped that by delivering constant news they would keep me connected to the world. They hoped that by ignoring my grief, I would forget Robin was gone.

I think they also hoped that if they talked and talked, they could cling to me, tie me to the world. That if they kept me here, I would not lose my mind.

A part of me was empty, but not my mind. A part of me had died with Robin. Perhaps a part of me had died with every person I had lost. There had always been another to continue on with. Before Robin there had been Kat, before Kat there had been my mother. Gone they all were and gone with them were parts of myself I had thought I could not do without. All those people I had offered my heart to, these precious chambers locked deep inside. All those people were lost to me. Would there be anything left of me when these ghosts ceased to steal? What was I without them?

Yet still I was here. Still I remained Elizabeth. With each loss, shattered bits had come together again, and reformed. One Elizabeth was dead, the girl Robin had known who had adored him, who had almost risked her independence and liberty for him, but I remained. The Queen remained.

I would not retreat into my chambers again, not in daylight. In the light of the sun, I had become the Queen once more. Only when darkness fell was I Elizabeth. The Queen, this shell of paint and powder, gowns and wigs, was a costume I wore. She was the mask presented to the world. Elizabeth had lost Robin. She was the person I allowed myself to become when darkness fell, when only my closest friends were with me.

And it was helping. There come times in life when we need to be other people, ones we construct so we may continue on. There are many people inside us, a new face for each event, each time. When one fails, we craft another. This was how I was coping, how I managed private sorrow and public duty.

My men feared to lose the Queen, feared that I would depart my mind, as ancestors of mine had before when the strain of the duty of the crown and throne became too much. Kings had fallen to madness, plunging the kingdom into war and confusion, but I would not fall. Not in that way. In little rooms inside me I boxed away my feelings, one for each chamber. When I needed comfort, I had a room for sweet memories. When I needed to be lost in grief I entered the chamber of sorrow, closed the door and became lost for a while.

And then I came out, I locked the door, and took to another room.

Little rooms. We all keep them inside our hearts; palaces of many tiny chambers in which shards of ourselves are kept. The more we are broken by life, the more rooms we make. My heart and soul had many rooms, perhaps too many to count. I did not try. It was enough that they were there, could be opened when I needed them. All the broken parts of me had been collected, shards of glass carefully plucked from the floor, kept safe inside me. Some would be repaired, some would stay as shards. And that was well. Some parts of me did not need to be whole again. Some parts of me made more sense as fractured, broken bits.

There was a relief in thinking that. So often people want you to be whole again after loss. They want you to grieve a while, then pick yourself up, stick yourself together and go on, a whole, complete being. I had come to learn I was not complete, and perhaps never would be. And that was not a bad thing. It did not have to be a confusing thing either. I made more sense to myself as a broken being. Inside my soul, I did not have to be anything but what I was. I showed a whole, the mask, to the world, but it was a part I played so people would not pester, would not drive me to become complete. Inside, I had accepted brokenness, and it was a relief. No more was I under pressure from my own self to become whole again. No more was I berating myself for not being fine.

I might not be fine again, and that was as it was. There was no shame in my model of grief. I was doing the best I could, and that is all anyone can ask of themselves or others.

This was not about longevity. It was about minutes, hours, days. It was about survival, carving time up into chunks that I could manage. That was all I could do to stay alive. That, and retreat behind my mask.

Robin was gone and I was living with a ghost of him. A real ghost might have been a comfort, but it was memories which haunted me. Everywhere he was in my palaces, my rooms. I could look up and remember that in that corner we had played chess, by that hearth we had sat upon cushions, sharing secrets and laughing. By that window we had kissed, by that door I had touched his face. If I listened, I could catch the last echo of his laughter. I could hear his voice in my mind. Never would it sound in my chambers again. Memories were all I had and I clung to them even as they tore into me, wounding me. I did not welcome the pain they brought, but I would not let go. Sometimes pain is worth it. Sometimes we must slice our hands, holding on to the things that matter.

"Some ships are reported to have taken shelter on the islands about Scotland," Walsingham went on. "I have sent men to aid James of Scotland in taking them."

I nodded. It helped my friends that I offered indications I was listening. I did not want them burdened with the notion they would lose me to grief.

"I am putting together a full report, a book, of the total losses of the Armada," Walsingham said. "And have sent word to Stafford in France to collect his own information and to expect ours."

"You hope our ambassador will send the news on to Phillip, to increase his mortification?" I asked.

"Indeed, madam. We will spread the news about the world, so the King of Spain will have nowhere to hide his crimson face."

I smiled gently at him, and Walsingham looked relieved. "I am worried by reports I hear of Spaniards roaming about Ireland," I said. "Forces were told to be ready if our Lord Deputy requires them. I would like them to remain ready."

"They are, madam, have no fear. No Spaniard will gain a lengthy or sure foothold in Ireland."

"I want no insecure ones either. No footholds, Walsingham. None at all."

He inclined his head and I continued. "What of our plan for pilfering from the silver fleet?"

He checked his notes, eyes running further down the page. "Drake's *Revenge* is taking on a new mainmast, Majesty," he said. "The former one was shot through, much decayed in the fighting. The *Victory* will require a new bowsprit and mizzen and the hulls of the *White Bear*, the *Hope*, *Marie Rose*, *Dreadnaught* and *Tiger* are all in need of repair. Some longboats need replacing. We think the costs will run at around three thousand pounds, which is a good estimate considering the work needed and time frame allowed. They should be ready to set out on schedule."

"Good. We need money and Phillip has it. I think we are justified in claiming redress from Spain." I toyed with my sleeve. "Some say the total English dead numbers six thousand," I said. "Is that true?"

Walsingham shook his head. "We think Spanish agents are putting that gossip about London, Majesty, and it is entirely false. There were only around seven thousand men serving on all your naval ships, so if that were the true figure almost all your men would have died. The true figure stands at about two to three thousand, and most died after the conflict, of fever."

"It is still not a good number," I said. "That makes a third or half our men dead."

"It is not an unusual number to lose, madam, in service at sea."

"What of our money?" I asked, looking at Cecil.

"The total spend of the conflict looks to be around one hundred and sixty thousand pounds for land and sea," he said. "By next year, with all the plans for loans and sales of estates from the Crown, the debt of the kingdom will have increased by around two hundred thousand."

I raised an eyebrow. Although a fearsome sum, it was far below what had been expected. "I checked the figures many times, Majesty," Cecil assured me. "With care and delicacy, this figure will be achieved. We still have a problem with the flow of money, to be fixed by raiding the silver fleet, but we should emerge fluid."

"Unless we pay all the men who served," I pointed out.

Cecil shifted uncomfortably. "The men of England will have to wait for their coin, Majesty. It is not unusual. They will understand."

I doubted that, but I remained silent on the matter.

"Payments are being made where they can be," Cecil said. "If we try to pay one company's wages, all will ask, and we have not the coin, but payments are going to captains for repairs, and for ships destroyed at Calais."

This was for the fireships. Cecil told me Drake had taken one thousand pounds, Hawkins six hundred, and others had claimed around the same. "Thomas Meldrun tried to convince us that his ship was stuffed full of prime beef, biscuit and beer when it was set alight and run at Sidonia, madam, but we have dismissed the claim." Cecil shook his head at the man's cheek.

I sighed. Some men would do anything to make more money. I was being forced to sell Crown lands to meet some of the costs, so this annoyed me only more. "The wounded that are not sick are going to their parishes?" I asked. This had been arranged, as it was the task of local parishes to care for those wounded in action. With wages still not paid, some men had refused to go, but some had, believing that when we had money they would be paid. I hoped after the silver fleet was taken this would be the case.

"They are, but some parishes are resisting," said Cecil. "They do not want the cost. Howard's licences for men to beg are aiding those who are struggling to get home."

"Parishes have a duty," I said, not wanting to think of my own responsibilities. "Tell the men they are all to repair home. Licences are all very well, but armies of beggars on the streets will do none of us any good. Ask churches and almshouses to offer food to those heading home, but get them home."

"We will, madam. Howard, Hawkins and Drake have paid off some companies and they are marching home even now."

"And what of what Spain spent on this enterprise?" I asked.

"We estimate the King of Spain parted with three million ducats, about one million, four hundred and thirty thousand pounds," said Cecil. "And there is word he is building again, another fleet, to attempt the same conflict again."

"And still money bleeds from him into the Netherlands and to the Catholic League of France," I said.

"With little to show for it," said Walsingham. "The Catholic League has no secure hold on France, and Phillip lost his chance to end war in the Netherlands when he attempted to invade England. Wars in both countries continue, so the King of Spain is paying for war in France, the Netherlands and preparing to try to attack England again."

"He wants the world to think him indestructible," I said. "He ignores his vulnerability, thinking that demonstrates invincibility, yet it does not."

I looked from the window, the last summer lights fading, bringing cool air and muted light. "The Armada failed because Phillip thought it could not be beaten. He refused to see where it was weak, where his plans were feeble, where they might fail. England won because our captains knew where they were vulnerable, and used that weakness to their advantage. We had fewer men, so could not face the wrath of Spain as always ships had at sea. Our men saw where we were vulnerable, and used it to become strong."

I looked back at my men. "They saw cracks in our armour and used them to make it impregnable. That is what strength is. As courage is knowledge of fear, strength is the recognition of weakness."

*

On the 8th of September, there was another service at St Paul's Cathedral. Captured standards of Spanish ships were displayed inside and out, and later were taken to Cheapside and the Southwark end of London Bridge, where they hung so people could flock about them to cheer England and mock Spain. I ordered that services of thanksgiving were to be held up and down the country, and sent out a prayer I had written, thanking God for delivering England from Spain.

The people of England celebrated as only the people of England can. Men of other lands often think us a joyless, composed race, yet we are stiff only with strangers. Inside, English hearts are untamed, feral creatures. We are people of passion. Bonfires were lit, night after night, in villages, towns and cities, and people danced about flickering flames, feet beating time with drums and pipes played by musicians. Paintings of me and my men were commissioned to adorn houses. Pictures of ships fighting at sea, and me rallying my men at Tilbury were printed and handed out in the streets. People called for a national day of thanksgiving for the defeat of the Armada, and the 19th of November, two days after my Accession Day, was chosen; a day on which we would celebrate our salvation.

Parishes prepared not only for bonfires and fireworks in November, but feasting. There would be free food and drink given out, some from noble houses and some from churches, and before that many impromptu celebrations went on. The Watch frequently had to be called in to herd drunken men home, although they reported most of them were merry rather than violent drunks.

Pamphlets about the defeat of the Armada and the triumph of England were everywhere, copies clasped in hands, ready for reading when a weary worker made their way to the hearth that night, or dropped upon the streets, drifting down the roads, collecting in piles and turning to mush. Some were by Catholics, so appalled by Phillip's tyrannical attempt to convert England to Catholicism that they had turned to the more peaceful Protestant faith. I had no doubt that if some of these were real, others were fakes put about by Walsingham and Cecil. They knew how to make the best of the story we had created.

And as people rejoiced for the defeat of the Armada, they celebrated Robin's death.

I knew my people had been wary of him, feared his influence upon me. They had thought him guilty of murdering his wife to take me as a bride, had blamed him for the deaths of other courtiers, but much of that I had thought jealousy, a natural feeling when someone rises to the highest peaks of life.

Their jubilation about his death compacted my sorrow. I had thought, when Robin died, people might come to see the good in him. It had been that way for my cousin of Scots. The moment she passed from life she became a saint. Not so for Robin. It was as though his death released bile in my people, stored for so long, becoming bitterer and sourer with each passing year. Never did I more believe the maxim that only good should be spoken of the dead than at that time. If they could say nothing good of my friend, this brother of my soul whom I had lost, I wished they had remained silent, so I might remember him without their scorn. But it was not so. As much as they rejoiced for the defeat of Spain, they gloried in the death of Robin.

It was the hardest thing to hear in that time of personal loss, that many were celebrating the same event which brought me such pain. That perhaps I alone, or I one of few, mourned Robin. Understanding how unpopular he had been brought further pain, and anger. I tucked it away. My grief was private, as my feelings for Robin had always been. No one, including me, had understood the depths of them, the ebb and flow, the always returning tide stroking the shores of my soul. That was what he was and always would be; the sea to my shore, water to my earth.

It brought Essex and me closer, for he was one of the few who mourned his stepfather. My other men, even Cecil, might miss Rob from time to time, they had learned to work with him over the years, but for them there was more gain than loss. Robin had left a space at court, a hole of power into which other men could insert themselves. His death brought opportunity, opened possibility.

Robin asked to be buried with his son, Denbigh, at the Beauchamp Chapel in Warwick. It was the seat of his ancestors and the resting place of his beloved child, but for a man who had served England so long and in so many roles, including her protection against invasion, a tomb in Westminster would have been more apt. His will said that if he could not be buried there, he would lay wherever I chose, but I insisted on Warwick because that was what he wanted.

I like to think Robin chose Warwick not only so he could be with his son in death, but to save me pain. Perhaps it was Rob's last move in the game of politics. If he knew how the people hated him, and chose a spot that was not public as Westminster was, it was to save me having to hold a state funeral in London, to save me having to hear people insult him as he went to his last resting place.

Perhaps he chose Warwick, too, because I would then not have a constant reminder of his death in London, near me all the time.

I think he was trying to save me grief. Trying to be a friend one last time. Trying to make my life a little easier.

In his will, Robin called me *"his most gracious sovereign,"* and said he had always been my creature. He did not have much to leave, his debts were larger than anyone had imagined, more than fifty thousand and half of that was owed to me, but Robin had set aside a large pendant of emeralds and diamonds and a rope of six hundred pearls, which he knew were my favourite decoration, for me, to keep in memory of him.

Perhaps thinking his wife would not want to part with these items, there were specific instructions commanding her to send them to me.

That Rob thought badly of his wife, not trusting her in this last, most personal matter, struck me hard, as did other things I heard. Many were accusing Lettice of murdering Robin, of slipping poison into his cup. They said she had done the same with the Earl of Essex, her first husband. Each day the rumours grew wilder.

There were times I wished I could believe them, but I knew it was not true. Robin provided generously for Lettice in terms of goods and estates if not in money. His will had been drawn up before he went to the Netherlands, and added to upon his death bed. If she had handed him a poisoned cup, I doubted he would have trusted her as executor of his will. He might not trust her to hand over jewels he had wanted to give to me, but that was another matter, one of jealousy between women, not murder in marriage.

But whilst I thought her not a murderess, I hated her with more fire than before. I needed to. I needed something to rage against, for unleash it elsewhere I could not. Turn that fire upon myself and I would burn for eternity. Show it to my people and they would run from me as a demon.

I did not blame Lettice for Robin's death. I blamed her for stealing his life from me, the person he should have shared it with. I had been the person he had shared life with every day, every moment, until she stole him from me.

All the moments they had had together had been taken from me, from my time with him. But for her I could have had more hours, more memories.

My anger at the world, for stealing Robin, I unleashed on Lettice. I had a legal reason to. She was named executor of his estates, so she was the one who had to settle his debts. Lettice owed me money, and I would hound her for it from the day after Robin's funeral until it was paid in full. No other did I ever treat as harshly as her. Often I waited on debts. I did not that time and not because I needed the money, which I did. I did it for vengeance. I did it because she owed me more than just money. She owed me Robin.

She had stolen time from us. She had taken him when he might have been mine. Precious more moments might we have had together and less anger, had she not chosen him. There would not have been the time of distrust and rage between us, would not have been the stilted talk, the uncomfortable hesitations, the times we became strangers to one another.

Without her, we always would have been friends. I would not have had to share his heart with anyone.

Lettice might have more loves, I never would. She could have picked anyone, but Robin was the only one who ever claimed my heart.

And she had been with him when he died. For that, there could be no forgiveness. That place, that moment, the last of life, should have been mine. I should have been with him as darkness fell, should have held his hand as fear came, as the unknown reached out for him. It should have been my voice in his ear, the warmth of my breath upon his cheek, whispering words of friendship, love and comfort so he had known he was not alone.

It should have been me holding back darkness, not her. She had been with him years. I had been with Robin his whole life.

All else she did to me, I might one day have forgiven. But not this. I seized some of her estates immediately, to ensure her debt was paid.

Time she had stolen from me before, and at the hour of his death. And no time would aid me to forget or forgive that.

Chapter Thirty-Five

England and Spain
September 1588

Death

September rolled on, and roads about England became muddy and wet. They were almost empty. Men who had drilled, preparing for war, had all gone home to set aside what small weapons they had been handed and take up reaping hooks and scythes, gathering in the harvest. It was late that year, months of rain and storms which had saved England, or at least contributed to her salvation, having slowed the period of ripening. But now wheat and corn was being cut, grain was gathered in. Vegetables were plucked from soggy soil and dried, stored in earthy-smelling shelters ready for the autumn and winter months.

The scent of vinegar perfumed the air along with the rich, sweet smell of fruit bubbling in water and sugar as foods were preserved and stored on shelves and in pantries. Spices sang on the breeze, flowing from the kitchens of the wealthy, sending nutmeg and mace, pepper and cinnamon to fly in the wind, sailing over green fields made lush by the ever-present rain.

In towns the ring of blacksmiths' hammers were heard again, forging horseshoes rather than blades, and carts carrying produce bound for market rather than the army trundled on sodden roads, drenching travellers walking on the wayside with sheets of foul water. In the fields there was the sound of people singing, songs pealing out like bells, alongside the swish of blades as long stems of green-gold grain were cut. In the hedgerows animals shuffled, seeking out the glut of autumn berries and fruits, as nearby maids gathered the first mushrooms in baskets woven from willow.

Farmers and yeomen were fattening hogs and sheep, ready to be herded to town for the feast of Martinmas in two months time, where they would be sold and slaughtered. The smell of woodsmoke was high on the air as people cleared spinney and pasture of bracken and bramble. Soon would come snow, when the golden days of autumn were passed. Nights would grow dark and darker still, sending people hurrying home, hands tucked deep into sleeves and buried in gloves, the bite of their silver breath upon the wind. But for now that time was to come, not yet here. Autumn is a good season, a time of plenty, a time of action, bright days and cool mornings, months when much is done.

Men looking about them saw change. Many woodlands where once pigs had rooted and berries and mushrooms grew were gone, their trees felled for the Queen's navy when the Armada had come, and now again, as many had heard there was a plan to steal once more from Spain. Great oaks that had stood since the time of the civil war had gone, shattered stumps the only evidence they had lived at all. Landlords did not mind; cleared land was land for pasture, which meant more profit, but to those who had drawn comfort from the trees and a living at least in part, it seemed England was naked, her skin bare.

The timber supply was needed, they were told. More than six hundred oak trees were required to build a warship. But there were problems other than grazing, for wood as fuel was in short supply. The price of wood was going up, and many now did not build houses of wood, they used brick, which before had always been more expensive. Some men told stories of when they were young and great forests had stood all over England. Now huge fields dominated the landscape. King Henry had started to cut them down, they said, building ships more for play than war.

These men did not begrudge the Queen taking them, for surely it had been seen ships were needed! But they missed them. People always miss trees when they go, even if they note them not when they are there. Sometimes loss is like that. Men realise not what they have until they have it no more, until there comes a day they look for shade and have to stand in harsh sunlight.

As autumn winds curled in London streets, chill winds still with a touch of summer to them, the almshouses were busy.

London had more than many other countries. There were five hospitals, offering relief for the poor, and not only beggars of the street, but those who earned small wages for a day's work, journeymen presently without employment, and those who were rendered unable to find work because of sickness or disability. Some who came to the gates of almshouses and hospitals were widows or widowers who could not support themselves, and an annual collection at St Paul's Cross provided for many who had not the means themselves. Benefactors left money in their wills for the formation of almshouses, and livery companies set aside sums for men once of their trade or house. And men, still unpaid from service in the navy or army, had need of them.

But if men of England were not entering an easy autumn, those of Spain were not either. Into ports along the coast of Spain's north, ships sailed that September, broken shells of the once colossal fleet. Some said that the Armada had lost half its ships either to sea, or shore or because they were too badly damaged ever to ride the waves again.

News that the English had lost only eight ships did not help. Even more dreadful was that news when the people of Spain came to understand the English had *purposefully* lost those ships. They had set them on fire to send against the Armada.

Other news that brought no cheer was the estimated dead of the English. Some whispered only one hundred and fifty had died in action. Only four thousand of eight thousand sailors returned to Spain, and nine and a half thousand soldiers. More than eighteen thousand had set out.

Four ships of Spain had been destroyed in the Battle of Gravelines, and two before through accidents along the Channel. All the rest had been lost on the way home. To some it seemed God had battered them with His own hand, teaching the prideful a lesson by inflicting humiliation.

And shame for Spain, it seemed, was not about to end. One returning ship blew up in the harbour of Santander, and another ran aground at Laredo because it had not men enough to bring it safe into port. One sank in a Spanish harbour after mooring, her hull battered too badly to keep afloat. Bit by bit, many ships in bits, the Armada crawled home. More than half the ships were missing.

Men were ordered to stay aboard their ships, for fever was rife and if they emerged the towns of Spain would be overcome. Soon it was said more than four thousand were sweating within the holds of ships they now hated. Others, eyes hollow and bodies skeletal, died from starvation, as the Spanish commissariat, overwhelmed as the English government had been, could not dispatch supplies fast enough.

There were few regions that had not lost men. In some places, entire male lines had been wiped out; sons, fathers, cousins… Those who were fortunate found out their loved ones were alive or dead. Some never discovered what happened to their men. They simply did not come home.

And their King hid in his palace, praying for guidance. Men went to him, asking for payment for the troops and commanders, for reimbursement for lost ships. They were told the King was under no obligation to pay them.

Sidonia returned to his homeland on the 21st of September, a broken man. As the *San Martin* crept into port at Santander, shots were fired to signal for aid. Listing badly in the water, she looked as though she might fall at any time. Fishing boats had to tow her in. The noble flagship was a walking wreak, thrashed by weather and wind, whipped by water, her sails hanging lifeless from masts riddled with holes. The pungent scent of death was upon the ship. Many below tossed in raging beds of fever and sweat. The few who manned her bore hollow, haunted eyes and skeletal frames.

The Admiral was carried from his ship on a stretcher, too weak with fever and low spirits to walk. When he reached the streets and was put in a carriage he pulled his hood over his head. As news spread through the port, Sidonia could hear the wailing of mourning people fill the air.

Like Howard and Drake, Sidonia paid for food and drink for the men starving aboard ships, because his sovereign would or could not. He appealed for clothing, food and drink, and said men were trapped on board ship for lack of pay.

Phillip sent a man to organise wages and food for the Armada and ships loaded with supplies were sent out to seek ships still missing at sea.

Sidonia knew Phillip's aid would not get to his men in time. Sending out orders for raisins, almonds and other foods to be found and distributed, Sidonia begged to return to his home to recover, rather than heading first for Madrid to explain his failure. The King told him to repair his health and then come, and Sidonia went home to the whispering, warm orange groves of San Lucar.

As he left, many noted that his hair had turned grey. It had been black before he departed for England.

Recalde died three days after his feet touched Spanish soil again. Before he died he sent a dossier to the King, condemning Sidonia. The King read it, then wished he had not, for it hurt too much. Phillip hid the dossier. It was enough that they had been trounced, he did not need everyone hearing of all the mistakes made.

In Rome, prayers for the success of the Armada began to falter on lips as news leaked through Europe of England's triumph. The Pope refused to send money to the King of Spain, and in Spain the commanders of the navy turned on one another, seeking to mitigate the blame by handing it to others.

In Valladolid, on his way home, Sidonia sat inside his lodgings, listening to young boys taunt him. They gathered about the house, shouting "Drake, Drake, Drake," over the walls, and calling him *el duque de gallina*, the chicken Duke. Sick and shamed, Sidonia placed his head in his hands, praying to God they would cease.

In France, Ambassador Mendoza, too, hid inside, for when he came into the streets boys and youths chased him shrieking, "Victoria, Victoria," at him, taunting him, for those were the words he had yelled as he rushed into the Notre Dame, sword drawn, thinking victory had come to his country.

And as men of Spain hid their faces, the Queen of England showed hers to all. She was seen about her palaces and moving between them. Her people were fooled by her pageant of pride, but I knew as I looked upon her it was not her true face. Courage is a show, sometimes strength is too. She played her part. She wore the mask of the Queen as inside her the woman she truly was curled up, cradling a broken heart in her arms.

Chapter Thirty-Six

Somerset House
October 1588

Elizabeth

They told me of the funeral.

I could not go, could not see Robin pass from memory. Monarchs were not permitted to attend funerals in case people saw us, thought of our deaths, and therein committed treason. Of the last chance to honour my friend was I robbed, by duty, by tradition.

It was apt. For the sake of keeping my position I had denied myself marriage with Robin in life, and I could not attend his death for the same reason.

It was so easy at that time to think of all I should have done, such as marrying Robin. It was all so very false. We create scenarios in our head, imagining things differently, thinking had we just changed one thing our lives would have played out in perfect joy. But had I married Robin, it would have changed him, as it would have changed our relationship. It would have altered the structure of power between us, and I was not one destined to become subordinate to any man save God.

Robin would have tried to master me, no matter if he started out with promises of equality. Some things are too hard-trained into us from birth to stand against, and the structure of the world, with men above women, is one of those things. Precious few men I ever met could grant the same freedoms they enjoyed to their wives, fewer still offered equality in marriage. Had I married Robin, it would have destroyed the man I knew, and the friendship we had. Somewhere in my dark dreams of bliss that would never be, I knew that. Rob would have succumbed to the temptation to master me, thinking other men would look down on him if he did not. That made him not weak, as you might think, but only human. It takes people of extraordinary power to break from the standards and expectations imposed on us by family, kin and society from the moment we are born.

By not marrying him, I had kept my power, my source of safety, and we had been friends. Even though I had ruled him, we had been more equal as we were, with me as Queen and Robin as subject, than ever we would have been had he become my husband.

I knew this only too well. Every time Robin had tried to woo me it had become as though he was *ordering* me to wed him. Hints of what he might become if we had married had scared me in the past. Instinct had kindled, reminding me that when a woman weds she surrenders power to her husband. It had been enough to frighten me away from the act of marriage, but never had I lost the love I had for him.

People think they are the same, love and marriage, and if a person does not wish to wed there is something wrong with them, something deficient in their heart. It is not so. I did not marry Robin *because* I loved him. Marriage would have killed our love, for I would not have been the person I was, and he would not have either. When we love someone we know them, perhaps better than they do themselves. I did right in not marrying Robin. I would have destroyed the good man he became before that man had a chance to draw breath. I would have lost the one I loved years ago, not through death, but as he became my master.

But when we think about what might have been, rarely are we honest about what would have happened. I thought a great deal in those barren, stark days about all the best ways my life could have turned out, had I chosen to take his hand.

Robin's funeral was large. A procession set out from Kenilworth of one hundred poor people and a hundred gentlemen servants in mourning cloaks. There were, too, a hundred of Robin's own men, attendants to carry his guidon and mourners of rank. Most were men. As it was custom for the Queen to not go to funerals, it was also tradition that more mourners of the same sex as the deceased attend. Of the few women, Robin's washerwomen, scullery maids and dairy women were there. All had served him long. He had always been generous to his people. There had been great loyalty in my friend.

Essex was the chief mourner. Sir Robert Sidney was his assistant. They escorted Robin's body with a trainbearer behind them, trailing yards of black cloth in his wake. Robin's brother Ambrose was not there. Too sick to attend, he mourned at his house nearby.

On Robin's tomb were engraved his many titles, and a line which noted that I had distinguished him with particular favour. Robin was laid to rest near the tomb of his son, the Noble Imp.

With that, my friend was gone. People started to talk of other things. Only I seemed to note the gaping hole at my side.

So many of my friends were now dead. I had entered the time of life where friends lost outnumber those made. I was leaving behind a time when people understood me without question, for they had been raised at the same time, seen the same things. I was becoming a creature of the past living in the present. Creatures of the future were already at court. They knew of things I had seen, people I had known, only as names from stories and books. I was growing old.

In his will, Robin said I had honoured him, maintaining him always in goodness and liberality. *"And as it was my greatest joy, in my life time, to serve her to her contentation, so it is not unwelcome to me, being the will of God to die, and end this life for her service."*

That part of his will had been written before he went to the Netherlands. He had thought he would meet death in glory, in battle, but had died in his bed of fever. Yet Robin had done what he had promised. He died in service to me. His health had been wreaked by gathering the army, his last strength given in protection of the country. It was a protection never required, but at no moment in his work had Robin known that. Had he been called upon to lead men of England in a last, desperate and doomed charge against Parma, he would have. Asked to give his blood for me, he would not have hesitated.

My friend had spent his life and exhausted his health in my service. He had used the last of his strength working to protect England, and had fallen to death only when he knew she and I were safe. I could ask nothing more of Robin.

On the day I had come to the throne, he had come riding towards me on a white steed, like a knight of old. Robin always knew how to play a part. I had never been one with much use for a knight, never had the inclination to wait for a man to save me when I could save myself, but had I called, Robin would have answered. Had I required rescue, he would have climbed the tower.

That was not the way I needed him, though, and he knew it. In our last years, we became as friends and siblings, yet still with an old fire burning between us.

On the day he was buried, I took out the last letter he had sent, that little note of little importance. Just a message telling me where he was and that he had my gift and appreciated my medicine. It was such a commonplace thing. Over decades of friendship and love, I had kept many of his letters, the important ones, or so I thought. I had kept ones which spoke of love, contained poetry, flowery phrases, messages of devotion.

And yet this one, this note of small significance was the most important. Not only because it was the last, but because it showed the ease, the everyday, of our relationship. It contained nothing that was significant and yet all the ways we were joined. It was all that bonded us, held us, in friendship, in years, in love.

This little note. This commonplace thing. It showed how Robin had become my everyday. Like the dawn, like the stars, like the air of the morning. Think on those things and imagine how it would be to lose them. Then you have an idea of what it was to lose Robin.

We think of that which is everyday as unimportant, we take it for granted, and then, when it is gone, we know how extraordinary it was, what we had and have lost. This letter, just a note from a friend, was that; the last piece of Robin as part of my everyday that I had; the last bit of commonplace between us. The last moment when he was so much a part of me and mine, of all that was me, that I had.

It was the last moment of the sun rising in the skies, of stars shining on the earth at night. The last moment everything was normal.

"His Last Letter," I wrote on the outside of the missive. I took it and placed it in a box by my bedside. In there were all the keepsakes of my family, of those I had loved and lost. Robin joined them that day.

I held my hand on the box as I closed it, thinking of so many people who, like the man I loved, had once been part of my everyday, and had left me to face every day after without them.

Chapter Thirty-Seven

Whitehall Palace
November 19th 1588

Elizabeth

And life carried on, because that is what life does.

Death seems to stop the world for a while, yet it is a false thought. About you the world carries on. You can stay behind a while, but soon you too must go on, start walking again. It feels wrong for a long time, as though sorrow should hold you in place, frozen like a fern frond in the first autumn snow. As though you should stay forever motionless, preserving the last moment, keeping company with the dead.

But all seasons change. There is no eternal winter for the human heart. Thaw comes, and you awake, slow and sluggish, but you wake. Only in fairytales do princesses get to sleep forever when sorrow comes, when darkness falls.

That was only more true for me.

It was November 19th, the day of celebration for the defeat of the Armada. Festivities had begun two days before, on the 17th, for my Accession day and continued, linking the two days as one in the minds and hearts of my people. It was on purpose. Cecil thought that bonding the two would fix an image of victory with me in the minds of the people. The 19th was also Saint Elizabeth's Day. Cecil was carving a holy icon out of living flesh. In truth, he hardly needed to make this happen. Already victory and Elizabeth Tudor were one and the same. Our story of glory had worked. The people believed.

They needed to keep believing.

That is the hard thing with a story, not the telling of it, but giving it life. So many fall to the wayside, become forgotten. England needed a tale that would last, one that would endure.

I glanced over at Hatton. He and Essex along with Henry Lee had organised the celebrations. If Robin were alive, the honour would have been his. They had done their best, but I felt there was a sparkle missing that would have been there upon the jousting, the services of thanksgiving, the bear baiting and cockfighting if Robin were still alive. Robin had always added a dusting of magic to all he had done.

But it was good for the people to have something. The days of celebration that now stood as holidays in November would continue, I was sure. Up and down the country there were bonfires and feasts going on in towns, cities and villages. Mummers were roaming, pageants were being enacted, and church bells were pealing. Companies of players had been acting out a performance about court for the last few days. Called *The Three Lords and The Three Ladies of London*, it was about the defeat of the Armada, done in allegory. Pride, Shame, Tyranny, Terror, Treachery and Ambition were played by men affecting to be Spaniards. The end, which made everyone laugh and cheer, had them chased off stage by a rabble of English schoolboys.

England had broken her idols and ceased to take holidays on the days of the Saints, but life must have tradition. My Accession Day and the day of thanks for our victory were replacing the old events of the Church. Man must have something to worship, and more than that, must have excuses to make merry.

Life brings great sorrow. When it offers joy, it should be honoured.

I was in the stalls, dressed as Cynthia, the moon goddess and Lady of the Sea. It was fitting I took that role on this first celebration of our triumph. Many talked of me as though I were divine. Dressing as a goddess was just playing into the myth we had made.

I glanced to one side, at Essex. He was preparing to leave my side to enter the lists. Seeing the fire of excitement in his dark eyes, I knew him for the rash, bold boy he was, yet there were times he looked so like Robin I thought my heart would break and heal all in the same moment. Sometimes, talking to him, I could forget Robin was dead.

We watched as knights entered, playing romantic parts as they had in the days of my father. There were wandering knights, come from foreign lands to worship at my feet. A blind knight knelt before me and his sight was restored, apparently by my beauty. The melancholy knights become cheerful near me, the unknown found their names. I watched my men enter, their servants dressed as wild men of the woods, fairies, or savages. I watched my children play.

As the joust began, knights upon their horses, hooves churning the ground, my mind was on real war. The Armada had been defeated, but Phillip had not. England and Spain were at war now, and were likely to remain so a long time. Word was the King of Spain was building a new fleet, bigger than before. The Spanish Parliament had promised him five million in gold and all their remaining sons so he could "chastise that woman and wipe out the stain" upon the pride of Spain. Provinces of Spain had offered ships, lords had promised to loan galleys and galleons. Walsingham had information from his spies in the Spanish court that they would be ready by April or May.

The possibility of another fleet setting out and managing to reach Parma this time was real enough. Phillip had made mistakes, but if he learned from them what would I defend England with? We had no money, our men were sick and broken. Our hope lay in our attack on the silver fleet and the incursion into Portugal. It was all a game of chess; we would try to get our pieces into position before Phillip.

Some of his pieces, however, were still upon our shores, but my men were dealing with them.

"We arranged for one of our men to sneak on board and light gunpowder they were drying on deck," Walsingham had reported a few days before. "He dropped a smouldering cloth and left. The rest you know, madam."

I did indeed. The *San Juan de Sicilla* was one of the ships left behind by the main Armada fleet and had dropped anchor in Tobermory Bay that September, on the tip of the Isle of Mull in Scotland. She had stayed, making repairs and taking on supplies. The local lord had hired some of the Spanish soldiers to use as he sorted out disputes with his neighbours. They had plundered the islands of Rum and Eigg, annoying the clans of the MacDonalds and Macleans. These lords had contacted Walsingham, who sent John Smollett, a merchant, to infiltrate the Spanish ship. On the 5th of November, the ship had blown up. Only fifteen men on the vessel survived.

"Of the men who were ashore when the explosion occurred," Walsingham had gone on, "some have been taken on by the lord of the isle as mercenaries. Of the rest of the Armada, we estimate forty ships at the very least are lost, and many who made it home are broken. One ship actually blew up in port."

"Your men again?" I had asked, arching an eyebrow.

"Actually, no, Majesty. It appears to have been an accident."

As I had watched with suspicious eyes, a smile had been growing on Walsingham's face. "It would seem something in that bag of missives has tickled you," I had said. "What is it?"

"A new proposition of marriage for Your Majesty," Walsingham said. "Although I think not one you would accept."

"I have never accepted one, unless my agreement with Anjou counts," I said. "Why would I be particularly averse to this one?"

"Because it comes from the Pope."

My eyebrows had shot up and Walsingham laughed. "He was jesting, of course," he said. "The Bishop of Rome seems rather merry that England was not invaded and he did not have to pay Phillip the promised money."

"The Pope has never liked him," I said. "He trusts his ambition not a whit."

"The Bishop of Rome likes *you* a great deal, Majesty," said Walsingham. "He chuckled to his, rather shocked, cardinals that he wished he was free to wed, so he could take your hand. 'What a wife she would make!' he said to his men, 'what children we would have!'"

"Of all the proposals I have had, this is the most ludicrous," I said.

"He also praised Drake, said he was a great captain of high courage."

The wind of the jousting ring brushed my face as I looked down at my hands. No ring from any husband would my fingers bear, and certainly not from the Pope. There was but one ring upon my fingers that day, the one containing the portrait of my mother and me. That was the way it would stay, until the end of my days.

But if the Pope was busy falling over his silk skirts to praise England, he was not alone. In so many ways we were in dire circumstances, but we had emerged from conflict with more friends than we had possessed before it. That is often the way of things. True friends stick with you in all weathers. Allies made for politics only wish to enjoy the sun with you.

King Henri was lauding my virtues in France, and sending word that if I helped him he would be my friend forever. I had written to Ahmad al-Mansur, Sultan of Morocco, of our victory and he sent back word. Celebrations in Morocco had been quite riotous, according to reports. English merchants led a procession through the city and there had been street banquets and dancing, all held with the Sultan's permission. Standards had flown showing me standing in triumph above Phillip, and effigies of the Pope had been burned. Al-Mansur wrote that some brawls had broken out, as his country had many Catholics within it, but the trouble had been contained. He sent congratulations on our victory over Spain, and asked permission to send his ambassador to my court, to talk of an alliance between us not based on trade alone. He was going to ask that our alliance become military, I could feel it.

His court historian was writing of the event, al-Mansur told me, and I was shown, as was true, as the defender of true faith against the infidel, Phillip. I had been aided by God, the Sultan's historian had said, and one passage had moved many of my men. It said God had sent a sharp wind, *reehan sarsaran*, against Spain. Al-Mansur had kindly explained the term was from their Holy Book, and was a sacred breath, akin to our Pentecostal wind. God had sent this wind against the enemies of the faith, punishing them for their sins in the past, wrote al-Mansur, and had again now, against Spain. It proved we were children of God, said the Sultan. Medals struck to commemorate the defeat of the Armada had upon them, *"Afflavit Deus et Dissipati Sunt" God blew, and they were scattered,* in honour of this thought.

Those were not actually my favourite of the medals struck. One had made me laugh when I held it in my hands.

"Venit, Vidit, *Fugit*?" I said, and a roar of laughter escaped my lips. I had stopped in surprise. It was the first laugh I had experienced since Robin died. In many ways it felt too soon to laugh.

"It came, it saw, it fled," Cecil translated with a grin. "Selected from the words of Julius Caesar as a treat for General Parma. He is a devotee of the works of Caesar."

"Most wonderful," I said, turning it in my hands.

"Would the Sultan be willing to help with the reclamation of Portugal, do you think, Majesty?" Essex had asked me when news that al-Mansur was sending an ambassador had spread. I had glanced at him, suspicious. I had told him he was not to go on this voyage, but it was all he could speak of.

"Perhaps," I said. "It would be to the Sultan's benefit to stand against Spain with us. The Ottomans have also sent letters. They too want to make alliance with England."

"We grow strong," Essex said, his eyes lost as he stared from the window.

We look strong, I had thought.

I looked up and saw clouds scattered in the skies, torn like shredded sails cast loose upon the water. I knew the importance of appearances. I sat there in the stalls, ten thousand people watching me. From a distance I looked like a maid, with my thin figure and full, thick hair, my face white as snow, lips red as blood. Grateful I was to the breeze, light and teasing, carrying a hint of winter to cool my cheeks. It was hot under all this paint, in this gown, under my mask of youth.

But no youth was I. I was fifty-five, the age my father had been when he died. I felt hale, better than I had for years in terms of health, but my time might be running short. I had escaped Death again. One day there would be no more running, no more dancing. Death would catch me unawares. That was how He had caught Robin.

I sighed, stretching my back a little as I tried to keep my mind from wandering towards Robin. I could not be seen with a sad face. Invincible Spain had been routed by tiny England. God was on our side. The future was ours.

Bonfires would be lit that night to honour the blazing beacons that had ripped along the coast, warning men of England that danger had come. Fireworks would rain in the night's sky in tribute to the battles fought, feasts would be held and all men would tell stories of what they had done to save England. To hear them now, you would think all men had fought, that all men had turned up when called, ready to fight to the death. Short memories there were indeed amongst my people. Many seemed to forget they had not turned up for militia service, more had forgotten they had deserted. I was not the only one telling tales of triumph and boundless courage.

Victory is no place for a good memory. Battles of the past tell us that. Armies that win write the histories of the world, so victories are always magnificent, men always brave, women always full of faith. We are the stuff of stories, we humans.

We Tudors had always been talented at telling tales. Perhaps it was the Welsh blood in us; somewhere in our lineage there had been a bard, perhaps, his tongue skilled at weaving stories and making people believe them. Like my grandfather's claim to the throne, like my father's split with Rome, the Armada would become the tale told of me. The bad I had done, mistakes made, were being brushed away. Only the good remained. It was the way it had to be, and I encouraged it.

It was the part I played, the mask I wore, not only for me but England. As I painted the mask of the Queen upon my face, the woman inside me was kept safe, kept hidden. Paint covered the signs of grief, somewhat. White lead slathered over reddened skin and hollow eyes. Under it I was aged, and I felt it. I was aware of my weaknesses, but I would not let others see.

So many of us wear a face as a shield, and it is as well, for the world is a realm of dangers, and we all need protection. But inside our shield we can admit who we are. We can trust ourselves with knowledge of our true souls.

We are creatures of the past, present and future. We are memory and moment. We carry scars and stories, and tell tales of where we are going and what we will do. We tell stories, and try to make them real.

I thought of the portrait being painted of me. "Paint me as in youth," I had told the painter. He had not dared to disagree. And so there I sat, a youthful, pretty Queen, before a picture of victory that showed nothing of the ugly underbelly that battle or its aftermath had possessed.

It was not a picture of me, in truth. I was a creature of earth; the future of England was upon the waves.

My hand on a globe, one finger pointing to the New World, I sat as behind me sailed the broken ships of the Armada and the victorious vessels of my fleet. My face was as young and fresh as on the day I claimed the throne, a terrible if necessary lie. My gown was black, trimmed with gold and colourful silks, and pearls were scattered upon me, symbols of my purity. Upon my sleeves were golden embroidered suns-in-splendour, along with flowers with pearls as their centre. Beside my elbow was the Crown Imperial. In my left hand was a feather. Upon my gown, where a codpiece would have lain had I been the son my father desired, was a bow with a pearl hanging from it. The bow was tied, demonstrating my virginity, untried and unchallenged. The body of the Queen was the emblem of the country. My body, virginal and youthful, had repelled the assault of Spain, the assault of men.

About my throat were the pearls Robin left to me before he died.

Upon the arm of my chair was carved a mermaid.

Between two visions of the world I rested in that portrait; between war and peace, victory and defeat. Just as I had proclaimed myself male and female, weak and powerful at Tilbury, I was all things in this portrait. I was possibility. I was not a woman, but a Queen, not a man, but a Prince. I was not old, but youthful, not broken, weighed down with years and grief, but eternal. My eyes were lost in the future, but about my throat were the pearls Robin gave me, and upon my chair the symbol my cousin of Scots had been defamed by; a touch of the past.

I was the centre, the balance.

Always I had been the emblem of England and that was what I became in that portrait. It was not me that was young, it was England. I would not see the future unfold in hope, exploration, and the certainty of courage and confidence. England would.

I was not the woman in that portrait. Neither was England that woman, yet. Both of us were broken, ruptured so deep we would never again be the same. My cousin once said that were she to compass my death it would make a shipwreck of her soul. The battle we had won, yet our souls were wrecked.

We would not let the world see our wounds, for enemies would take hold and rip them wider. Battles had been fought. Much had died. But something survived. And this I would harness. I had let my people down. My men were starving and poor. My coffers were empty. My heart was broken as never it had been before. Those men who had fought should have been offered salvation not starvation, and yet, in the end, I had little left to offer but something born in imagination.

We would become this image I had created, this shield, this future of hope.

I understood now. I wore the shell of the perfect, strong Queen to protect myself, to protect my people. Inside, I was broken. But I had learned much. In falling apart, we get to see what we are made of.

When sorrow comes, when shadows fall, when grief shatters us, we may look down. There on the floor at our feet are little shards, like broken glass, shining up at us. And we can pick them up; a piece of dignity, a shard of courage, a sliver of kindness, a splinter of love. From them we can build something new, leaving what we do not need upon the floor.

Each time we are broken we have this chance to build ourselves anew, better, stronger than before, carrying only what we need.

Broken things are all about us. Countries are lines on maps, places where man decided to break apart from other men using ink and parchment. Soil is torn asunder so seeds may be planted. In darkness, stars shine, fracturing the blackness.

What we hide is what we are. We pretend to be whole, and perhaps that is as well, so we do not scare those we love, so those who would harm us cannot, but in ourselves there is no shame in accepting our brokenness. We do not have to be complete. Whole is not a state we reach one day and continue in forever. Such perfection is not for us. If human beings were meant to be perfect, life would not throw challenges and loss and sorrow and joy our way. We would be stagnant and unchanging, never capable of altering our minds, hearts, or souls, never finding new friends, connecting with old ones, or falling in love.

We are not beings of stagnation, but change, not souls of completeness, but alteration. We are the soil the plough breaks, the dark recesses in which seeds are planted. We are crumbling earth which falls aside, allowing flowers to grow. We are the cracks in shutters through which morning light shines. We are the night sky where stars glimmer.

And this is life, this changing, our adaptations. Life is change. Death is where our souls stop, frozen. There is a reason ghosts are seen enacting the last moment of life over and over again. To survive, one must change. Only in death can a person stop, never altering, for eternity.

Brokenness brings change, new life, new hope. As perfection is a face of cold marble, brokenness is an expanse of warm earth, waiting for shoots to come, trembling from the soil. Death shows us that we are and will be broken, becoming something new from the remnants of the old. This is Death's truth, and if, in life, we have the wit to learn it, we may become wise.

What cannot change remains in the past. What cannot adapt has no future. Without dreams we die, and that which knows itself not, never can succeed. In an ever-changing world, we must accept our changing selves. That is how we survive. As long as we know what we are inside, we can be anything we want on the outside. The world does not have to know our secret hearts, but we must.

All things are measured by their opposites. Courage comes when we bear honest witness to the fear within, rising to fight despite it. Grief teaches us how deep and precious the gift of love is. The evils of greed demonstrate the purity of charity. And the worth of life is measured by death, by life having an end, showing us that time should be treasured.

In this knowledge of ourselves we can become that which cannot be defeated.

To the world, England would be youth, beauty, power and might. Inside, we would be broken, always able to transform. On the surface cracks would not show. We would wear a mask. We would be pure, impregnable.

We would be strong, understanding our weakness. In acceptance of our inner chaos we would become tranquil. From understanding our timidity, we would learn to roar into the darkness of fear. In seeing our rage we would learn the value of temperance.

From knowledge of our vulnerability, we would become invincible.

Epilogue

Richmond Palace
February 1603

"How can I look upon you?" I ask Robin, "knowing you are so close, and yet so far away?"

I cannot bring myself to look up, for I know he is there. This man who was my friend in childhood, who stole my heart as a girl, and broke it not once but many times, the last by leaving me alone in the world?

And yet rebellious eyes steal upwards. I see his shadow, there behind Death. I see those dark eyes, lit with a fire that was born as he was and never left him, even in death.

"In my time as Queen I have moved palaces every few months. I owned vast expanses of land, castles with more chambers than any might count; palaces along the river, and in the countryside." I stare into Robin's eyes. "But you were home, Robin. When you died, I no longer knew where I belonged."

I look away to the window again, leaning on the sill, my hands trembling. "And now you are here, standing there, tempting me to go, to walk away from life before I have completed my tale. You always could tempt where others failed. You knew how to steal my eyes so I could see no other but you."

Robin does not speak. Like the other shades at his back, he remains in the power of the hooded figure of Death.

"Was it a trade?" I ask Death. "Was it as I thought; that I was granted the impossible for my people, and in return what I thought I could not live without was taken?"

He bows. Confirmation of my thoughts. I always wondered if I had offered up this bargain, this deal. Always I hated people striking bargains with God, and yet I too had done the same. My happiness in return for the liberty of the people of England.

"I always said I would give anything for England," I say. "And I did. I risked my life many times. I endangered my soul when I killed my own cousin. And in trade for victory, for freedom, my heart was taken from me. For that was how it felt, every day from that day onwards. I was living but not alive. I stood where I should have shattered, glass upon the hard rocks of the shore. On the day Robin was taken, I became a person no more, I truly was become an emblem. England asked and I gave myself to her."

Behind Death, I see Robin take hands with a woman. It is Mary. He bows to her, a hated enemy in life, yet in death they are become friends, it seems. I watch as they dance, a slow, sad, yet somehow merry dance, much as the dance of life is. As they come to the close, he stands waiting, his dark, bright eyes shining at me. And I laugh, for I know he is saving the last dance for me.

Partners we were in life. We will be once more in death. When I am ready, he will be waiting. He will take my hand, lead me out, and in the darkness of death will we dance, two souls joined by a bond everlasting, two beings twisting away from the noise and clamour of life, into the hushed, serene twilight of eternity.

Here ends *Invincible*,
Book Eight of the Elizabeth of England Chronicles.
In Book Nine, *Old Foxes*, Elizabeth must face death and loss as war with Spain rages and games of court grow dangerous.

Author's Notes

This is a work of fiction. Although I try to stick to known facts, there are certain elements I created in this book. All conversations are fiction, although where the words of the characters were set down in historical record, those words are used. The characters of the people involved are my invention, although based on study of their lives and actions. Although I used a great deal of sources for this book, and mean to include those in the bibliography at the end of the series, I would recommend the following books if you are interested in the Armada, as I found these the most valuable when researching this book. They are: *The Spanish Armada*, by Robert Huchinson, *Drake* by John Sugden, *The Pirate Queen: Queen Elizabeth I, her Pirate Adventurers and the Dawn of Empire* by Susan Ronald, *The Confident Hope of a Miracle*, by Neil Hanson, and *Elizabeth's Sea Dogs*, by Hugh Bicheno.

The story of Drake and his men playing bowls on the Hoe at Plymouth is fairly likely to be a myth. The earliest reports of it arise at least thirty-six years after the events, and come from a Spanish source. That no English sources of the time mention this event does make it suspicious. It is not, however, impossible. Some say that with the Armada bearing upon them, there is no way the men of the English fleet would have delayed to finish a game of bowls, but the fact is that there was little they could do. The tide was against them as was the wind. The fleet was stuck in port. The Hoe was a good look out point, and if they had started a game, finishing it might have been the best way to reassure the other men that all was well, and the comment certainly sounds like Drake. He was known to be boastful and had a swagger to him. I included the story for several reasons. The first is that I lived near Plymouth for years, and frankly, if I left it out friends would rise in rebellion against me. The second is that in every myth there is a grain of truth, and it is a great story. Since this is a work of fiction, I allowed myself a little liberty with this part of the tale.

Villages named in the first chapters are mentioned because I used to live there, and my friends still do. Millbrook, Cawsands, Kingsands and Liskeard are fine places. Do go and see them if you go to Cornwall. The Mount Edgcumbe estate still exists, too. A beautiful place, where you can wander the grounds for free, and the house is worth a look. St Nicholas's Island, once called St Michael's Island, is in the Plymouth Sound. It is now known as Drake's Island.

Sidonia did not order the *Disdain* to be left alone when it fired the first shot of the conflict, I invented this, but Drake did run off after the *Rosario* in the night after the first battle. Some sources say he really *did* believe he was going after a wandering Spanish ship. I don't believe this for a moment. I think he knew what he was doing, and took a huge gamble. Drake was a man known for taking risks, as he was known for being lucky. It paid off for him that time, but leaving the fleet that night as he did could have spelt the end for England.

I have given commanders like Frobisher and Recalde the benefit of the doubt when it comes to their tactics. Some historians put a great deal of daring tactics down as accidents; they suppose Frobisher *was* trapped in the Portland Race and then the St Catherine's Race; Recalde became separated from his squadron by accident. I put these manoeuvres down to deliberate tactics used by experienced men to try to trap their enemy. It is not impossible that some of these events were accidents, even the best commanders can make mistakes, but I think these events were deliberate, and gave credit to the men of the Armada and English fleet for them. Plenty of mistakes were made in this campaign on both sides, it was not, in so many ways, an organised campaign, but I think we should give the benefit of the doubt on some events.

I included a lot of detail on wind, direction and strength, because it is all too easy to forget, in our days of engines and machinery, how reliant the ships of that time were on the wind. The tales of the English fleet warping out of Plymouth and pulling themselves into battle formation out at sea using oar and man power when there was no wind are true.

The numbers of ground troops England had ready vary wildly depending on which source you read. Some say that there were barely any, and others that there were tens of thousands. Whatever the true number, what is for sure is that England did not have as many men as Spain, they were not well armed, and many deserted. The idea of the whole country coming together to face the might of Spain is a great story, but it is not true. Many men did not turn up, many more left their posts. I think the reason was as I said in the book; most men would rather defend their homes than that of others. The other reason was that England had not seen war for generations, so was simply not prepared.

A lot of the problems with preparation were down to Elizabeth, that cannot be denied. She tried to hold off war using talks of peace. That they did not work is not necessarily something she could have anticipated. In all other situations and times she had achieved a great deal with the same tactics, and *had* it worked this time, the Armada never would have been. Avoiding war would have saved her and her people money as well as lives, so I do not blame her for her delay and negotiations. That she failed to prepare once it was obvious war was upon her was due to money. We should also consider that when we look back we *know* when the Armada set out. Since we know this, Elizabeth looks foolhardy for delaying so long. But Elizabeth did not know when the Armada set out. She didn't know her talks would fail. She was trying moves which had served her well for thirty years. That they did not work this time wasn't something she could have known.

Elizabeth comes in for a lot of condemnation with regards to the Armada. Some of it deserved, and some not. One of the oddest things I have read is that some doubt her speech at Tilbury. Quite why people have a hard time believing Elizabeth made the famous Tilbury speech, I have no idea. She was well known for her speeches to Parliament, and was famous for her command of words. The speech certainly sounds like her. I have no problem believing she wrote it, and delivered it as recorded. Whether or not she wore armour is debatable, as this doesn't appear in all the sources, but again, it is not unbelievable. Wearing armour did not mean she had any actual intention of fighting; she may well have worn it as a costume, and Elizabeth wore many costumes before court and her people. Her sister and her cousin, Mary of Scots, both donned armour or carried weapons in times of conflict and no one believed they were about to go into battle. Costumes were there so monarchs, particularly female ones, could inspire their troops.

Some sneer at her speech, pointing out that by the time she delivered it the Armada had been defeated. But Elizabeth *did not know* the Armada had been defeated. That she chose to stay with her men, after learning (falsely, as it turned out) that Parma was on his way, is just as brave as her sister Queen Mary staying in London when Wyatt's rebels came pouring in. Looking back with the benefit of knowing what happened it is rather easy to dismiss Elizabeth's courage, but the fact is she remained in London despite the danger the Armada posed, and stayed at Tilbury with her men when it was announced Parma had invaded. Elizabeth stayed to bring courage to her people. She made mistakes at this time in her life, but we should not condemn everything she did. Let us allow that she made mistakes, as her men did, and also that she demonstrated courage, as they did too.

There is no denying that the treatment of English sailors after the Armada was appalling. The fault was certainly that of Elizabeth and her government, and although it was true that she had very little money by this time, and therefore few options but to delay pay, or not pay at all if she could, this must be held up as one of her worst acts as Queen. I am not sure, however, it should be such a surprise.

Perhaps it is only a surprise as the Armada was a famous victory, so we expect that all commanders and generals on the field and off acted with honour. This never happens. It is a sad and terrible fact that few soldiers or sailors who fought and died, or survived, for their country have ever been treated well. After the First World War, men returning with mutilated bodies or with shell shock were cast aside from society; their mental issues were ignored as something that was embarrassing. The same happened to many after the Second World War. There are still men and women on the street in the USA who fought in the Korean and Vietnam wars, and service men and women are not cared for as they should in the UK either. PTSD is something that is only just becoming understood, and some who suffer from it also suffer the stigma of being misunderstood by society; so many mental illnesses are misunderstood, which only increases the suffering for those who have them.

The simple fact that charities exist to aid men and women who have served in the army and navy should tell us that our governments now, and kings and queens before that, did not and do not support those who fight for their countries as they should. It would be nice to think that we had moved on in the five hundred years or more that have passed, but any improvements in care or support for soldiers and sailors has been recent, has largely been driven by ordinary men and women rather than governments, and is still not enough. If we, in this modern day and age, cannot treat men and women who fought for their countries well, why do we expect people of the past to have? They lived in a time supposedly more brutal than ours, and yet for some reason we expect their treatment of army and navy to have been better. I find that odd.

Ship's fever, mentioned in the book, generally is thought of as typhus, but it could have been any number of diseases. The close-packed quarters, the rats and lice, the blood and vomit all would have spread any sickness rapidly.

On the treatment of sailors and soldiers in Spain, some sources say that Phillip immediately set to action to pay them all, and some say there was a delay. Since Sidonia paid for food and drink for his men, and had Phillip immediately sent provisions there would be no need for this, I have followed the theory of the delay.

As for Sidonia himself, I think him underrated. He had good instincts, and acted with courage many times. Everyone remembers Drake, but Howard and Sidonia don't get the credit they deserve. Sidonia went to the rescue of ships, he put himself in grave danger, and had his hands not been tied by his fanatical King, he might have done a lot better than he did. As it was, Sidonia, with very little experience, faced one of the best fleets in the world, got the Armada past them in the Channel, and got many ships home after suffering terrible defeat at Gravelines. He made mistakes, but considering his lack of experience, his achievements were remarkable. I think he deserves to be remembered better than he is. Howard too, deserves more recognition. He untied the captains of the English fleet in a way which allowed them to fight as a team. The English tactics were brilliant at times, baffling at others. The captains were all used to being their own master, and not following directions. This led to many a battle being incomplete in the Armada conflict.

The fact is that the Armada had too much discipline hampering it, and the English too little. Had the Armada had more freedom and the English fleet had a little less, the battles could have been wildly different, as might the outcomes.

What struck me the most when researching this book was how disorganised both sides were, the English in terms of actually preparing for war, and truthfully had they faced Spain on land they would have lost, and the Spanish in terms of Phillip's ambitious, if unrealistic, plan of invasion. The other aspect that struck me was the ingenuity of the battles. We think now of ships making war upon each other as commonplace, but this was a new thing at the time of the Armada. The English came up with a new way of making war at sea, which should be recognised. That their execution was far from perfect, and most of the Spanish ships escaped, does not detract from the fact that naval warfare altered from that day onwards. People love to say the weather saved England, but actually the weather only battered the Spanish fleet after Gravelines. Before that, the English are due credit for innovative techniques, just as the ships of Spain are due some for standing against those tactics and surviving almost intact.

Perhaps my most lingering memory of this are the acts of admirable lunacy: Men leading ships and battles who had almost no experience of naval warfare, and extremely limited forms of communication; Admirals with no experience who showed not only sagacious, wily tactics, but extraordinary courage; The ships of Spain which, during the Battle of Gravelines, sailed into battle, armed with *nothing* but muskets against cannons, to save fellow ships; Captains and Admirals who, seeing their government were failing their men, bought them food and drink from their own purses, and set up charities to aid them.

The courage of the men who fought in this conflict, on both sides, should be remembered, as should the acts of mercy and charity that happened after.

One other thing I think we should keep in mind; a tradition we seem to have lost. Most of us are unaware, in the UK, that when we celebrate Guy Fawkes Night also known as Bonfire Night on the 5th of November, we are actually celebrating an older festival; one created after the defeat of the Armada. The two events were combined after the Gunpowder Plot and the earlier festival became forgotten, but the lighting of bonfires and the eruption of fireworks actually come from Elizabeth's time. The bonfires honour the beacons that lit to warn of the Armada, and the fireworks commemorate the battles at sea. It is, to my mind, a better thing to mark the Armada, not so much the defeat of Spain, but the courage of the men who fought in that conflict, the innovate tactics, the admirable courage shown, than to mark the death of Guy Fawkes and his fellow conspirators. I always thought celebrating the execution of those men unsettling, but after writing this book, I will not be honouring the execution of Catholics trying to blow up Parliament and their King out of desperation on Bonfire Night. I will be honouring the men who fought on both sides during the assault of the Armada, men who made mistakes, who did much wrong, but who deserve to be remembered for their wit, courage, and their sacrifice.

Thank You

…to so many people for helping me make this book possible… to my proof reader, Julia Gibbs, who gave me her time, her wonderful guidance and also her encouragement. To my family for their ongoing love and support; this includes not only my own blood in my mother and father, sister and brother, but also their families, their partners and all my nieces who I am sure are set to take the world by storm as they grow. To my friend Petra who took a tour of Tudor palaces and places with me back in 2010 which helped me to prepare for this book and others; her enthusiasm for that strange but amazing holiday brought an early ally to the idea I could actually write a book. To my friend Nessa for her support and affection, and to another friend, Anne, my dedicated dog walking partner, to whom this book is dedicated. To Sue and Annette, more friends who read my books and cheer me on. To Terry for getting me into writing and indie publishing in the first place. To Katie and Jooles, often there in times of trial. To all my wonderful readers, who took a chance on an unknown author, and have followed my career and books since. To those who have left reviews or contacted me by email or Twitter, I give great thanks, as you have shown support for my career as an author, and enabled me to continue writing. Thank you for allowing me to live my dream.

And lastly, to the people who wrote all the books I read in order to write this book… all the historical biographers and masters of their craft who brought Elizabeth, and her times, to life in my head. I intend to include a bibliography at the end of the last book in this series.

Thank you to all of you; you'll never know how much you've helped me, but I know what I owe to you.

Gemma Lawrence
2019

About The Author

I find people talking about themselves in the third person to be entirely unsettling, so, since this section is written by me, I will use my own voice rather than try to make you believe that another person is writing about me to make me sound terribly important.

I am an independent author, publishing my books by myself, with the help of my lovely proof reader. I left my day job in 2016 and am now a fully-fledged, full time author, and proud to be so!

My passion for history, in particular perhaps the era of the Tudors, began early in life. As a child I lived in Croydon, near London, and my schools were lucky enough to be close to such glorious places as Hampton Court and the Tower of London, allowing field trips to take us to those castles. I think it's hard not to find characters from history infectious when you hear their stories, especially when surrounded by the bricks and mortar they built their reigns and legends within. There is heroism and scandal, betrayal and belief, politics and passion and a seemingly never-ending cast list of truly fascinating people. So when I sat down to start writing, I could think of no better place to start than a time and place I loved and was slightly obsessed with.

Expect *many* books from me, but do not necessarily expect them all to be of one era. I write as many of you read, I suspect; in many genres. My own bookshelves are weighted down with historical volumes and biographies, but they also contain dystopias, sci-fi, horror, humour, children's books, fairy tales, romance and adventure. I can't promise I'll manage to write in *all* the areas I've mentioned there, but I'd love to give it a go. If anything I've published isn't your thing, that's fine, I just hope you like the ones I write which *are* your thing!

The majority of my books *are* historical fiction, however, so I hope that if you liked this volume you will give the others in this series (and perhaps not in this series), a look. I want to divert you as readers, to please you with my writing and to have you join me on these adventures.

A book is nothing without a reader.

As to the rest of me; I am in my thirties and live in Wales with a rescued dog, and a rescued cat. I studied Literature at University after I fell in love with books as a small child. When I was little I could often be found nestled halfway up the stairs with a pile of books in my lap and my head lost in another world. There is nothing more satisfying to me than finding a new book I adore, to place next to the multitudes I own and love… and nothing more disappointing to me to find a book I am willing to never open again. I do hope that this book was not a disappointment to you; I loved writing it and I hope that showed through the pages.

This is only one of a large selection of titles coming to you on Amazon. I hope you will try the others.

If you would like to contact me, please do so.

On Twitter, I am @TudorTweep and am more than happy to follow back and reply to any and all messages. I may avoid you if you decide to say anything worrying or anything abusive, but I figure that's acceptable.

Via email, I am tudortweep@gmail.com a dedicated email account for my readers to reach me on. I'll try and reply within a few days.

I publish some first drafts and short stories on Wattpad where I can be found at www.wattpad.com/user/GemmaLawrence31 . Wattpad was the first place I ever showed my stories, *to anyone*, and in many ways its readers and their response to my works were the influence which pushed me into self-publishing. If you have never been on the site I recommend you try it out. It's free, it's fun and it's chock-full of real emerging talent. I love Wattpad because its members and their encouragement gave me the boost I needed as a fearful waif to get some confidence in myself and make a go of a life as a real, published writer.

Thank you for taking a risk with an unknown author and reading my book. I do hope now that you've read one you'll want to read more. If you'd like to leave me a review, that would be very much appreciated also!

Gemma Lawrence
Wales
2019

Printed in Great Britain
by Amazon

78129376R00222